Spindle and the Wheel Re-Living Text and Context in Translation Studies

Spindle and the Wheel
Re-Living Text and Context in Translation Studies

Binod Mishra

ADHYAYAN
ADHYAYAN PUBLISHERS & DISTRIBUTORS
NEW DELHI (INDIA)

Published by

ADHYAYAN PUBLISHERS & DISTRIBUTORS

4378/4B, 105, J.M.D. House, Murari Lal Street
Ansari Road Darya Ganj, New Delhi - 110002
Ph.: 011-23263018, 011-23277156, Fax: 011-23280028
Email: adhyayanpublishers@yahoo.com

Spindle and the Wheel Re-Living Text and Context in Translation Studies

Edition 2011
ISBN 978-81-8435-255-9

Printed in India

Published by Harish Chandra Yadav for Adhyayan Publishers & Distributors, Laser Typeseting at A.V. Rao and Printed at Tarun Offset Printers, Delhi

Dedicated

to

My parents, (My Source Language)

whose essence

I have always struggled to translate into

Target Language

and yet am craving

for acceptability.

FOREWORD

I

The translated is always in need of translation of itself in an endless regress. It evokes Blake's Urisen who is chained into his own thunderbolts of realon, which he thought, would liberate him. It was for this reason that God had asked Adam and Eve not to eat the fruit of good and evil for that would lead to emasculation-a kind of self-closure which man would call knowledge. God's expulsion of Adam and Eve from the garden of Eden led to the birth of language which begot binaries in an endless process-a science of counter productivity that had Nachiketas and Savitris in the Indian tradition and Socrates and Jesus in the Western. They wanted to get back to the original, the essence, manifest in the word as Logos. Vedanta talks of Brahma, who can only be attained through neti, neti- 'not this,' not this' because Brahma cannot be compared with anything else in the world. Hence He can be attained anly through extreme forms of negation. An original work of art or literature enjoys the status of samadhi while the translation evokes the process of disturbing that state of equanimity, that economy of desire, which has come to its own kind of stillness in an ever evaporating world. The ontic status we get to is that of the constant versus variation and viceversa.

To escape the variorum edition of the translation energies, Vedas were called apaurusheya which is a denial of the authorship altogether. revealed text are grossly because text are not revealed; they are as they ever have been. To escape binaries and reason which man calls mistakenly, enlightenment, Buddha evolved sunya, emptiness, which, he thought, is the essence of all our taxonomical exercises. Dignaga had propounded the theory of apoha- contextual elimination of one word by another in an endless process which exhausts our performative being leading to the stillness beyond words and reason. This, in Yoga School becomes kaivalya, loneness, away from itself, distanced from the distance itself, the Upanishadic 'beyond the beyond'. Nagarjuna, the 4th century A.D. Buddhist monk expounded upon the theory of emptiness in his classic *Mulmadhyamak-Karika.* Agam and Nigam Shastras end a tradition rather than beginning it. Translation, thus, is a necessary evil which ultimately discovers the original else it falls piteously on an endless road to eternity. The birth of the script ennobles the mysteries of heaven and the realities of the earth. The latter provides a low-mimetic version to what is already high-mimetic in its original shape and contour and context. Translation, thus, is low-mimetic trying to become the high-mimetic in an endless process of transformation which may involve millenniums not to speak of men, generations and societies.

At the Tower of Babel God had confused the speech of man because our science of scriptology had failed to deliver the goods. Translation is textuality's endless bias. In *Truth and Method*, H.G. Gadamer gave primacy to prejudice- a sort of volitional power that helps us create, understand and transform ourselves. Translation must better be understood as textual appropriation, for the original has to be appropriated rater than translated. It requires meditation which alone can get us to the wavelength in which the onticity of the original manifests itself. In that sense, one does not have to begin from a low-mimetic subversion of the textual energies. The text is always an intertext, not only beyond time but across it too. Harold Bloom propounded the theory of misreading for this reason. In his theory of revisionism Bloom said that there is a text standing before a text in an endless process. Derrida, too, questioned the very concept of the original just as Plato had talked of the carbon copy logic. Oral traditions speak volumes of this transference.

The mind of the creative writer, for that matter, is like a satellite that receives signals from planetary bodies to authenticate its own existence. The writer and the translator, therefore, are forms of medium. In truth, they do not originate any thing for they cannot. The source is the beyond. Krishna tells Arjuna not to understand Him with the help of words for He is much beyond them. The three-fourth of the Purusha in the Rig Veda is visible, the rest invisible. William Blake said that man perceives more than his senses do. Translation is the *play* not with the text in question but in millenniums that we have constructed in order to account for our tiny endeavours. The cosmic angle annuls it all. Krishna tells Arjuna that a Sumeru mountain can be raised out of his bones if He were to tell him all about his previous births and deaths. This is precisely the genealogical burden of the text which we consider as a printed document written by a particular author who lived from a certain time to a certain time. Authors are forms of disseminations just as textual bodies are. We are trying to reconstruct them for our pleasure, for the access to meaning makes us knowledgeable human beings.

Ancient cultures of the world do have a tradition of primary and secondary texts, the latter being exegetical exercises which beget the commentatorial culture. The intractability of the Vedas begot Upanishads- theistic, atheistic, monotheistic and polytheistic. This is textual variance and freedom that a reappropriator enjoys while gaining access to the anterior text not necessarily original. The source and target languages are belittled by the phenomenology of experience which carries existential burdens. Source and target languages do smack of an empirical psychology that simply is inadequate to generate the intuitional manifolds equivalent to the text that is being processed. The text is the convergence of the intentionalities that a creative writer might have had over known and unkown periods of time spanning across births and deaths. Convergence is a play and not a sedimentation; therefore, connotation is the only way out, evoking the original states of mind rather than translating it. Adi Shankaracharya wrote his *bhashya* upon the Upanishads as Brahma Sutras. His endeavour to establish Hinduism over the length and breadth of the country brought him to Benaras where he had to engage himself in shastrath, a logical form for affirming God through point and counterpoint argument. Mandan Mishra was the scholar with whom Adi Shankara had good exchanges. When Shankara's victory became apparent, Mandan Mishra's wife put a question to Shankara which did not pertain to the Shastra. The question begged Shankara to answer how does a man feel when he becomes a father. This was deliberately asked knowing that Shankara was a celibate and he would never have access to such experiences. Shankara asked for two days time during which he left his own body and entered into the body of a dying king who was married and had sons. He gathered all the experiences, got back to the stage and answered the question successfully. In Yoga, this is known as par-kaya-pravesh. It is precisely this that a translator has to accomplish. He has to enter into the consciousness of the writer he is translating- his volitions, his *karmic* deposits- have to be the translators'. The doctrine of metempsychosis had early inroads into Greek philosophy and the theory of avatar is God's translation of Himself. God multiplies himself into myriad forms, words, syntaxes, syllables, etc. His pleasure is that of variance; hence there is no correct translation. Translations can have degrees of appropriateness seeking eternity in a grain of sand Translation, in other words, is the continuity of the creative process, difference being that of the level and the degree of consciousness. The calibre and context of engagement shall have premonitions of a different kind for entering into the soul of the author, imbibing and assimilating his samskaras which is an uphill task. Buddha's sermons were never written or recorded. His voice translated itself in an oral tradition for two hundred years. The original Buddha word got cirulated through different bodily ambiences, blood relationalities and kept itself alive with changes that no one had access to know as true or false. Hence, Thervadins claimed to possess the original Buddha Word while the Mahayanists claimed the same. The original became a fiction and dissemination became the name of the game. Similarly, in the Western tradition, there was nothing like Christianity for two hundred years after the crucifixion of Jesus. Then the power of the word asserted itself and the Truth component manifested itself as the New Testament. Translations are meaningful to the extent that they preserve the sanctity of the essence element; the moment they violate the virginity of the idea and the ideation process, they get off the target, become banal even.

II

Translations are carried out intra-culturally and contra-culturally as historicity masks itself in distinct periodicities of time. The advent of the Greeks, Muslims and the British in India asked for an change in our perspectival expositions of reality The influence of Greek art can be seen in the sculpture of the period with many Buddha images carrying Greek patterns in the shape of the eyes, nose, ears and the mouth. This is translation at the level of sculpture. The Greek yavanikas influenced Indian classical drama to some extent is now well accepted. William Jones was the first comparative linguist of note, who drew vital parallels among different ancient languages of the world in including Sanskrit Comparing the Gods of Greek, Italy and India in an essay of that name as the first president of the Asiatic Society of Bengal. Muslim invasion saw change in architecture that were radical. Textuality is ideational in content and the translation is always made made of the ideas that might carry patterns of organisation varied, vast and culture-specific.

The founding of the East India Company in the sixteenth century is a landmark event in the history of the translation of Indian Sanskrit texts into English. Destinguished scholarxs like Sir Charles Wilkins, william Jones, N.B. Halhed, J.Z. Holwell, A.J. Arberry, among many others inaugurated an era of translation that became the projected India for the western imagination. Translation, there fore, is just not communcation; it transforms and overhauls our being as an endless continuity. The publication of the Bhagavadgita in 1785 in English is a landmark event in the history of transtations. Wilkins had learnt Sanskrit from Bengali teachers just as Holwell and Halhed had also done. Therefore, the peculiarities of usage remain. Kreeshna for Krishna, Arjoo for Arjun will serve as examples. The word for Hindu is Gentoo in Holwell and jal become jhoale. William Hones' translation of the hymns from the vedas, the story of Shakuntala from the Mahabharata and the Laws of Manu are now monumental pieces, Many of these translations travelled to Europe, England and America influencing a whole generation of creative writers, philosophers and historians. Schhlegel and Schiller brothers in Germany, the poet Goethe, and later, Max Muller were Indic scholars of great repute. Kant had read Paul Duessen's translation of the Upanishade, and more recently, Heidegger acquired his knowledge of Buddhism through D.T. Suzuki's work on India. Dara Sikoh had a persian translation of the upanishads from which an English version was made. The founding of the Sanskrit Chairs in Germany, England and at various other places established Indic studies as a discipline in the West. The translations carry their own cultural bias but a major part recognises the value of India as a distinct cultural entity which it is difficult to parallel any where in the world. H.H. Wilson was the the first Sanskrit Professor at Oxford who transtated *Vishnu Purana* in 1855. The British Romantic Movement would not have been what it is if it was not for the translations from the Indian soil transported into the West. It was in this context that the Northrop Frye remarked in his *Fearful Symmetry* that Blake was among the first of Euopean idealists able to link his own tradition of thought with that of the Bhagavadgita. When Romanticism reached America, the New York Public Library had in forty four volumes the knowledge about India its culture and literature. The whole transcendental school made use of it. The Harvard oriental series bridged further gaps in translation studies with Sanskritists like Charles Lenman and James Hottenwoods teaching Sanskrit at Harvard. T.S. Eliot studied under them and had read the *Gita* and Patanjali's *Yog-Sutras* in the original Sanskrit. In fact Eliot's wide readings in Hindu scriptures had made him confess that now he must stop reading Hindu scriptures else he might become a Hindu. Translation can also generate such cultural predilections as faced by Eliot. Organised religions like Christianity and Mohammedanism do have this problem for translation gets you out of your boots in a cosmicity of experince that one's own culture cannot provide. For example, Eliot's translation into various Indian languages has influenced modern Indian literatures in regional languages. Macaulay's *Minutes* and the englishing of India is now a historical reality. The acceptance of English as a mode of creative expression gained circularity and wider acceptance. Mahatma Gandhi, J.L. Nehru, Aurobindo Ghosh, Dutt sisters, Sarojini Naidu, among the rest- all wrote in English but not without Indianising it. Cultural constructs must bear the stamp of the culture they emanate from. Regional specificities cannot be doled out to cultures not our own. Time and Space regimes magnify rather than diminish the quality of a work of art or literature.

III

Indian literature is unlike any other literature in the world since it is not written in one language nor does it come from identical cultural regimes. Folk and oral traditions add to this number and it becomes a cosmic body of sort that it is difficult for a non-Indian to decode or decipher. Sanskrit is the most ancient language of the world leave alone India. It has originated semantic fields that regions have shaped into their own cultural needs. Multi-culturalism, linguistic pluralism, mythology, folk traditions- all add up to a complicated situation. Yet there are homonymies, semantic identites within dialogical variance. It is vital for a country like India to forge a link among its various literatures through a language that is commonly acceptable. English even has performed this task successfully well binding India in a common thread though it happens to be a language imported into India.Translation in different literary genres poses challenges of a very difficult order. One canot translate colloquialisms in Shakespeare's plays for that would ruin the textual multivalence and its polyphoniec character. Text is a vibrant mode of existence and its rendering in the same mode may always fall short of expectations. Indian English drama does not use very many colloquialisms because English is not a spoken language at every aspect of our social life. All the same, Indian drama in regional language is borne out of the local theatrical traditions and its rendering into English is more a necessity than a measure of its correctness. Linguistic registers, stage-craft, sound patterns, speech deliveries are untranslatable but such drawbacks can easily be filled up by a *sahradaya's* imaginative skills which can be generated out of one's readings in that culture into whose language the text is being translated. Fiction is story-telling in which Indians have excelled others. Myth, folk-tale combine into a narrative full of adventure, war, victory and defeat that ultimately leads to salvation. This is peculiarly an Indian trait that Indian katha literature leads to salvation and all translators need to understand this. Typologies of character, corresponding ideologies, metaphysical intentionalities constitute the fabric of indian narratology and a translator needs to understan the basic Indian episteme originating from the *Mahabharata* and the *Ramayana* S.K. Dey and P. V. Kane have done yeoman service to the scholarly community by making it available the basic principles of sanskrit Poetics in English. Bharata's *Natya Shastra* as translated by Man Mohan Ghosh is again a landmark event. It is imperative for a translator to know the principles of literary appreciation of the culture whose text he is translating. A knowledge of rasa, dhvani, alankara, riti, vakrokti, among other concepts is what a translator is supposed to possess within warmth of his blood that must generate his creative imagination. All translations involve a dynamics of reading as wolfgang Iser says and the proof of a good reading is that it creates an identical/ parallel textin simultaneities that are ever trying to become thmselves. The translation of Kalhan's *Rajtarangini*, in the Penguin edition, for example, carries a thorough lack of cultural understanding by the translator at various places. The translation of dhvani, to take another example, is not suggestion as it is made out in Daniel Ingall, Mason and Patwardhan's translation of *Dhvnyaloka* in the Harvard Oriental Series, vol. 49. Suggestion is the import of dhvani not its meaning. Dhavni is the non-material sound, nada is whose trans-temporal essence. Similarly, *rasa* is not juice or flavour; it is medition leading to samadhi. Region and place beget their own kind of tonalities, hence *gaudi*, *vidharbha* and *panchali* are stylistic modes that further divide into miniature styles. A translator has to know and understand this variety and pluralistic character of the Indian reality before making the text yield its meaning.

Dr. Binod Mishra has been doing excellent work for quite some time and he has earned the love and respect of the scholarly community for editing volumes that have come to stay in the libraries. I congratulate him for getting articles from senior scholars and translators who have been engaged in the field for a considerable period of time. Translations are definitely globalising mental colonies but it is vital to preserve the sanctity of the local and the regional. Eliot called himself a cosmpolitan in literature therely losing touch with the local. William Carles Williams said that Eliot does not show any respect for time and place. Northrop fvye remarked in creation and Decreation that in order that a creative work of art might preserve its universal value, it is essential for it to respect the local and the regional. I am glad Binod Mishra's anthology raises issues that are vital to the art of translation in the modern times. This is more so because our existence as a nation depends upon our transcreation of the textual traditions both in the mainstresm and in the substream.

Charu Sheel Singh

Preface

Indian writing in English is expanding its horizon year after year. The growing number of creative writers in English in India has made it a force to reckon with. But for any writing to become representative, the participation of regional literatures too is mandatory. Thus it is through translation of regional texts into English that the various myths and superstitious beliefs, traditional practices, customs good or bad, and the continuation of certain taboos can be rectified and their remedies found. A large number of Indian sacred texts that have enlightened the thought processes of the world have resulted because of their translation into English. It is doubtless to say that the diversity of any nation is tantamount to its unity. And for such a unity, respect to languages other than English becomes compulsory. In a globalized world of today every language enriches other languages in contact through various devices. Today it is not language alone that influences but it is also through language that users learn new and novel ways of accommodating in an alien surrounding. Celebrated philosophers, mathematicians, reformers, mythological figures and various gods and goddesses show their presence worldwide, thanks to the services of translation studies. Though translators facilitate languages, their role has become challenging in the changing scenario when meaning is not a slave to words but it assimilates non-words and contexts too.

The present anthology is an endeavour to record the scenario of translation studies and to understand its relevance in literary world. It comprises twenty two essays both from Indian and foreign scholars. Some of the articles focus on the problematics of translation while some provide solutions too. While a good number of articles include discussions on translated texts from Hindi, regional texts such as Punjabi, Urdu, Marathi, Konkani, Tamil,Telugu, and Kannad have also been referred to. The anthology also includes a translated work of a South African text.

The anthology opens with an insightful essay which paves a background of translation studies. **Prof. Z.N. Patil** provides a historical background of Indian English novels attempted at sustaining the local culture even while translating from regional language to English. A translator, according to Prof. Patil, runs on a double edged sword, i.e he has to retain the content as well as the colour and local flavour of the source language and also facilitate the readability in the target language. He emphasizes that it is time that translators drew a line between verbatim translation and culture bound translation for a better tomorrow.

Prashant Mishra considers translation as an important device to learn language use. He finds enough scope of translation as a tool in language teaching and learning. Dr. Mishra underlines the need of teaching language and its subtle nuances more through translation than merely through theoretical concepts of language. He believes that as a task based learning, translation can enhance the quality of language learning through proper selection of tasks keeping into consideration the choice and interest of learners. He asserts that it can be an effective tool to teach language especially in rural areas. In his yet another article, Mishra feels the need of postmodern factors into consideration while translating a text. Postmodernism, according to him, has added a new dimension to translation studies and it can free a text from closed-ended transliteration process and open the door for creativity and inventiveness.

Prof. C.R. Kar in his scholarly article raises certain issues of translation and laments how most of us still have a misunderstanding about it. He believes translation to be 'communicative equivalence' and not word-for-word translation. Prof. Kar suggests that a subtle translation should rise above the considerations of Source Language and Target Language. It should rather be a creative communication and look like original.

José Carlos Redondo Olmedilla considers chaos and imperfection as two necessary principles in computer assisted language learning and computer translation. In his scholarly paper, he discusses how recent developments in electronic instrumentation and computer science have changed the way we think about language operating. Though these methods have also led to computer translation yet we cannot ignore the role of human aspects such as flexibility and evolutionary dynamics of language. He advises that we ought to be aware of the difference between language and biology and also realize that the closer we get to the biological analogy of language, the better the understanding we will have about some important aspects.

C.L.Khatri discusses the problems a translator faces while translating a drama. In his very authentic paper, he emphatically mentions that the translators, despite having many other pre-requisites, must also have the practical knowledge of theatre, of light, sound and colour mechanism. Moreover, he also must have the knowledge of how to use non verbals and other clues that may affect the meaning of the dialogues and the overall impact. The translation of a play in the target language, according to Khatri, must be equally stage-able, the dialogues natural, expressive and convenient to deliver in target language for the characters.

Aruna Bommareddi discusses the translation of Amrita Preetam's short story and unveils the the complexity of the narrative of the city as projected in it. Aruna examines how the familial concerns and dilemmas that women encounter in her writings are not confined to a particular language and region. Amrita's writings stand true to the expectations of new thinking, new psychology and morality and newer conflicts that depict the aspirations and frustrations of the modern India.

T.Sai Chandra Mouli in his thought- provoking essay mentions the challenge that a translator faces in a globalized world. Mouli considers Translation as a creative activity, which offers gratification to the person who renders it and also the audience who receives and interprets it. He finds much substance in translators' demand that they should be treated as interpreters only. Still Mouli warns translators to be more conscious of the content and culture of the source language.

G.A. Ghanshyam's brilliant essay underlines the fact that translation is not only a transfer of content but also transference of culture. Translational literature, as Ghanshyam believes is a hybrid product of the multicultural world. A device to enrich World literature with the inclusion of native and regional variants of linguistic modes and cultural variations, translation encourages cultural exchange and mutual transference of meaning provided in the translator is well versed in Source language as well as target language.

Basavraj Naikar in his exhaustive and scholarly paper analyses the translation of Veerappa Moily's Kannada play *Tembare*. Naikar appreciates C.N. Ramchandran whose translation liberates the local text from the regional bondage releasing it into the global realm of letters and giving it an opportunity of international recognition. Naikar's essay asserts that in a postcolonial situation and the multi-cultural context of India, recognition of the otherness of cultures assumes enormous significance. *Tembare* also testifies to the fact that a man (novelist) from the subaltern strata of Indian society can not only speak but also write artistically about his experiences. *Tembare* easily brings to our mind similar ethnic novels from Africa like those of Chinua Achebe and Ngugi Wa Thiang'O.

Naikar in yet another article analyses Dharmaveer Bharati's play, *Andha Yug*, translated into English by Alok Bhalla, and traces the echoes of the epical theme of conflict between the Kauravas and the Pandavas culminating into climax on the eighteenth day of Kurukshetra war. Though borrowed from the last part of Vyasa's *Mahabharata*, Dharmaveer Bharati's deft handling and Bhalla's exemplary translation make it relevant for all ages and all humans.

Prof. Naikar's third article meticulously discusses the transition of Konkani society from tradition to modernity by depicting the subtle changes in the social, political and moral values of rural life. Originally written by Pundalik N.Naik and translated by Vidya Pai, Naikar's analysis of *The Upheaval* adds to our knowledge the mores and chores of a neglected part of rural India. The essayist believes that the translator has offered a minutia of human experience and cultural background of Goan part of Konkani belt and enlarged the canvas of Indian Literature in English Translation.

Translation not only links two languages and nations but also acquaints readers with various cultural rites and practices. **Deepa S. Mathur** in her incisive essay discusses the stories of Bessie Head, who portrays the experiences of South African rural dwellers. Head's stories foreground the consciousness and agency of ordinary village characters in the historical context of the transition from pre-colonial tradition and custom-bound communities to post-colonial modernity and the political mutation from colonial rule to independence. Head's South African inheritance prompted her to reveal the social unconscious or the darkly uncongenial aspects of the seemingly placid Botswana rural communities. According to Ms. Mathur, Head's representation of Botswana village characters is distinguished by its abiding concern with and empathy for ordinary or non-elite and socially subordinated individuals and groups.

Sudhir K Arora makes a close examination of the Marathi poems of Namdeo Dhasal translated by famous Indian English poet, Dilip Chitre. Dr. Arora applauds Chitre, who succeeds in retaining the depth of Namdeo's poems as he is bilingual and aware of the ethos other than his own. Chitre's bilingual knowledge helped him ward off all fears related to the stylistic and linguistic paradigms that often bring an obstacle in maintaining the very ethos. The English translation of Dhasal's poetry reveals his vision of unification, integrity and love for all human beings to the core.

Saurabh Shukla and Anurag Kumar Pandey in their article focus on the difficulties faced by Gillian Wright while translating Rahi Masoom Reza's *Aadha Gaon.* They are of the view that

Gillian underwent enough ordeals to translate the original text in order to retain the content and the context, yet certain lapses couldn't be avoided. The scholars have appreciated Gillian's effort and called her a transcreator.

Vandana Pathak mentions the practical problems of translating a Marathi Dalit autobiography into English. The intricacies involved in translation comprise the issues of address, certain customs and also various pet expressions unable to be translated. Ms. Pathak believes that the success of the translated text should be tested on the touchstone of the 'readability criterion' and 'the acceptability criterion'. Despite the problems of equivalences in lexicon and culture, a translator has to ensure that translated text has maintained the essentialities of the source text both in matter and manner.

Madhavi Nikam discusses Naikar's translation of M.M.Kalburgi's Kannad play *Kettittu Kalyana,* which disseminates Mahatma Basaveswara's progressive ideology. Ms. Nikam makes it clear that Naikar's translation of this play brings to light the various issues which frustrated many social reformers. The essay substantiates the fact that translation is a cultural link that familiarizes readers with various customs and also helps in bringing to mainstream many reformers confined to a particular community, culture and language.

Mudita Agnihotri and **Alok Pandey** make a very close examination of Manjhan's *Madhumalati*, an Indian Sufi Romance. the book, a translated version of exemplary love story faces the translator's dilemma of finding the real English substitute of certain words and feelings, which stand dwarf as regards the proper essence embedded in them in a particular ambience.

Pratima Chaitanya analyses Naikar's translation of a popular folk play of North-Karnataka, *Sangya-Balya* into English. She emphasizes that the play despite its traditional theatrical features also correspond to the more contemporary and modern idea of defamiliarisation, which enables audience to think hard about the problems and the issues, which surround them rather than identify with them.

Swatantra Asija makes an exhaustive study of Kabir's poetry and explores how love becomes a uniting force between humans and divine forces. She asserts that Kabir's poetry unifies people of every sect. His poetry is not only soaked in love but is also a sojourn of soul towards the Supreme and reflects the different facets experienced by every individual without any discrimination of caste, creed and sex.

Neeta Modi's article though second last in the anthology makes a bold attempt to explore the untranslatability and the cultural snags faced by a translator while translating Munshi Premchand's famous Hindi novel *"Godaan"* into English. She affirms that despite various innovative techniques to overcome cultural obstacles, a translated text often lacks in the essence, and evocative-associative value, besides rich connotations of culturally loaded texts. Translated texts most often fail to register and evoke proper responses in the hearts of Target language readers as compared to texts in Source language.

The last article of the anthology by **N.Sharda Iyer** presents a historical account of Indian literatures both national and regional ones which have brought them world recognition only after their being translated into English. Dr. Iyer advocates that despite having problems of translation, these translated texts can bring great acclaim and acceptance if a proper harmony between the authors of the original text and contemporary translators as well as readers is honestly maintained.

The anthology is an outcome of the growing realization of the need and relevance of translation studies. The book in the present shape could not have been possible without the ever increasing faith of scholar critics and contributors whose articles have always helped me translate my dreams into reality. I register my thanks to all the contributors who have always ennobled my sagging spirits. Their frequent queries at times made me aware of my responsibilities. However, I also express my inability not to complete the project in time though because of certain limitations. I express my deep sense of gratitude to my teachers whose inspiration always keeps me ignited to take up new challenges every time. The torchbearers in my creative and critical path include Prof. P.N. Jha (LNMU, Darbhanga), Prof. Pashupati Jha (IIT Roorkee), Prof. M.R. Verma (GKU, Haridwar), Prof. A.K. Bachchan, (LNMU Darbhanga), Dr. R.C.Shukla(Moradabad), Dr. R.S.Nath (R.C.C, Majuli, Assam), Prof. B.K.Khan(GIT, Sonepat), Prof. A.A. Khan(Durg), Dr. S.K.Pandey(NDA, Khadagvasla), Dr. Suresh Nath(Editor, Creative Writing & Criticism), Prof. Krishna Mohan(Pilani), and Dr. G.S. Jha(Arunachal Pradesh). I place on record my profound regards to Prof. Charusheel Singh (MKV, Varanasi), who despite his busy academic sessions, readily agrees to write the foreword to my book. In fact, it is always his foreword, which acts as a cocktail for my future literary feasts.

I am also indebted to my friend, Shri S.S. Jha (JMC, Majuli, Assam) for his mature and timely suggestions. I shall be failing in my duty if I do not thank my wife, Meena and my children Prerna Priyadarshini and Abhyudaya Anand Mishra, who provided me with a cordial and serene atmosphere in an age of ranting T.V. and Video shows. Shree Harish Chandra Yadav and his team (Adhyayan Publishers, New Delhi) also deserve special mention for their unwavering faith in my endeavours. Their readiness to publish my work and make it reader friendly is the dual realization of retaining content and quality often needed for translation studies. I sincerely hope that the anthology will provide enough food for thought to the students and scholars working in the field of translation studies.

Binod Mishra
Janmashtmi, 2010

List of Contributors

Alok Pandey, A.S.O. IIT Roorkee, Uttarakhand, India.

Anurag Kr. Pandey, Research Scholar, Departmet of Humanities & Social Sciences, IIT Roorkee, Uttarakhand, India.

Aruna Bommareddi, Lecturer, Humanities and Social Sceinces Group, Birla Institute of Technology & Science Goa Campus, Zuari Nagar GOA-403 726,India.

Basavaraj Naikar, Professor & Chairman, Department of English, Karnataka University, Dharwad -580 003, Karnataka, India.

C.L.Khatri, Editor, Cyber Literature Department of English, T.P.S College, Patna, Bihar, India.

Deepa S.P. Mathur, Assistant Professor, Department of English, University of Rajasthan, Jaipur,Rajasthan,India.

C.R.Kar, School of Studies in Literature & Languages, Pt. Ravishankar Shukla Univerity, Raipur, Chattisgarh , India.

G A. Ghanshyam, Associate Professor of English, Govt. M. L. Shukla College, Seepat, Bilaspur, Chattisgarh, India.

José Carlos Redondo Olmedilla, Departamento de Filología Inglesa y Alemana, Universidad de Almería- 04120 La Cañada de San Urbano, Almería Spain.

Madhavi Nikam, P.G. Dept. of English, R.K.Talreja College,University of Mumbai,Ulhasnagar,Maharashtra, India.

Mudita Agnihotri, Reader & Head, Department of English,Kanya Gurukul Mahavidyalaya, Jwalapur, Haridwar, Uttarkhand,India.

Neeta Modi, Head, Dept. of English, Navjivan Arts & Commerce College, Dahod, Gujarat, India.

N.Sharda Iyer, Head, Deptt of English, Vasanta College for Women, Varanasi.

Prashant Mishra, Professor and Head, Department of English, Government P.G. College Neemuch (M.P.) Neemuch –458 441, Madhya Pradesh,India.

Pratima Chaitanya, Department of English & Modern European Languages, University of Allahabad, Allahabad, Uttar Pradesh, India.

Sudhir K. Arora, Department of English, Maharaja Harishchandra PG College, Moradabad- 244001, Uttar Pradesh , India.

Saurabh Shukla, Lecturer, Department of English, SMS Institute of Technology, Lucknow, Uttar Pradesh,India.

Swatantra Asija, Reader, Deapartment of Applied Science & Humanities, G.L.A. Institute of Technology & Management, Mathura, Uttar Pradesh, India.

T. Sai Chandra Mouli, A/93, Bapuji Nagar, Nacharam, Hyderabad-500076, Andhra Pradesh, India.

Vandana Pathak, Head, Dept. of English, L.A.D.& Smt.R.P. College for Women, Nagpur-10.Maharashtra,India.

Z.N.Patil, Professor of English, Department of Training, Development and Education, School of English Language Education, The English and Foreign Languages University, Hyderabad, India

CONTENTS

1

Role and Relevance of Translation Studies in India: An Interpretation

Z. N. Patil

Translation is a kind of cross-cultural communication. First, in a country like India, which has eighteen official languages, translation is a part of everyday life. Signboards, names of shops, bus and train stations, airports, and banks are written in at least three languages: English, Hindi and the regional language. Paper currency denominations are written in at least fifteen languages. Movie titles and sub-titles and safety instructions are in English and the regional language. Many application and feedback forms are multilingual. Food packets and medicine wrappers carry information in more than one language.

Secondly, in many countries where English is taught as a second or foreign language translation from English into the first language of the learners is used to facilitate teaching and learning. For example, in India teachers and students of English make extensive use of the local language. As we know, translation method of language teaching has been quite popular throughout the history of language teaching.

Thirdly, translation has always been used as a carrier of India's rich literary tradition. There are more than eighteen official languages in India. Each one of these languages has a wealthy literary heritage. Scholars have untiringly translated literary classics from one Indian language into others. Moreover, discourses and treatises on theory, linguistics, grammar, and philosophy have been translated from time to time.

In addition to these three major uses of translation in Indian context, there is an interesting use of translation, which is found in the novels of Mulk Raj Anand, Raja Rao, Khushwant Singh and a few others. In this context we need to understand the nature and role of the English language as what I call a 'twice born language'.

English as a twice born language in India

What is a "twice-born language"? A language that is transplanted from its native soil to an alien soil is a twice-born language. We say that such a language is born again in the sense that it has to carry the weight of new cultural experiences. English is a twice-born language in those countries where it is used as a native language. One can think of the use of English in terms of three circles: the inner circle, the outer circle, and the expanding circle. English is a once-born language in the countries that belong to the inner circle, whereas it is a twice-born language in the context of the countries in the outer and expanding circles. The non-native varieties of English are characterized by socio-linguistic or pragmatic transfer. The use of rules of speaking and writing from one's own native speech community when speaking and writing a second or foreign language is known as socio-linguistic or pragmatic transfer. There are two types of transfer: unconscious or unintentional, and conscious or intentional (Pandharipade 1987: 155). Learners of English as a second/foreign language, for instance, unconsciously transfer the rules of the use from their mother tongue. Similarly, general users of English in India unwittingly impose the rules of their mother tongue on the other tongue. Characters in Indian English novels, for example, are producers of unconscious deviation. On the other hand, creative writers are conscious creators of deviation from Standard English. The very idea of standard implies stability. But language is of its nature unstable. It is essentially protean in nature, adapting its shape to suit changing circumstances. It would otherwise lose its vitality and its communicative and communal value. The users of English exploit its protean potential and fashion it to their need, thereby demonstrating a high degree of linguistic capacity. The innovation indicates that English has been learned, not just as a set of fixed conventions to conform to but also as an adaptable resource for making meaning. And meaning making is a personal as well as a communal activity. The creative users of English as a second or foreign language are proficient in that language to am extent that they possess it, make it their own, bend it to their will, assert themselves through it rather than submit to dictates of its form. They take possession of the language, turn it to their advantage, and make it real for them. This is what mastery means. So, in a way, proficiency only comes with nonconformity, when people can take the initiative and strike out on their own. Let us consider the remarks of the Nigerian writer, Achebe (1975: 67): "I feel that the English language will be able to carry the weight of my African experience... But it has to be new English, still in communion with its ancestral home but altered to suit its new African surroundings."

Achebe is a novelist, and here he is talking about creative writing. But what he says has clearly wider relevance and applies to other varieties of English. The point is that all users of language are creative in the sense that they draw on linguistic resources to express different perceptions of reality. English is called upon to carry the weight of all kinds of experience, much of it very remote indeed from its ancestral home. The new English which Achebe refers to is locally developed. Ojaide expresses a similar view (1987): "...The English I write and speak is neither mainstream British nor American, and I cherish this uniqueness. In addition, I express the African sensibility in my writing. This sensibility is different from the Western and the Asian, a little closer to the Asian. Western universals crumble in the African worldview... (p. 165)

Knowing my audience and deliberately not aiming at British or American cultural tradition, I emphasize content and meaning in my poetry. I write not to develop the English language, but to articulate ideas as clearly as possible. I do not follow English metric patterns; that is not relevant to my message. For me English is the supra-language on top of my own personal language... My writing, though in English, has its roots in Africa, not in England or North America. (165-66)

African values also give different connotations to English words. English has become indigenized in Nigeria and West Africa... In any case, there is now an established West African usage of English. Let me give examples of words and expressions that have different meaning in Nigeria and the United States. Somebody with a deep throat in Nigeria is greedy: I know what deep throat connotes in the United States. If among my people somebody eats grass, it means that the person is miserably poor. That person has nothing to do with marijuana. Somebody could be gay in Nigeria in a positive sense of being convivial, because homosexuality, a natural aberration, does not exist among my people. Our family is bigger than yours because we are our brother and sisters' keepers and are not traditionally individualistic. My brothers are a thousand and one...

Language becomes old and worn-out as do human beings and other things, and consequently they lose their color and vigor. Non-native English as in Nigeria is still fresh, exciting and vigorous... Paradoxically, I believe I have an advantage in Urhobo as my mother tongue, belonging to a different culture and 'world', and writing poetry in English, which is different from the mainstream English of American language. I am cultural standard hearer of the African world, not of the British or Western world. And in that freedom I can manipulate English to my advantage." (166-67)

A translator has mastery over the source language as well as the target language. He renders a literary creation into a recreation. In addition to full-length translations of various genres, we encounter translation of words, phrases, sentences and small stretches of discourse in novels written by non-native writers writing in English. A very striking case in point is that of Indo-Anglian writers. These writers feel that they cannot reach out to wider readership if they write in their mother tongues. Therefore, the obvious choice for them is English. Some of these writers use a neutral variety of English, which gives few, if any, clues to their regional identity. Their subject matter is Indian to the core; they write about people, places and events in India. However, from their language itself, it is difficult to know whether they are users of Indian English.

On the other hand, there are other writers like Mulk Raj Anand, Raja Rao, and Khushwant Singh who clearly show their regional identity through the variety of English they use. As Platt, et al (1984: 178) point out, these writers "translate narrative and speech styles of another language. Kachru (1982: 342) mentions the predicament of a non-native writer in English who has to reflect their culture-bound styles and codes. However, a number of Indian writers have Indianized the English language to represent the speech of their characters who otherwise speak Indian languages.

Now, let us dwell upon how Indo-Anglian writers give a local flavor to their English. There are a couple of ways in which they do this. They may deliberately translate from their mother tongue to convey Indianness or they may use Indian English unconsciously. Platt et al (1984: 183) list three main ways that these writers follow:

1. They use a neutral variety of English, but include some words and expressions from the language (s), which the characters would actually use.
2. They translate expressions and structures from local languages, but include words and expressions from local languages.
3. They include dialogue in another language.

Use of translation as a literary device

Now let us discuss the use of translation as a literary device by Indian writers in English in their novels from the point of view of the characters involved in the interaction as well as from the point of view of a non-Indian reader of Indian English fiction. We will talk about cross-cultural communication with reference to interpersonal interaction happening in fictional discourse. The illustrations that we are going to cite are from Indo-Anglian novels and can be categorized into the following types:

i) Two characters belonging to Indian culture are engaged in fictional conversation. They use culture-bound expressions and speech functions. But readers are not familiar with the culture-specific expressions and speech acts. As a result, they find this culture-specific language (a) intelligible but amusing, confusing, or even shocking, or (b) find it unintelligible.

ii) Two characters engaged in fictional dialogue come from different cultures. Therefore, when they interact, two things may happen: (a) one of the two characters receives a culture shock, or (b) both of them receive a culture shock.

iii) Just as characters may receive culture shocks while interacting with each other, readers belonging to cultures other than Indian culture may also receive a culture shock.

iv) The culture of a character may affect their interpretation of what is said or done by a character from another culture. By the same token, the culture of a translator or interpreter may also influence their interpretation of what is said and done by characters and what is written or left unwritten by the author they attempt to translate.

Use of translation as a vehicle of culture

It is common knowledge that the nexus between language and literature on the one hand and language and culture on the other is a very strong one. Probably the most widely accepted views on the relationship between language and culture are those of Malinowski (1964: 40) whose focus on the study of culture as a system led him to the conclusion that linguistic behavior could best be delineated and interpreted in its appropriate socio-cultural context. As we know, culture is like gravity: we do not experience it until we jump six feet into the air. It is like an iceberg, with its largest implicit part beneath the water. It is a shared system of meaning, a mental program. Culture comes in layers, like an onion. To understand it we have to peel it layer by layer. The outer layer comprises explicit products such as language, literature, food, buildings, houses, monuments, agriculture, shrines, markets, fashion and art. The middle layer consists of the norms and values of what is right and wrong, and what is good and bad. The inner layer consists of assumptions. The best way to test of something is a basic assumption is when a question provokes confusion or irritation. Lazar (1993: 65-66) offers a list of thirteen aspect of culture, which can be a useful starting-point in reading literary texts from any culture. They are as follows:

(i) Objects of products that exist in one society, but not in another, e.g. cucumber sandwiches;

(ii) Proverbs, idioms, or formulaic expressions which embody cultural values, e. g., "Marriages are made in heaven";

(iii) Social structures, roles and relationships, e.g. Superwoman;

(iv) Customs/rituals/traditions/festivals, e. g. , arranged marriages;

(v) Beliefs/values/superstitions

(vi) Political, historic and economic background;

(vii) Institutions;

(viii) Taboos;

(ix) Metaphorical/connotative meaning, e. g., "doing harijan work";

(x) Humour;

(xi) Representativeness;

(xii) Genre; and

(xiii) The status of the written language.

It would be in the fitness of things to mention the major culture-types people belong to Characters in novels as well as writers and readers are products of the following types of culture:

(i) Universalist versus Particularist

(ii) Individualist versus Communitarian

(iii) Neutral versus Emotional

(iv) Specific versus Diffuse

(v) Achievement versus Ascription

(vi) Sequential versus Polychronic

To a large extent, what a character says and how he says it, is determined by his culture-type. Similarly, what a character perceives and how he perceives it is influenced by his culture-type. The question most pertinent to our topic here is "How does a writer convey culture-specific ideas, concepts, norms and values, situations and perception? Obviously, to convey most of these culture-bound things, he has to deploy various strategies. However, probably the handiest strategy is that of indigenizing the medium of literature. And translation is one major device that he exploits. It is devices like translation, which make his language a "twice-born language".

Use of translation of compliments and blessings

And this point applies to all other new Englishes, which have been created to carry the weight of different experiences in different surroundings. All non-native writers of English literature "write with an accent, as it were. As one read a non-native variety text, it becomes immediately clear that there are devices and elements that are acceptable to the non-native variety author, which are not the same as those in a native-variety text. From the level of lexical redefinition to that of stylistic features and discourse arrangement and speech functions, the text is marked as non-native (Nelson 1985: 245). Here, we will look at some examples of translation of the speech functions of complimenting and blessing as marked features of the discourse in Indian English novels.

i) Compliments

Different cultures employ different compliment and compliment response strategies which reflect the value system of the particular speech community. The why of complimenting and compliment-response is usually assumed to be culturally universal: compliments are offered with a view to making the hearer and receiver of compliments feel happy. The how of compliment, on the other hand, seems to be culture-bound. Some cultures might sound in their use of compliments as obsequious, diffident and miserly; others might sound unappreciative and smug, generous and prolific. We can prepare cultural value profiles of societies on the basis of compliments. Let us look at the following compliment and the response to it from *Inside the Haveli* as culturally loaded speech acts:

"Where is Binniji?" asked the wife of Daulat Singhji. "Hukkum, you have been blessed with many things but your daughter-in-law is the haveli's greatest ornament."

"You have always been generous in your praises for this haveli," replied Bhagwat Singhji's wife with customary humility.

ii) Blessings

Now, let us look at some of the blessings selected from Mehta's *Inside the Haveli*.

(i) "God bless you. We are proud of your success. May you continue to excel in your studies." (p. 174)

(ii) "Vijay Bai Sa God bless her, is the daughter of this haveli." (p. 7.9)

(iii) "May you have eight sons." (p. 16)

(iv) "May you have many sons and may you always wear red." (p. 29)

(v) "May you have eight sons; may the gods bless you. May this haveli flourish forever." (p. 29)

(vi) "May you always wear red and live to see your great grandsons." (p. 72)

(vii) "May you always wear red and may your sons carry on the illustrious name of this haveli." (p. 161)

(viii) "Binniji.... God bless you. May you always wear red. May gold always shine on your hand." (p. 208)

(ix) "May you live in your husband's shadow for a hundred years." (p. 86)

These blessings are translations of blessings from Rajasthani language. The first two blessings are relatively neutral or culture-free. In other words, they may be exchanged in any culture. The rest of the blessings, however, are different. There are two frequent topics of blessings: (a) wish for the addressee's and/or her husband's longevity, and (b) prayer for the addressee's sexual fertility. A woman, who passes away before her husband, is considered lucky. She 'wears red' till the end of her life. It is interesting that a woman carries with her the mark of being married whereas a man does not carry with him such a mark. She walks and lives in her 'husband's shadow.' Secondly, a woman would long to be a mother. Hence we have the blessings 'May you have many sons' and 'May you have eight sons'.

Foreign readers and use of translation in Indian English novels

Now, let us look at the compliments and the blessings from the point of view of a foreign reader. How would he respond to these speech acts? The compliment 'your daughter-in-law is the haveli's greatest ornament' is not likely to cause unintelligibility. However, a non-Indian reader may not be quite comfortable with the comparison of the daughter-in-law with an ornament. Talking about the blessings, the language here is unlikely to create problem for a non-Indian. But she/he would be wondering why a Hindu woman in India should always 'wear red' and why she should have 'many sons' and why she should always live in her husband's shadow. A non-Indian reader is likely to be amused by such avatars of the speech act of blessing.

As we move from implicit translations to the explicit ones, we can draw a continuum with three types of translation shown at different points: (i) intelligible but amusing, (ii) unintelligible, and (iii) culturally shocking. Let us list them in that order.

i) Intelligible

1) "Wah, Wah," he exploded warmly, "you are sitting outside and this is your own home! Come inside." (*I Shall not Hear the Nightingale*, p.121)

2) "Sardar Sahib, it is your own house; you are most welcome. What could give us greater pleasure?" (*I Shall not Hear the Nightingale*, p. 87)

3) "Bring yourself and all the children for a meal. You must not light the oven in your own house". (*The Financial Expert*, p. 86)

4) "Ohe, your stomach is your own, even though the food you are eating has been provided by His Highness?" (*The Private Life*, p. 195)

5) "I'm your slave" said the peasant, touching Sher Singh's knee, "the slave of your salve. You must come to my humble home for some water or something."

"Do not shame me. I am not short of money. By the Guru's blessings, I have plenty to eat and drink. I only need your kindness. If you step into the hut of Jhimma Singh I will ask nothing more. Your slave is named Jhimma Singh." (*I Shall not Hear the Nightingale*, pp. 10-11)

ii) Unintelligible

6) "I have eaten your salt." (*The Private Life*, p. 153)

7) "So you betrayed my salt." (*The Private Life*, p. 153)

8) "Munoo, Ohe Munooa, Oh Mundu! Where have you died?" (*Coolie*, p. 9)

9) "You have blessed my hovel with the good dust of your feet."(*So Many Hungers*, p. 62)

10) "Sardar Sahib, you are a big man and we are but small radishes from an unknown garden." (*I Shall not Hear the Nightingale*, p. 27)

11) "When shall we present ourselves?" (*I Shall not Hear the Nightingale*, p. 61)

12) "What honourable noun does your honour bear?"

"My name is Iqbal.

"Where does your wealth reside. Babu Sahib?"

"My poor house is in Jhelum district." (*Train to Pakistan*, p. 35)

iii) Culturally shocking

13) "Is this your son?"

"No sir. No. He is your son only." (*Azadi, p.* 20)

14) The Babu took up two dishes in his hands and brought them up to Mr.

England's nose... He recoiled from the attack of the syrupy stuff on his senses with a murmur of 'No, thank you.'

"Oh yes, sir, yes, sir," urged Babu Nathoo Ram

"Some pakoras, then?" said the Babu. "They are a speciality of my wife."

The peon brought up the dish of the maize-flour dumplings. Mr. England looked at it as if it were poison and said, "No, no, thank you, really, I had late lunch."

"Well, if you don't care for Indian sweets sir," said Nathoo Ram in a hurt voice, "then please eat English-made pastry that I specially ordered from Stiffles. You must, Sir"

"No, thanks really I can't eat in this hot weather," said Mr. England, trying to give a plausible excuse.

"Sir, sir", he protested, thrusting the food again under Mr. England's nose. 'Do please eat something - just a little bit of a thing.'

"No, thank you very much, Nahoo Ram." (*Coolie*, pp. 56-57)

Savile-Troike (1982: 36) reports a very interesting experience of indirectness related to a host guest situations. It shows how visitors from Middle East and Asia remain hungry in England and the States because they are ignorant of English and American table manners. Whenever the hosts coax these visitors they say 'no' which in fact means 'Ask me again'; but the hosts, equally ignorant of the table manners prevalent in the respective countries of the guests, fail to understand the indirect illocutionary force of the negative and mistake it for a literal negative and do not offer the guests any more food or drinks. Englishmen have probably the opposite experience in countries like India where their 'no' is interpreted as a polite refusal and consequently they are forced to eat food they really do not want to.

Conclusion

In conclusion, we can raise certain issues regarding the use of word by word translation and also that of culture-bound behavioural patterns in Indian English fiction:

- Should Indian writers in English transiate word by word?
- Must they translate word by word? Why?
- If it is necessary and if Indian English writers do that, what are the advantages and disadvantages?
- How far does the culture-type of the reader/translator influence his interpretation and translation? And does it affect his interpretation and translation directly and explicitly or does it influence them indirectly subconsciously and implicitly?
- Just as we can elicit a foreigner's response to these (i) intelligible, but amusing, (ii) unintelligible, and (iii) culturally shocking translations, can we conduct a reverse exercise by asking Indian readers to read, say a culturally loaded African American novel?

Works Cited

Achehe, C. (1975) The African Writer and the English language. In *Morning Yet on Creation Day*. London: Heinemann

Anand, M. R. (1972) *Coolie*. Delhi: Arnold-Heinemann.

Anand, M. R. (1966) *Two Leaves and a Bud*. Mumbai: Kutub Popular

Anand, M. R. (1970) *The Private Life of an Indian Prince*. London: The Bodley Head

Bhattacharya, B. (1978) *So Many Hungers*. Delhi: Orient Paperbacks.

Kachru, B. B. (1982) Meaning in deviation: Toward understanding non-native English texts. in B. B. Kachru (ed.) *The Other Tongue: English Acros Cultures*. Urbana: University of Illinois Press

Lazar, G. (1193) *Literature and Language Teaching*. Cambridge: Cambridge University Press

Malinowski, B. (1964) *A Scientific Theory of Culture and Other Essays*. Chapel Hill N.C: University of North Carolina Press

Mehta, R. (1977) *Inside the Haveli*. New Delhi: Arnold. Heinemann

Nahal, C. (1975) *Azadi*. New Delhi: Orient Paperbacks.

Narayan, R. K. (1958) *The Financial Expert*. Mysore: Indian Thought Publications.

Nelson, C. L. (1985) "My language, Your culture: Whose communicative competence?" in *World Englishes*, 4(2): 243-250

Nemade, B. (1984) "The Problem of Equivalence in Translation". In G.S. Amur, B.V. Nemade, P. S. Deshpande and K. R. Shirwadkar (eds.) *Essays in Comparative Literature and Linguistics*. New Delhi: Sterling, 37-43

Ojaide, T. (1987) "My Poetry: English Language and the African Tradition". in *World Englishes*, 6 (2): 165-167

Pandey, S. (1984) "A Note on Possessive Clauses in Hindi". in S. Kumar (ed.) *Gaveshana*. Agra: Kendriya Hindi Samsthan, 37-48

Pandharipande, R. (1987) "On Nativization of English". in *World Englishes*, 6 (2): 149-158

Platt J., Weber, H. S, and Ho, M. L. (1984) *The New Englishes*. London: Routledge and Kegan Paul

Saville-Troike, M. (1982) *The Ethnography of Communication: An Introduction*. Oxford: Basil Blackwell

Singh, K. (1967) *Train to Pakistan*. Mumbai: Pearl Publications

Singh, K. (1970) *I Shall not Hear the Nightingale*. Mumbai: India Book House

2

Postmodernism and Its Implications for Translation Studies

Prashant Mishra

The traditional concept of translation aimed at translating a text literally from source language to a target language. The centre of attention was the literal translation of words and forms. However, with the development of linguistic, semiotic, semantic and literary theories the concept of translation evolved over a period of time, grew and underwent a sea- change. During Structuralism, translation no longer remained a literal translation of isolated verbal units but extended to translate words in relation to the wider structures of the whole or the main text. Instead of isolated words, the whole text in which words occur in a syntagmatic relationship with each other and contribute to the core, was emphasized in translation. Now a text is regarded as a composite unit where parts contribute to the whole through a sequential relationship between them and therefore the aim is to translate a text as a whole maintaining the relationship between the parts. Noam Chomsky through his concept of surface and deep structures pointed towards the limits of Structuralism, which confines itself to the surface level of a text and ignores the deep level that exists in the mind of the speakers. Chomskian Generative Theory implies the translation of the deep meanings of a text rather than the surface ones which may be ambiguous and deviant from the deep level. However, Chomsky too, emphasizes on the textual translation that confine to linguistic competence of the native speakers. Further socio-linguist Dell Hymes and the Functionalist Halliday and, Leech regard language- centered studies inadequate and advocate the socio-cultural contexts important in determining the meaning of a text. In translation too language centered translation which regards that it is the deep level structures which provide us knowledge to translate the elements of the original text from source language to a target language was challenged by the functionalists. Socio-linguists and Functionalists further extended the scope of translation by regarding context as a deciding factor in the process of signification. According to them, a translation exercise requires not only linguistic competence but also pragmatic competence.

Postmodernism became popular in 1960s and 1970s and welcomed skeptic stand towards all meta-theories and meta-narratives. It questions all the traditionallly established notions, hierarchies and systems of knowledge and instead welcomes plurality, heterogeneity, individualism, localism, incompleteness, relativism, approximation, contingency and instability. Indeterminacy of meaning is central to postmodern theory. The indeterminacy of meaning of words and the ambiguity, uncertainty, plurality and postponement of meaning in a text due to the presence of allusiveness, figurativeness and inter-textuality in literary language and the concept of reader response problematize the work of a translator. Postmodernism advocates liberty as against fidelity in translation. Due to indeterminacy of meaning postmodernism rejects 'transliteration' (literal translation) and prefers 'transcreation'. What a writer creates is to be recreated by a translator. Hence, translation cannot be regarded as a mere mechanical copy of a text from source language into target language. It is something more and beyond that. Since translation recreates source language text into target language text, it goes beyond the original. A translated text is, therefore, regarded as the 'post life' of a source language text. In the process of translation a text is dismantled and deconstructed. A text, according to Postmodernism, is always in a state of flux. It does not have one fixed meaning but innately marked by fluidity, indeterminacy, instability and dynamism. A translator, therefore, when translates a text, in the process of its recreation, he fills his own meaning into it and in this way deviates from the original.

Pioneer of Structuralism Ferdinand de Saussure regards language a system of signs. According to him, a sign consists of a signifier and a signified. However, the relationship between signifier and signified is arbitrary and not logical and scientific one. Therefore, in order to know the meaning of words one has to depend on binary pair of signs which are in opposition to each other. As there is no inherent and logical relationship between signifier and signified, the signification depends on their contrast and differences. According to Pramod K. Nayar, "Meaning is seen as differential (see post structuralism and deconstruction above), contingent and purely arbitrary. Signification and narration are seen as ends in themselves, rather than as sources of any Truth. That is, the process of representation seeks not to offer any insights into reality (truth), but to call attention to itself as nothing more than a game of representation" (Nayar2002:218). Derrida extended Saussure's concept of language as a sign system in his theory of Deconstruction. Derrida begins from Saussure's concept of 'difference'. He argues with Saussure that through 'difference' or 'binary opposition' between signs, one can understand their meaning. But Derrida regards the process of signification as the endless one as meaning of signs are not found within a sign but scattered in a whole series of signifiers where it oscillates between presence and absence. According to Derrida, meanings not only differ but are also deferred endlessly. This concept of 'deferment'is relevant to Translation Studies as the meaning of a text is deferred endlessly and no final and absolute translation of a text can be achieved. As there is no transcendental and absolute meaning of a text, it is open to multiple significations. The process of deferment also takes place in Translation of a text. According to P.K.Kalyani, "The concept of other/difference provides a bigger room for translation to play. Instead of fixing the meaning, translation can extend boundaries and open up new avenues for further differences...He (Derrida) sees translation as a continuing process which aims at modifying the original text. It is a continuous process that thwarts and distorts original meaning and simultaneously reveals a network of texts both enabling and prohibiting inter-lingual communication. The process of translation as suggested by Derrida not only rejuvenates the text but also rejuvenates the language." (Kalyani2001:62). Thus, Translation as viewed by Postmodernist no longer remained a mere transformational activity from source language into a target language but it goes beyond that. Translation is a creative activity. What is created by a writer is recreated by a Translator. The creation of the source language text into target language text is never its replica but a reinvention of the original source language text into target language text. Since meaning of a text is something like a mirage seen in desert, it cannot be replicated through translation. Translation breathes a new life into a source text. It is, thus, a creative activity.

The traditional view of translation regards it as an exercise that aims at similitude of the original. A translator is to create a copy of the source language into target language. But deconstruction and Postmodernism opposed all types of absolutisms, perfection, totalities and transcendentalism in literature. They rather worshipped tentativeness, approximation, localization and ambiguity. According to postmodern view, translation cannot create exact copy of a text. In the process of translation, a text is dismantled and deconstructed and scattered into multiple significations. The socio-cultural environment, from which a language evolves, grows and functions differs from one language to another. Due to dialectal, registral and cultural idiosyncrasies present in various languages their natures differ from each other. Therefore, it is impossible to replicate the lexemes and culturemes of source language text into target language. The source language is uprooted from its native soil (culture) and replanted in the culture of the alien soil. The idiosyncrasies inherent in human languages always influence translation and make it an open-ended activity. Cultural differences always come in the way of creating an exact copy of a text in another language. According to Professor Bijay Kumar Das, "Language is largely culture oriented, and therefore, translators face the problem of translating certain culture based words into another language with a different culture. Colloquial expressions, culture words, slang, proverbs are difficult to translate for there is no one to one correspondence between one culture and another or one language and another. Equivalence of words in two or more languages is hard to come by. Hence the difficulty arises in finding equivalent swear words in another language. Socio-cultural matrix plays a vital role in checking the nuances of the words in both languages – SL and TL" (Das 2008:40). Hence a translator aims to use the nearest possible substitutes to approximate the intended meaning of the source language text.

Reader-response theory further strengthened the idea of subjectivism, individualism and pluralism in the reading of a text opposed to the idea of fixity of meaning. Reader-response regards that a text cannot mean the same to all the readers who have different schemata and who use translation for different purposes. A translator too is a reader who reads a text in order to translate it. The meaning of a scientific text may be in a frozen state but the meaning of a creative or an emotive text is open-ended. Different translators read an emotive text differently and provide their own significations of it. A postmodern reader sees multiple interpretations of a text and regards all monolithic and homogeneous interpretations as illusions. According to Barthes, "The text is plural, which is not simply to say that it has several meanings, but that it accomplishes the very plurality of meaning: an irreducible (and not merely an acceptable) plural. The text is not a co-existence of meanings but a passage, an over-crossing; thus it answers not to an interpretation, even a liberal one, but to an explosion, dissemination" (Barthes1989:168). Since the authorial meaning is lost with the completion of his work, text is open to multiple interpretations when it comes in the hands of readers who have different reading backgrounds and assign meanings to a text accordingly. A translator takes liberty with a text as he understands it. According to Stanley Fish (1980), meaning is not inherent in a text but it is the reader who supplies meaning and content to a text. Fish says that "the place where sense is made or not made is the reader's mind rather than the printed page or the space between the covers of a book" (Fish1974:397). Wolfgang Iser believes that the author leaves the 'gaps' which the readers are expected to fill. According to him, "These gaps have a different effect on the virtual dimension, for they may be filled in different ways. For this reason, one text is potentially capable of several different realizations, and no reading can ever exhaust the full potential, for each individual reader will fill in the gaps in his own way, thereby excluding the various other possibilities, as he reads, he will make his own decision as to how the gap is to be filled" (Iser 1989:79) Thus a translator only endeavours to approximate the authorial intentions. His work may be relative and approximate to the meaning of the author but it cannot be regarded as a substitute of the original. Talking about the creative aspect of translation and the freedom a translator enjoys, Professor Mohit K. Ray writes, "Fortunately, in this age of emphasis on reader-reception, when the reader has returned with a vengeance as the co-author, the critical climate is eminently congenial to the translator for an exercise of his freedom. Every act of reading is, in a profound sense, an act of translation and literary translation involves an interpretative retranslation of the source text" (Ray2008: vi). R. Shanti traces the indeterminacy in translation to the readers who translate for different aims. According to her, "The translator has to adopt a particular type of translation according to the readers who use translations for different purposes. Translation depends on the requirements of the reader and hence the translator has to select a method of translation accordingly. Thus the concept of reader is important in dealing with the type of translation" (Shanti 2008:29).

When a text is translated, it never remains the same text as it is in its original content and form in the source language. No two languages are of the same nature and culture. Different languages hail from different cultural backgrounds. Languages are codified in their culture. The conventions, codes, culturemes used in human languages differ from one language to another. Hence, the lexemes used to express ideational, interpersonal and textual functions differ from one language to another. Therefore, when a text is recreated in a target language, it has to be re-codified to suit the culture of the target language. The source language text is processed to meet the cultural demands of the target language text. Due to difference in cultures, translation cannot produce a copy of the original. It is recreation of the source language text. Therefore, the translator's attempt is to approximate the culture of the target language as he knows that due to linguistic and socio-cultural differences existing in various languages, exact translation from source language to target language is impossible. Exercise in translation transcends lexical and grammatical boundaries and ultimately involves socio-cultural considerations. Hence appropriateness of translation depends on various pragmatic considerations where creativity plays an important role. Professor Mohit K. Ray discusses the liberty a translator has to take in translating a source text. He writes, "Even if we accept the conservative view that recommends strict fidelity of the translation to the source text the fact remains, nevertheless, that on account of linguistic and cultural differences, and not infrequently, difference of historical periods (when one is translating an ancient text), the translation is never equal to the source text; it is always equal to a subtext of the source text" (Ray2008: vi).

To conclude, now translation no longer remains "replacement of textual material in one language (SL) by equivalent textual material in another language (TL)" as thought of by J.C.Catford and the other linguists but a creative enterprise that breathes a new life and meaning into SL text and in this way creates a new text. Postmodernism has added a new dimension to translation studies by freeing it from closed-ended transliteration process and opened the door for creativity and inventiveness. According to Professor A.K.Singh, "Translation is an extension of creative exercise characterized by almost the same process. Translator is a creative reader critic and not a failed writer or a disappointed author. He reads, interprets, criticizes and creates, for translation is a way of reading, interpreting, criticizing and in the same process creating a new text for those who have no access to literature in an alien language system"(Singh1996:8).

WORKS CITED

Barthes, Roland.1989. "From Work to Text".in Rice,Philip and Patrica Waugh(Eds.) Modern Literary Theory A Reader.London:Edward Arnold.

Catford, J.C. 1965.*A Linguistic Theory of Translation.* London:OUP.

Das,B.K. 2008. *A Handbook of Translation Studies.* New Delhi: Atlantic Publishers and Distributors.

Fish, Stanley.1974. Self-Consuming Artifacts. Berkley: University of California Press.

Iser, Wolfgang. "From 'The Reading Process': A Phenomenological Approach". in Rice, Philip and Patricia Waugh(Eds.). *Modern Literary Theory A Reader*. London:Edward Arnold.

Kalyani, P.K. 2001. *Translation Studies.* New Delhi: Creative Books.

Nayar, Pramod K. 2002. *Literary Theory Today*. New Delhi: Prestige Books.

Ray, Mohit K. 2008. (Eds.) Studies in Translation. New Delhi: Atlantic Publishers and Distributors.

Rice, Philip and Patricia Waugh. 1989. (Eds.) *Modern Literary Theory:* A Reader. London: Edward Arnold.

Singh, A.K. 1996. (Eds.) *Translation: Its Theory and Practice.* New Delhi: Creative Books.

Shanti, R.2008. "Translation Theory" In Ray, Mohit Kumar (Eds.) *Studies in Translation.*, Delhi: Atlantic Publishers and Distributors.

3

Subtleties and Sublimities of Translation

C.R. Kar

The first question that comes to my mind is to know what actually we translate. Most often we come across a question like "Translate the following Hindi/English/.... passage into English/Hindi/...." In my 25 years of teaching translation, in the first lecture of each session, I have heard students answering the question as 'a language is translated into another', and probably this is that misunderstanding which complicates the act of translation. As Saussure once said, "Language is a form, not a substance," no language can ever be translated. What we translate is the meaning underlying the utterance.

The next question is equally not easy to answer. It is what a bilingual dictionary provides. If somebody relies fully on the word-for-word meaning while translating, can it suffice the purpose? Certainly not. "Bilingual dictionaries and easy word-by-word translations are inevitably misleading; the shortcut of asking what a form means must ultimately be supplemented by active participation in the life of the community that speaks the language." (Hockett, 1973: 141)

'Meaning' means what the speaker or writer means, intends, wants, thinks, or proposes to convey or communicate to the hearer/reader. Thus, while talking of meaning, we have two ends - one, the speaker's/ writer's intention or proposition, and two, the hearer's/reader's interpretation. Unless and until these two are considered equally important, anything that we do may not be called appropriate. The intention of the speaker/writer is wreathed not only in words, phrases, clauses, and sentences, but also in their relationships. Whatever the hearer/reader receives as the content of speech/writing is the outcome of the context -'a complex network comprising the speaker/writer, the hearer/reader, the subject-matter, the language, the mode, the purpose, the time, the place, etc. In translation, meaning is what and how the translator interprets the text.

Each and every successive reading results in a closer and finer interpretation of the text. Davidson treats the problem of interpretation as domestic as well as foreign (1973/1984 : 125) The translator interprets a text in most of the cases accordingly as the linguistic structure permits and where cultural gaps are there, (s)he fills them either with domestication or with foreignisation. The former is assimilation into the target language convention and the latter non-transparent translation. The more the translator is well versed in the SL and TL conventions, the better is the interpretation. Bassnett (1998) has proposed a kind of balance between domesticating and foreignising in terms of acculturation.

The word 'Translation' has various renderings, viz. 're-composition' (Nida, 1964 : 68-9), 'co-writing' (Harris, 1983 : 121), 'trans-coding' (Greimas), 'creative transformation' (Matilal, 1990 : 122), 'trans-relating' (Kar, 2005). What appears from the variety of nomenclature is that translation is an indefinable act more difficult than writing and/or creating a new in that the translator is not free to write anything. He/She is in such a house where everything is his/her own but can't touch and use without the permission of the spouse. Translators are never mediators nor do they deserve low status as "Translation is no longer seen merely as a bridge between given cultural entity and is increasingly considered as a creative cultural activity." (Andone, 2002: 136)

Roman Jakobson (1959:232-239) views 'equivalence in differences' as the basic problem of every language. In translating, the problem of equivalence must not be over-emphasized at the cost of differences. "Overemphasis on the equivalence of the source and target texts in structure, intention and function only obscures the roles of the translators in intercultural communication and the independent status of target texts in target cultures." (Yunxing, 2001: 18) Any attempt of equivalence is actually a balancing act: "...the translator's skill must reside in achieving a balance between the two." (Malmkjaer : 2010 : 83) The translator appropriates the foreign text, but, at the same time, employs "domestic cultural materials" (Venuti,

1998 : 61) This is the way how balancing for the sake of originality may be achieved as can be seen in instances of greetings, exclamations, request, thanksgiving, command, delight, pity, regret, etc. in different languages.

What appears from the above is that for better results in the field of translation 'communicative equivalence' ought to be preferred to word-for-word translation. For developing communicative competence, original parallel texts have always proved better than mere structures of two different languages.

It has always been difficult to judge whether a native or a non-native speaker with a sufficient knowledge of the non-native language is a better translator while rendering the SL into TL, but the adverse is not true. A translation is assessed on the basis of comparison between SL text and TL text, "A recurrent issue in the assessment of contrastive phenomena is the relative weight of determining typological factors on the one hand and stylistic ideals on the other." (Magnusson, 2000: 126) TL speakers/readers seldom compare, the translated text to the SL original text "...the product of translation is usually a target language that is read without comparison to the original." (Phillips, 2001: 23)

The best translation is one that has the feel of the original, i.e. as if un-translated. Here originality must not be taken a one-sided phenomenon. Newmark talks of two types of translation - semantic and communicative. The latter, he defines as "attempts to produce on its readers an effect as close as possible to that obtained on the readers of the original." (1981: 39) Thus, the translator has to tread on two plains - originality of the SL and that of the TL. Aschen Mikoyan views it as the ability to create coherent and natural discourse in the target language (2002: 70). That is, "one needs to possess the critical as well as creative faculty. A truly professional translator needs to know languages, but also the social norms, reading habits, and stylistic preferences of the culture from which he takes, as well as the one to which he contributes." (Kuhiwczak, 2010 : 116)

Taking for granted that translation is a dynamic activity, no translation can be thought of as an ultimate rendering of the original. However, the noble translators, like Chaucer, have their aim "to be faithful to the content, not the form, of the original text." (Malaczkov, 2001 : 43) Thus, comparison at all levels is the starting point in translation assessment. To make the translation adequate, the translator must be more semiotic than structural. "Such a semiotic reading would bring into focus an important aspect of translation endeavours.... Semantic choices are filtered by communicative qua pragmatic intentions. Just as in the ST the meanings are the underpinnings of its communicative function, their reconstruction in the TT should serve the same purpose, provided the translation is supposed to have the same intent as the original... A communicatively satisfying translation can just as well be semantically congruous. At least, there is always a scale applying to units of translation from single words to phrases up to the whole text. To render them into the TT, translators negotiate semantic-cum-pragmatic choices. At the same time semantic deficiencies have to be consistently eliminated without jeopardising communicative effects, i.e. pragmatic adequacy." (Neubert, 2010 : 72)

Elsewhere, Neubert (2000 : 17) has devised five parameters to evaluate the competence of the translator. He terms it 'Translation competence', which, however, may be applied to translation assessment. They are: language competence, textual competence, subject competence, cultural competence, and transfer competence. Cay Dollerup (2000: 68) offers an innovative as well as an empirical approach to translation evaluation: "The principle of having a first translation done by a target language speaker and then revised by a source language reviser might, possibly, work just as well, and perhaps even better... than the present policy of having target language translators and target language revisers. It might, at least, be worth a try..." This can be reversed to maintain the reciprocity as a first translation done by a source language speaker and then revised by a target language speaker. It recalls Nietzsche's "trans-valuating", i.e. the role-values of both SL and TL are equally important in translation (Kar, 2005).

Adab (2000) has proposed translation assessment to be carried out in three stages: first holistically without reference to the source text, then more critically with reference to the source text, and finally with a view to comparing and synthesizing the two previous assessments.

A tentative checklist for the purpose of translation assessment may be as follows:

i. Skopos or purpose of translation

ii. Translation situation

iii. Coherence (intra-textual, inter-textual)

iv. Similarities

v. Contrasts

vi. Compensation

vii. Innovation

Translation has not been treated as important as an original work only because it has to depend on the SL, but the fact is that "....in the dialectic tension between the source and target poles, the latter enjoys a hegemonic position. Translation is ethnocentric." (Aaltonen, 2000 : 6). Actually, translation is a special act of communication and is a challenging task. Newmark rightly says that, "any old fool can learn a language... but it takes an intelligent person to become a translator." (1969: 85)

REFERENCES

Aaltonen, Sirkku : (2000) : quoted in Marco, Josep : 'Teaching Drama Translation', *Perspectives : Studies in Translatology,* vol. 10 : 1 (2002), pp. 55-68.

Andone, Oana-Helena : (2002) : 'Gender Issues in Translation', *Perspectives : Studies in Translatology,* vol. : 2, pp. 135-150.

Adab, Beverly : (2000) : in Review of Schaffer, Christina & Adab Beverly (eds) *Developing Translation Competence,Perpectives :Studies in Translatology*, vol. 9 : 1, p. 66. Bassnett, Susan : (1998) : Quoted in Marco, ibid.

Davidson, D. : (1984) : *Inquiries into Truth and Interpretation,* Clarendon Press, Oxford.

Dollerup. Cay (2000) : in Review of Grossman, Meta et al (eds.) *Translation into Non-Mother Tongues in Professional Practice and Training*, Tiibingen Stauffenburg Verlag, *Perspectives Studies in Translatology,* (2002) vol. 10-1 (2002) p. 71.

Greimas, A. : Cited in Chandler, Daniel, 2003 : *Semiotics : The Basics*, Routledge; First Indian Reprint. Harris, B. 1983 : Quoted in Neubert, 2010.

Hockett, C.F. (1973) : *A Course in Modern Linguistics*, Oxford and IBH Publishing Co., New Delhi-Bombay-Calcutta.

Jakobson, Roman (1959) : 'On Linguistic Aspect of Translation', in R.A. Brewer (ed.) *On Translation*, Cambridge, pp. 232-239.

Kar, C.R. (2005) : 'Translating as Transrelating', *Indian Journal of Language & Literature*, vol. 1, No. 2, 2005, pp. 45-48.

Kuhiwzak, P. (2010) : The Troubled Identity of Literary Translation', in G. Anderman & M. Rogers (ed.) *Translation Today : Trends & Perspectives*, Viva Books, New Delhi. pp. 112-124.

Magnusson, G. (2010) : 'Interlinear Translation and Discours a La Mark Twain., in G. Anderman & M. Rogers (ed.) ibid, pp. 125-139.

Malaczkov, S. (2001) : 'Geoffrey Chaucer's Translation Strategy', *Perspectives : Studies in Translatology,* Vol. 9 : 1, pp. 33-44.

Malmkjaer, K. (2010) : 'Looking Forward to the Translation : On 'ADynamic Reflection of Human Activities', in G. Anderman & M. Rogers (ed.) ibid, pp. 76-85.

Matilal, B.K. (1990) : *The Word and the World*, Oxford University Press.

Mikoyan, A. (2000) : in Review of Grossman, Meta et al (eds.) *Translation into Non-Mother Tongues in Professional Practice and Training*, Tiibingen Stauffenburg Verlag, *Perspectives : Studies in Translatology,* (2002) vol. 10-1.

Neubert, A. (2000) : in Review of Schaffer, Christina & Adab Beverly(eds) *Developing Translation Competence, Perpectives :Studies in Translatology*, vol. 9 : 1, pp. 63.

Neubert, A. (2010) : 'Some of Peter Newmark's Translation Categorie Revisited', in G. Anderman & M. Rogers (eds.) ibid, pp. 68-75.

Newmark, Peter : (1969) Quoted in Malmkjaer, 2010.

Newmark, Peter (1981) : *Approaches to Translation*, Oxford, Pergamon Press.

Nida, Eugene A. (1964) : *Towards a Science of Translating : With Special Reference to Principles and Procedures Involved in Bible Translating*, E.J. Brill, Leiden.

Phillips, P. (2001): 'Dethroning the Dictionary', *Perspectives : Studies in Translatology*, vol. 9 : a, pp. 23-32.

Venuti, Lawrence)1998) : *The Scandals of Translation*, Routledge,London & New York.

Yunxing, Li (2001) : 'Translation Evaluation in a Systemic Perspective', *Perspectives : Studies in Translatelogy*, vol. 9 : 1, pp. 15-22.

4

Chaos and Imperfection: Two Necessary Principles in Computer Assisted Language Learning and Computer Translation

José Carlos Redondo Olmedilla

Introduction

We know that for many scholars the tone of any good study that intends to be scientific must be characterized by detachment from any personal emotion. This is the hallmark that is normally associated with the triumph of the scientific method. Since we recognize that many researchers have taken this approach for granted, it may be interesting to equally account for the fact that other scholars have precisely found the language force of diction in the natural expression of emotions. The conveyance of emotions is one of the challenges of Computer Assisted Language Learning and Computer Translation, but prior to this analysis; two other core principles must be accounted for: chaos and imperfection.

At first sight, the beginnings of language are veiled from us by time, but we have had access to the study of it through different means. One of these has been through the study of primitive languages and in this case we know that, as J. H. Robinson (156) affirmed: "Words are fundamentally acts". It is evident that somebody can state that acts can be confined to words, but in the same way words can be expanded into acts. To set an example, we can see how whole professions can restrict their activities to words: lawyers, clerks, brokers… words are effective acts or, at least they lead to effective acts. It is a semiosis principle. In the same way that we know that words enhance the clarity of our memory; they can constitute random and imperfect material. In this sense and apart from the biochemical composition of some relevant brain building materials, we know little or less about the data storing system of language. One simply tends to see certain principles in language use and acquisition as imperfect and random because they are viewed through the optics of our rationale.

The Nobel Prize winner for Physics in 1979, Steven Weinberg (546), stated once that "although physicists are only interested in explaining general principles, it is not so clear what is a principle and what is mere accident". Therefore, one may be prompted to think that what is a fundamental law of nature could be an accident. Until now and well within the same frame one tends to think that there is a clear random character in language production and acquisition, but how can we perceive this? An approximate statistical explanation can give us details about language production, but this is information merely about the output. We are more interested in the haphazard and transformational character of language during the input process.

We know that languages are not static and that phonological systems tend to change methodically but unpredictably. Wilhelm Von Humboldt and Heymann Steinhal presented this idea openly and we have a clear example of it in Grimm's Law. Garrett Michener and Novak referred to the fact that, given an unrestricted set of languages: "It is difficult to model a language change by using tools from evolutionary game dynamics" (Garrett Michener and Nowak 1). We certainly marvel at the phenomenon of language acquisition, but its greatness relies precisely on its imperfection. Partha Niyogi, when referring to the robustness and reliability of language learning by children, transmitted in her work the idea that the process of language acquisition cannot be perfect or languages would never change (*The Computational Nature of Language Learning and Evolution*, 2006). Here, paradoxically lies one of the great principles of language: imperfection. The latter can be understood as mutability, facility for change or flexibility, but the parameter that best suits its meaning is its lack of perfection.

Children's language acquisition is a good evolutionary example and perhaps one of the most clearly established plastic windows in nature. Francisco Mora (77) remembers how in 1705 a Jesuit, Father Catrou, mentioned the Moghul emperor Akbar Khan and how he had ordered to isolate twelve new-born babies under the care of deaf and dumb people. It was done in such a way that any kind of verbal contact was avoided and forbidden. He wanted to know which was man's genuine language, the one given by God in the beginning, and the one used for the very first time with other men. The boys were called before him, but, prior to this moment, he gathered all kinds of language scholars to try to determine and decipher the possible language from the boys. What was unexpected and astonishing for the emperor was that once the boys were before him, they uttered nothing. The boys were dumb and were only able to communicate through signs. This experience serves to illustrate that speech is not something you are born with.

One is born with the potentiality to speak, but only learning materializes that potential. Nevertheless, more things need to be said and some questions still linger in this field, questions such as, has the random and imperfect character of language little or much to do with phylogeny? Can one have access to the phylogeny of language? If so, how? Can we have access to the random processes of language through inference? If so, how?

It is known that the random character of language has been simulated through the stochastic processes of Maths, and then they have been applied to computer software. However, we cannot forget that computers are based upon a rational and only simulated randomness imperfectly because the guiding principle is non-random-like. In other words, the way to achieve randomness in language through stochastic processes is finally organized through deduction, not inference. The question that arises is, Have we wondered if the way to find the explanation of chaos and imperfection in language can be reached through (biological) philogenetic inference.

John R. Searle remarked that the sense of information processing that is used in cognitive science is "too high a level of abstraction to capture the concrete biological reality of intrinsic intentionality" (Searle: 33) and this is only one of the lesser mitigating factors when considering the conveying of language through machines. If we wish to improve our abilities at reproducing human language through machines and at using them for teaching and language learning purposes, this intrinsic fact is capital at this level. We have mimicked human language through computers, thanks to a forward process, a course of action based upon the conception of human language as output. Researchers of different departments: Statistics, Linguistics,

Computer Science... have provided us with very good learning and teaching material used nowadays, but most people still feel there is a void in language representation through machines and their different applications. Have we wondered if the direction to solve the problem is just the opposite, not the forward one? We know that there are forward and backward analyses and that some tools can be used in any direction. For example, Linguistic phylogenetic reconstruction offers an inference problem, and Evans Ringe and Warnow admitted in the presentation to their work that this kind of reconstruction gives rise to a statistical inverse problem. Statistics constitute a forward method, but it is applied backwards in order to deduce information. So we can see how a kind of reverse engineering can be used to determine the internal structure of some things. The author of this article believes that the randomness and imperfect character of language are associated and linked. He also believes that they are in the potential interior, and that they belong to the backward or "biological inward" direction of the study of language.

Inference

The mathematician, philosopher and Nobel Prize for literature winner, Bertrand Russell (1950), reminded us in *An Outline of Philosophy* (63) that inference is considered to be a sign of intelligence that marks the superiority of man in respect to machines. The problem is how to have access to that level. A good way to achieve this could be through inductive inference. Bertrand Russell explained (186-187) that inference can be applied both to deduction and induction. As we know, induction and deduction are taken as different ways of interpreting and having access to reality. The difference lies in the consideration that inference assumes in deduction: a sign as a sign of two different things, while in induction two different signs are the sign of the same thing. In my opinion, the two elements that could well be interpreted as the signs of the same mark of language are imperfection and the random character. If we are able to understand the nature of these signs and how they operate, we will know much about a priori input generator or backward stage of language production. We will also be able to replicate language and thus work with a more natural state of language and, of course, be able to transfer it to Computer Assisted Language Learning and Computer Translation.

The problem is that we know little about putting the process of inference into practice. It is, using an Evans, Ringe and Warnow term "a priori winnowing" (4). But how do we winnow? In a related field, Franz Och, Google's machine translation expert boasted that the search-engine giant would probably have a key role in the future of machine translation, since it has such a huge repository of text (*The Economist Technology Quarterly*, 21). These future systems and modern day systems seem to be voracious systems fed with huge data banks: vocabulary items, sentences, training texts..., but problems like mobility, suppleness, adaptability, capacity for suitability still remain. It is clear that some frequencies and patterns may change from one generation to the next, but some frames are stable. However, if the situation requires it, even these stable frames are liable to change. What is/are the element/s that offer/s explanation for this?

Niyogi (447) alluded to the fact that much of the learning theory in language acquisition is based upon the classical Chomskian idealization of "ideal speaker- hearer in a homogeneous linguistic environment", which implies an artificial regard of language. Nevertheless, in the same way, Pinker (97) reminds us how Chomsky demonstrated that the linking word systems are not only somewhat suspicious, but are radical and basically incorrect explanations about the way language works. It is true that they are direct combinatory systems, but they are of an erroneous nature. This nature is what constitutes the good news. This allows the relationship between communicative efficiency and appropriateness, social connectivity, 'learnability' and the possibility of shared systems. This is the key to the evolutionary sequence of language

Linguists and mathematicians have been working with coherent linguistic elements and have been able to use model constructions. Nevertheless, these models, though based upon empirical data, are speculative, because they do not reach the correct fortuitous flexibility. Chaos and imperfection are part of the evolutionary dynamics of language and language learning. If, as Niyogi states "there are strong synergies between the methods and concerns of evolutionary biology and those of evolutionary linguistics" (456), inference on a backward or a priori stage of language could be explained through the exploration of natural evolutionary questions in the context of animal communication. It may equally be that the explanation of chaos and imperfection as part of a type of evolutionary linguistics may be a part concern of evolutionary biology. Of course, language is more than biology, it is cultural, social, unconscious, but the latter elements are by-products of the first and form part of the deductive behaviour realm. Chaos and imperfection form part of the inductive inference realm.

The State of the Art

Paradoxical as it may seem, and as Bertrand Russell asserted in *An Outline of Philosophy*, there has always been a subordination of induction to deduction. This is so much so that induction theories in logic are simply invented reasoning to prove that what we have done is rational. This subordination of induction and the insistence on the ubiquitous role of deduction leave some elements unexplained, especially when dealing with language operations: translation, language learning... From a mathematical perspective, language learning is grounded on the assumption that no language can be in an evolutionary stable equilibrium because two fundamental principles, random and imperfection, are actively determining the nature of language and subsequently of its operations: language learning, language translation.... However, this assumption is incorrect as it does not heed the arbitrary behaviour and nature of language. This fact is well reflected when simple learning or translation errors lead to complex, unpredictable and seemingly stochastic changes in languages over time. Steven Pinker in *The Language Instinct* (1995) affirmed that the essential fact in language is its extreme improbability. On equal terms he stated that if there was a system able to duplicate human language, this would have to account for a series of rules, but they would have to be necessarily non-prescriptive. We have advanced a lot as far as logical deduction is concerned and it could well be that the next revolution will concern inference. As inference is not a popular topic or due to the fact that we do not have the necessary tools to explore inference, we can build a device to diminish this gap in our knowledge. The inclusion of a stochastic process is a step further into the fallacy that we are closer to the brain processes through computers, but in the meantime, it is not a complete misconception.

One must also keep in mind that what we call the laws of language or the constants of language may be accidental features constrained by form and use. It is also true that some language phenomena that we regard now as mere accidents will one day be understood as mathematical or even physical principles. However, till that day comes, a useful tool is to account for them through the simulation of polyvalent elements of random character. Recent research in Computer Assisted Language Learning and Computer Translation has produced a lot of positive work through working with deductive-logic material. However, Evans, Ringe and Warnow left it clear that any future research in Computer Assisted Languages Learning and its related or derivatives must account for certain stochastic models where the answer for some linguistic haphazard behaviours may lie in the nature of linguistic phylogeny and not in the rationale of administering words as groups of data (Evans, Ringe and Warnow 2004). Indeed more than this, it may be time to complete the task with inductive natural and language-like material of a non-deductive nature. Only if that facet is developed, we will have truly-resembling ways to learning languages and translating through computers.

Conclusion

There is no doubt that recent developments in electronic instrumentation and computer science have changed the way we think about language operating. The capacity of language learning methods through computers and computer translation has made it possible to expect answers to questions that it would not have been viable to ask a generation ago. However, though there are simulators, there seem to be no efficient substitute replacements for chaos and imperfection as inherent elements in the flexibility and evolutionary dynamics of language. Secondly, though there is a difference between language and biology, mostly because genetic transmission in nature is vertical –carried out from parents to sons– and linguistic transmission allows horizontal possibilities –among non-related individuals– (Redondo Olmedilla 203), we must take into account that the closer we get to the biological analogy of language, the better the understanding we will have about some important aspects. David Crystal (438) presented the stages of language acquisition through stages of grammatical growth. Grammar was clearly presented as a continuous process. Nevertheless, the earliest stage, the so called "holophrastic stage" –because the children put the equivalent of a whole sentence into a single word– is, according to Crystal 'hardly like a grammar at all'. This is an important fact, because our handling of language is realised through computers with elements that behave like grammar rules, but that ignore this earliest stage.

My proposal is that the answer to chaos and imperfection as basic constituents of language operations: language acquisition, translation... is in a primal state. If we check the meaning of 'chaos' in any well reputed dictionary, such as the third edition of the *American Heritage Dictionary*, we realize that, apart from the standard meaning, basically "condition or place of state disorder or confusion", we find that the etymology dates back to ancient Greek where it was a "formal primordial space". What strikes us even more is that its astronomy related meaning is "the disordered state of unformed matter and infinite space supposed in some cosmogonist views to have existed before the ordered universe". If one is to link it to this present attempt for clarification, my suggestion leads towards the search of this primal, "before the ordered universe", state that appears in the last cited meaning. It is attainable through inference and more feasible and explicable, as it is an early state, in the context of animal communication.

Whether chaos and imperfection really behave through stable implicit evolutionary dynamics or not is another issue. What we do know is that David Crystal (440) and Partha Niyogi (446) recognized the important role of interaction in language acquisition and its derivatives and we consequently know that learning to speak and listen is a process that takes place spontaneously as part of natural interaction. I simply dare say that spontaneity, imperfection and chaos belong to the equation of interaction and that interaction is central to language acquisition and language translation. The cogent proposal offered in this article so far is that language, language acquisition and translation as derivatives are coherent, thanks to chaos and imperfection. Needless to say, we cannot ignore them in any implementation via Computer Assisted Language Learning or Computer Translation.

WORKS CITED

Crystal, D. (2003) *The Cambridge Encyclopaedia of the English Language(2nd.ed.)*. Cambridge: Cambridge University Press

Cunnigham, K. (2000) "Integrating CALL into the Writing Curriculum", *The Internet TESL Journal*, Vol VI, No 5, May.

Evans, S.N., Ringe, D. & Warnow, T. (2004) "Inference of divergence times as a statistical inverse problem", *Phylogenetic Methods and the Prehistory of Languages*. Cambridge: Cambridge University Press.

"How to build a Babel Fish" (2006) *The Economist Technology Quarterly*, June 10th (20-21).

Mitchener, W.G. & Nowak, M. A. (2004) *Chaos and Language: Proceedings of the Royal Society of London. Series B, Biological Sciences.* 271(1540), 701-704.

Mora, F. (2001) *El reloj de la sabiduría. Tiempos y espacios en el cerebro humano*, Madrid: Alianza Editorial

Pinker, S. (1994) *The Language Instinct. How the Mind Creates Language*. London: Penguin.

Redondo Olmedilla, J. C. (2003) "James Fenimore Cooper: La desaparición de lenguas y la necesidad de Babel", Revista *A Distancia*, Universidad Nacional de Educación a Distancia, vol. 21, nº 1 febrero, pp. 201-205.

Robinson, J. H. (1992) Civilization. In: Clifton, F. (ed.), *The Treasury of the Encyclopaedia Britannica*. New York: Viking, 156-174.

Searle, John R. (1990) "Is the Brain a Digital Computer?", *Proceedings and Addresses of the American Philosophical Association*, Vol. 64, No. 3 , 21-37.

Weinberg, S. (2004) Can Science explain everything? Anything? in: Peterson, L. H. & Bereton, J. C. (eds.), *The Norton Reader*. New York: Norton, 539-550.

Niyogi, P. (2006) *The Computational Nature of Language Learning and Evolution*. Cambridge, Mass. The M I T Press.

5

Problems in Translation of Drama: A Case Study of Mohan Rakesh's *Halfway House*

C.L.Khatri

In a multi-lingual country like India translation is indispensable. It has played a leading role in enriching the dramatic corpus of both Hindi and English. Many of the popular plays have come to their folds from regional languages. For example, from Kannad, Grish Karnad's *Tughlaq, Hayavadana* and his other plays, from Bengali Badal Sircar's *Pagla Ghora, Baki Itihas, Juloos* and the plays of Rabindranath Tagore, from Marathi Vijay Tendulkar's *Khamosh, Sakharam Binder, Ghasi Ram Kotwal, Kanyadan* etc. were translated into, Hindi, English and other languages and were successfully performed on the stage in both source language and target languages. Not only this but translation of the plays of Shakespeare, Ibsen, Shaw, Osborne, Arthur Miller, Brecht and of other foreign playwrights have provided the well needed stage worthy plays to the body of Hindi drama.

Problems in Translation

Translation is a complex process of transmitting not only the meaning and intention but the socio-cultural specialties and the composite effect of the original text to the readers into the target language (TL). According to Dr. Rabindranath Srivastava, translation is a creative reconstruction of the underlying facts of the text of source language into target language on the principle of approximation. However, translation involves explanation also. In ancient India translation was intra-language. It meant restatement in terms of explanation of the earlier text of teachings. In those days scriptures like the Vedas and the Upanishads were in the form of Shruti transmitted orally by Rishis to their disciples. Later on, they were translated into written form in the same language.

Translation of any genre of literature is a tight rope walk. It is more difficult than the original writing. Because the translation is to reach the nearest to the text in contents, intents, structure and the total effect but it should not be literal. Each language has its own distinct rhythm, music, linguistic and cultural delicacies that are near impossible to reproduce in target language. The art of translation is all the more difficult because it is pre-requisite for the translator to be proficient in source language (SL), target language (TL) and he should understand the subject in its totality. The best translation is the one that is most approximate to the text without giving the feeling to the readers of reading a translation. A practical problem that a translator faces in the course of translation is to find the proper synonyms of words and phrases in the target language and they should express not the literal meaning but the contextual meaning of those words and phrases.

Problems in the Translation of Drama

In translation of drama besides the aforesaid pre-requisites, the translator must have the practical knowledge of theatre, of light, sound and colour mechanism. Physical and facial expressions also add to the meaning of the dialogues and the translator has to take them into account. The translation of a play in the target language must be equally stage-able and the dialogues should be natural, expressive and convenient to deliver in target language for the characters. This is a challenge for a translator.

There are certain architectural problems which have to be taken into account. Nemi Chandra Jain rightly says that the problem involved in the translation of drama lies in the genre of drama itself. Drama is an entirely dialogue oriented form of literature in which the story, emotional and practical dilemmas, conflict, struggle, objective and thought process of the playwright and characters are expressed through dialogues. In fact dialogues throw light on the overall personality of characters – their educational standard, socio-cultural moorings, general habits and mental condition. It is the language they speak that distinguishes one character from other. And this poses a great problem. Where the language of dialogue is colloquial, short and pointed as we find in *Aadhe Adhure,* it becomes sometimes difficult to find the equivalent expression of the same nature in target language. In such cases one has to add explanation to it and sometimes to omit a clause or even a dialogue. But this is a risky affair because explanation may spoil the poignancy and naturalness of the dialogues of source language. If it is not given it may affect the expressiveness of the dialogue and things may not be clear.

Dialects, proverbs, idioms and multi-lingual references in the dialogues create problem in the process of translation. Now the question is whether to retain the terms of regional dialects or foreign words in the translation or not. From a realistic point of view retention of foreign terms can be advocated. But if the same effect can be reproduced in some other ways it will be good for stage-ability and communication.

An important aspect of translation is the creation of a particular environment. For each play has a particularbackground-political, social, industrial or spiritual. The environment is an integral factor in the composite effect in the TL through sounds and words what a director produces on the stage with the help of sound, colour and light mechanism.

Sometimes motive implied in a dialogue is different from the explicit meaning as in the case of ironical and satiric expression and in dramatic irony. A translator is expected to preserve the feeling and tone of the source language.

A Case Study of Halfway House

The most popular drama of Mohan Rakesh-*Aadhe Adhure*-is translated into English under the title *Halfway House* by Bindu Batra. A comparative study of the original text and the translation reveals the problems involved in its translation, the points of approximation, variation between the two texts and omissions in the translation. It also shows how far Bindu Batra has succeeded in her job. Bindu Batra began her career as a translator and art journalist. Later on, she worked in the area of film and performing arts. She has been close to Mohan Rakesh and has translated the play in continuous consultation with Mohan Rakesh. The final draft was approved by Rakesh himself. Despite being placed in a privileged position it was not an easy job for her to translate the play into English.

One of the significant achievements of Bindu Batra is that she has produced a translation which is perfectly stage-able. Dialogues in English are colloquial and can be delivered eloquently on the stage. Another achievement is that the translation does not disturb the dramatic thrusts of the Hindi text. The overall effect of the translation is approximate to the Hindi text and the thematic content is well expressed.

However, there are variations and omissions in the translation. Lines move away from here and there, a few dialogues are dropped and some others are abridged. Descriptive passages in brackets are cut to size. Such passages are well needed in the stage performance and have to be supplied. They not only give the background but also create the right atmosphere for the play. I do not subscribe to the view that it is desirable as Dilip Kumar Basu feels in his 'Note on the Translation' Published in the *Halfway House:*

The translation of the title is not literal. 'Halfway House' is not a lexical equivalent of 'Aadhe Adhure'. 'Aadhe Adhure' connotes mainly a sense of incompleteness, imperfection and half-hearted attempt. The play deals with incomplete men, disintegrating family and disordered house. Title of the translation Halfway House aptly conveys the sense. But I doubt if it conveys the second meaning. In most of the studies of Aadhe Adhure the tragedy has drawn little attention. Savitri, the heroine struggles for twenty two years to make a happy home, to keep the house in order but fails. She strives in the quest of perfection but in vain. Even in her feminist approach to life when she tries other men-Juneja, Shivjeet, Jagmohan and Manoj to replace her husband, she is half-hearted. And a half-hearted attempt seldom if ever meets success. Even when she leaves the house in dejection to live her own life on her own terms, she is not decisive and returns to her 'hell' defeated. But the title cannot be disapproved of. It is pleasing, and it reflects the focus of the play.

Omissions and Deviations

Bindu Batra does not give details of age, dress, mood and other features of the characters in the beginning as they are given in the original play. She has only given the list of dramatis personae with their age. Even the details of the living room where action takes place is abridged In fact, the details given in the beginning set the tone of the play and are necessary guidelines for stage production. In fact, facial expression, gesture and posture of the characters have bearings on the meaning of the dialogues delivered. Take for example the first dialogue of the play by the woman when she returns home from office.

Estri: (Thakan nikalney key Swar main) Oh Hola HoHa Ho Ha (Kuch Hatash Bhaw se) Phir Ghar Main Koi Nahin! (A.A.13)
English Translation

"The Woman: Phe-e-ew! No one's ever at home!"

By reading the Hindi version one can visualize the actual picture of the woman. Above all 'Phew' in itself expresses the feelings of astonishment, impatience, discomfort, disgust, etc. So it was desirable to express the mood and feelings of the character in the translation. Such details describing the general mood or demeanour of characters are left out at several places in the play. Again in the same dialogue 'Ashok' in place of 'Ashok Babu' does not communicate the tone and feeling of the speaker. It misses the derision and exasperation implied in it. 'Babu' in Hindi is a term of affection and respect. But it is also used to ridicule someone in the mood of exasperation.

At one point in Act I she calls her husband 'aadami': (A.A. 19). The word aadami gives the socio-cultural background of the heroine, Savitri, and it cannot be expressed with 'you' or 'husband'.

A translator should refrain from omitting actions or making changes in actions of the original play. One wonders why she does so in *Halfway House* several times. For example, in the very first scene Savitri calls Kinni looking at the inside door. But in the translation looking at the 'inside door' is omitted. Then she picks up a book from Kinni's bag. But Bindu Batra writes that she 'goes towards books'. Again when she encounters the first man while carrying the tray towards the courtyard door, the facial reaction and the movement of two are left out in the translation. When the man calls the woman "Listen" while she was going to make tea, the woman stops and turns to him but it is left out in the translation. These and the like omissions do not affect the overall impact of the drama. But in stage performance they will be missed.

Omission in action or even in dialogue is fraught with serious risk. One should opt for omission of a dialogue only when it is redundant in the target language or is inevitable keeping in mind the demands of stage-acting. Most of her omissions and deviations in dialogue can be approved of. As in page 16 of the translation where the older girl sharply reacts to her father's query, "Is consumption the only thing one can have?" (16) Look at the literal translation of her dialogue and the transcreation by Bindu Batra:

Literal Translation

The Older Girl: "So what else can one have? Sans eyes? Crooked nose and ear? Sans lips? Does my face look like that to you?"

Transcreation by Bindu Batra

The Older Girl: "What else can one have? Cancer? Polio? Leprosy? (H.H. 16)

Certainly the latter reads natural in English and recaptures the mood and tone of the original speech with greater precision. Again for Singa (horns) on Singhania's head (in a sketch drawn by Ashok) the translator uses 'ears' because 'horns' would have sent misleading signals in English for in Hindi the saying is that "asses don't grow horns".

But omission of dialogues in page 10, 17 and 54 in the translation does not seem necessary. In page 10 the omitted dialogue runs like this:

The First Man (stands up in anger):You talk as if...

The woman: Why did you stand up like this?

The first Man: Can't I?

The woman (in weary reproof): You can. But within these walls. (Translation mine)

This is the first candid statement of Savitri that shows how she views her husband and it throws ample light on the spineless personality of Mahendranath. Therefore, it should not have been dropped.

One may point out a few words and sentences which do not properly communicate the feelings implied in their original version. For example, "Go ahead, provoke one if you want." (11) does not convey the real sense of the Hindi statement expressing apprehension. "Tum Lar Bhi Sakte Ho Ees Wakta." (19) The translation in imperative gives a different sense. A literal translation may serve the purpose here-'you may quarrel'.

But in many other cases literal translation will not do and is rightly avoided wherever necessary. In Act two when Juneja comes to Binni, she asks "Chaya Banaun Aapake Liye?" may not be proper in the context where Binni has already made tea for Jagmohan who leaves the venue without taking tea. What she means here is just to pour tea. So the translation "May I pour you a cup of tea?" (62) is appropriate. In the same Act she says to Juneja about Mahendranath-Apana do Pair Kabhi They Uske Pass. (83) A literal translation in English would be erroneous. So what it implies is expressed in translation: "When was he ever capable of doing anything?" (67)

Let us have another example. Mahendranath says "Larkey-Larki Kee Convent Kee Fees Jati Thi." (19) A literal translation would sound unnatural in English. So an approximate sense is conveyed through "School Fees" in 'Halfway House'. But school in itself does not always mean convent school. This is a limitation of translation.

A close study of the original text and the translation of Aadhe Adhure reveals two important points of this translation. First, most of the long speeches have context based translation and not literal translation. They do not give the impression of reading a translation. However, short and crisp dialogues are largely rendered in English literally to gain the approximate strength of pointed colloquial conversation particularly between the man and the woman, and the woman and the older girl.

A good translator is expected to make their characters speak in their own language and not in his language. So the language of the characters reflects their personality, their social, economic and educational standard, their habits and mental condition. Bindu Batra to a great extent succeeds in this difficult task. So the language of Singhania is typical of his character and is different from that of Juneja or Mahendranath. Again the agitated mind of a young child, Kinni, who is crying, is well reflected in her language.

"If n-no one's wanted they all c-crowd around... and when the they're wanted, not a s-soul's to be seen." (59)

Finally one can say that Halfway House is to a great extent a successful translation of Mohan Rakesh's Aadha Adhure, despite omissions and deviations.

WORKS CITED

Dr. Nagendda, (ed.) Anuvada Vigyan: Sidhanta Anuprayog: 1983, Delhi University, Delhi.

Rakesh,Mohan Aadha Adhure. New Delhi.: Radhakrishna Prakashan. 1977,

Batra, Bindu, Halfway House, A translation of Aadha Adhure. Delhi: Worldview Publication.

6

Text and Context in Amrita Pritam's "*Death of a City*"[1]

Aruna Bomma Reddy

I

Amrita Pritam (1919-2005) is undoubtedly one of the pioneers of 20th century women writing in India. Though she was born in Gurjanwala, now in Pakistan, she chose to live in Delhi after the partition of India and continued to write in Punjabi and Hindi. Although she lived in Delhi, her writing bears the mark of a cultural ethos that is uniquely Punjabi. She discussed women-centric themes much before the feminist movement became active in India. In her writings she vociferously argues for the dignity of women as individuals; men and women caught up in their familial and societal relationships is the underlying theme of most of her works. Amrita Pritam explores women's sexuality through her works by which she extends an unmatched sensitivity and understanding towards women's plight in a predominantly patriarchal society. Her writings appear to be informed by a personal note as she herself has had a tumultuous family life and was perceived to be a rebel during her times. The rebellion born of her life is reflected in her short stories like "The Stench of Kerosene", "The Wild Flower" and "Sahiban in Exile"[2] and in her poems like "Jada" and "Ek Baat".[3] The familial concerns and dilemmas that women encounter in her writings are not far removed from the reality of her own life. Amrita Pritam's concerns in her fiction are shared by other contemporary women writers like Kamala Das, Ismat Chugtai, Shashi Deshpande, Kamala Markandaya and many others.

This paper is an attempt to study the complexity of the narrative of the city as projected in her short story "Death of a City". The story is a symbolic expression of how society smothers women's desire for self-expression and freedom in making decisions of their life. It is particularly interesting as Amrita Pritam draws parallels between the life of a woman and that of a dead city. The story moves in the structural pattern of a city and this paper highlights the architecture of the dead city and the pattern of life of the female protagonist. The city referred to in the story is far different from the industrial cities that we are familiar with. The city here stands as a metaphor for the inner life or the sexuality of a woman. The existential angst of the protagonist is envisaged through a dead Italian city Pompeii. The paper has the twin objectives of (i) looking at the images of death, damnation and the desolation within, while unveiling the structure or rather the architecture of the city (I call it architecture as it is about city) and (ii) of examining protagonist's search for identity, and her exploration of her sexuality — finally connecting it up with the dead city and the possibility of suggesting answers for her quest.

In the story "Death of a City" the conflicts and the aspirations of a young woman are symbolized in the many images of the city. For the sake of convenience, I'll give a brief account of the story. The protagonist Ms. Singh is a school teacher in London, whose individuality has been oppressed by an overpowering father who objects to her marriage with her lover Veerinder because he belongs to a different community from hers; she feels that her desire for freedom is damned like that of the city of Pompeii. Her lover, Veerinder deceives her and marries another woman without her knowledge. Ms. Singh in her search for happiness often escapes into the memory of the city of Pompeii which she visits on a weekend. The dead city comes alive to her bringing back the memories of her childhood city: the city which she has left in search of freedom. The 'city' discussed in the story represents the inner life of the protagonist as also the ancient Italian city of Pompeii. Pompeii was a port city in Italy which sent Roman ships back without allowing it to the port. In an attempt to avenge the insult Pompeii was attacked and subsequently annexed and made a colony by Rome. Later, Pompeii also suffers an earthquake in which people experience death in a unique way. People were found transfixed in their living postures in agonizing positions while lava from the Vesuvius engulfed them and thus reducing a living city to ashes.

The multi-layered structure of the story unfurls the imagery of death and desolation. The city is dead and so also her desire for a family, home and ultimately the desire to fall into the moral code itself. Ms. Singh wants to fall out of the dominant patterns of the moral code, once she discovers the myth of the much celebrated values of love, morality and family. From then onwards, love becomes an elusive goal for her. It is equivalent to death. The death of the city is the death of her desires. But the true love she seems to search for becomes more and more elusive. The images of death at every point illustrate the death of desire and the inner desolation of the protagonist. Ms. Singh internalizes the death of the city as her own.

The story begins with the images of death as is captured in the title of story itself and then leads to the damnation of Pompeii and consequently to the desolation of the city. As the story unfurls, we are informed that the Romans attacked Pompeii and imposed their language and customs on the 20,000 citizens living in Pompeii. Similarly, the central character of the story Ms. Singh's father doesn't allow her to marry Veerinder, a man of her choice. Likewise in encountering the coercive power of the colonizer and a patriarchal father, both the people of Pompeii and the protagonist suffer humiliation and loss of identity; secondly the analogy between the city and Ms. Singh is that of the desolation. The city has been attacked and the attempts to resurrect the city have been thwarted by the earthquake and an eventual volcanic eruption. Ms. Singh's attempts to free her life from the power and authority of her father and her desire to marry Veerinder fail because the man she is in love gets married to another woman without her knowledge. Thus the purpose of her defiance -of her father's authority- is defeated. She has been betrayed. Like the city, she feels lonely and abandoned too being unable to connect with either the family that she has left or the family that she desires to build.

Another interesting aspect of the story is the dominant geometrical pattern that emerges in the story; the story "Death of a City" moves in triangles; there are three cities in the story: one is the actual setting of the story that of London where the central character lives; the second one is the city of Pompeii into which she often escapes in her loneliness and in her search for identity; and the third one is the city of lost happiness, where she has spent her childhood. To take the point further, the protagonist identifies herself with the city at each turn of her life. The three dimensional architecture of the story, in fact, helps us understand the predicament of the protagonist as well as her existential crisis. Her silences, her desires, her wanderings find a resonance in the dead city. The triangular aspect is again manifest in the cycle of love, life and death as represented by the three women characters in the story, Ms. Singh, the mother and a friend of hers, Claire. Ms. Singh in her pining for love symbolizes love, while the mother stands for life as the creator and nurturer and finally Claire with her irredeemable predicament stands for death. Incidentally there are three lovers in Ms. Singh's life.

While the story is fraught with the images of death, damnation and desolation the three stages which the city experiences and the stages which the protagonist relives and easily identifies with, it also oscillates between the spatial and the temporal dimensions. It would be useful to look at the spatial and temporal dimension of the story for a better understanding of Ms. Singh's predicament/search for the self.

Spatially there are three dimensions to the story:

- the city of Pompeii
- the industrial city of London and
- the inner city of childhood.

Temporally it again shows three kinds of time sense:

- the present (her own)
- the past (hers and that of the city's)
- (no)future (as represented in her friend)

The spatial dimension throws light on the inner and outer moorings of the protagonist. The story discusses three different yet related spaces: one is the actual setting of the story the industrial city of London where the protagonist Ms. Singh teaches. The second place is the ancient city of Pompeii: where the protagonist constantly escapes and finds an image of herself and the more interesting space is the space within the mind of every young woman- which the author describes as the third space- that is the city within. It represents the complex situation of her life and the desperation for love and the eventual denial of it. The loveless life that Ms. Singh leads and the apathy with which she deals with her lovers is a response to her parents' cruelty to her own situation. The city inside her mind is the city in which she grew up- which stands for her autocratic parental home. "I was no different from Pompeii. For fifteen long years I remained quietly embraced to the London frost and the silence within me". [4] The torture that she undergoes is not spoken out. She suffers silently and witnesses her childhood dream dissolve quietly. Her Indian city was big like Pompeii. Her childhood city was full of hopes and aspirations and it was a land of promises. Hence she compares "the history of my city is no different from that of Pompeii and that is why, perhaps I came to the ruins of my own city while moving amidst the ruins of Pompeii. [5] The glory of Pompeii and her own happy life which is lost are brought to bear a similarity.

The desolation drives her into shifting planes of time: the present, the past and (no) future. The present represents the conflict ridden life of Ms. Singh and the past of Pompeii is nothing but the remains of destruction, of a gory past and Ms. Singh also stands as a witness to the violence caused by her parental authority and the deceptive lover. If father opposes to the community of her lover as a hurdle for their marriage, mother attacks her sensitivity with her abusive language. And Veerinder whom she loves and for whose sake she deserts her family deceives her for the security and comfort of another woman. The situation of (no) future is not represented by Ms. Singh herself but a friend of hers, Claire, an ageing English woman who is a divorcee and has no hope of getting lovers. in order to gratify the needs of the flesh makes love to an electronic instrument. This situation, as Ms. Singh finds has (no) future because it is not life-giving but simply a damning experience. She doesn't want an electronic gadget to become part of her fate.

The city of Pompeii loses its freedom and also its future after the volcanic eruption and Ms. Singh too doesn't find any future after her lover Veerinder gets married to another woman. And there begins her search for identity. She wants to get away from that happy city of childhood which has now been turned into bitter memory, but she finds herself transfixed in an act of escape like the many images of Pompeii which were found dead in their living postures. Symbolically she identifies herself with a figure in Pompeii and in actuality also she cannot get away from the memories of her childhood/adolescent city and hence driven by desperation, she constantly finds solace only in the dead city. Hence both the protagonist and her city of fantasy have no future as Pompeii is not a city of future.

II

At this point it would be pertinent to probe into some of the questions that the story raises; "city" in all its connotations represents the desires and aspirations of a woman here in the story. It doesn't denote the complex industrial life. Why does she constantly escape into Pompeii which is dead? Why is it set in London and not in India? Usually, rural life and rural space are celebrated as romantic escape hatches. As a foil to the polluted, space-crammed city life, village is celebrated and treated as an anchoring position for all human emotions. But Ms. Singh constantly harps on to images of Pompeii in her efforts to bring together the loose ends of her life. It could perhaps be explained that her desires for love and family and the absence of it in later life and the lack of meaning in all these sexual acts that she indulges in, make her constantly compare herself to the dead city of Pompeii. At one point of time in her life, concepts like family, love and morality seem to have had some meaning. Because she nurtures hopes of fulfilment of love, she finds hope in marriage and family. But as her dreams begin to shatter her search for fulfilling yet elusive love begins. The first time she takes a lover she says the moral code doesn't bother her. The quest for meaning, in other words, for some sense of love, leads to her encounters with the entrenched system of values and the subsequent disillusionment with the system. And hence the complacent notions of love, morality, marriage, family are shattered and the comparison of herself and her life with a dead city rather than a living city with population.

The quest for fulfilling love seems to continue as indicated by her inclination to take lovers occasionally and the men do not mean much to her and moreover she's not intrigued by any sense of morality. The second question is the mystery of why the story is set in London, far away from India? The possible answer could be that the protagonist Ms. Singh's exploration of her sexuality in her attempts to find the meaning of life, love and ultimately her own existence are inevitably surrounded by questions of morality. She has defied all moral codes and the possibility of a role model such a story can set to the contemporary Indian society will be underplayed if it is set in a far off land; where the moral code perhaps would be different and also Ms. Singh being an Indian, cannot be fixed into either the British moral code or can she be judged according to the Indian codes of conduct. The story being set in London gives her the leverage of not being judged by any of these societies. It is a device; an exploration of the sexuality of man would definitely form part of the cultural ethos of any nation. But a woman's exploration of the same needed a setting far removed from India because of the possible implications such an act would have on the contemporary Indian family and society. Though the editor of the volume claims that the time period presents a transitional period in Indian society "since the beginning of the sixties a new generation of writers has emerged, beginning a new period in Indian Literature. Their writings are a testimony to the new thinking about human relations, a new type of psychology and morality, newer conflicts- depicting the aspirations and frustrations of the modern Indian"[1] **(Endnotes)**

"The Death of a City" presents these conflicts and struggles in a situation far away from the actual site of happening.

REFERENCES

1. While the stories "Stench of Kerosene" and "The Wild Flower" are translated by Kushwanth Singh, the other story referred to in this paper "Sahiban in Exile" is translated by Nirupama Dutt.
2. These two poems are anthologized in Tharu and K.Lalitha edited volume Women Writing in India Vol. I; the poems are translated by Kesava Rao and Vasantha Kannabhiran.
3. See Modern Indian Short Stories Kohli (eds). (1974). Arnold Heinman: New Delhi, 1983, p.4
4. Ibid
5. See text p. (xv)

WORKS CONSULTED

Kohli, Suresh (eds). *Modern Indian Short Stories* (1974). Arnold Heinemann: New Delhi,1983.

Pritam, Amrita. "The Stench of Kerosene" (http://www.sikh-history.com/literature/stories/kerosene.html)

— ."The Wild Flower". (http://www.littlemag.com/jan-feb01/amrita.html)

— . "Sahiban in Exile". (http://www.littlemag.com/belonging/amrita.html)

— . "Death of a City". *Modern Indian Short Stories.* Kohli (eds). (1974). Arnold Heinemann: New Delhi,1983.

Tharu and Lalitha.(Ed) *Women Writing in India Vol.I.* New Delhi: OUP, 1993, P. 160-164.

7

Nuances of Translation

T.Sai Chandra Mouli

Translation is an integral part of human life. If Verbal communication connects people, non verbal communication plays an equally significant role in cementing and reinforcing inter- personal relationships. It is translation of the *said* and *unsaid* that makes it possible to bring people and their cultures together. In fact, translation or transcreation is a very important aspect of comparative literature.

> Translation as a sub-text of the original text is comparatively a modern concept. Maybe it is the later requirement of straight jacketed faithfulness to the original which had a debilitating effect. In Indian tradition it never used to be so as the transference of text from one language into another was more of the nature of adaptation, retelling and redoing which went on over a period of time. [Gopi Chand Narang, 2005].

Serious practitioners and lovers of translation are exposed to countless theories and counter theories of translation. Unequivocally it is accepted as inspiring, as creative as the original writing in the source language (S.L.). In this context terms like source language (S.L.),source text (S.T.), target language(T.L.) and target text(T.T) assume significance.

Early theories of translation focused attention on literal translation only. Shift in focus generated diverse theories subsequently. It is often said if a translation is beautiful it is not faithful and if it is faithful it cannot be beautiful. One wonders whether male chauvinism influenced such an idea. A close scrutiny of the history of translation and the methodology followed reveals that the emphasis was more on retaining loyalty to the source language (S.L.) and the source text (S.T.). ~~No~~ attention was paid to the target reader (T.R). The translator took delight in exhibiting his extraordinary comprehension and communication skills (linguistically). The aesthetic value of S.L text was given greater importance. Faithful translation generally tends to be rigid and uncompromising. Semantic translation is more flexible in giving a little freedom to the translator in employing his intuition. The following observation seems quite noteworthy in this context:

> Badly / inaccurately written passages should be corrected in communicative translation."(Newmark). A discerning reader appreciates communicative translation rather than semantic translation, which is generally perceived inferior to the original. Viewed in the hierarchical context of high and low, primary and secondary, the larger and wide-spread hierarchy/creativity//non-creativity/is reinforced implying that while text is creative, translation is non-creative. [GopiChand Narang, 2005].

The Sahitya Akademi President feels that the word '*creative*' is euphuistic. The marginalization is certainly a construct and it needs to be looked into, since a good translation certainly is not possible without creative involvement. It is further observed that it is not possible to evaluate creativity through fossilized constructs.

> Creativity is a product of love; it comes from your soul, your inner self. It is not in the thing being done, it is in your attitude towards things and how you approach a work. Any attainment where one has bestowed one's love and care is always positive and this sort of positivity is always creative....Creativity is not in a particular work per se, it's in your attitude towards work...Whatever one does, if one does it lovingly, if one does it joyfully, if one's act of doing it not purely economical, then it is creative. Those who make translation a love affair achieve creativity. [GopiChand Narang, 2005].

A translator and translation activity have acquired due respect in recent times. Post colonial theories concern themselves thoroughly with cultural transference. Cultural implications have a wider spectrum encompassing lexical content, syntax, ideologies and ways of life. Here the translator's role assumes greater significance as he prioritizes his concerns and evolves suitable strategies.

Homi K. Bhabha, in his interview states that psycho analysis connected to the issue of identity suggests that all forms of identification are partial and ambivalent. He states:

> All subjects are constituted in a liminal wrong. Ambivalence is thus very important in my understanding of social processes and social relations. Similarly, semiotics, the theory and understanding signs. suggests that a particular sign has a set of meanings, based on a systemic location and a discursive use of that sign. Every sign gains its meaning in a particular language system. Words have to be read in given social context. Thus, for me, semiotics suggested that you could not ascribe universal values to literary texts. You had to understand the burden of interpretation and the burden of representation on those specific texts. [Sachidananda Mohanty, The Hindu, 3-7-2005].

Homi Bhabha further affirms that an attempt at making new connections, articulating new meanings always takes the risk of being not immediately comprehensible to readers.

Translation is a creative activity offering gratification to the person who renders it and the audience. Translators often felt that they should be treated as interpreters. This inclination overshadowed the earlier concept of invisibility of the translator. If the translator happens to be a creative writer the resultant product can be termed '*excessive translation*'. Excessive translation tends to foreignise/ exoticise i.e. use of source language [S.L] terms in the target language text [T.T], to a level that is now acceptable.

Target language [T.L] terms can be enlightening to a reader in reflecting source culture in a meaningful way. Globalization influenced tremendously in rendering the texts more exotic. In this context, these translations contribute a great deal in a better and correct understanding of the source culture.

1. Globalization has greatly affected our lives and culture.
2. It has equally influenced a translator's life and work.
3. Translation has acquired greater significance in bridging cultures.

4. Unfamiliarity as regards people and their culture have been replaced emphatically by the concept of familiarity.
5. The practice of foreignising or exoticising has undergone a great deal of transformation.

Globalization has come to mean rendering source text [S.T] global in understanding or application. Here, application refers to teaching and learning about different cultures. A translator takes advantage of the present context in extending greater exposure to unknown cultures and languages. This counters the earlier practice of glorifying dominant cultures. More so studies dedicated to analyzing western languages and cultures.

Globalization also offered a touchstone to test the competence of the translator and the audience. This concept is a significant aspect of translation. As is well known translation studies attempt tying divergent cultures together leading to fusion of boundaries. In the context of globalization a translator has some options:

a) Adopting the foreign word without any explanation;
b) Adopting the foreign word with extensive explanation;
c) Rewriting the text to make it lucid to the target language audience.

A translator has to make a choice:

1. to make the text understood quite easily
2. to render the text more exotic and more foreign.
3. to retain proximity to source culture.
4. to enable the target language audience get better understanding of source culture.

Internet has become a household name and a part and parcel of our daily activities. Distances are shrinking, cultures are coming closer, differences are diminishing, and fusions are flowering. Though globalization has a better connotation in commercial parlance, its existence and efficacy cannot be dismissed light heartedly. Search engines on the Internet provide a lot more information in a jiffy than what more could be collected through years of carefully conducted search of useful material in libraries across the land.

Literary translation in a global context deserves special mention. A translator can be defined here, as an expert in inter-cultural communication in an internationalized context. When machine translation and allied activities have come to dominate, literary translation is not given due regard. Dominant cultures have always enjoyed glorification .But in the changed context less known cultures and languages demand more attention, exploration and exposure. It is here translation studies assume greater significance.

English, enjoying an undisputed global status, beckons be witchingly the bemused translators to render service the cause of their own less known language and culture. A translator with bi-cultural awareness, bilingual capability is supposed to play a more serious role .In the prevailing situation language, literary or otherwise is viewed as a means of communication. In the proliferation of commercial vistas and ensuing opportunities a translator's role has to be accorded due recognition.

Globalization decreases foreignness. A text cannot become more foreign or less familiar. In the present context more foreign elements sneak into target text and thus offer more of the source text to the audience. More elements of source culture are preserved in the target text. Hence, transfer of culture is more authentic.

A careful study of translations in the last three decades offers some brilliant insights. In earlier versions a translator strained to domesticate the text to the target audiences (he made it closer to the comprehension of target audience). Subsequently, we notice translators striking a balancing brilliantly between foreignizing and domesticating a rendered text. In the context of globalization more elements and culture specifics of the source language are preserved in the translated text, giving foot notes and detailed explanation where necessary.

M.Sridhar and Alladi Uma have translated *Avval Kalma* (written by Yakoob in Telugu) into English retaining the title as it is. In this poem the poet talks about the peculiar predicament of a Muslim in Andhra Pradesh. His yearning for acceptability and recognition as a fellow human being is brilliantly depicted. The translators retained the title deliberately and a number of culture specific words.

> You may not believe me.
> but nobody gives expression to our suffering...

Festivals for us only mean rice with pickle,
biryani, talavs, pulavs, sheer khurmas are for you....
Wonder of wonders—the language we know is not ours,
I believe the language which is supposed to be ours
we do not know.

The poet feels sorry that he is neither accepted by the Muslim community nor by others. For speaking Telugu he is looked down upon and humiliated by his own people.

A curious dilemma whether to laugh or to cry.
When all said and done our dreams are Telugu,
our tears are Telugu.
Whether we ask for food when hungry,
whether we cry out in distress,
the expression of our feelings is Telugu.
When we were asked to perform namaz
we were dazed not knowing what to do.
We were startled listening to the azas,
We could only look for the ragas in the sound of the suras.
When we were asked to pray in the language we didn't
know
we even lost the pleasure of praying.
You may not believe me,
but nobody gives expression to our suffering. [M.Sridhar,
A.Uma, *Avval Kalma*]

Words like *Oyamma, abbu, abbajaan ,haveli, nawab, muslim ,sahib, turaka, ammijaan ,pappa, chaar deewar, khilwat, pardah, Bismillah hir Rehamaan, Allah ho Akbar,jihad, biryani, pulavs, talavs, sheer kurmas, shervaanis, laddhaf* are retained in the English version. Terms referring to the castes like *laddaf, doodekula, kasabu, pinjaari, dhobis, dhobans, hajjams , mehters,* also are retained to reflect the native tint of the text in S.L. The translators have chosen to give a detailed glossary at the end of the poem. Perhaps, it is aimed at making the rendered text target audience friendly. *"No language can exist unless it is steeped in the context of culture and no culture can exist which does not have at its centre the structure of natural language."* It is pertinent to recall how Susan Bassnett (1980) highlights the importance of cultural component in translation. According to her, language is 'the heart within the body of culture.'

Dalits have written moving poems expressing their anguish and misery. Sikhamani's poem *Maa Baappa* reveals how a Dalit woman toils for a living. Quite often in Indian context a Dalit person is socially ill-treated and physically abused. In the case of a lady sexual exploitation adds fuel to the consuming flames of economic and social exploitation. The poem mentioned above has been translated as *Baappa* by T.S.Chandra Mouli and B.B.Sarojini.

Except a hamlet, villageless...
except a caste nameless...
except hard labour, pleasureless...
story of my Baappa, will you listen?

Baappa is not an ordinary one...
like a tall papaya tree,
like a river that never looks back,
like a slender casurina tree
that challenges the sky
a very tall lady she was!
....
What a lovely blackness!
Blackness of clusters of rose apples,
blackness of a slice of tilled black cotton soil field,
blackness of black lotus blooming in abundance
in the irrigation channel.
....
Apparently black in complexion only,
but my Baappa's tenderness was
white as the flowers of watermelon,
soft as silk cotton,
soothing as chilled gruel.
....
I regret why my Baappa
who could shred coir in coconut shop
keeping the fruit on her thigh,
was not born at KaramcheDu!*

I wonder why my Baappa
who kept guard along riverbank

with a lantern in hand
and some chilly powder in her chengu**
whenever there were clashes with the village
was not born at Tsunduru !***

Unlike other times,
my Baappa's presence is
all the more needed now!

[T.S.Chandramouli&B.B.Sarojini,*Baapp*]

In the above translation only a few words like-*Chengu*, place names like *KaramcheDu and Tsunduru* have been retained. Explication was appended to the poem.

Translators interested and involved in translating Telugu poetry into English have ignored social stratifications and temporal ideological differences. It is heartening to note that a majority of them are not Dalits nor do they belong to minority Muslim sections. What obtains in a speech community can be extended to other speech communities as well in India. Through such selfless service rendered by self-effacing translators, realization dawns that the strife and struggle of the downtrodden are not restricted to one region or religion, but are pan-Indian.

Translations do awaken hibernating conscience of fellow countrymen and spur them to undertake remedial measure sincerely. Wherever people are oppressed resistance develops resulting in revolt, regeneration of life and reconstruction of a social order. Translations carry cultures across the frontiers convincingly and conveniently, forging bonds of fraternity and bridging chasms in comprehension of man's destined role in this universe. Solutions are offered, problems are solved and inner spirit of man is purged through translations and transference of culture .m

Autonomy of translator

Present day translators have almost dispensed with the practice of faithfully translating titles of texts, poems or fiction. Most of the titles are related to the theme, an expression there in or a term in the text itself. This is a welcome change in achieving the autonomy of the translator. Though he operates between two sign systems, severely handicapped by the conservative, archaic notions and norms, a realization has to dawn that autonomy of the text in T.L and translator's craft have to be accorded due respect by writers in S.L and critics. This is in no way related to the concept of invisibility of the translator.

Translation is no longer perceived as a mere linguistic exercise. Enterprising translators extended hitherto unheard of charm and charisma to a translated text, where their scholarship is certainly not sought to be on display but only their creativity. Ability to enjoy the work one does and the one on display matters most here.

Reduction

Some translators have deliberately chosen this as a translation tool. Poets, in particular in Indian languages keep repeating the same idea ad nauseam, at times using end rhyming, alliteration and onomatopoeic expression, just to enjoy applause from audience in poetry recitation sessions. So far so good.

But in translating the same text for publication, all those elements need not be carried in the T.T. '*MO'* [V. Mohan Prasad], a prominent poet and reputed translator believes in this strategy and practises it to perfection. To an ordinary reader it may look as though he had taken too much liberty with the text in S.L. But the end product, text in T.L, looks elegant with crisp expression devoid of redundancy and monotony. He also believes in the concept of *transportation* of a text and culture from one port [S.L] to another [T.L].Here, he states that a translator exports the text from one speech community to another. In the process he imports some features of T.L which hones his skill as a translator.

Interactive Translation

When I translated a Telugu poem *warthamaanam* by K.Siva Reddy I was at a loss to fix the title, as the word in Telugu means 'communication', 'message' or 'present time'. The word *warthamaanam* occurs in the poem many times .Any shade of meaning offered lends beauty to the poem equally well. The poet intends to convey the idea that poetry connects him to the world around. He himself suggested *Link* as the title and the poem in translation acquired a rare appeal.

Saleem's novel *Kaaluthunna Puula tho Ta* was translated by me as Smouldering Garden. [literal translation].He wanted a different title. The novel was sent to press with the title Stigma, since the theme highlights the need to dispel misconceptions about HIV and AIDS. Thus, writers in S.L, at times, help translators by giving required freedom and suggestions.

I am not diffident or indifferent to experiment in translations. My earlier experiences with eminent and elderly writers who demanded emphatically that titles of their works should be literally translated made me wary of getting adventurous.

Young poets and writers offer full freedom to translators and are concerned with the final product in T.L. Yakoob, an eminent poet, requested me to translate his poem *KuDikaalu* ['Right Foot'] at short notice. Literal translation of the title was not to my liking or his. A careful reading of the poem riveted my attention to the expression '*My Soul.*' which explicates the poet's intention exceptionally, as he describes his intimacy with the muse of poetry and impact of her entry into his life. Yakoob's wife 'Silalolitha ' is also a poet and writer, whose influence on his career is quite perceptible. It is said that behind the success of a man there is always a lady. Thus, the title *My Soul* served the purpose splendidly.

If a translator can interact with a writer in S.L while translating a text, many layers of meanings of words , normally beyond the reach of an ordinary eye are explained and acquaintance with personal life and experiences of a writer help a translator immensely. A point missed or a reference not understood properly, symbolic significance of titles, historical, political , social associations with certain expressions when explained by the writer in S.L, enable a receptive translator acquit himself judiciously and present the text in T.L convincingly.

It may not be always possible to meet the writers in person. Telephonic conversations, online interviews help .Once the pulse of a writer is read properly; a translator's job becomes facile and effective. Sharing texts and views with seniors in the craft also facilitate in shaping a translated text tantalizingly. Peer reviews always are rewarding.

As subaltern studies acquired prominence, retention of meaning potential and terms in S.L strengthened the hands of translators. *Pidgin* cannot be accurately translated. Only approximation can be accomplished. Likewise, speech practices of the elite and the uninitiated cannot be uniformly translated into Standard English. In Indian languages it can be attempted. So, a translator is left with an awkward choice of employing '*butler-English*' or broken English.in T.T (Target Text) . Debunking such intelligent device as *inelegant English* or *substandard English* is quite unbecoming of a reviewer or a sensible critic.

Before pronouncing value judgment , what compelled the translator choose a particular pattern of expression in T.L has to be explored ,sympathetically understood and then only a comment , if an uncharitable one, has to be made. Mere sophistication in expression can never lend grandeur to a text in translation.

Psychological factors, inner conflicts, social hierarchy of characters influence their expression in some texts. A translator who is also a creative writer, in the full knowledge of the situation in which a character operates, chooses an appropriate mode for his text in T.L. This has to be sympathetically realized by a reviewer or reader. A reviewer needs to be more charitable to extend due regard to the labour of love and craftsmanship of a translator.

In conclusion, it may be stated that globalization has extended more glow to translation studies forcing a translator to be highly conscious of his role in fusing cultures through his creative art. While machine and man continue to function dismantling barriers effecting fusion of cultures, the importance of intellectual contribution of a translator should be appropriately appreciated.

WORKS CONSULTED

1. Basnett ,Susan & Trivedi, Harish. *Post-Colonial Translation*. London: Routledge.1999.

3. Catford, J.C. *A Linguistic Theory of Translation*. Delhi : Oxford University Press.1965

4 Lakshmi, H. *Problem of Translation: A Study of Literary& Technical Texts.* Hyderabad: Book Links Corporation. 1993

5. Mohan Prasad V. This Tense Time (*Modern Telugu Poetry*). Vijayawada: New Directions. 1981

5. Mehta, Amrit & Lakshmi H ed. *Translating Alien Cultures.* Hyderabad: CIEFL. 2000

6. Prakasam, V., *Stylistics of Poetry.* Hyderabad: Omkar Publications.1996.

7. Rao Prabhakar, S.S. Post Independence Poetry. Calcutta: Writers' Workshop, 1993.

8. Singh, A.K. (ed.) Translation, Its Theory & Practice. New Delhi: CreativeBooks.1966

9. Talgeri , Pramod. "*Inter Cultural Hermeneutics and Literary Translation*" in Literary Translation. ed. R.S. Gupta. New Delhi: Creative Books.1999

8

Cultural Transference through Translation

A Two-Way Traffic

G A. Ghanshyam

> *A translation is no translation unless it will give you the music of a poem along with the words of it.*
>
> ***J. M. Synge***

Man is indebted to translation as a process which has ensured the survival and continuity of cultural heritage. Literature pertaining to any part of the world is a gift of translation that has been handed down to us through the ages. In fact, "This art is as old as written language." ("Translation" 12) The classical literature of the Western world or the ancient literature of the East have transgressed the barriers of time and place only because they have been successfully translated; the Greek epics of Homer or the Sanskrit renditions of Kalidasa are still a source of inspiration today.

Translation is a process through which one language is transformed through the act of translation into another language. But translation is not only transformation of the 'source language' (SL) into 'target language' (TL); it is a vastly comprehensive process of translation of one culture into another that is from 'source culture' into 'target culture'. A language carries within itself the nuance of the culture of which it's a creation. A true translation requires an authentic transference of not only the literal meaning of the text but also the genuine transference of the inherent ethos in it. To put it in the words of Wail S. Hassan, translation is essentially a "component of cross-cultural contact." (Hassan 754).

India has a rich cultural heritage which has come down to us with the help of some expert translators. The colonial experience has further enriched this multi-lingual cross over with the influence of a language and culture that were initially alien to the socio-cultural milieu of the land. English being the alien language was the product of the cross cultural encounter between the Western and the Eastern culture that left a profound impact on both; each was enriched by the other. Translation effects a change both linguistically and culturally for, "The change of language changes us. All languages permit slightly varying forms of thought, imagination and play." (Rushdie 434).

Translation is however a process that requires not only a precision of language but also a precision of thought and feelings; and the task of the translator becomes all the more crucial and tough when the source language and the target language are grounded in milieus culturally different. "A good translation is one that preserves as far as possible all the formal, linguistic and cultural peculiarities of the original text." (Nair 'Conclusion' 112). If the translator is grossly ignorant of the culture to which the source text belongs then it's obvious that the resultant work of translation will surely not be of a good standard. It is not only the language that is a hindrance in this case, though there may be the problem of the target language's inadequacy to interpret certain peculiarities of expression of the source language like expressions of happiness, greetings, sadness, pain, blessings or angry words of abuse: 'Tere muh meh ghee shakkar', 'Are yaar', 'Jug jug jiyo', 'Keede pade tere muh meh', etc. Sometimes a word common to both the languages however has different connotations like 'Hai', which is a form of greeting in English while an expression of pain and anguish in Hindi.

In the Indian context which is multicultural and multi-lingual in character, translation is difficult but not so complicated and impossible from one regional language to another because a common thread of cultural values connects them all. The base of all Indian languages is Sanskrit, which is the creator or mother of all regional languages that have evolved with the change in society and culture at every turn of the country's geography. However, when translation involves a language originated in alien environs then the scenario becomes quite different. The situation has nevertheless changed in the postcolonial set-up when an Indian no longer has to explain at each and every turn of text the use of peculiar Indian expressions or the Indian sensibilities in question. Common practices like chewing of betel leaves and nuts or the various cultural and religious ceremonies like mehendi, navratri, upnayan sanskar, etc. are no longer explained by giving foot notes or end notes. 'Hanuman' is no longer the monkey god but a revered symbol of strength, power and devotion.

This amalgamation of indigenous nuances of Indian life into the English language is an important step in the process of appropriation through which English has transformed as an Indian language. In fact English language has become more enriched in the process as has been the other Indian languages with the inclusion of various English words in the native idiom. Translation generates and encourages this two-way traffic of linguistic change and adaptation. However a translation is not true translation if it fails to keep the spirit of the work alive that is, ". . . giving life to a work was more important than just giving its outline accurately." (Nair 'Concepts and Applicability'25). Here it is worth citing the example of Rabindranath Tagore's Gitanjali that was originally written in Bengali and later translated or to be more precise transcreated into its English renditions.

The amalgamation of the native words and nuances into English and vice versa has helped this process of translation immensely. However, language is essentially the by-product of the culture and society, hence knowledge of culture, society and the nature of language is necessary for the act of translation to be effective and successful. Ignorance regarding these variants and aspects of language results in misrepresentation and misinterpretation like the one cited by Rushdie in an essay in *Step Across this Line* wherein he describes David Lean's film adaptation of *Forster's A Passage to India.* In a particular scene in the film Dr. Aziz climbs up on Fielding's bed with his shoes on; an action that might not even raise an eyebrow amongst the Western readers it would certainly be an act of utter disregard of conventions and culture of the East.

Cultural translation is, thus, the transference of cultures that have brought the varied cultures of the world together, bridging all the distances in between. In the present context when the world has become a globalized village and societies earlier dominated by colonial powers have become empowered themselves, assertion of one's identity is one of the most important issues addressed by the writers in their works. Keeping in view the above trend in literature, Indian writers have endeavoured to represent the culture, the sensibility, the ethos of essentially Indian life and society. In this connection it is worthwhile to acknowledge the contribution of writers writing in / translating into English, starting from the initial renderings of Indian stories through narratives constructed in imitation of the Western modes of literature to the modern day postcolonial representations of essentially Indian stories through Indian form of narratives and expressions.

Girish Karnad is a writer who is one of the foremost exponents of the process of cultural transference through translation. A bi-lingual writer he writes primarily in Kannada, which he eventually translates into English. Many of his works can be metaphorically called as the odes to cultural translation. Through his various plays Karnad has successfully translated or transcreated the cultural peculiarities and nuances of India. "He has represented India in foreign lands as an emissary of art and culture." (Dhawan 13) In his plays like *Yayati, Hayavadana, Nagamandala, Tale-Daṇḍa, Bali: The Sacrifice, The Fire and the Rain,* etc. Karnad presents the social, cultural, religious and mythical aspects of India. For his stories Karnad takes his inspiration from myth and folk tales, and transforms them into important dialogues of cultural exchange through his imagination and by employing the techniques of folk theatre. 'Language carries culture' said Ngugi wa Thiong'o and Indian culture forms the core of all of Karnad's plays. Mythology and folk tales are important signifiers of culture that are translated for the modern generation giving these age old traditions of the nation a modern garb.

Yayati is a story taken from the epic of Mahabharata focusing on the central theme of responsibility, and the importance of sacrifice and renunciation of materialistic and sensual pleasures in the pursuit of spiritualism and salvation. If *Yayati* affirms the supremacy of the soul over the body then *Hayavadana* depicts the primacy of buddhi (wisdom) over body, which is another aspect of Indian ideology and belief. Based on an ancient story taken from Kathasaritsagar, Karnad's narrative extends the tale to include the human quest for completion.

Nagamandala is a play based on the folk lore surrounding the snake myth that represents the close knit and community based life of India, beliefs in supernatural elements and miracles. In *Tale-Danda* Karnad takes his story from ancient Kannada history portraying the caste based divided society of the nation while in *Bali-The Sacrifice* he presents the ideology of non-violence inherent in the religious belief of Jainism. Karnad's play *The Fire and the Rain* evokes the religious rituals and sacrifices adhered to in the Indian way of life and tradition.

Translating the essential Indian cultural context in the English language Karnad contributes immensely to the cross cultural transference between the cultures of the East and the West. Various Indian references, words, expressions are carried over to the Target language and culture through Karnad's plays and his presentation in the form of the folk theatre like Yakshgana, Bayalata, etc.

In *Hayavadana* (Karnad Vol. I 2006), the play starts in the traditional manner of the folk theatre with an invocation of Ganesha in whose praise the Bhagwata sings, "May Vighneshwara, the destroyer of obstacles, who removes all hurdles and crowns all endeavours with success, bless our performance now." (*Hayavadana* 105) Even the play starts in the manner of a folk play with the description of the city, "This is the city of Dharmapura, ruled by King Dharmasheela whose fame and empire have already reached the ends of the eight directions." *(Hayavadana 106).* Various words and Indian forms of expressions that have been used in the narrative like Punya; "Shyam Nayika" (*Hayavadana* 120); "Come, come" (*Hayavadana* 116); Kapila in mock exasperation to Padmini calls her, "My mother, can I at least talk to a servant?" (*Hayavadana* 125) or Padmini when she says, "Sorry, I forgot. I apologize-I slap myself on the cheeks." (*Hayavadana* 129); Fortunate Lady's flower; Dhoti; Mangalarati; Namaskara; Shastras; Vetala; Rishi; "Tut-tut" (Hayavadana 152); Alpanas; Arati; Sati; Makarandas; Pativrata; Ram Ram!; Sree Hari!; Nata. Sanskrit verses, "Tanvee Shyāma- . . . nimnanabhih." *(Hayavadana* 119) and Hindi songs, Jhanda Ooncha . . . Hammara" (*Hayavadana* 179), with or without subsequent explanations are incorporated into the text transforming the Indian ethos into a language whose origins are alien to such expressions and peculiarities of life typically Indian.

Nagamandala (Karnad Vol. I 2006) has several usages of Indian expressions and words like Sari; "Chih! Chih!" (*Nagamandala* 259), Koel, Yaksha woman, etc. Tale-Danda (Karnad Vol. II 2006) depicts the caste ridden Indian society. It takes inspiration from the life of the famous Kannada poet Basavanna and the Sharanas in their effort to remove all divisions from society. Expressions like "son of a whore" (*Tale-Danda* 17), "You shouldn't rush in like this-without aarti or saffron-water to cast out the evil eye." (*Tale-Danda* 17), "I am a Kalachurya. Katta Churra. A barber." (*Tale-Danda* 21), "Jagadeva, go sweep the floor after him and apply cowdung, so the ground he's stepped on is purified again." (Tale-Danda 35), "Om namah Shivaya" (Tale-Danda 39), "Ayyo, Shiva-Shiva!" (Tale-Danda 47), "Thoo, you, you blackguard!" (*Tale-Danda* 69); words like Bhakti, "Tale-danda" (*Tale-Danda* 30), Mantras, Linga, Varnashrama dharma, Bhakta, "sanatana religion" (*Tale-Danda* 46), Dharma, Artha Shastra; and Sanskrit titles like "Maharajadhiraja Kalanjarapuradhishwara . . ." (*Tale-Danda* 24), "Yuvarajendra . . . Bho parak!" (Tale-Danda 65) abound throughout the text.

Similar expressions, words and nuances are present in the other plays as well. In Bali-*The Sacrifice* (Karnad Vol. I 2006): "Tcha!" (*Bali-The Sacrifice* 205), "If you don't tell me what's on your mind, let my skull splinter into a thousand shards." (*Bali-The Sacrifice* 219); and in *The Fire and the Rain* (Karnad Vol. II 2006): "fire sacrifice (yagna)" (*The Fire and the Rain* 105), "conducting priest (adhvaryu)" (*The Fire and the Rain* 105), Brahma Rakshasa, Kritya, Kamandalu, Moksha, Dhoti, are some of the examples of Karnad's deftness and expertise in dealing with the peculiarities and distinctive traits of Indian life, culture and society.

Various Indian characteristics related to religion, popular beliefs like myths and superstitions, rituals and social structure are represented with care and authenticity by translating them into English expressions and words. Lighting up of funeral pyre by son and yearly rituals to commemorate the day, Snake ordeal, village elders sitting on judgment at the village square, touching the feet in reverence, prostrating before gods, sacrifice offered to deities, acceptance of divine intervention and miracles etc. are depicted by the playwright in order to infuse the narrative in a typically Indian flavour and essence. The use of folk theatre techniques like the character of Sutradhar or Bhagwata, imagery of a dilapidated and ruined temple dotting the Indian country side, invocation of a deity before the play, use of chorus and symbolism to depict the village atmosphere of gossips and tales, all lend their particular magic to the conjuring up an image of an indisputably Indian traditional society and culture.

The heavy layering of Indian words, expressions or their translation into English in plays rendered in English enriches the Target language and culture with new terms of meaning and expressions. In return the Source language and culture finds a wider ranging audience and acceptance and a greater level of comprehension. Viewed from this context, translation cannot be taken in a narrow sense of the term restraining its applicability to the confines of mere linguistic exchange between languages. In fact, in this age of Globalization and emergence of Knowledge Society the indispensability of translation as a process of cultural transference cannot be denied.

"In so far as international communication is an indispensability for the progress of mankind, translations are bound to play a very crucial role in the years to come." (Nair 'Concepts and Applicability' 42).

Translational literature is, therefore, a hybrid product of the multicultural world of ours that augments and enriches World literature with the inclusion of native and regional variants of linguistic modes and cultural variations. The task of the translator is, thereby, that of a facilitator of cultural exchange and mutual transference of meaning. The act not only bridges the distances between cultures and languages but also empowers the languages, level of comprehension, vocabulary and perspectives of SLC (Source language and culture) and TLC (Target language and culture) through its two-way mutual exchange of traffic. James Clifford rightly says: In the kind of translation that interests me most, you learn a lot about peoples, cultures, and histories different from your own, enough to begin to know what you're missing.

WORKS CITED

1. "Translation", Encyclopaedia Americana, vol.27 New York: American Corporation, 1974.
2. Hassan, Wail S. "Agency and Translational Literature: Ahdaf Soueif's The Map of Love". PMLA Vol.121 No.3 May 2006. 753-768.
3. Rushdie, Salman. "Step Across this Line", *Step Across this Line.* London: Vintage Books, 2003.
4. Nair, Sreedevi K. 'Conclusion', *Aspects of Translation.* New Delhi: Creative Books, 1996.
5. Nair 'Concepts and Applicability', *Aspects of Translation.*
6. Dhawan, R. K. 'Girish Karnad: The Man and the Writer', *The Plays of Girish Karnad: Critical Perspectives.* Ed. Jaydipsinh Dodiya. New Delhi: Prestige Books, 1999. 11-20.
7. Karnad, Girish. 'Hayavadana' Collected Plays. Vol. I. New Delhi: OUP, 2006. 101-186. (All parenthetical references to the text are to this edition.)
8. Karnad, Girish. 'Nagamandala', Collected Plays.Vol. I. 243-300. (All parenthetical references to the text are to this edition.)
9. Karnad, Girish. 'Tale-Danda', Collected Plays.Vol. II. New Delhi: OUP, 2006. 1-102. (All parenthetical references to the text are to this edition.)
10. Karnad, Girish. 'Bali-The Sacrifice', Collected Plays. Vol. I. 187-241.
11. Karnad, Girish. 'The Fire and the Rain', Collected Plays. Vol. II 103-176.
12. Nair 'Concepts and Applicability', Aspects of Translation.

9

Translation as a Task-Based Language Teaching and Learning

Prashant Mishra

Introduction

The purpose of the present paper is to explore the effective use of Translation as a Task-based language teaching and learning. Task-based approach to teaching and learning is based on the concept that effective language learning will take place only when students are engaged in different types of language tasks and activities as providing theoretical knowledge of only rules will not contribute to the development of learner's communicative competence. Translation as a pedagogical tool of language teaching has been used since the medieval period in Europe. However, until 17th century, it was confined only to the teaching of vocabulary and form and that also only to the written skill as priorities of language teaching were different. Currently due to globalization, priorities of language learning have changed and targets in language learning have been extended from learning of vocabulary and form to the achievement of fluency in its use. Task-based approach that came into existence as a result of Prabhu's work (1987) engages students in various types of language tasks and activates their inherent communicative potential. A pedagogue through the use of various interesting and entertaining translating tasks like translation of jokes, stories, dialogues, speeches, films, cartoons can ensure the participation of the learners in the learning process. Through extending the task-based approach further to oral skills learners can be facilitated to achieve communicative competence in the use of target language.

Translation as a Tool Used in ELT: A Brief Review

The need to learn a foreign language is felt in all the ages and in all the countries. Human beings use different languages to communicate among themselves in different parts of the world. Hence the need to learn other's language is always felt in human society. Trade, commerce, diplomatic relations, military campaigns, higher education, tourism and now the need to collect, store and disseminate knowledge due to web revolution compel people to communicate with the people of other countries and societies. Linguists and pedagogues have been busy in exploring and devising different methods and strategies to simplify and understand the process of learning a foreign language since the ancient times. Roger Ascham(1515–68) initiated a method of teaching Latin to the English pupils based on translation of Cicero's Latin epistles. The pupils were asked to translate Cicero's Latin epistles into English and the teacher repeated the translation many times so that the students are able to consolidate the understanding of the letters. After this activity, students were asked to retranslate the English translated versions into Latin once again to compare it with Cicero's original letters. William Bath (1564–1614) who found vocabulary learning an important factor in learning a foreign tongue used translation method in his Latin-Spanish book "Janua Linguarum". He selected 1200 sentences of Latin containing within them the most commonly and frequently used Latin words and provided their translation equivalents in Spanish. However, these vocabulary items were not taught in isolation but as they were used in meaningful sentences. John Lock (1632 – 1704) introduced Interlinear Translation in which Latin sentences along with their equivalents in vernaculars were given one below the other to enable the learners to establish links between the two. James Hamilton (1769–1831) extended the scope of interlinear translation from writing to include oral skills so that proficiency in target language is acquired through practice. Unlike Locke by avoiding teaching of grammatical rules and by including oral practice of translated passages, Hamilton moved towards natural method. But in the second half of the 19th century Otto Jespersen (1860–1943) rejected the translation method and by recognizing communication as the main goal of language learning paved the way for natural and oral methods. In the 19th century Structuralism and further Transformational Generative Grammar of Noam Chomsky too recognized the importance of communication in language studies. Hymes(1972) even rejected Chomsky's theory of Generative Grammar(1965) that limits itself to grammatical competence. Hymes extended the meaning of competence to communicative competence which he defines as the knowledge and ability to use a language in multiple social situations. Hymes's concept of communicative competence opened the way for communicative language teaching that has currently been in vogue and used widely in classrooms due to increasing need of contact and exchange of information between various societies as a result of the phenomena of globalization and information technology. Communicative language teaching recognizes language as a means of communication. Task-based approach to language learning exposes learners to language through task-based communication activities like different types of games, role plays etc. The later part of the paper provides a brief account of Task-Based Approach.

Task-Based Approach: A Brief Account

Prabhu (1987) stressed the importance of tasks in language learning and pioneered the task-based approach to language teaching and learning. This approach is based on the premise that abstract theorizing and teaching of rules do not effectively contribute to language learning. Unless L2 learners are fully engaged in different types of language tasks, they will not be able to use the target language fluently. Rebecca L. Oxford (2006) defines the task as "an outcome-oriented segment of work in a curriculum or lesson plan". Breen (1987)defines a pedagogical task as "range of work plans which have the overall purposes of facilitating language learning – from the simple and brief exercise type, to more complex and lengthy activities such as group problem-solving or simulations and decision-making"(Breen 1987:23). Professor David Nunan(2006) regards a task "a piece of classroom work that involves learners in comprehending, manipulating, producing or interacting in the target language while their attention is focused on mobilizing their grammatical knowledge in order to express meaning, and in which the intention is to convey meaning rather than to manipulate form. The task should also have a sense of completeness, being able to stand alone as a communicative act in its own right with a beginning, middle and an end". A task-based approach is a learner-centered approach in which the participation of the learner is ensured in the learning process through setting of different tasks by the teacher to facilitate language learning. Through tasks of various types the learner is exposed to a target language to achieve an outcome. A Pedagogue plans different tasks to engage students in various skills – oral and written – to make the learning process conducive to communicative goals.

Selection of Tasks: Some important Criteria

Selection of Medium: Translation is a decoding of the source language text and re-encoding it into target language text. In the traditional teaching methodology, translation exercises on writing skills were given to the students and oral skills wore completely ignored. However, translation exercises on writing only improves the writing skills and do not address to the communicative needs of the learners. Translation as a task-based activity cannot be confined to the translation of written texts into written medium in target language only. In order to aid a learner in acquiring competency in the use of a language, translation as a task-based approach has to be extended to include oral skills also. As a task-based approach translation can be used extensively for ELT purposes to improve different skills of the learners by providing tasks to translate written texts into written medium, written texts into oral mode, oral texts into written medium and oral texts into oral. When translation from one medium of communication is undertaken into another medium of communication, it will improve competencies of different skills of the learners. When both written and oral translations and tasks are introduced in a class room, students will be exposed to a greater chunk of language in formal as well as informal communicative situations.

Selection of Content: The ultimate aim of any language teaching programme is to facilitate the learners to achieve communicative competence in its use. However L2 learners cannot reach this goal directly as exposure to target language is not spontaneous, natural and sufficient. Therefore, before achieving communicative competence, they have to acquire competence in the use of meaning and form i.e. semantic competence and grammatical competence. In the initial stages of learning, a learner should be given those tasks for translation which include the most common and widely used vocabulary and the core structural items and rules which are indispensable for learning the target language. However, once students become well versed in semantic and grammatical items of the target language, they can be later on exposed to the task related to the culture of the target language. Culture specific tasks peculiarly related to the target language should not be introduced at the early stages of learning as content and tasks related to the culture of the target language if it is an alien one will put impediments in its comprehension.

Selection of Genre: In the selection of translation tasks, selection of type of genre according to the needs, interests, academic or professional requirements and aptitude of the learner plays an important role. Earlier religious and literary texts were used for translation studies. Due to globalization and web revolution, the need to improve communicational skills has been felt. To improve interpersonal skills of the learners, oral translation of important passages and dialogues from plays, or speeches of popular personalities can be given to the students as recently speeches of Barak Obama have drawn the attention of the people and children and people in Japan and in many other countries have started learning English through these speeches. A pedagogue can prepare translation tasks based on any recently hit book, movie, speech, joke, anecdote keeping in view the standard, needs and interests of the learners.

Pre-task, In-task and Post-task support inputs by a teacher: In a task-based learning a teacher acts as a facilitator throughout the learning process. A task based approach is goal-directed approach in which a teacher monitors the learning progress of the learner and assists him to move ahead to complete the assigned task whenever he comes to a halt. A teacher if necessary provides pre-task, in-task and post-task support to the learners to enable them to accelerate the task towards completion. Poor vocabulary, grammatical errors, limited exposure, ignorance of structural patterns and lack of socio-cultural awareness are the main hurdles faced by students while translating from source language into a target language. Hence it becomes necessary for a teacher to assist the learners at various stages of translation – semantic level, form level and function level. At the pre-task level a teacher should prepare and gear up the students by introducing them to those vocabularies, grammatical and cultural items which he thinks may put constraint in the completion of the translation task. Once students start translation they may also get stuck in between the translating process. Here a teacher, in order to get a task going, can provide them in-task support in the problematic areas. Different task requires highly technical registral items, simple structural patterns to complex ones, plain language features to highly figurative and stylistic features. Therefore in-task supports to students are very necessary to smoother and accelerate the learning process to achieve the final target. Even if a task is accomplished by the students, a teacher as a post-task activity should provide feedback to the learners by bringing to his notice the errors, the lapses that remain in the accomplished task and the means and tips to improve in future.

Different Translation Tasks for Practice: Translation exercises, games, activities and miscellaneous tasks can be used in a language classroom to provide exposure to students to improve their proficiency in different language skills. Earlier in Indian classrooms, translation method was confined to the teaching of vocabulary and grammatical items and isolated sentences estranged from any content and situation were given to the students to translate them from source language into target language. Divorcing translation exercise from any content and providing isolated sentences for translation created monotony and ultimately resulted in the failure of translation method. Another reason for the failure of translation method in the past was confining translation activities to written texts only and particularly to literary and religious ones. In the English language classroom, translation as a method of teaching and learning was confined only to writing skills and completely ignored the oral skills of the learners. Hence, it provided only partial exposure to students. Consequently, with the advent of oral and communicative approach to language learning, it lost ground and was banished from the classroom. Currently due to globalization and the greater interaction between various societies, individuals and nations, the need of translation is felt more strongly. Translation as a task-based approach to teaching and learning ensures the participation of the learner in the learning process and caters to the communicative needs of the L2 learners. By introducing translation tasks based on translation of jokes, anecdotes, short stories, dialogues, speeches, cartoons, animation films, short filmic stories a pedagogue can make the learning process exciting and stimulating. The following interesting tasks can be used to ensure the active participation of the learner and to make the teaching programme interesting:

1. Translation of jokes, anecdotes.
2. Translation of cartoons and animation films.
3. Translation of comics.
4. Translation of short filmic stories.
5. Translation of dialogues from one act plays.
6. Translation of some popular speeches.

Besides, interviews on T.V. shows, tasks based on interesting and entertaining material extracted from various books and audio-visual material downloaded from the Internet can be used for preparing various tasks for translation purposes. Newspapers contain so many news iteins and columns of the interest of the learners. News items range from political, social, educational, commercial, current affairs, youths, environment, travel, sports and games and entertainments. A teacher may cull some interesting news items of contemporary concern and interest and ask students to translate them from source language into target language or vice-versa. As newspapers are easily available and within the reach of most of the students, task based on news items can be fruitfully used in a class-room. Cartoons highlighting current themes and subjects of interest and relevance can be chosen for preparing various translation tasks. Inter-semiotic translation from film into stories which involves re-encoding the visual images into words either written or oral can be also given to the students as most of the students like films and often after watching movies narrate the stories to their friends. They can be asked to do the same in the class-room also. Translation tasks based on video films, documentaries and T.V serials of the interest of the students – written as well as oral – can be offered to students. Translation tasks based on entertaining, absorbing and readable contents taken from the prescribed text books of history, geography, sociology and science can also be employed for learning a second language as students will be more comfortable and at ease with the subjects and contexts they are already familiar with.

Internet that provides facility for browsing on the world-wide-web (www) contains textual material of different type and nature and is a rich source of translation practice. Not only written texts can be obtained from the net but visual texts including voice can also be taken from the net. Various written and audio-visual texts can be downloaded from the net and can be used for preparing various tasks to be assigned to the students in the classroom. Entertaining and stimulating texts, relevant to the contemporary life, society and the world, can be culled from the web for preparing translation tasks. The material may include short prose passages, narratives, dialogues from plays, interviews, speeches, blogs and visual material like animation films, short documentaries etc. Film strips, recorded audio-video material, news and entertaining T.V. programmes can also be used for preparing various translation tasks. CALL can also be used for preparing various translation tasks. CALL which makes use of both audio and visual material can be fruitfully used for translation activities. According to E. Nageswar Rao, "CALL is learner-centered unlike several traditional modes of learning and teaching. It takes into account the learner's strengths, weaknesses and problems and it is geared to the learner's specific needs. Yet another great advantage of CALL is its outreach. It can be used and used effectively even in such places as hospitals, prisons and offices which are generally considered not conducive to learning" (Rao2001:88).

Conclusion

Translation as a Task-based approach will be more relevant and advantageous in rural and semi-urban classrooms where students are too shy and poor to respond to teacher's instructions and questions in English. Translation which involves bilingualism may be used to motivate and encourage students of underprivileged regions to overcome their lingophobia. By providing translating tasks of their choice, students can be actively engaged in the learning process. Different translating tasks based on students' favourite books, games, films, serials, topics and day to-day activities can be provided to students to ensure their participation in the learning process. The teacher can act as a facilitator to assist the students in pre-task activities to help them overcome the vocabulary and structural gaps arising out of their insufficient exposure to a foreign language but later on withdraw him when students gain confidence and are keen to do translation tasks themselves. To conclude, tasks based translation teaching and learning will make the class room vibrant and ensure greater language use by the students.

(Note: This paper was presented in the National Seminar on "Translation As a Site of Cultural Traffic" organized by the School of Studies in English, Vikram University, Ujjain from 9 –10 February, 2009.)

WORKS CONSULTED

Breen, M.1987. "Learner Contributions to Task Design". In c. Candlin and U. Murphy(Ed.) Language Learning Tasks(pp. 23-46). Englewood Cliffs,NJ: Prentice Hall.

Nunan, David.2006. "Task-based language Teaching in the Asia Context:Defining Task". In Asian EFL Journal Volume 8. Issue 3. Article I. http://asian-efl-journal.com/Sept-06-ro.php.

Oxford,R.L.2006. "Task-Based Language Teaching and Learning :An Overview". In Asian EFL Journal Vol 8. Issue 3. Article 5. http://asian-efl-journal.com/Sept-06-ro.php.

Prabhu,N.S. 1987. Second Language Pedagogy. Oxford:OUP.

Rao,E.N. 2008. "Challenges in English Language Teaching in the Twenty First Century". In IT Revolution, Globalilzation and the Teaching of English. Ed. G. Damodar, P. Shallaja and M. Rajeshwar. New Delhi: Atlantic Publisher and Distributors.

10

Transition from Tradition to Modernity in *The Upheaval*

Basavaraj Naikar

Pundalik N.Naik (1952—) has been a very prolific writer in Konkani language. He is a poet, short story writer, novelist, playwright and screenwriter. He has forty books and two films to his credit. He is not educated highly, but has studied up to the first year B.A.degree. He has taught Hindi, Marathi and Konkani in Santacruz High School, Goa (1974-80). Then for some time he worked as Assistant Editor (script) in All India Radio, Panaji (1980-84). Presently he runs a printing press. He has won many prizes for his stories. His *Ganvdhani Ganvkar* (*Villager, the Village Boss,* 1975) is a collection of one-act plays. *Khon Khan Mati* (*Go on Digging the Earth*, 1977), *Raktakhev* (*Bloodbath*, 1978), *Rakhan* (*Protection*, 1979) and *Muktatay* (*Freedom*, 1980) are his full-length plays. *Bambar* (*The Muck*, 1976) is a novelette known for its bold contents and style. *Muthay* (*Bunch of Corn*, 1977) shows him as storywriter of outstanding merit. *Achhev* (*Havoc*, 1977), winner of Kala Academy Award is a "powerful novel depicting life in a Goan village set against the background of impending mining industry, which brings about moral and social degeneration of traditional values"[1]

He has won many awards for his plays and novels. He has articulated the Konkani sensibility in all his works. Being deeply steeped in the Konkani culture, which is basically rural but which is slowly influenced by the forces of modernization in terms of industrialization, he has the fine sensitivity to capture the minutia of common people's experience. A regional writer to the core and deeply interested in human nature and the rural background, he is able to record the joys and sorrows, hopes and despairs and good and evil of the Konkani people. Konkani is said to be a cultural space from Malabar to Mumbai on the western coast of India touching four States of Kerala, Karnataka, Goa and Mumbai. Konkan, obviously, does not have a separate political administration. Within the Konkan region there are minor variations in the dialect, custom and manners. For example, the Konkani of Mangalore region may be slightly different from that of Goa or that of Mumbai. The common geographical factor i.e. Western coastal belt has given them some common features of culture. Since Pundalik Naik hails from a Goan village, he foregrounds the Goan context of Konkani culture and language in his novel *The Upheaval* (*Acchev*). Pundalik Naik is passionately attached to his mother-tongue, Konkani and therefore has articulated his artistic vision through it. His mission is obviously to assert his identity and get the due recognition for the Konkani language, which has no separate script of its own. (Incidentally Konkani has been written in Latin, Portuguese, Devanagari and Kannada scripts respectively.) "He recalls his decision to write in Konkani when as a teenager he read the description of a cattle festival in Marathi short story so vastly different from the cattle festival in his own village that he felt the compulsion to write about it and understood that he could only bring the experience to life in Konkani"[2]

The novel is set in the villages of Ponda district in Goa, where the Portuguese influence has been insignificant. Goa is generally associated in the minds of people, with 'fun, frolic and feny', and Christianity. But Pundalik Naik annuls the general impression by depicting the humdrum life of the villagers, their predicament and struggle for survival against all kinds of odds — man-made, natural and God-made. In *The Upheaval* the novelist holds mirror to the transition of Konkani society from tradition to modernity by depicting the subtle changes in the social, political and moral values of rural life. That is because Pundalik Naik has a first-hand experience of the rural life of Goa, which is characterized by poverty and suffering and dependence upon agriculture for the bare sustenance. As he has confessed, "I belonged to a family of farmers and have experienced poverty and suffering. As a boy, besides helping the elders in the field, I had also to look after the cattle. Wonderful surroundings —hills and rivers — had a profound impact on my mind. Nature inspired me and instilled in me a competitive spirit. I had a lot to say and started with poems"[3] Deeply rooted in the Konkani agrarian culture, the novelist has an intimate knowledge of the inner intricacies of his culture, which he expresses in the form of the novel. "Pundalik Naik's writing illuminates peasant life in all its variety, not least the changing landscape of modernity and industrialization, which has fragmented village communities and disturbed a rural ethos without necessarily alleviating poverty"[4]

The novelist offers a microscopic picture of a Goan village, Kolamba in postcolonial era. He creates a strong impression of the distinctive and picturesque Konkani culture through his thick description of the landscape, the climate, and the social milieu, mores and manners of the villagers. The rural society is patriarchal and quite traditional in its framework of values. Agriculture, which provides the substratum for all the superstructure of culture, happens to be the chief preoccupation and means of livelihood for the people of Kolamba and other neighbouring villages.

The novel is divided into two parts. Whereas the first part depicts the traditional society of Kolamba into which the element of industrialism has been slowly creeping. Half a dozen important characters, representing different professions and sections of the society play significant roles. Pandhari, the protagonist of the novel, is an agriculturist, who depends on land and its cultivation for his livelihood. His wife, Rukmini and his children implicitly believe in and encourage his agricultural profession. Their agricultural calendar of events is marked by a number of rites and rituals, fairs and festivals, singing and dancing, worship and entertainment at regular intervals. On the one hand agriculture is conditioned by the cycle of seasons, on the other hand, it also provides the economic basis of the village society and the mutual dependence of people, on the basis of bartering of goods. At the beginning of the novel, Pandhari is busy attending to the strengthening of the embankment of his field, after completing the ploughing in the morning. Since the land is well prepared for sowing, he has fixed the sowing on the next day. But he also knows the difficulty of getting labour due to the slow but steady commercialization . Shanu points out the difference between the past and the present, "But you don't get labour like you used to in the old days. Earlier, all you had to do was to feed them well and give them enough to drink, but today they work only for daily wages" (P.5). His opinion is corroborated by Pandhari also, "Yes, is there anything left of the past? The firangis went away and so did everything that was connected with them...those loaves of bread, that easy life. Today even men are measured by money" (P.5). Pandhari goes to the country-bar in the evening and invites a couple of labourers for sowing in his field the next morning. "Pandhari hailed a couple of labourers, who had come to the *gadi* for a drink and told them to come to his field the next day. He asked one of them to bring the *nivolo* and told the other to bring a bundle of fifty plantain leaves" (P.8). Agriculture requires a lot of dedication and patience on the part of the farmer, who should be willing to accept the unexpected losses due to the vagaries of Nature. Pandhari is used to this kind of life of hard labour and poverty.

But the agrarian society slowly comes under the influence of industrialization, with its promise of quick money. In 1950s there was a mining boom in Goa, which changed the landscape and had an adverse effect upon the moral life of the villagers, in spite of its promise of profitable jobs for them. It is this social change that has been captured realistically by Pundalik Naik. Just as Pandhari is planning to sow his field, some unexpected event happens. At night an acquaintance called Babuso brings a Gujarati contractor of the mining industry, namely Prasad Babu and introduces him to Pandhari. Then Babuso explains the importance of the mining industry that has been started in the area and how it provides an excellent opportunity for the villagers to earn more than ten times of what they earn from other labour. He points out how the wages in the mining industry are by far higher than those of other professions, "'Five rupees is what they get at the mine for breaking up the stones. Not by hand... the company provides explosives. Remember how we used gelatine to blast those huge rocks by the lake?' Babuso came to him and squatting beside Pandhari lowered his voice to a conspiratorial whisper, 'If you have a bullock-cart it's easy to make money. Just bring the stone chips down from the mine, they'll weigh the cart and they'll pay. The more you bring, the more you earn" (P.12). Babuso explains further that they have to transport the stone from Naveli down to the river at Shenori and they will be paid seventy rupees per trip by Prasad Babu. Pandhari is easily tempted by the high rate, which he can never earn from any other kind of labour. Babuso advises Pandhari to lose no time lest the work should be entrusted to some other man, "Take the cart to Naveli tomorrow. But go tomorrow and see him or he might hire someone else. You needn't go the next two days" (P.13). Tempted by the prospects of high wages and pressed by the urgency of the situation Pandhari agrees to accept the contract from Prasad Babu by postponing the programme of sowing his field. He is easily attracted by the materialistic profit promised by the mining industry and is ready to neglect his agriculture. But his Rukmini does not approve of his decision and asks him angrily, "Has the Spirit of the Lake turned your head?"(P.13) She accuses him that he has forsaken his gods and his duties for money. Instead of sprinkling cow-dung water on the sprouts as directed by her husband, Rukmini says that she wants to boil them, make them a bitter broth done at a funeral and to mourn her husband. Her inauspicious words exasperate him so much that he calls her a bitch and strikes her uncontrollably. "Pandhari struck her just once but the blow sent her reeling against the wall, stunned. The whole hut seemed to shake with the impact" (P.14). Thus Pandhari and some other villagers of Kolamba are attracted by the lucrative jobs offered by the mining industry. They ignore the agricultural work and start going to the mine to earn high wages. Babuso, who lures these people to the mining industry acts as a tempter in the village society. Unscrupulous and shameless by nature, he tries to ruin the life of people around him.

The rural society of Kolamba has its tradition and custom to be followed by the villagers. The traditional values of life are represented by an old man called Abu, who is sixty-year-old. He is a disciplinarian and conscience-keeper of the society. He is easily the wise old man figure in the novel, who upholds the moral values of the society. He does not hesitate to scold and advise people whenever they violate the morals or make some mistake. He, thus, acts as a reminder of the traditional values and ideals of the Konkani society of Kolamba. A man of discipline by nature Abu gets up early in the morning, goes near the lake for nature call, brushes his teeth and offers prayer to the sun in the east with palms joined together. Then he warms himself by the fire of twigs. He admonishes the children, who squat for nature call very near the lake thereby reminding them of the religious importance of the lake in their lives. "Who was that squatting so close to the lake?' Abu turned his piercing gaze on the children but no one dared own up. 'Don't you know that the Barmo, the Holy Spirit, lives by the lake? You must keep the whole place clean. If you squat there and dirty the area, worms will crawl all over your buttocks. The Barmo will catch you and never let you go...' he thundered. 'Don't you know of that woman, who washed dirty clothes at that spot during her monthly cycle...she kept washing them month after month and remained childless...' " (P.16). He does not approve of the laziness of children. He, therefore, advises Savlo Master to teach them to overcome their laziness. " 'Lazy? The rascals! We've given them to you Master, only you can drive some wisdom into their heads. Teach them, beat them if you have to. No one will say a word. I'll take care of that…' said Abu with feeling" (P.17). Abu is known for his carping tongue, but he does not like the people of Kolamba, especially the new generation, to speak foul language. He alerts and implores Savlo Master, "All of us are the same, here in Kolamba. We barely speak two words without cursing and using foul language. The children learn to speak like their parents…you can tell the crop from the quality of the seed. People, who come from other places are shocked at the language we use…but the new generation must learn to speak well…teach them, Master" (P.17). At the same time Abu wants to control his own tongue, "I'm the worst of the lot. I must learn to control my tongue" (P.17).

Abu, the elderly man participates in all the important festivals of the village and advises or admonishes people and tries to put them on the right track. For example, he is invited by the women to inaugurate the *dhalo* festival in the month of *Poush* and requested by them to apply oil, *kajal*, *kunkum* and sandal paste on the deity and to offer flowers and prayers on their behalf. Abu, therefore, obliges them by participating in the festival. He intones the prayer solemnly, "Look after us O deity of the *maand*," and invokes the divine blessings and protection. He breaks the coconut and passes the slivers around. Then signalling to the women to let the *dhalo* begin, he moves off to seek the blessings of the Spirit of the Lake.

Abu takes the liberty of scolding and advising people freely. All the sensible villagers respect him for his moral stature and take his advice in the right spirit. When Abu visits Shanu's shack during the harvesting season and appreciates the healthy grains of paddy as a result of hard labour, Shanu asks him to 'sit down. Have a *beedi*..." (P.42). Abu reacts instantly, "You rascal! Want to buy my good wishes with a *beedi*? But no, I was only joking. May your good fortune increase! This old man gives you his blessings" (P.42). Then he starts to move away and comments on Pandhari, "...that wretch has sold himself to the mine!" (P.42) Abu does not like the villagers like Pandhari and others neglecting their traditional agricultural work and going to the mining industry with a profitarian motive. When he visits Pandhari's field he thunders at Pandhari, "Who is that wretched creature whistling on the threshing platform?" (P.43). He does not like the friendship between Pandhari and Babuso because of the latter's adverse influence upon the former. Refusing the rice gruel offered by Rukmini (wife of Pandhari) he offers her moral advice, which has a note of warning and a prophetic value about it, "Find your husband. And that Babuso. You might be a good wife, wearing yourself out like the broom that sweeps the house. But if a woman isn't smart enough, there's trouble ahead for her husband...But why am I telling you all this? It's like reciting the *Gita* to a donkey" (P.43). Then he scolds Pandhari for neglecting his agriculture and for being lured to the mine, "Shame on you. You were always the first man in the village to finish the ploughing, the first one to sow and the first one to reap his field" (P.43). In order to drive home the moral, Abu tells the story of Baba Gavas, who was a rich landlord but who was finally reduced to the level of a beggar due to his negligence of agriculture caused by his recklessness, alcoholism and womanization. After narrating the story in details, he advises Pandhari explicitly, "What are you nodding your head like an ox for? I am sure that you are turning into another Babu Gavas, at least as far as your fields are concerned. Your wife is strong and healthy, so you don't know what wretched things you do at Naveli! No wonder your crop is as bad as this. And look at the scoundrels who come to help you! It is like pulling down a great house to build a shack!" (P.44) Abu's advice is taken in the right spirit by Pandhari and Rukmini, but Babuso does not like Abu's intermeddling with others' affairs.

Savlo Master is a school teacher in Kolamba village. He plays an important role in the village as an educator thereby leading the school children from ignorance to knowledge and from darkness to light. The Students revere him. But the teacher feels a special difficulty in educating his students when their parents remain crass ignorant and follow uncultured way of life thereby contaminating the minds of their children. He expresses his views to Abu, "It's not the children's faults, you must learn to change your ways. I can teach them in school but…" (P.17). His problem is how to educate the parents who set wrong morals to their children.

Savlo Master is a sincere teacher, who does his duty religiously. He teaches them sums, controls their mischievous behaviour, checks their homework and educates them morally. His school is meant exclusively for boys and girls are not allowed at all there. Savlo Master is not paid regular salary in cash every month. On the contrary he is paid annually in kind, i.e. in the form of corn and paddy. Then Savlo Master closes his school for a couple of days and goes to his native village Volvoi carrying the paddy given by the villagers.

He returns to Kolamba after a few days and resumes his teaching. Savlol master plays not only the role of a teacher within four walls, but also the role of a protector of the local culture. For example, he trains his students for participation in *taalgadi* performance and *divli* dance. Nanu has rehearsed his *divli* dance to the master's satisfaction. Next day when the villagers of Kolamba gather at the *maand*, Savlo Master plays on the harmonium accompanied by somebody on the *pakhwaj* and help the schoolboys perform the *taalgadi* play about Srikrisna and Radha. Finally when they have to do the *divli* dance, Nanu dressed as a woman in a saffron sari and a shiny red blouse edged with gold, begins to dance gracefully by jingling the bells strapped to his ankles. It is a difficult dance for a boy or anybody for that matter, to perform. "Savlo Master took out a copper coin and placed it on the ground in front of the boy. Nanu would now lie prone and pick it up with his tongue, balancing the lamp on his head all the while, following what Master said" (P.49). People watch the scene with fear and anxiety. "Nanu lowered himself carefully to the ground, bracing his shoulders as he strove to balance the weight on his head. His tongue inched forward in search of the coin, as everyone's eyes remained transfixed. It was at the very last moment, when his tongue had almost reached its goal that Nanu's neck twitched convulsively, his head fell forward, and everything before him turned dark" (P.49-50). The fall of the lamp from Nanu's head is interpreted by the superstitious villagers as inauspicious. They curse Savlo Master as a mad fellow and mock at him. Savlo Master does not understand why such an unfortunate thing happened. Some people think that "May be the gods are angry" (P.50). Some people suspect that Abu might not have performed the rituals properly. But Abu reacts strongly, "May be one of you went to bathe in the lake or come here to the *maand* when she was still unclean..." (P.50). Some people suggest that they should ask the Oracle but some others remind them that they cannot do so in the month of the Shigmo. Intent on knowing the exact reason, Savlo Master asks Nanu, "What happened to your neck all of a sudden?" (P.51) Then Nanu confesses hesitantly, "I went to Naveli yesterday and the day before... Yes. I went in the daytime. Bappa said not to tell anyone... He took me to work at the mine. To carry stones on my head to fill the cart. It's our own cart so if we do the work ourselves we can make more money...Then my neck began to ache. I didn't tell you. I was scared you'd be angry. When the lamp was on my head my neck began to ache and suddenly it snapped forward... and... Master don't tell anyone...Bappa will hit me..."(P.51). Savlo Master learns from Nanu's answer that Pandhari has been forcing his son to join the work at the mining industry and neglect his school. Savlo Master does not like Pandhari's wrong prioritization, commercial attitude and short sightedness. He, therefore, makes a vain attempt of advising Pandhari against such a wrong path. But Pandhari pretends to be absent from home when Savlo Master visits his home. Savlo Master tells Rukmini, "Don't keep Nanu away from school..." (P.56).

It is a pity that Savlo Master's noble intention of educating the younger generation of Kolamba village is not taken seriously by the parents, who are not sufficiently enlightened. The people are too poor and therefore have become too materialistic to care for education. Once when Savlo Master reminds Pandhari about the importance of sending his son to school, Pandhari does not take his advice seriously. Pandhari and his wife think rather narrow mindedly that Savlo Master is serving there in their village merely for his salary. But they do not have the higher perspective of the cultural significance of education in society. This shortsighted materialistic approach is due to their attraction for the mining work which is more profitable than learning. Deeply hurt by this kind of public indifference, Savlo Master expresses his sense of frustration, "Pandhari, it is not your fault. It takes one man to recognize another. And in all of Kolamba there is no one who recognizes Savlo Master any more" (P.15). Pandhari feels insulted by Savlo Master's words, especially in the presence of the village barber. He, therefore, talks disrespectfully to Savlo Master. Then Rukmini and the barber also heap abuse on the teacher for teaching *divli* dance to Nanu and for being responsible for the inauspicious omen of the fall of the lamp from Nanu's head. But Savlo Master's compassion for the boy prevents him from betraying the latter. Savlo Master realizes that an educator is not respected in a society, which understands only the language of money and nothing else. He, therefore, takes the right decision of leaving Kolamba village for good. "Savlo Master went home. He bundled up his clothes and walked out of the village. As soon as Shankar heard, he rushed from house to house in consternation telling everyone the news, just as he had done after Abu's death. But no one stopped Master. Though shut when he passed by, just as they had been when Abu's corpse had been carried past. And long after Savlo Master disappeared into the distance, the leaves of the *lajja* creeper that had drooped shut as he passed by, raised their heads again" (P.76). The illiterate people of Kolamba do not like a teacher or an educator to disturb their bliss of ignorance and smugness. The villagers are too busy in their struggle for survival to be provident of the future.

Abu is another interesting character created by Pundalik Naik. He attracts our attention by his frankness and straight forwardness. He is a sharp-tongued man who does not spare anyone in the village for their deviation from the moral path. He is rather unhappy about the people's growing materialism and sinfulness. As he speaks directly to people about their moral degeneration, they feel embarrassed but they try to keep quiet in deference of his age. Once when Abu meets Savlo Master he sympathizes with the latter, who was wrongly blamed for Nanu's mistake. He says further, "We're wretched sinners, Master... but you're a saint!...Would our people forsake their fields to go and break stones at the mine otherwise? Would our women go and lie with those wretched strangers even though their husbands are healthy and strong? We've forsaken our homes...cast ourselves into the wind... This isn't an eclipse that will pass... leaving everything as pure as it was before. Everything has been defiled. Our food is impure... the work we do...who knows whose seed grows in those field these days...only the Spirit of the Lake sees everything" (P.68-69). Abu knows the sinfulness of the priest, who has almost gone mad. He tells Savlo Master how Datta the priest carried the rice-dolls of the ritual of Baras to immerse in water and how the dolls were stinking because they were infested with big worms inside them. Abu rightly interprets the priest's sinful nature, "After all, he carried the symbol of sin on his head" (P.69).

Abu has been ailing and taken to bed since the Baras ritual. One day he dies quietly in his hut. As he is a childless man there is no relative to conduct his funeral rites. The people of Kolamba are not willing to do it either because they hate his abusive nature. Truth hurts people. They comment upon his nature, "That's why they say you must always do good to others, talk well of them. But this old man! So abusive! Didn't care to see if it was a relative or a guest, his sharp tongue spared no one! He lashed out at Babuso at the threshing this year. Interfered in everything and everyone's affairs" (P.70). But sensible people like Savlo Master understand Abu's moral height and idealism. He closes the scholar and sends word to some people, about Abu's death. He feels a pang of grief for Abu and waits on his dead body in the hut throughout the night. He collects some villagers including Nanu and Babuso and buries Abu by sprinkling some blossoms on his dead body. He says rather sadly to Babuso, "Forget about religion. And tradition. All that ended in Kolamba with Abu's death" (P.72). Abu has, obviously, been a spokesman of the traditional ideals and moral values of the Kolamba society. The villagers, who could not conform to his expectations tended to dislike him and called him an intermeddler. When Rukmini, wife of Pandhari, talks disrespectfully about Abu, Savlo Master chides her because it is only he who knows the visionary nature of Abu's personality, "Don't take that saint's name with your vile tongue! He was the last of the real men in Kolamba, and passed away empty and unfulfilled. He had visions of a new generation of worthy young men in Kolamba..." (P.75). The irony is that nobody except Savlo Master in Kolamba is able to understand Abu's moral idealism and optimism beneath his apparently harsh language.

Babuso happens to act as an agent of evil in the Kolamba society. For it is he who brings the Gujarati contractor Prasad Babu to Pandhari and tempts the latter economically. Due to the promise of relatively high rate of wages, Pandhari neglects his traditional agriculture and concentrates on the mining work. Thus money happens to be the greatest attraction for the villagers. Babuso has, obviously, succeeded in directing the attention of Pandhari and others to the moneymaking business. Consequently, Pandhari and such others tend to neglect the age-old profession of agriculture and the related rituals, which is almost tantamount to sin.

Babuso is a mean-minded and cunning opportunist. After tempting Pandhari away from agriculture and to the mining work, he begins to concentrate on Pandhari's wife, Rukmini. He tries to make friends with her by frequenting her hut in the absence of her husband. Rukmini instinctively understands his ulterior motives and curses him inwardly, "This man has already made two or three trips to our house and each time he comes when Pandhari isn't home. He'll destroy not only my home but all of Kolamba, she thought bitterly" (P.26). When Babuso visits her for the first time at dusk, he finds her bathing in the backyard. She feels annoyed at his attempt to forge kinship. But he tries to assure her, "Never mind, don't be embarrassed. You're like a sister to me" (P.27). He earns the sympathy of Rukmini by telling her the sad story of the death by drowning of his own twelve-year-old sister, who was as big as Kesar. He hypocritically addresses her as a sister, "Rukminiakka... you don't mind if I call you that, do you? ... Now that I have sister like you I'm quite happy" (P.27). He offers a few biscuits to Rukmini to be given to her children and lies to her that he is still unmarried and that nobody offers his daughter to a no-gooder like him. But his carnal desire cannot be suppressed. "Rukmini crossed the courtyard in her wet clothes, hurried up the steps and into the hut. Though the lamp light flickered but dimly, Babuso did not fail to notice the damp cloth sticking to her fair calves or the heavy swell of her breasts hat moved as freely as she hurried indoors" (P.27).

Next time when he goes to her, she is smearing the cowdung paste on the inner wall by the light of a glass lamp. As usual Pandhari has not returned home yet. Babuso tries to ingratiate her, "Rukminiakka, I've brought fireworks for the children. Ten pieces here. They can light them tomorrow" (P.58). He finds out from her that her son Nanu and daughter Kesar have gone to the *chowk* and that her husband has gone across the river to Volvoi. Babuso thinks that it is a golden opportunity to seduce her. He, therefore, sits comfortably there exposing his crotch. Then he takes the lamp from her hand and holds it up so that he could gaze at her breasts, pities her for thinness and gradually tempts and seduces her,

> 'Rukiminiakka, you've become thin,' he said.
> 'What?
> 'Yes. Look at your thighs. They were taut...like plantain stems...
> 'What are you up to... Give me that lamp..."
> Rukmini giggled, scrambling to her feet.
> 'Wait...don't get up.'
> 'I must. There's no cowdung left in the pot. I must get some more.'

Rukmini clutched the pot in her left hand and tried to free the lamp, which was in her right but Babuso would not let go. The strip of cloth tossed over her shoulder slipped as she moved and Babuso gazed freely at her breasts. She bit her lips shyly blowing out the lamp. Her bangles tinkled as she rinsed her hands. Babuso tugged at the cloth around her waist and began to stroke her back.

> There...now I've got cowdung all over my face...'
> 'Let it be Rukminiakka...'
> 'Still calling me akka?'
> 'Well... you're my sister when there is light...but Rukmini in the darkness...' he murmured, 'Did you like the sari I got for you the other day?'
> 'Yes. Looks good.'
> 'Not as good as you look with this cloth wrapped around you... and even better without it...'
> 'Oh God! Your mouth smells.'
> ...

Rukmini hastily lit the lamp unmindful of the state of her clothes. Babuso pulled up his shorts, flustered at the sudden change that had come over her. (Pp.59-60).

Thus Babuso succeeds in fucking Rukmini although he addresses her as sister publicly. The seduction testifies to Babuso's hypocrisy, opportunism and betrayal and to Rukmini's vulnerability, fallibility and compromise with wifely chastity.

Babuso has stolen a *kegdi* flower from the lake to be offered as a gift to his beloved. But Rukmini does not approve of his irreligious act. She shouts at him, "You fool! All of Kolamba has seen that flower! It was kept for the Ganapati on the *chowk*. If anybody gets to know it in our house, we'll be swallowed alive by the villagers" (P.60). Then she orders him to get out of her hut with the bag containing the flower. Babuso has thus, ruined his post-coital pleasure by his foolish act. "Babuso scrambled out of the hut hardly comprehending how everything had changed in so short a time" (P.60). On the whole Babuso is an unscrupulous and shameless opportunist.

There is a long interval of time between the first part and the second part of the novel. The second part depicts the negative effect of the mining work on the physical, cultural and moral life of the village. One may easily see the transition of the rural society from the agricultural to the industrial and from the moral to the immoral. The forces of industrialization and modernization contribute to the materialistic philosophy of life, opportunism and immorality.

Although the mining industry has given the village labourers better wages; it has also made serious demands on their life. The villagers have been forced to sacrifice something or the other for the so-called high wages. For example, Pandhari, who neglected the agriculture and opted for the mining work, seems to have grown prematurely old due to restless and strenuous labour. He was the first one to lease out his cart for carrying the ore, but he has to pay the price for this materialistic deed. Now his cart is broken and his bullock has died due to stress and strain. As he has no more the earlier physical strength and enthusiasm, he has been reduced almost to the level of a pauper and intends to set up a tea-stall at Chinchey Devni for drivers and workers. On an auspicious day he starts his tea-stall and keeps on earning a bit of livelihood.

The mining industry at Naveli has become so attractive to the villagers that every young man and woman has started working there for livelihood. Pandhari's son, Nanu and daughter, Kesar have been working there in different capacities. Whereas Kesar works as a labourer, her brother Nanu works as a truck driver. Now Nanu is no longer an innocent boy. On the contrary, he keeps away from home for days together and visits his parents very rarely. He befriends other truck drivers and learns from them the bad habits of alcoholism and womanization. Manuel happens to be close friend of Nanu. They meet regularly in the evening and chat over a cup of tea or a peg of whisky. Once when Kesar is taking her lunch box to the mine, Manuel stops his truck and gives her a lift and introduces himself as a friend of her brother. Later he tells Nanu that he met his sister and that his mother is ill. Then he suggests to Nanu to protect his sister and her honour by their working together in the same company instead of in two different ones. "Sure, you can drink as much as you like and sleep around! But what I'm saying is this...your sister works at our mine. If both of you worked for the same company, you could keep an eye on her. You know how they treat young girls here...like a heap of ore... any man picks up a hoe and thrusts it in" (P.91). The mining industry has both positive and negative effect upon the life of the villagers. On the positive side, it has given jobs, hence means of livelihood to people. But on the negative side, it has also given them a chance to indulge in bad habits like alcoholism, whoring and womanization.

Once when Nanu is driving his truck to the mine in the afternoon, he happens to see a woman of thirty or thirty-five walking on the way. He takes pity on her and gives her a lift in his truck. On the way she tells him that her labourers' settlement at Dingnya village was burnt by a fire; that she lives alone though her husband is alive and living elsewhere. Hers is really a pitiable condition. She tells him, "At the worst, I'll swallow poison...no parents... no husband, no home. No money either. Got on to your truck to escape the heat but I don't know where to get off" (P.93). Nanu takes pity on the forlorn woman, Devki and arranges to appoint her as a cook for the drivers and labourers in a boarding hut at Chinchey Devni, adjacent to his father's tea-stall.

Babuso, who was the initiator of Pandhari into the mining work, is an unscrupulous and shameless scoundrel. He has already seduced Rukmini and cuckolded Pandhari. Still he hypocritically addresses her as 'sister.' One day he visits Rukmini at the twilight hour as usual. Rukmini is not happy at his arrival and comments, "Come to torment us all" (P.95) loud enough to be heard by Babuso. She curses him as "low-caste vermin" (P.95). When he enquires about

Kesar, Rukmini retorts, "Have you come to ask about me or to see Kesar?" (P.96) Then Babuso enquires about Nanu. After a little while Kesar returns home, changes her dress and goes to the Lake for bathing. But Babuso, in spite of his failing eyesight tries to see the beauty of Kesar's figure. "His failing eyesight didn't permit him to see too well and the flickering light of the lamp made everything indistinct, yet, as he stared at Kesar's lissome figure he thought of Rukmini as she had been some fifteen or twenty years ago" (P.99). Obviously Babuso sees the mother in her daughter. At night Rukmini cooks rice-gruel and all the three of them including Babuso eat it. Then they keep the front door open so that Pandhari may not disturb them on returning home late. All the three of them sleep in different parts of the hut: Rukmini in the back room, Kesar in the middle room and Babuso in the front room "Babuso curled up on the mud seat but couldn't get to sleep. Rukmini lay on her bed and snuffed out the lamp and as Kesar tossed and turned in the other room, she couldn't get any sleep either" (P.100). In the middle of the night Rukmini hears a scream. She, therefore, lights the lamp and asks her daughter, "Kesar…oh my dear…Why did you scream like that? Was it a bad dream…? When she rushes to Kesar's room she sees her daughter in disarray. "Kesar was sitting up in bed drenched in sweat, her hair in disarray. Her blouse was unbuttoned and her skirt had ridden way below her hips. Rukmini threw a sheet over her, breaking out into cold sweat herself. 'O my dear girl…oh my child…' she said again and again, stroking the girl's back, not quite aware what had brought her to that state. Suddenly a faint doubt rose in her mind and she darted a swift glance around the room" (P.101). Rukmini takes some time to guess that her innocent daughter has been raped by Babuso. "There, behind the door in the shadows stood Babuso, one hand clutching his tattered shorts, the other pressing against the wall as he tried to merge into the darkness. He was dripping sweat as though he had just emerged from a dip in the lake" (P.101). Rukmini takes a stick and rains blows on Babuso.

> You sister—! You wild creature with nothing but sex on your mind!… Destroyed me…and here I am bed-ridden…you diseased creature…low caste vermin…!
>
> 'Stop! Akka! You'll kill me…'

> 'You...who will sleep with your own mother...called me sister and then lay with me! Now what are you here for? To sleep with your niece...?'
> 'Stop...stop! You've broken my leg...!
> 'Let it break! Your wife is running around with other men...go show her what you can do! You make her sleep with other men, and you come here to...'
> 'I'm going...I'm going...!'
> 'And don't ever cross this threshold again...or I'll put you in your grave. (P.)

Thus Babuso has been so unscrupulous and shameless that he has robbed the chastity of Pandhari's wife as well as the virginity of his daughter. He has demoralized the family of his own friend without any compunction.

The mining industry has upset the ecological rhythm also. "No one relied on the rooster announcing daybreak any more these days. The continuous rumble of machinery around the mine seemed to confuse the birds who crowed at odd hours, sometimes in the afternoons, or even after dusk" (P.102). Likewise it has also offered new temptations in their life thereby upsetting the normal human relationships. For example, Nanu has helped Devki with a job mainly on humanitarian grounds. She has been working as a cook for the drivers. Her shack is just adjacent to Pandhari's tea stall. Nanu comes to meet her every evening. But the labourers talk loosely about their relation. The two customers in Pandhari's tea-stall talk derogatorily about Nanu and Devki. One of them says, "What his son earns is blown up on drink and whores! That Devki, who lives in the next shack...she's his mistress..." (P.104). When the other customer opines that Devki being quite old, Nanu might not be attracted to her, the first customer says in his characteristic uncultured manner, "Old she is, but her body is young enough. And anyway, what does it matter in the dark? He is a driver after all, as long as the gears function smoothly, he is happy enough!" (P.104). Pandhari, who hears the loose talk about his son's connection with Devki, wants to take him to task. When Nanu comes to the tea-stall, Pandhari accuses him of unrespectable behaviour and asks him, "Just get rid of that whore...That Devki. That married whore, who is youı mistress. And you, a young man. Not even married yet!" (P.111).

Nanu is so exasperated by his father's accusation that he strikes his father forcefully, "The force of the blow spun Pandhari around and he sprawled against the wall, rubbing his cheek"(P.111). Some drivers, who are eating, rush out of the shack and try to control the situation. Nanu shouts angrily at his father, "Listen! Devki will stay right here! If you act too smart I'll set fire to the shack. Yes! I've kept Devki here! She's my mistress! Tell all those bastards who ask you... go spread the news in Kolamba too!"(P.111).

Nanu is so deeply insulted by his father's references to the sex-scandal that he wants to convert the myth into reality. One night Nanu is suddenly awakened by his own mental anxiety. He drinks half a bottle of *feni* and happens to see Devki return in her wet clothes after bathing outside the hovel. He is, therefore, sexually aroused and begins to make advances on her. Devki draws his attention to the gap between her old age and his youth and the one between his status and hers. But he does not bother about that. He retorts, "Young? I've so many women...been between so many thighs..."(P.113). Devki tries to ward him off. But Nanu shouts at her, "You've left your husband. You're a whore. Everyone knows that. They say you're my mistress. I don't care. If you don't come to me now, I'm going. There are thousands of others who'll come...you...you whore" (P.113). Deeply humiliated by his words Devki grows desperate and retorts, "Yes. I'm a whore. Slept with hundreds...no thousands...of men. You want me, too? Come. See. I've dropped my clothes. You say I'm your mistress? Why should I be shy with you then? Come, hold me tight. Where has all your strength gone now...?" (P.114) Nanu is so much fuddled with liquor that he is not able to meet the challenge. "Nanu lost his balance and almost keeled over. Devki tried to grab him, dropping the sari she had been holding against herself all this while. But the weight of his unconscious frame was too much for her to bear and he fell against her breasts, then slid down her belly and crumpled in a heap at her feet. Babuso, peeping through a chink in the reed mat wall, drooled silently as he stared" (P.114). Nanu, who was an innocent boy and student of Savlo Master in the past, has now become a rake and been ruining himself due to the evil habits of alcoholism and womanization. He has forgotten all the traditional values of life like respect for parents and self-control due to the evil effect of working in the mines.

Because of the job opportunities at the mines, girls are no longer confined to their homes. But when they go to their work-place they naturally come in contact with young men. Then they tend to get into trouble due to either external temptation or biological urge. Kesar, the young daughter of Pandhari and Rukmini, who has been working at the mine at Naveli, has unfortunately got into trouble by becoming premaritally pregnant. Now she has got to approach a country abortionist to induce abortion secretly. It is Rukmini's responsibility as a mother to help her daughter out of the difficulty. Rukmini expresses her helplessness, "Don't worry about me. I've lived my life, only a little remains of it. And even that seems too long to bear. Lord knows what more I'll have to see with these eyes!" (P.115) Both Rukmini and Kesar lie to the neighbours that they are going to the Ravalnath Temple, but actually they go to Parab's house. They are under the impression that nobody is watching their movements. But unfortunately Manuel happens to see them going to Parab's house and shows it to Nanu also. Both of them hide themselves behind the truck and observe everything. Manuel in his characteristically crude and hurting manner casts aspersions on Nanu's sister and explains the reason as to why his (Nanu's) mother and sister have gone to Parab's house,

> 'Must have come to the Ravalnath temple. They come sometimes. To get holy water and to pray. To check their forecasts.'
>
> 'You liar! Telling me a story? Don't you know why people come here early morning?'
>
> 'No. Why?'
>
> 'You Hindus are very smart! You come to the temple to pray. And then you go and get holy water from that Parab's house!'
>
> 'Who's that Parab?'
>
> 'Don't pretend you don't know. Or do you mean that you only know those doctors who live in Kudney and Digne?'
>
> 'You mean this Parab gives that sort of medicine?'
>
> 'What else will he give your sister?'
>
> 'Manuel...!'

> 'Don't yell! I am telling the truth. And you're getting furious only because she's your sister...but she's a girl like any of other workers...don't they get pregnant from time to time?'
>
> 'Manuel...I am warning you...!'
>
> 'Don't feel so insulted...if what I say is false, I'll do anything you say...come! Never mind if we get to Sankhle a bit late today' (P.118).

Manuel shows Nanu how the latter's mother was hiding the medicine bottle under her sari. Then Manuel takes Nanu near Parab's house and makes him wait there while he goes to Parab's house and brings another bottle of medicine. He convinces Nanu beyond any doubt, "Look! Open your eyes wide and look.' Manuel shoved the bottle into Nanu's trembling hands. 'What's this? Holy water from the Ravalnath temple? How many times have you bought this sort of medicine for girls two or three months pregnant?'" (P.119) Nanu is deeply embarrassed by the revelation of the bitter truth about his sister's predicament.

After becoming aware of his sister's pregnancy, Nanu begins to think seriously about his own evil habits like drinking and whoring. He knows that it is mainly men who tempt young women and get them into trouble. He, therefore, thinks that men should not do so. Thus Nanu has a belated realization of the nature of reality. But Manuel, who is a shameless rogue, tries to justify the evil habits of men and women. He is rather surprised by Nanu's philosophical awakening. Nanu tells Manuel, "I'm not good enough to tell you all this, but experience has taught me a few things...and I must tell you what I feel...' Nanu spoke quietly, as though nothing strange had occurred. 'We drivers are steeped in vice. No worker at the mine or at the loading platform earns as much as we do...two hundred and fifty rupees plus overtime, plus whatever the unions can get for us and of course whatever we can collect from the passengers we carry on our trips. Is there anyone in the mine who earns as much as we do? ...Why do we spend so much on drink? On whores?" (P.121) But Manuel argues from an opposite point of view and defends their hedonistic way of life, "Nanu, we don't plan to live like this, but we have to. And then it becomes a habit we can't shake off. We eat a lot, spend fifty or sixty rupees on tea alone, but we have to maintain our strength. Drink a lot, too. To be rid of the tension and weariness that comes after driving continuously through all this dust. Our bodies demand satisfaction, so we go to those whores. These aren't vices, they're needs! Don't you see?'" (P.121) Manuel and others laugh and joke about Nanu's sudden change of heart. But Nanu continues to say, "We have no right to lead these young girls astray!" (P.122) But Manuel does not approve of Nanu's sudden change of heart. He, therefore, taunts Nanu, "Go burn yourself! Drinking and playing around with young girls was all right for you too all these days. Didn't you ever think that those girls had brothers too? Just because someone got your sister into trouble...'" (P.122) Then there ensues an exchange of blows between Nanu and Manuel.

Kesar's pre-marital pregnancy has become the subject of women's gossip at the lake of the village. Kesar, who overhears the gossip, burns silently with embarrassment. Nanu, who has been awakened morally now, tells his mother, "*Avai*, don't send Kesar to work at the mine from tomorrow... No more working at the mine" (P.125). Nanu has grown wise enough to realize the evil effect of working in a mine for a young girl like his sister. He wants to safeguard the honour of his sister (hence of his family) according to the norms of the patriarchal society. Rukmini wants to send Kesar the next day to the mine only to collect her wages and never to continue with the job.

But things go beyond their control. The next day when Pandhari returns home in the evening, he sees Rukmini crying. When he asks her for the reason, she replies, "She has smeared tar on our faces, she has! ... The whole village has been buzzing with the news since this afternoon... She has run away...this Kesar...with that Christian driver Manuel!" (P.126). Obviously Pandhari is shocked out of his wits.

Pandhari has to endure the humiliation and a sense of embarrassment when people gossip openly about his daughter's elopement with Manuel. He has to see and hear so many unhappy events. For example Savlo Master is dead now. Although Pandhari never cared for Savlo Master in the past, now he seems to have grown mature enough to understand the importance of the sincere teacher retrospectively. "My shop can't stay open while Savlo Master is being cremated. I must go there. Out you go. This shop is closed. In memory of Savlo Master" (P.129). Besides, Pandhari has been suffering from tuberculosis and vomits blood frequently. Rukmini also has been suffering from old-age sickness.

Nanu, who used to lead a reckless life in the bad company of drivers by neglecting his home and by squandering the money on drinks and whores, has now become a sober youth, especially after discovering his sister's pre-marital pregnancy. He has returned home now and feels nostalgic about his lost childhood. He wants to go to the lake for bathing in the cold water. But Rukmini wants to rub oil on his head to prevent him from getting cold in the lake water, "Come, I'll rub oil on your head. Sit here.' Rukmini braced herself against the wall as Nanu crouched before her. Pouring some oil into the hollow of her palm, she began to rub it slowly into his scalp. Nanu felt like a little boy once more and quite unconsciously, sat with his legs outstretched the way he used to when he was a child. Slowly he felt his head grow light" (P.136).

But the irony of life is such that Nanu cannot live and enjoy his life though he has sobered now. One day he drives his truck to the mine where tragedy awaits him. As it is very hot and no trees or bushes are around to provide a patch of shade, Nanu walks towards the huge mound of mineral dust to take refuse from the sun. But suddenly and rather unexpectedly the sand on the top of the mound begins to slide. Consequently Nanu is buried under that heap of dust. Then pressurized by the workers the operator of the mechanical shovel starts the machine. Two scoops yield nothing. But when the shovel digs deeper for the third time, Nanu's head is severed from his trunk. By that time Rukmini rushes there, "My son! Oh my son…!' Rukmini pushed through the crowd of men and women and leapt into the dust. One of the workers tried to hold her back and jumped into the dust right behind her. Rukmini grabbed Nanu's head as it emerged from the dust, the head that she had so lovingly smeared oil upon, only that morning. One of the workers caught hold of her trying to draw her back when horrifyingly, everyone screamed as Nanu's head slipped into her hands, severed neatly from his body" (P.138-9). Nanu's death seems to be the final punishment for him as well as his parents, who neglected their traditional agricultural way of life and chose the lucrative job in the mining industry. But again the question remains as to why they chose the lucrative jobs. The answer is — their crushing poverty, illiteracy, ignorance and helplessness. They are the puppets in the hands of circumstances, which might be again due to their *karma* of previous life according to Hindu philosophy.

The mining industry has not only weaned the people of Kolamba from their agricultural profession, but also destroyed the fertility of the arable land thereby converting it further into the mining arena. This ecological violence and imbalance is noticed only by sensible people like Shanudada, who are too helpless to do anything about it. When Shankar (Yeso's son) meets Shanudada, the latter explains the nature of destruction of fertility of their land, "Our wretched fate! Even grass doesn't grow in these fields any longer...Don't you see? During the rains the lake fills with water and overflows, its banks and all this area where you are sitting now is waist deep in water. That road there, that goes up to the mine at Shenori...during the rains, water gushes down that road into the lake bringing with it dust ana stones and ore and the whole lake turns read like the paint we use on our walls. This is the water that runs into the fields leaving behind a thick layer of mud...mud that destroys the earth so no amount of manure or fertilizer can have any effect. The fields around Surla village were destroyed in this way. Now it is our turn" (P.131). He tells Shankar further how even the Sarpanch does not bother about the destruction of land because of his deep commercial involvement with mining work. He feels that the god of Kolamba i.e. the Spirit of the Lake has deserted the village. He expresses his anxiety in some detail, "When the mine is exhausted and closes down, what will we Kolambakars eat? We begged the Sarpanch to talk to the mine owners... Those bastards declared that if the fields turned barren they were willing to buy the land! What will we do with the money we get by selling our land? Pile it on our graves? At least you have an education...but what sort of education is that? When you should have been in school, you youngsters were carrying heavy loads on your heads in the mines! Why don't you write about this in the papers...let everyone know..."(P.132). But Shankar expresses his helplessness against the situation, "The mine owners own the newspapers. Will they paint anything that is critical of them?"(P.132) Shanu thus remains a representative of the old times and the attendant values of life, who deplores the negative change that has come over the landscape as well as the morality of the village.

The transition of the society in Kolamba from the traditional-agricultural to the modern-industrial may be seen in its cultural dimension also. For example, the people of Kolamba village celebrate and take part in many religious and cultural festivals like harvest festival, *dhalo*, *bhang* dance, *shigmo* festival, *taalgad* and *divli* dance, Ganesh festival, ritual of *Baras*, with great enthusiasm. But after the people like Pandhari and his family come under the influence of mining industry, they become too busy with their lucrative job to spare their time for cultural activities.

In the early days the people of Kolamba used to celebrate the New Year with a Satyanarayana Puja. After the competition of the worship and distribution of *tirtha* and *prasada*, the fruits and vegetables would be auctioned to the highest bidder. The man, who offers the highest bid, would establish his superior status in the eyes of the villagers. Accordingly, the auction begins with a bid for ten rupees and rises up to fifteen, twenty and so on. Finally Jaidev Volvoikar (brother) offers the highest bid of Rs.51 and buys the holy items thereby exhibiting his respect for religion and establishing his superior status. He is so happy about his victory (true to his name) that he talks about it enthusiastically, "This is an honour I look forward to every year, what do you say, Abu?... Accepting the holy *veedo* and coconut worshipped in this village is our right. Someday we'll come here and take a girl, our daughter-in law from this village too" (P.54). But the mining industry has helped the labour class to have quick money and improved their financial condition. During the intervening period of about ten years many changes have taken place in the village. Now when the Satyanarayana Puja is arranged at the advent of the New Year, Jaidev comes again from Volvoi to buy the *veedo* and coconut at the highest bid. But this time he cannot have the success that he used to have in the past. The auction begins with a bid for twenty-five rupees and goes up to seventy-five rupees. Jaidev is surprised to know that it is not the wealthy men from Naveli but the truck-drivers from the mining companies, who are able and ready to buy the *veedo* and coconut at the highest rate. Jaidev feels crestfallen. "Jaidev sat open-mouthed, quite unable to get a word in. The bid flew back and forth with drivers from rival mining companies pitting themselves against each other. Deeply shaken, Jaidev was forced to admit defeat. The honour, ours by right, has been wrested away by these drivers. Tomorrow they may lay claim to our womenfolk and our daughters-in-law...he thought" (P.88). In this changed situation due to mining industry, more money has been flowing into the hands of uncultured truck-drivers thereby making them richer than the others i.e. cultured people.

Another feature of the transition of Kolamba society may be seen in the degeneration or vulgarization of culture. The traditional beauty and dignity of cultural activities have given place to so-called modernity with its tendency to cheapen or trivialize culture. For example, in the early days before the mining industry entered the Goan part of Konkan belt, the people of Kolamba used to arrange the performance of Dashavatari plays during the New Year celebrations and enjoy the cultural feat. "The auction was followed by the Dashavatari, a homespun play performed by some villagers. Cries of *'ditta thom, tattha tom'* rent the night air as the villagers watched, enraptured... Everyone was engrossed in the happenings on stage where Devyani was edging up to Kacch, who was trying desperately to move away" (P.54). The people, who have put up the folk play, have great respect for mythological themes, traditional costumes, melodious music and graceful dance, which together provide a feast for the eyes and ears of spectators. But after the entry of the mining industry in the area with its attendant evils like easy money and vulgarization of taste, respect and love for traditional culture are lost. The truck-drivers of the mining companies stage not classical plays but modern plays now, which are as realistic as drab. Manuel, the Christian driver and friend of Nanu tells him how there was a modern play performed in Kolamba, which was not appreciated by the villagers due to its ordinariness. As Manuel tells Nanu, "Do you think they understand this sort of play? First they yell, wanting to know why we are wearing ordinary clothes!" (P.90) When Nanu refers to the people's liking for the traditional plays, "Yes. They're only familiar with the *'ditta thom...tattha tom'* sort of Dashavatari plays or the Har Har Mahadev sort of dances with naked swords" (P.90). But Manuel shows his inclination for modern plays for a change, "You mean a Shivaji story every day? Why, do we drink *caju feni* all the time? Sometimes whiskey, sometimes brandy ... and if we don't get a tipper don't we mount a wooden body to soothe the itch? But these country bumpkins of yours...yelled and screamed because we were wearing ordinary clothes! ... Not me. I'm a Christian, can't speak Marathi well, but the rest were no better! Marathi play where everyone was speaking Konkani!" (P.90) The classical grandeur and purity of traditional Dashavatari plays have given way to modern realistic and drab plays thereby holding mirror to the vulgarization of taste and culture.

We have already seen how the life of Kolamba village has suffered a great deal due to the adverse effect of the mining industry in the area, during the last ten years. Shankar, (Yes's son) had left Kolamba then and returned his village after an interval of ten years. He grows nostalgic and tearfully remembers things and beings of the past years. For example, when he happens to cast his eyes on Abu's grave he grows sad, "His eyes were heavy with tears as he recalled that day ten years ago, the day when Abu died. Like a picture unfolding before him, he saw Abu's body being carried out of the hut" (P.130). Shankar is so much depressed by the ugly sight of the village that he asks himself, "Why did I ever come back to Kolamba?" (P.130) He notices the physical ugliness and dirt that have crept into the village due to the mining industry. "A large yellow truck stood on the far edge splashing basketful of water over it. The dirty water ran back into the lake, covering the surface with a film of dust, oil and diesel that gleamed in the sun" (P.130) Obviously the environmental beauty and cleanliness have been robbed by the industry.

But Shankar feels that he is lucky enough to have escaped from the trammels of industrial life of Kolamba. In a way he thinks that he has achieved a sort of spiritual detachment from the mundane life. The *santon* tree that he sees in the village acts as an objective correlative of his inner feelings." The man tore his eyes away from the sight and prepared to walk off when he suddenly noticed the *santon*, tall and erect as ever, its top seeming to brush the sky. But even the *santon* seemed to have lost its zest for life. It still stood there keeping watch over Kolamba but the joys and sorrows of the villagers didn't seem to touch it any longer, it continued to live but was passive, disinterested, aloof. The wild creeper that had grown unhindered all over the santon, however, was gone. It was as though the proud tree had finally managed to liberate itself. He was glad to see that the *santon*, like himself, was finally free"(P.130). Obviously the *santon* happens to be an external symbol of Shankar's spiritual liberation.

Shankar is unhappy to learn from Shanudada how the industrial waste-material has wrought an adverse chemical effect on the arable land thereby rendering it barren. "Don't you see? During the rains the lake fills with water and overflows, its banks and all this area where you are sitting now is waist deep in water. That road there, that goes up to the mine at Shenori… during the rains, water gushes down that road into the lake bringing with it dust and stones and ore and the whole lake turns red like the paint we use on our walls. This is the water that runs into the fields leaving behind a thick layer of mud…mud that destroys the earth so no amount of manure or fertilizer can have any effect. The fields around Surla village were destroyed in this way. Now it's our turn" (P.131). The physical barrenness of land suggests the spiritual barrenness as well.

Shankar and Nanu are like binary opposites. Whereas Shankar is an idealist and respects the higher values of life, Nanu happens to be a pragmatist and materialist, who is too busy in the enjoyment of material and sensuous pleasures of life to think of higher values of life. The contrast in their personalities may be seen in their words. Nanu says sadly to Shankar, "We didn't realize what Savlo Master was worth… or Abu, for that matter… I know that you're laughing at me Shankar…you were present at Abu's funeral. And yesterday at Savlo Master's too… but I was at the mine both times" (P.133).

Shankar has chosen the vocation of a painter, not for a living but for spiritual satisfaction. He has cleared the repaired the hovel which once belonged to Abu. He has painted a few pictures showing the scenes of the past life in Kolamba — like the *chowk*, children reading *Ramvijay*, bullocks on the threshing platform and a typical woman of Kolamba. On seeing these pictures Nanu complements Shankar, "You're the first artist Kolamba has ever produced" (P.134). But Shankar corrects him by saying, "That's not true. Abu was the first artist Kolamba produced. But he drew visions with his imagination" (P.134). Nanu admires Shankar's pictures so much that he wants them to be framed. But Shankar destroys those pictures because "They have no relevance today. They were dreams dreamt ten years ago" (P.134). Shankar wants to draw pictures that express Abu's dreams. He, refuses to accept Nanu's invitation for dinner at his house, as he wants to draw his pictures in Abu's hovel itself.

"No. I must draw the pictures right here, so that Abu's spirit can see them" (P.135). Like Abu, Shankar also happens to be a dreamer, who looks far ahead of his life and therefore is not understood properly by his contemporary villagers of Kolamba.

The Upheaval may be described as a typically provincial novel about the Konkani life in Kolamba village around 1950s. It offers an authentic picture of the socio-economic and cultural life of the villagers. The economic poverty is the main reason, which drives the villagers represented by Pandhari and his children from agriculture to mining industry. But apart from the economic factors there are other socio-religious factors also to their life, which are minutely captured by Pundhalik Naik. The novel contains many sociological details of Kolamba life. For example, the villagers practice the bartering system, which is very common in the rural society of India. The teacher, the priest, the barber, the washerman etc., whoever renders some service or the other to the village farmers, are not paid on the spot in cash. On the contrary, they have to render their professional service to the farmers throughout the year and collect their fee only at the time of harvest, that too in kind, i.e. in the form of paddy or grain. In Kolamba, Savlo Master and the barber, for example, are paid by Pandhari in the form of paddy and grain.

Since the rural people of Kolamba are generally illiterate, they celebrate their festivals and religious rituals, which are folksy and deeply flavoured with local colour. Like in all folk cultures, many of their festivals like *Baras* festivals are decided by the cycle of seasons. The New Year festival, the *jatras* following the harvest seasons, *dhalo* songs and dance, *bhang* dance, *shigmo* festival, *divli* dance, *taalgadi* dance, *Phugdi* dance, Satyanarayana Puja, Ganesh Chavath etc are celebrated by the villagers of Kolamba very enthusiastically. Especially the younger men and women take a very active part in them. They believe in their own folk form of religion. For example they visit the shrine of Gram Purush and believe in the Spirit of the Lake, which is a sort of moral referee and ideal for them. They conduct a variety of rituals and festivals only to please the Spirit of the Lake, which acts as their guardian.

That geography has a deep influence on culture is a commonplace truth. The landscape of the village, and the flora and fauna of the region are recreated microscopically, poetically as well as photographically. Trees or bushes like *bheda, champa, channadi, lajja, pitkoli, santon* and *taikilo*; flowers like *aboli, chameli, kegdi, raat-ki-rani* and *shankara*; food items like *ambil, bhakri, kanji, khathkhatho, kulith, nassanoy* and *panchakhadya;* and miscellaneous culture-specific words like *bhang, bhatkar, bhavin, bund, chowk, chumbal, dakshina, godhuli, Jalmi, kudav, matka, patrao, sompo, vaddo and yajman* etc create a rich texture of the local Konkani culture thereby adding to the ethnic and exotic beauty of the novel.

Pundalik Naik follows the realistic mode of presenting the picture of Kolamba life. Since the villagers and miners are uneducated and without much refinement, they indulge in crude and vulgar jokes and remarks without any inhibitions. None of them is offended by such crude statements and observations. Far from being a Puritanical writer, Pundalik Naik writes very realistically, candidly and boldly about the villagers. The villagers and miners indulge in vulgar jokes whenever they meet somewhere, especially in taverns and gossip, thereby achieving a kind of relief the tension of their hard life. For example when Nanu and Manuel meet at a bar they compare and contrast the Indian trucks with foreign tippers with analogies from married and unmarried women. Manuel says, "look at our company trucks. Indian trucks have wooden bodies. Rattle...groan...! But the foreign ones! Isuzu...Nissan... Chevrolet...Bedford...! Not a single part makes a noise. Except the horn! You take it from me...if it's fifty years old and has a wooden body, it's Indian. Understand? .... My arse, you do! A truck with a wooden body is like a married woman but a foreign-body tipper is ...like this...like twenty-year-old with high breasts...like the top of a truck. Understand?"(P.89) They continue their sexual jokes by using the same vehicular metaphorical language.

Sometimes they borrow metaphors from the mining industry to express their ideas. Commenting on the possibility of sexual exploitation of girls in the industry, Manuel alerts Nanu, "Sure, you can drink as much as you like and sleep around! But what I'm saying is this...your sister works at our mine. If both of you worked for the same company, you could keep and eye on her. You know how they treat young girls here...like a heap of ore...any man picks up a hoe and thrusts it in" (P.91).

One of the two customers in Pandhari's tea stall refers to Nanu's love affair with Devki by using a vehicular and mechanical metaphor. "Old she is, but her body is young enough. And anyway, what does it matter in the dark? He is a driver after all, as long as the gears function smoothly, he is happy enough!" (P.104) The same customer refers to the supervisor's concessions to women by using Freudian metaphors, "He doesn't say anything to the women. After all, they have a ring and two pumpkins to keep him charmed, what do we have?" (P.104)

The Upheaval offers an interesting picture of Konkani life and adds to our knowledge of a neglected part of rural India. It has been ably translated by Vidya Pai, who has amply succeeded in capturing the minutia of human experience and cultural background of Goan part of Konkani belt. It is a welcome addition to the emerging academic field of Indian Literature in English Translation

WORKS CITED

1. Datta, Amaresh. *Encyclopaedia of Indian Literature, Vol.III.* New Delhi: Sahitya Academy, 1989. P.2847.
2. Couto, Maria Aurora. Introduction, *The Upheaval*, By. Pundalik N. Naik. New Delhi: Oxford University Press. 2002. P.XXVII.
3. Naik, Pundalik N. *The Upheaval.* Tr. Vidya Pai. New Delhi: Oxford University Press. P.XXVI. All the subsequent page references are to this edition.
4. Ibid. P.XXVI.

11

Discarding the Encumbrance of Tradition

Libertarian Impulses in Bessie Head's *Botswana Tales*"

Deepa S.P. Mathur

In the short story collection The *Collector of Treasures* Bessie Head portrays the experiences of rural dwellers. The stories foreground the consciousness and agency of ordinary village characters in the historical context of the transition from pre-colonial tradition and custom-bound communities to post-colonial modernity and the political mutation from colonial rule to independence. The stories sensitively engage with the texture of village life by evocatively depicting the configuration of belief systems, the contours of emotional and moral economy, the processes of individuation, formation of desire, distribution of status, power relations, patterns of perceptions, and the institutionalization of pride and prejudice among individuals and groups in Botswana rural communities.

Bessie Head was born and brought up in South Africa and later lived in exile in Serowe, the setting, though fictionalized of most of her novels and short stories. It is to her credit that she originally wrote into "Setswana", one of the regional languages in Botswana and later translated the same in English in order to display the creativity of African Women writers and also to fight back the empire.

In her aesthetic representation of Botswana's unevenly distributed state of independence, Head recuperates subaltern experiences and voices that colonial narratives and elitist nationalist historiographies often fail to take into consideration. The stories, in my view, constitute a consequential fictional archive of Botswana's village life that accentuates the experience of individuals, especially women and children, who live through the history of grinding poverty, neglect, humiliation, abandonment, and shame yet tenaciously manage to muster the strength to cope with minimal resources in acutely uncongenial circumstances. The stories call attention to cruelties of a patriarchal, ageist, and xenophobic order that victimizes women, children, elderly people, and outsiders. The repression and victimization of women, children, elderly, and infirm people is a gnawing feature in Head's stories. The psychological distress resulting from the conflict between Christian and Setswana beliefs, customs, and practices is also given prominence in Head's village tales. In terms of ideological disposition, Head eschews both the orientation of a cultural preservationist and the advocacy of modern elite-driven nationalism and shows inclination towards a broad-based humanism that incorporates and accommodates all humane peculiarities.

"Heaven is not Closed"

"Heaven is not Closed" pivots on the spiritual agony afflicting Galethebege, an elderly woman in her nineties. Galethebege is racked with distress due to a community-wide discord between Tswana ancestral beliefs and customs and a bigoted brand of Christianity that sanctions colonial governance while displaying wanton contempt for the values and practices of the Tswana way of life. In her youth, Galethebege responds to the seductions of the Christian religion with great zeal. Her heart is thrilled by "the austere rituals of the Church, the mass, the sermons, the intimate communication in prayers with God" (11). Throughout her life she remains a convinced and devoted Christian. She leads a quiet and worshipful life. She is always on her way to church and at home she spends hours on end diligently reading the Bible.

Galethebege's fidelity to Christian religion is put to a severe test when she falls in love with Ralokae and consents to be his spouse. Her marriage to Ralokae results in her being ex-communicated from the church. Ralokae is a zestful and cheerful village gent. He is a devout traditionalist and a stickler when it comes to adhering to and upholding Setswana custom. He firmly believes that his community would experience untold adversity and degenerate into moral turpitude should it jettison Setswana customs and laws. He is also deeply distrustful of the missionaries and is inclined to "reject all things foreign" (10). There is palpable mutual hostility between Ralokae and the resident missionary. The vertically challenged and bespectacled resident missionary is contemptuous of ordinary village people who are not part of village elite. In the resident missionary's jaundiced view, the village people, inclusive of members of his congregation, are a "vague blur" of "terrible beggars and rather stupid" (10). Ralokae has little time for the cultural intolerance and racial prejudice exhibited by the missionary and his ilk. He speaks out against the exploitative and despotic tendencies of "the people who brought the word of the Gospel to the land. Their love was enslaving people and he could not stand it" (9). His reasoning blows to smithereens the hypocritical colonial claim of embarking on a God-inspired civilising mission of rescuing the souls of primitive heathens from the raging fires of hell: "They were full of tricks. They were a people who, at the sight of a black man, pointed a finger in the air, looked away into the distance and said impatiently; 'Boy! Will you carry this! Will you fetch this!' They had brought a new order of things into the land and they made people cry for love" (10).

Galethebege's decision to marry Ralokae in accordance with Setswana custom is not an act of premeditated defiance. Though Christianity is her chosen religion, she remains sensitive to "the ancient stream of holiness that people had lived with before any white man had set foot in the land, [...]" (11). She is a Christian convert who also remains firmly rooted in the Setswana life and custom. Her ardent wish in the acrimonious situation of conflicting belief systems is for "a compromise of tenderness". She is not a self-conscious protester like Ralokae. Her life is described as worshipful, orderly, and quiet. She is a well-respected member of her community whose integrity has never been called into question. As a person with "natural goodness of heart", she genuinely falls in love with Ralokae, whom she knows and accepts as an unbeliever (8). In good faith, she approaches the bigoted resident missionary for advice only to be crudely dismissed and rejected. Galethebege without any sign of indignation goes through a ritualistic Setswana wedding ceremony. To wish the couple luck and prosperity in their marriage, bags made from portions of a cow's intestines are placed around the necks of Galethebege and Ralokae in accordance with Setswana custom. In the merriment punctuated by ululation, the wedding guests enjoy porridge and meat dished up in *mogopo* bowls. Ralokae and Galethebege are showered with adulation for observing Setswana marriage procedures. Throughout her married life, Galethebege dutifully performs her duties as a woman married in line with Setswana tradition. Significantly and true to her calling, Galethebege finds a comer in which to pray to her Christian God. After the death of Ralokae, Galethebege devotes the remaining five years of her life to her Christian worship. During Galethebege's funeral, in their funeral eulogies, her grandchildren solemnly recount anecdotes to the gathered mourners of how "all her pent-up d suppressed love for God burst forth and she talked only of Him, day and night-[...]" (7). She openly, frequently, and fervently declares her wholehearted devotion to God until her dying day.

Though she is not outwardly defiant, Galethebege's actions are cast in a heroic mode. In contrast to Ralokae's more open rebellion, Galethebege pursues the dictates of her conscience with quiet but firm resolution. The lofty dignity with which she conducts herself throughout her life is legendary. Her uncanny death posture in which "she lay on her side with her right arm thrust out above her head" (7) may be taken as a disturbing unconscious reflex action to keep the doors of heaven open even for unbelievers like Ralokae. This gesture symbolically resists the resident missionary's cruel pronouncement that heaven is closed to the unbeliever. Galethebege's death posture as well as her remarkable life story captures the imagination of the villagers who "talked about it for days afterwards" (7). The seemingly uneventful life as well as Galethebege's seemingly innocuous death posture complicates, expands, and challenges the horizons of her community, imaginatively and conceptually. Galethebege's experience is remarkable and significant enough to become a consequential part of the community's oral archives. Four or five decades down the line Ralokae's brother, the elderly Modise, tells Galethebege's story to his children and grandchildren as they sit around the fire for an evening meal. The riveting story of Galethebege sets people asking themselves pointed questions that open up space for debate on religious and cultural syncretism based on the values of mutual respect and tolerance: "had Christian custom been so intolerant of Setswana custom that it could not hear the holiness of

Setswana custom? Wasn't there a place in heaven too for Setswana custom?" (12). Galethebege's story foregrounds the autonomous and independent consciousness and agency of ordinary villagers, their endeavour to overcome the problems posed by their specific historical conjuncture. The story registers the dignified resilience and ingenuity of ordinary villagers in the struggle to forge a sense of identity and cultural validity in the face of forces bent of erasing their humanity.

"The Village Saint"

"The Village Saint" is a moral tale set in a Bamangwato village. The tale, "written into the very stones and earth of village life" (13), depicts a rural community that sneers at ethical venality and phony mannerisms. The story traces how the protagonist Mma-Mompati's almost foolproof facade of saintliness is exposed after almost twenty-six years. Mma-Mompati and her spouse Rra-Mompati are village notables. They have wealth and status. Rra-Mompati holds a position of eminence in community affairs. The family's white-washed, colonial styled mansion is a regular meeting place where top-secret community issues are discussed and where political intrigues are hatched. In contrast to the cloak-and-dagger political meetings of her home, Mma-Mompati cultivates an image of a "great lady of the town" and a "patron saint". She earns her reputation of saintliness by attending the funerals in the village regardless of the social station of the deceased. She also makes regular rounds at the village hospital to pray for sick people.

A critical situation that leads to the eventual shattering of Mma-Mompati's elaborate social image emerges when Rra-Mompati turns his back on his family and leaves his job to live with another woman. This scandal sets the village rumour machine in top gear. The majority of the village people condemn and curse Rra-Mompati for forsaking his noble spouse who was "matchless in perfection". Mma-Mompati makes a divorce court oration that impresses many villagers and sways their sympathy towards her. She speaks about "God, the Church, the Bible, the Sick, the Poor, the Suffering, the Honour of an Honourable Woman, The Blessings of Holy Matrimony [...]" (15). Mma-Mompati's speech casts her as a noble woman who has been wronged by a callous spouse. The villagers do not hide their disdain for Rra-Mompati and his lover. In utter indignation Rra-Mompati retires to his cattle-post. Mompati, the couple's only child, suffers a nervous breakdown when his attempt to follow his father to the cattle post flounders. He later recovers, and together with his mother, he manages to restore their life to normalcy.

Mma-Mompati's angelic image is shattered when a month after Mompati's marriage, his mother insists on being the first one to open her son's pay packet and fishing out as much money as she wants, leaving the married couple with barely enough to afford a week's groceries. She does so mainly to spite Mary, her daughter-in-law, whom she despises for being weak and plaintive. She feels an urge to dominate her daughter-in-law. She devises a number of devious plans to humiliate and emotionally abuse Mary. When Mompati summons enough courage to hand over his pay-packet to his wife instead of his mother, Mma-Mompati's pose of graciousness is blown to pieces. She shows her evil streak. She even denies her daughter-in-law permission to draw water from the tap in her yard. Mary has to walk a mile from her home in order to draw water from the village taps. Mma-Mompati's malicious and demeaning treatment of her daughter-in-law reveals the villainy and viciousness that has been shielded by her pretensions of saintliness and piety. Village people stop believing in Mma-Mompati's "God or her Jesus Christ" (18). In the eyes of the community, her tragically decrepit character has been revealed and the phony halo of righteousness and rectitude has evaporated. They see her for what she is, a control freak and phony saint. Not only does the tale highlight the complex moral economy of village life, it also foregrounds the moral vigilance of ordinary rural people who "were never fooled by facades" (13). Mma-Mompati's redeeming qualities are her resilience and social fluidity. Though a particularly ugly aspect of her personality has been exposed, she continues to make her social presence felt when she "buried the dead and prayed for the sick" (18).

"Jacob: The Story of a Faith-Healing Priest"

"Jacob: The Story of a Faith-Healing Priest" is set in the quiet. sleepy village of Makaleng, a settlement of about five hundred people situated in Northern Botswana. The village is depicted as an uncanny and intriguing locale, "one of those far-away wonders of the world which people sometimes visited but never thought of inhabiting·· (19). In an arid country that experiences drought regularly, "Makaleng village never failed to receive its yearly quota of twenty-two inches of rain" (19). The mystery of Makaleng village's bountiful rainfall and agricultural prosperity is further compounded by the antics of two famous prophets of the faith-healing type active in the village. The moral universe of the tale orbits around the activities of the two rural-based faith-healers.

The tale casts Jacob as its hero while Lebojang is the villain. Jacob lives on the sunrise side of the village. He is poor and lives in a mud hut. He walks around bare-footed. His church is mostly attended by children. Although he lives in poverty, in his dealings with people he exhibits astounding selflessness. Lebojang, on the other hand, lives in a mansion on the sunset side of Makaleng. He drives around in a posh car. Lebojang is a serial ritual murderer who uses the word of God to hide his ghastly acts. At the time of his arrest he is almost a millionaire. He is sentenced to death for killing men, women, and children for ritual purposes. Together with the traditional doctor and local aristocrat who were his partners in crime, he had for twenty years been involved in horrendous activities of cutting up the body parts of their victims and selling the potions to other greedy and selfish people who wanted to increase their power and wealth. Lebojang is a killer posing as a "priest of a Christian church with a big blue cross down the back of his cloak" (36).

Jacob, the star of the tale, after years of hardship and suffering finds peace and happiness in the embrace of Johannah, a lovely, lone parent to several children whose fathers had promised to marry her and then disappeared. Jacob, whose father was a German-born cattle speculator who moved to Botswana to establish a cattle ranch, had been affected by tragedy at an early age. He was only six years old when his father and his Motswana mother were killed in a car crash. Jacob and his brother Isaac were robbed of their inheritance by a rapacious uncle assisted by an opportunistic local aristocrat. The uncle ill-treated his nephews and also tried to justify his wicked campaign by claiming that the orphans "were of inferior status because they were not pure Botswana by birth" (24). Isaac died of starvation, hard labour, and exposure to the elements. While in the throes of this suffering, Jacob heard the voice of his God. The voice said "Jacob, one day I shall call you to do my work. All the suffering you endure now is but a preparation for the work you have to do" (25). Jacob, by dint of diligence, overcomes adversity and rises to prosperity. He establishes a thriving store and a profit-making beer brewing enterprise in a railway village thirty miles from Makaleng. Together with his high-living spouse and children, he indulges in lavish living and wallows "in the roar of prosperity" (21) until thieves break into his shop and take his household property and almost all his money. It is during this disaster that Jacob experiences yet another visitation from his God. Jacob's God reminds him that his prosperity turned him away from his calling. Jacob at the prompting of his God leaves his empty house and his even emptier spouse to go and establish a church in Makaleng.

Jacob in his simple and sincere manner builds "one of the oddest churches in the whole wide world" (25). Jacob receives strict instructions from his God not to canvass for membership. He is to share his daily bread with whoever comes to his hut. The majority of the members of Jacob's congregation are children. The children inform Jacob about people in distress who need his ministering. In all the cases, the ailing and sorrow-struck people recover and go about with their daily activities. Jacob is popular with many ordinary villagers because of his generosity: "No one ever left Jacob's hut without a parcel" (29). He distributes gifts he receives from grateful "seekers of help" to destitute people. Jacob supports his family by doing odd jobs in the village. Jacob is an eccentric village faith-healer whose emotional intelligence, moral integrity, and humble approach to faith-healing endear him to a lot of ordinary villagers and children. His style of ministering may be slightly unorthodox, but it is premised on the enduring principles of simplicity, humility, generosity, and sincerity. The story shows how goodness of heart triumphs over greed and moral turpitude.

The tale also sheds some light on the plight of children in Botswana society. Children are subject to all kinds of harsh treatment by adults. Jacob identifies with the struggle for children's rights because as a child he had also experienced torture, humiliation, and exploitation at the hands of his uncle who robbed him of his inheritance. His own brother died of starvation and hard labour. Children are also subject to adult cruelty as victims of ritual murder. In response to these issues Jacob establishes his church around specific physical and spiritual needs of children.

"Witchcraft"

This story deals with the phenomenon of witchcraft or sorcery. The tale's narrative voice describes witchcraft as "one of the most potent evils", "a dark thing", "a force of destruction" and "a lingering and malignant ailment" (47) that Botswana have carried along with them from ancestral times. In this tale, Head provides a critique of some of the retrogressive aspects of Setswana belief system in which "every villager believes that at some stage in his life 'something' got hold 0: him; all his animals died and his life was completely smashed up" (47 . The narrative voice observes that the belief in witchcraft is so entrenched in Setswana society that "when an ordinary villager started a new yard and before he put up his fence, he would call the Tswana doctor to place protective charms and medicines all around the yard" (47). For almost every event, a *ngaka* or traditional doctor is consulted: when children are born, when marriage rites are performed, for protection of crops and livestock, for job-related issues, and for undertakings like embarking on long journeys.

The tale chronicles the agony of Mma-Mabele, a single parent who struggles to make ends meet by taking up odd jobs around the villages. Mma-Mabele comes from a family of regular church-goers who have deeply embraced Christianity. As a Christian, she feels n need to consult traditional doctors. She does not believe that she can be bewitched until the day her son points out to her that a patch 00her hair has been shaved off. This mysterious incident makes Mma-Mabele to conclude that she has been bewitched. Her plight attracts, unsavoury characters like the local quack traditional doctor Lekena who attempts to defraud her by offering to throw bones for her and to give her some medicine for a fee. Uncanny and disturbing visions and sensations trouble her. At night she has a feeling of being strangled or being dashed about this way and that way in a high windstorm. At night she is haunted by a grotesque figure of a man who laughs at her anguish and her tormented prayers. Her affliction makes her lose a great deal of weight and saps all her energy until she is reduced to a skeletal frame lying in bed for many days.

Villagers are taken aback when she suddenly recovers, regains her appetite, and goes about doing her daily chores. Her response to the queries of fellow villagers is that "there was no one to help, not even God. I could not sit down because I am too poor and there is no one else to feed my children" (56). Mma-Mabele's recovery suggests that she has summoned her spiritual and physical resources to discard the incubus of believing in witchcraft. Her abjection leads her to marshal her strength as a hardworking woman and to grow out of the infantilism of blaming other people for her woes. As a woman who has been betrayed by male lovers and stigmatised as a "he-man" for refusing to offer sexual favours to callous men who treat women as sexual objects; she comes to the realisation that she has to rely on her own abilities. This quantum leap in understanding implies a move towards more autonomy, independence, and liberty.

Mma-Mabele disentangles herself from the albatross of negative traditional beliefs and the stranglehold of Christianity for a spiritual identity more favourable to her interests as a poor, rural, single, female, working parent living in post-independence Botswana. She moves from the prison-house of spiritual dependence and conceptual servitude to the more congenial halls of self-determination and self-reliance. Mma-Mabele triumphs over the hobgoblins of her imagination, regains self-confidence and takes her destiny into her hands by engaging in practical activities such as fending for her children and ending her dependence on God, men, and energy-sapping belief systems. She becomes conscious of her identity as "a woman alone" and comes to terms with her existential situation.

Conclusion

This paper has considered how Head orchestrates characterization as a narrative appliance to depict fortitude and resilience of the human spirit in the face of powerfully entrenched and repressive social forces as well as jaded ideological rigidities. Each of the stories deals with challenges faced by individual characters embroiled in a vortex of change. The weight of ancient traditions, the political and psychological injuries associated with colonialism, the modern pressures of newly attained independence, and the opportunities and constrictions of a patriarchal and elite-driven nationalism conspire to elicit multifarious responses in Head's characters.

Head's stories evince emergent forms of social consciousness that defy and transcend the constraints and restrictions of traditional culture and the constrictions of colonial and neo-colonial culture to more democratic "structures of feeling" that embrace change, diversity and difference. As Huma Ibrahim puts it, Head in her work examines "power relationships, as they inform and are informed by exiled identities who seek to subvert the social and individual institutions of the nation, [...]" (3). The stories also reveal the social unconscious or the darkly uncongenial aspects of the seemingly placid Botswana rural communities. Head's representation of Botswana village characters is distinguished by its abiding concern with and empathy for ordinary or non-elite and socially subordinated individuals and groups. This paper affirms the libertarian impulses inherent in Head's aesthetic oeuvre.

WORKS CITED

Head, Bessie. *The Collector of Treasures and other Botswana Village Tales*. 1977. Oxford: Heinemann, 1992.

——."Heaven is not Closed." The Collector o/Treasures 7-12.

——."Jacob: The Story of a Faith-Healing Priest." *The Collector Treasures* 19-36.

——."The Village Saint." The Collector o/Treasures 13-18.

——."Witchcraft." *The Collector of Treasures* 47-56.

Ibrahim, Huma. *Bessie Head: Subversive Identities in Exile*. Charlottesville and London: UP of Virginia, 1996.

12

Namdeo Dhasal's Marathi Muse in Dilip Chitre's English Mirror: A Critique

Sudhir K. Arora

"Translation is the medium that has offered scores of alternatives to know, to identify, to understand, to recognize, to learn and to evaluate oneself by the comparative touchstone. It has proved to be the best way of importing others' literature and exporting one's own for reciprocal advancement since Renaissance. It is translation that has made us able to peep into others' psyche and interact with them in order to improve us in adopting the best and making them improve by giving our best. The reciprocal enrichment would have not been possible without translation. Hence, it has become almost a tradition to translate literatures for reciprocal enhancement. To minimize the space among people and phobia of being alien in one's native land, regional literatures are being translated. This new trend has fashioned a locale where man is at ease with his own fellows" (*Poetcrit* 12). Indian poetry is being translated successfully in English and other languages so that anyone can read and be benefited by the richness and beauty of thoughts and ethos. The task of translator is not an easy one as he has to go into the very spirit of the author whom he is translating. He cannot do it until or unless he is bilingual and aware of the ethos other than his own. It is generally believed that poetry is difficult to translate because of the stylistic and linguistic paradigms that carry the very ethos. It is feared that poetry is lost in translation but it is also true that something new is gained. While discussing the difference between a poem and its translation, Sreedevi K. Nair writes: "A poet writes about a particular thing or experience because his deep perception of it has strongly moved him to give it a verbal expression. Thus, it is his own emotional, imaginative, or intellectual apprehension of facts and experiences that a poet tries to express. In the case of a translation, the cause for its genesis is the existing poem. This original work stimulates the translator so much that he experiences a deep affinity for the work which, in turn, prompts him to create a version of that experience in his own language. But he is not a person who merely collects the meaning contained in the original poem's linguistic and textual structure or who merely interprets the text's surface signs. Yet, the most frequent criticism against translation is that it lacks the spontaneity and power of the original work as the translator is trying to render the original poet's views faithfully. It is true, that no man can think another man's thoughts or feel another man's feelings exactly and in totality, but this is not what is expected of a translator either. The basic qualification that a goc ' translator should meet is that he should be able to peruse a literary work in such a way that he can make a sensible reading of it" (*Aspects of Translation* 48).

Dilip Chitre, a bilingual poet who has translated Namdeo Dhasal's Muse from Marathi into English is quite aware of the hazards that lie on the path of translation. It is not an easy task to enter the body of the text, feel the very spirit and then come out in order to share the felt experiences. A translator has not only to feel the spirit of the original author for a successful translation but also to listen to "the voice of another human, identifying it, empathizing with it and making it one's own" (*Namdeo Dhasal* 174). The point that favours Chitre in translation is that he is well-versed in Marathi and its culture. Even then, he feels problem in translating some of Dhasal's major poems which are landmark in Marathi simply because of their linguistic and stylistic paradigms which are too complex for translation. He himself admits: "I have been compelled to omit some of my favourite Namdeo poems that are major landmarks in the evolution of modern Marathi and Indian poetry, for the simple reason that they are linguistically too complex and deeply embedded in their own ethos" (*Namdeo Dhasal* 179-80).

Chitre knows that while translating one has to be "possessed and occupied by another human voice that is located elsewhere". He believes that "this 'elsewhere' is a larger, deeper repository of human voices, real as well as imagined. It is a shared and sharable universe; and it is the very stem of all languages and acts of speech (and writing)" (*Namdeo Dhasal* 174). While translating Dhasal's work, sometimes he has felt a kind of despair because of his inability to find out literary equivalents. He believes that "Nothing can be an adequate substitute for the empathy and the imagination that enables us to perceive poetry and to translate it into our own inner language of soulful intimacy" (*Namdeo Dhasal* 179). Even then, he has succeeded in translating Dhasal's poetry because of his understanding of "its deeper resonances, its roots that reach the rich subterranean resources of language and culture, the source that propels his metaphor and his startling imagery, the music of his ideas and the dance of his awareness" (*Namdeo Dhasal* 178).

Namdeo Dhasal is not a regional poet in spite of his writing in Marathi. He has a potential for a global poet as he understands that "great poetry integrates—rather than divides—humanity" (*Namdeo Dhasal* 12). He is a poet who cannot be confined to any boundary or nation. His poetry talks of beyond nation, race and caste. For him a man is a human being only and herein lies his achievement in developing his creative identity for claiming man not as confined to caste or race or nation but as a human being. Hence, his poetry has a universal appeal that claims for a larger audience. It is Dhasal's creative identity with broad vision that motivated Chitre to introduce Namdeo Dhasal to the world which for him "is rooted in a shared anguish and a glimmer of hope for humanity" (*Namdeo Dhasal* 30). No doubt, he has translated Dhasal but he does not claim originality for the sameness in the source text and the target text. Between these two texts, for him, there lies "a highly contested area where meta-textual reading differ" (*Namdeo Dhasal* 29). In spite of some errors that may occur, Dilip Chitre's *Namdeo Dhasal: Poet of the Underworld* is a modest attempt to introduce Dhasal's Muse to the world.

Namdeo Dhasal, the maverick Marathi poet who hardly had any formal education was born in a former 'untouchable' community in Pur-Kanersar village near Pune in Maharashtra in 1949. As he was a taxi-driver, he came in touch with pimps, prostitutes, petty criminals, drug peddlers, gangsters and illicit traders in Mumbai's sinister and sordid underworld. On the model of Black Panther, he founded Dalit

Panther in 1972. In 2004, the Sahitya Akademi conferred on him the only 'Life Time Achievement Award' for his exceptional contribution. Dilip Chitre, who considers Dhasal to be "one of the outstanding poets of twentieth century", has translated some selected poems from his eight poetic collections, namely, *Golpitha* (1972), *Moorkha Mhatarayane Dongar Halavile* (1975), *Tuhi Yatta Kanchi* (1981) , *Khel* (1983) , *Gandu Bagicha* (1986) , *Ya Sattet Jeev Ramat Nahi* (1995) , *Mee Marale Sooryachya Rathache Ghode Saat* (2005) and *Tujhe Bot Dharoon Chalalo Ahe Mee* (2006). In these poetic volumes he articulates not only for the scheduled caste or the scheduled tribes but for any caste that has become a victim of subjugation and exploitation. It is by virtue of Chitre's translation of Dhasal's poetic volumes in English that the people of the world have come to know about his comprehensive vision.

What Dhasal writes is real to the core as it reflects the lived experiences of life. He does not care for rules because they bind him to the conventionality which he does not like. For the lived experiences, he has boozed and visited brothels. Not only this, he has gone to meet mujra dancing women's establishment and also visited the houses of prostitutes who gave him a peep into life. He wished to be free in his poetic expression as he himself was. He admits: "My poetry was as free as I was. I wrote what I felt like writing and how I felt like writing. I had found my weapons and I sharpened them. Nothing was going to stop me now. I went on writing, unshackled and liberated" (*Namdeo Dhasal* 166). He loves literature at his own conditions. He feels a kind of "inner disturbance" when he sees the people being exploited and harassed. His heart forces his head to articulate the exploited. He writes: "For what makes one speak or write are the themes that create an excruciating turmoil inside you, heighten your sensitivity and leave you tenderly troubled" (*Namdeo Dhasal* 167). Prostitutes, Pimps, hijras, loan sharks, corrupt cops, drug addicts, petty criminals, street urchins, sexually transmitted diseases, physicians and general practitioners, gangster, supari killers, singers and mujra dancers, folk balladeers, tamasha artistes, coolies, immigrant labourers, food vendors, paan shopwallaahs etc. are the people who move in the streets of Dhasal's poetic world. He opposes exploitation in any form and this very determination gives an outlet for his poetic expression. He admits: "My poetry is a product of my spontaneous commitment to my mission. What I write is spontaneous, natural. I make no compromise there" (*Namdeo Dhasal* 171).

Irrespective of caste, creed or nationality, a person who is ostracized and not given the status of a human being is dalit for Dhasal who does not wish for those oppressions, insults and tortures which he himself faced in life for being a dalit. A kind of alienation entered him as he, being a dalit was made aware that "dalits are a product of a different soil, an infertile patch of land that others do not wish to till" (*Namdeo Dhasal* 156). He also saw other people who were not shudra but treated as dalits. For him, dalit means "all people discarded by society as useless to its organization" (*Namdeo Dhasal* 20). All the socio-economically ostracized people have the claims to be dalits. Hence, dalit is not confined to India as such ostracized people are scattered all over the world. He does not talk of only Indian dalits but dalits of the whole world. This is the broad perspective that makes his vision quite positive and mission ideal. He is a world poet beyond border and order. He has a deep belief in humanity which differentiates him from other dalit poets. He states: "In my view, there should be no borders of nations confining us. There should be no armies. After all we belong to this world. Whatever that happens in this world is done for the sake of humanity, and while this is being done, humanity faces obstacles; and I will say that I love those obstacles too. My vision is not restricted to the ground under my feet" (*Namdeo Dhasal* 172).

Namdeo Dhasal first shocks and then mocks finally stirring the reader's heart that begins to feel the love that he has for human beings. In the beginning he categorizes Dhasal's poetic corpus as scatological literature as he feels nausea or revulsion. But, he appreciates when he comes to know the real motive. As he writes for dalits, his pen becomes abusive for the oppressors and exploiters. To these oppressors, a dalit is 'the other', an untouchable. He writes with fire—the fire that burns the reader who fails to understand as he is not in himself. Mark the lines that shock the reader's sense of understanding:

> One should hang to death the descendant of Jesus, the Paighamber, the Buddha and Vishnu
> One should crumble up temples, churches, mosques, sculptures, museums

...
Man, one should tear off all the pages of all the sacred books in the world
And give them to people for wiping shit off their arses
...
Wage class wars, caste wars, communal wars, party wars, crusades, world wars
One should become totally savage, ferocious, and primitive
One should become devil-may-care and create anarchy (*Namdeo Dhasal* 35)

Dhasal upsets the reader when he talks of hanging the people of all religions. He is not satisfied with this as he advises to tear off the pages of the sacred books and use them for wiping shit off their arses. No one can tolerate such abusive and dirty suggestions. His advice to create anarchy seems to be insane. But, when the reader goes through the poem, he understands the logic and realizes the great soul that has a vision of a world—the world where there will be no caste, colour or creed. He surprises the reader with the technique of juxtaposition. To say in a contradictory way adds the charm to the text. One cannot help appreciating the great idea presented here in these lines:

After this those who survive should stop robbing anyone or making others their slaves
After this they should stop calling one another names—white or black, brahmin, kshatriya, vaishya or shudra;
Stop creating political parties, stop building property, stop committing
The crime of not recognizing one's kin, not recognizing one's mother or sister
One should regard the sky as one's grandpa, the earth as one's grandma
And coddled by them everybody should bask in mutual love
Man, one should act so bright as to make the Sun and the Moon seem pale
To humanity itself, man, man should sing the song of man. (*Namdeo Dhasal* 36)

For him, construction lies in destruction. He envisions a utopia where man will only be man, neither dalit nor non-dalit. It is his faith in humanity which causes him to think on this line. He is not satisfied with the present system and so he talks of its destruction so that he may create a world where man will sing the song of man.

Woman, particularly a prostitute, for Dhasal, deserves respect as she is a true dalit because of her exploitation by all. No doubt, she is an object of carnal love but is still loathed. She has no sanction like a wife and so loses the claim of having dignity of a human being. It is strange that she is considered as degraded while the truth is that man himself degrades while exploiting her body with his carnal passions. She is untouchable but how one who touches her and enjoys sex with her can remain touchable and sacred. Dhasal feels no hesitation in declaring his relationship with prostitute. He loves her and feels her to explore himself. Mark the lines for his frank confession:

> Manda
> Your mind is neither of ash nor of marble
> I feel your hair, your clothes, your nails, your breasts
> as though they were my own: they reveal to me, within myself
> colonies of the dead; hunchbacks left to die in the streets; (*Namdeo Dhasal* 56-57)

Dhasal becomes informal when he talks about the beloved and the lover as whore and pimp. In the manner of Shaw, he forces the reader to think. Mark the lines that give a shock to any sensible reader:

> The beloved is only a sanctified form of a whore;
> the lover is just a glorified pimp
> Women are merely printed whores of men.
> Men are just pimps of women.
> The relationship of men and women is just like—
> Take a few whores; take a few pimps; take a few chewing sticks to clean the teeth;
> And throw them away after use; and then gargle with the holy water of the river. (*Namdeo Dhasal* 58)

But, Dhasal respects women and never wishes to degrade them. For him, even a prostitute has a personality of her own. What he wants to bring out is the hollowness of men for whom women are nothing except the means of sexual gratification. Outwardly they show their sacredness while inwardly they make the Ganga impure. He fails to understand why a man's love for woman is limited only to coitus. If he does so, he is merely a beast, not a human being. He speaks in a candid manner:

I didn't dare to redefine love
There are many ways beasts and human make love;
The limit of their is coitus
If a human being begins to behave as a beast
It can't be human love. (*Namdeo Dhasal* 128)

Love of and for coitus is an animal love, not a human love. He recommends for the human love that does not know any limit or caste or any boundary.

Water and land have always been the means of dalits' exploitation. Water is a free gift of nature but is controlled by the so-called landlords or the non-dalits. Hence, water became the root cause as man cannot live without it. Dhasal says:

When water is brought to despair
A desperate life-or-death struggle reaches its critical point
And the folk-song withers away (*Namdeo Dhasal* 43)

He becomes aggressive against the touchables who exploited the untouchables even for water. Out of fury, he abuses them saying:

Away, away you daughterfucker,
You fistfucker, you shithead, you jerk,
You pedigreed bastard,
Get away, get away , you block in the way of water.
'You get out of here. Don't make my blood boil.
I'll shred you to pieces; I'll set the whole world on fire
Out, out,' (*Namdeo Dhasal* 46)

He voices for Dalits who own nothing except the tag of being dalits. All the things are under the high caste Hindus' or the landlords' control. This has made the dalits helpless to the extent that they even feel disgusting to be human. Mark the lines for the dalits' crying over their miserable condition:

In this lowered life imposed on us, not even a pavement belongs to us
They've made us so helpless; being human's become nauseating to us
We can't find even dust to fill up our scorched bowels
The rising day of justice, like a bribed person, favours only them
While we are being slaughtered, not even a sigh for us escapes their generous hands (*Namdeo Dhasal* 47)

Such is the painful outcry of all dalits irrespective of their caste, colour or creed. Dhasal's voice is every dalit's voice. In the poem, 'I Slew the Seven Horses of the Chariot of the Sun', he speaks against the Sun who is none other than God, the mighty, the powerful, the Capitalist and the exploiter in the guise of Messiah known for impartiality. He asks the Sun to:

> Punish the landowners and the feudal lords
> Whom caste and money have made powerful and arrogant
> Return to us the rain that belongs to us
> And irrigates our crops
> Returns to us our autumns and winters;
> Give back to us our months of receding rains
> When sunlight and showers play hide and seek
> (*Namdeo Dhasal* 123)

For dalits, the Sun is insensitive and indifferent. He reminds the Sun of the bond which he had forgotten. He threatens him that dalits will slay the horses of his chariot as now they have become quite conscious of his disguise and insensitiveness towards them. Mark the lines for his threatening to the Sun:

> From now on. live for us; die for us.
> And if that does not happen,
> As of now, you're nobody to us.
> O great brazenfaced one!
> I slay the seven horses of your chariot
> And break its wheel.
> (*Namdeo Dhasal* 126)

Identity crisis lies somewhere in the very conscious of every dalit who struggles to get over it. Dhasal knows it and so voices this fear. He feels that he is "a venereal sore in the private part of language" (*Namdeo Dhasal* 100) and when he sees that people have forsaken him, he is broken by the revolt that begins to explode inside him. He wishes to be released from his infernal identity. He is frustrated and finds himself on the "seashore of pain" sculpting "with a chisel an image of many-faceted wounds" (*Namdeo Dhasal* 112). When he says: "As for me I still have to worry / about tomorrow's bread", he narrates every dalit's story. Mark the lines for voicing dalits' pain, suffering, dreams and longings:

Pain and roti are being roasted in the same tandoor's fire.
The flame of the clothless dwells in mythologies and folklore.
The rock of whoring is meeting live roots;
A sigh is standing up on lame legs;
Satan has started drumming the long hollowness
A young green leaf is beginning to swing at the door of desire
(*Namdeo Dhasal* 101)

When he sees the terror dance of the touchables over the bodies of the untouchables, a volcano erupts in him. He makes up his mind to commit violence. "Perhaps these usurpers' heads can be brought back to sense / if they are hit hard" (*Namdeo Dhasal* 110).

It has always been Namdeo Dhasal's endeavour to translate the vision though it changed many times with time. Without vision, a man is a problem not only to others but also to himself. Dhasal had never been a problem to himself. He himself admits: "If you do not have a vision, you become a problem unto yourself. I never became a problem to myself. I became a socialist; but as soon as I saw the hollowness of it, I turned to communism. However, whatever I did, my foundation was Ambedkar's vision" (*Namdeo Dhasal* 166). Whatever vision he has, he never forgets Ambedkar and his teachings. It is Ambedkar's vision which prepared his foundation. He is Ambedkarite to the core. Ambedkar never liked idolatry but Dhasal cannot live without appreciating him. He invokes him and believes that Babasaheb will forgive him for worshipping him. He states:

I couldn't do without writing
The poetry of your achievement.
Babasaheb, I bow my head before you.
I'm ready t suffer for life time
Any punishment you award me. (*Namdeo Dhasal* 134)

It is Baba Ambedkar who proved to be the Sun for all dalits as he saved them from being exploited. He is the "only charioteer" who belongs to them. He has grown "larger than the name of the nation" as he changed dalits' lives like "a great flow of thought" (*Namdeo Dhasal* 83). With his liberal vision, he proved to "the human pivot for all dalits" (*Namdeo Dhasal* 83). His main aim was not just to liberate man but to change him for betterment on the foundation of study and service. Mark the lines for Dhasal's respect for Ambedkar:

You spoke out hard and clear:
For your purpose was to liberate man.
The same heart in which you contained all tolerance,
You let the volcano of revolt become active.
Yours was not a blind revolt.
it was for changing oneself, for changing the world.
New eyes; a new heart.
You believed in awakening; not in terrorizing
Your awakening was founded upon study and service. (*Namdeo Dhasal* 84)

No doubt, the Marathi poet in Namdeo Dhasal is everybody's poet because of his catholicity of vision and mission. He talks of integration of humanity, never of its disintegration. Thanks to Dilip Chitre who has made his face popular through his English mirror that reflects the face which is similar to the face of the viewer. Dhasal's Marathi Muse reflects Dalits' pain and suffering in Dilip Chitre's English mirror realistically to the extent that the agony seems to be of all the people who are denied full human status by other human beings. As a true follower of Ambedker, he attempts to unite all dalits not only of his nation but of the whole world. Exploitation in any form is quite allergic to him and his muse treats literature as "an instrument of cultural change and as an expression of all deeper concerns such as the quality of life and the realization of liberty, the striving for equality and the achievement of excellence" (*Namdeo Dhasal* 158).

WORKS CITED

Arora, Sudhir K. "Fragrant Regional Flowers in Indian Poetic Vase: A Note on Indian Poetry Translated in English." *Poetcrit*. (ed.) D. C. Chambial, Vol. XXI, January 2008, No. 1, 12-19.

Dhasal, Namdeo. *Namdeo Dhasal: Poet of the Underworld Poems of 1972-2006* (translated by Dilip Chitre). Chennai: Navayana, 2007.

Dhasal, Namdeo. "Namdeo on Namdeo", *Namdeo Dhasal: Poet of the Underworld Poems of 1972-2006* (translated by Dilip Chitre). Chennai: Navayana, 2007. 163-173.

Chitre, Dilip. "Poetry of the Scum of the Earth." *Namdeo Dhasal: Poet of the Underworld Poems of 1972-2006* (translated by Dilip Chitre). Chennai: Navayana, 2007. 7-30.

Chitre, Dilip. "Namdeo's Mumbai." *Namdeo Dhasal: Poet of the Underworld Poems of 1972-2006* (translated by Dilip Chitre). Chennai: Navayana, 2007. 149-162.

Chitre, Dilip. "A Translator's Delight and Despair." *Namdeo Dhasal: Poet of the Underworld Poems of 1972-2006* (translated by Dilip Chitre). Chennai: Navayana, 2007. 174-180.

Nair, Sreedevi K. "Is Poetry Lost in Translation?" *Aspects of Translation*. New Delhi: Creative Books, 1996. 46-69.

13

Translator as Transcreator: Reading Gillian Wright's translation of Dr. Rahi Masoom Reza's *Aadha Gaon*

Saurabh Shukla
Anurag Kr. Pandey

There has been numerous debate on translation and both writers and critics have often landed themselves in unending discussions on it as an art or skill. Translation has been called as 'the eternal profession'. J.C. Catford regards translation as 'the replacement of textual material in one language by equivalent textual material in another language'.[1] According to J.B. Casargrande, 'One doesn't translate Languages, one translates Cultures'.[2] Ivir Opines, 'Translation is a way of establishing contacts between cultures'.[3] Steiner rightly observes that 'Language is a science but translation is an art.'

The need of translation is as ancient as the 'Tower of Babel'. In the absence of translation, much literature would have remained unnoticed like 'full many a flower' blushing unseen 'in the dark unfathomed caves of ocean'. Along with serving as a sort of bridge in a multilingual situation, translation helps in preserving ancient literary and cultural heritage. It helps in crystallizing various Indian literatures at national level and national literature at international level. The prime purpose of translation is of placing source writer's concerned feelings and thoughts in totality in proper perspective for its target readers.

Translation is a complex, painstaking, and demanding task. A translator has to operate from multiple choices to choicelessness. The translator hangs like *Trisanku* between two languages. Cicero gave vent to the translator's dilemma when he said, 'If I render word for word, the result will sound uncouth, and if compelled by necessity I alter anything in the order or wording, I shall seem to have departed from the function of a translator'.[4]

The translator has to bear in mind that a language is not merely a medium through which experience is communicated but is something inseparable from the experience it communicates. A common expression 'tu tu main main' communicates for too much than its translated version 'you youing me meing' suggested by P. Lal and N. Nopany'.[5] In Hindi, 'abhiman' and 'ghamand' are two different feelings; so are 'lajja' and 'sharm'. Each of these pairs cannot be translated by one and the same term. The inadequacy of literal translation is beautifully expressed in an Italian proverb, 'Tradultore traditore', which means 'A translator is a traitor'. William Cowper once remarked, 'total fidelity is also unfaithfulness' in translation.

Dr. Rahi Masoom Reza and Gillian Wright are two different authors with completely different personalities, connected by a great work called *Aadha Gaon.* One is an Indian, the other a British. One was born in Ghazipur in eastern Uttar Pradesh in 1927, the other was born in Hertfordshire in 1957 and resides in New Delhi. The former was educated in Ghazipur and later at the Aligarh Muslim University, where he took a Ph.D., while the latter graduated from London University. The first was a brilliant student of Urdu, Hindi and Sanskrit and a proponent of Urdu in the Devnagari Script. He, later, moved to Bombay and became a successful screenplay writer and wrote the screenplays and dialogues for over 300 films including B.R. Chopra's television series, Mahabharat and died on 15 March 1992 in Bombay. The second is a journalist and has studied both Hindi and Urdu at London University and has translated two modern classics of Hindi literature, Shrilal Shukla's *Raag Darbari* and Rahi Masoom Reza's *Aadha Gaon.*

Widely acclaimed for his writing on communal discourse and tragedy of partition in contemporary Hindi fiction, Rahi Masoom Reza published his *Aadha Gaon* in 1966. Reza sets this novel in his native Avadh Village offering a vibrant Indian blend of Muslim and Hindu cultures. Rahi Masoom Reza's honest and controversial novel unfolds during the latter years of the Raj and the first decade of Independence and portrays the rival halve of a zamindar family, their loves, fights and litigations. It attacks the creation of Pakistan and explores the abolition of the Zamindari system and its impact at the village level. The novel is also semi-autobiographical work set in the author's village of Gangauli in Ghazipur district on the fringes of Avadh. *Aadha Gaon* is possibly the first novel in Hindi which depicts the life style of Shia Muslims and related people in a village with full realism. *Aadha Gaon*, is Gangauli, a village with Muslim majority. In this novel there is an artistic description of the time period of partition, the condition of Muslims, their mindset and their cordial relationship with Hindus. The novel is a creative stroke against communalism and supports nationality. Not only *Aadha Gaon*, several other works of Reza like *Katra Bi Arzoo*, *Topi Shukla*, *Neem ka Ped*, *Os ki Boond,* vividly depict the agony and turmoil of the consequences of partition and its effect on the Hindu-Muslim relationship in the Indian sub-continent, along with the social tension among different social groups of India.

Dr. Reza is one of the finest literary talents in terms of his content, context and style. He mixes Urdu and Hindi so brilliantly that it tastes extremely Indian. Whatever one says, but India, as a nation belongs to these two languages equally. No language matches Urdu for its sweetness and style. And when Hindi forms the soul on which Urdu writes the mannerisms, it's as good as it gets. And what is interesting that Dr. Reza is of the viewpoint that Urdu is no different language. Urdu is only a branch of Hindi which differs primarily in mannerisms and style. That gives a different flavour to his novels.

Being a foreigner, the translation of *Aadha Gaon* was a Herculean task for Gillian Wright. Earlier, she translated the novel with the title *'The Feuding Families of Village Gangauli,* but after revision she changed the title. And now it is *A Village Divided.* During translation she was called upon to render Avadhi proverbs, idiomatic expressions, colloquial expressions, slang and figures of speech. Wright left no stone unturned in doing justice to the work she had undertaken. But, as every rose has a thorn, Wright's translation suffers from some lacunae.

She took sufficient liberty for the effective transmission of the 'spirit of the work. She has provided a detailed description of Muslim culture as well as the hierarchical structure of different families of village in form of Translator's introduction. In a way, Wright became a transcreator while rendering translation.

At the outset the title of the novel *'Aadha Gaon'* is well translated *'A Village Divided'*. And in the opening chapter, the line 'Laga Jhoolani Ka Dhakka, Balam Kalkatta Chale Gaye' been translated as 'A Nudge of my bridal nose ring sent, my love as far as Calcutta' (Pg.2). It can be observed easily that instead of performing literal translation, Wright remains true to the content.

Similarly, 'Uumme Laila Pukari ye rokar : Shaam hoti hai, Ghar aoo Akbar....' has been translated as 'Laila wept and cried, It's eventide, come home Akbar.... (P.20)

Wright shows a lot of creativity in her translation of typical Hindi dialectical expressions for example.

'Bhai hoti hongi randiya bevafa... meri Gulaabi Jaan to wafa ki Putali hai. Har Jumerat ko masha ka sadka utarti hai'.

Becomes

'Bhai, I suppose whores must be unfaithful... but my whore Gulabi Jaan is the image of fidelity. Every Thursday she wards off the evil eye from me with an offering of blackdal'. (P.78).

The line 'Ee ta Kauno roeka bakat na hai Ummul!' is translated as 'What sort of time is this to cry, Ummul!' (p.105). and the dialogues like, 'Uu to randi na hai: Baki hamahu bivayane me rahila. Kachhu Keh deib ta aap chichiyavat nunahra tak chal jai hain.' Are translated as,

'She is not a whore. In fact, we live in zenana. And if I say anything, you will run yelping & whinning back to Naunahra'. (P.99)

Even to maintain the locale touch, some words of Urdu as well as the slang's and abusive words are used as it is. Wright has no hesitation in using words like 'Baqra', 'Asharh', 'Chamar', 'Matimile', Jharumare', ' Behenchod', 'Matam', 'Zenana' etc. to maintain the originality of the text.

A glimpse of Wright's innovation is very clear in her translation of popular idioms. Instead of using the parallel English idiom, Wright tries to remain close to the Hindi one. For example 'Dunia dekhe hona' is translated as 'had seen the world' (Pg.80), 'Doodh Ka Doodh our Pani Ka Pani karna' as 'To separate the milk from the water' (P. 96) and 'Ankho me chirag jalna' as 'A kind of light burning in eyes' (P.30).

But the translation which speaks volumes of Wright's creativity is that of 'Gaari : a kind of folk song usually sung at marriage ceremony',

'Badi dhoom Gajar se aaya ri banna,
Kumhar ki gali ho aya ri banna,
Apni amma nachata aya ri banna,
Sab log kahe kumhar ka jana.'
Is translated as,

'With lots of noise and drums, here he comes, re,
Down the alley of the potters, here he comes re
He's got his mother up to dance, so he has re,
He was fathered by a potter, so he was re.' (P. 147)

And

'Kothe se bada lamba hamara banna
Banne Ki amma baansbareli
Banne ki abba teni murga hamara banna
Kothe se bada lamba hamara banna'
As,

'Taller than the roof is our young bridegroom
The mother of groom is a Bareilly bamboo
The father of the groom is a fighting cockeral
Taller than the roof is our young bridegroom.' (P.149)

But, as every rose has a thorn, Wright's, translation suffers from some defects. She has made a lot of words literally translated like the term 'lament' is used for 'nauha', Marsia' and 'Salaam'. The word 'Bastered' is used both for 'heramzade' and 'Sale', 'had a feeling' for 'Maatha Thanka', and use of many original words which can be translated, Wright also skips the translation of some passages of pure dialectical expressions.

Thus, we can observe that in *A Village Divided* Wright has tried to focus on the content while remaining faithful to her own vision. In this process, she has recreated the text for the readers. Speaking about translation Salman Rushdie once remarked. "It is generally believed that something is always lost in translation; I cling to the notion- and use, in evidence, the success of Fitzgerald-Khayyam - that something can also be gained."[6] The same thing is applicable to Gillian Wright's transcreation of Aadha *Gaon* as *A Village Divided.*

REFERENCES

1. Catford., J.C.A Linguistic Theory of Translation. London. OUP.1965.p.20
2. Casagrande., J.B. "The Ends of Translation". International Journal of American Linguistics 20/4(1954). P.338
3. Vladimir, Ivir. *Translation Across Cultures*(ed.). 1987.p.35
4. Quoted in Sisan Bassnett-McGuire. Translation Studies. London.1980.p.43
5. Cited in R.Gargesh. "On Equivalence:A Comparitive Study of Three Translations of a Hindi Short Story". International Journal of Translation1/1(Jan.1989).p.72
6. Rushdie, Salman. Midnight's Children.Delhi.Rupa Publication.1983.p29

WORKS CONSULTED

Reza, Rahi Masoom. *Adha Gaon*. New Delhi. Rajkamal Publication. 1966.

Wright, Gillian.*A Village Divided*. .New Delhi. Penguin.2003.

Newmark, Peter. *Approaches to Translation*. Oxford. Pergamon Press.1981.

Mc Guire, S.B. *Translation Studies*. Methuen London and Newyork.1980.

Rai, Chandra Dev. *Abhinav Qadam*. Mau. Sahityik Sanskritik Manthan Pub. 2002.

14

Protean Interstices between Praxis and Gnosis: Hands on Experience of Translating a Female Dalit Autobiography

Vandana Pathak

I

In India, there is a vast majority of castes and sub –castes. Their literature is a reflection of their woes and miseries. The Dalits are the most poor, marginalized, oppressed, ostracized and exploited people. They have been deprived of many rights since ages. Dalit literature acts as a powerful tool to create social, political awareness, thus becoming an important social, political and cultural document in the process.

Dalit autobiographies are based on real life experiences. Naturally, the main strength of these autobiographies is reality of experiences and proximity. In other genres, detachment can easily be achieved. Yet the involvement of 'Atma' makes this detachment rather difficult.[1] These Dalit writers bring their own experiences, awareness, and language into literature. Bhalchandra Phadke too concurs, "The Dalit writer wants to say something. His rejection, protest and agony will be expressed in his language."[2]

The genesis of Dalit literature has taken place in the womb of Dalit litterateurs.[3] Dalit literature is literature of protest. It is a manifesto for revolutionary transformation of society and human consciousness. It is an attempt to arouse Dalit awareness. Hence, it is written in the language of the Dalits. Rural colloquial language becomes an apt vehicle to reveal in all honesty the agony, pain, exploitation, marginalization, poverty, anger and protest of the Dalits. The translation of such a document into a foreign language is a tedious task.

II

Shantabai Kamble's *Mazhya Jalmachi Chittarkatha* is widely acclaimed as the first female Dalit autobiography in Marathi. She wrote it after superannuation from service as an education extension officer on 28 February 1981. It was first published in a magazine called 'Purva' in a serialized form in March 1983. A T.V. serial entitled 'Najuka' based on this particular text was shown on Mumbai T.V. from 10 August 1990. When I read this text for the first time without any prior introduction, it struck a chord in my heart. Young Naja's story from subjugation and marginalization to empowerment was a chronicle, a socio-cultural-historical document which was in itself a revelation- a candid record of her own life and the life of her community in general. The juxtaposition of 'I' and 'we' in the text lent to it an additional dimension and significance. Her son, Dr. Arun Kamble, described its genesis. Shantabai actively participated in all discussions of and on Dalit autobiographies. These discussions whetted her curiosity and she read all these 'Swakathans' with great interest. Shankarrao Kharat (*Taral Antaral* fame) was her contemporary. His autobiography made her realize that she too had similar experiences and on her mentioning this to her son, he asked her to write them down without any delay. "Perhaps while reading Dalit autobiographies she felt", says Dr. Arun Kamble, "that she too should write, she had too many things to narrate."[4] Shantabai's own comment in this context is very relevant. She says, "Nanasheb Zodage and Shankarao Kharat were writers from my side of the country. I read their writing with great affection. I felt warmth for it. Similar incidents had taken place in my life. I had too many things to narrate. I too should write; that my life as a woman was very different from their life, I realized."[5] Shantabai had realized the significance of gynocentric experiences of her life. Her son highlighting the same remarks, "Everywhere the scenario of Dalit life is the same- same neglect, same humiliation, barbarism, life of hellish agonies... the life of a Dalit woman is that of a Dalit amongst Dalits-a slave's slave. If a reading of this life results in removing the slavery of an Indian woman and paves way for the removal of Dalitness from their lives, it would not be a mean achievement."[6] Her son suggested the title *Mazhya Jalmachi Chittarkatha*. Shantabai had often heard other women use this word '*chittarkatha*' for her life and felt that it reflected her life perfectly and so she too decided to use the same title.[7]

III

Shantabai Kamble's life was influenced by the ideology of Mahatma Phule and Dr. Ambedkar. She was an active participant in the Ambedkarite movement. Her autobiography also reflects these twin influences and life of all other Dalits, especially of the Mahar community. Her life's narrative is a saga of untouchability, social discrimination and exploitation rampant in the society. Through various incidents, Shantabai narrates, how since childhood, she had searing experiences of untouchability. Her request for water at a well at Pandharpur, or seeking Vithoba's darshan from outside the temple, offering of malida to the Pir from outside the mosque, her being addressed as the '*mharache por*' etc. are many such incidents depicted in the text. As a teacher trainee and headmistress too, she faced similar discrimination. Shantabai subtly describes the internal discrimination practised by the lower castes amongst their hierarchies and how the *Rayrands* performed exclusively for the Mahars. Shantabai has very aptly described various social customs, traditions and superstitions prevalent in the Dalit community. Her mother died without proper medical treatment because she felt that she was the victim of sorcery. Shantabai too as a child went into a delirium due to fever but all felt that it was a magical spell. She describes how offerings were made to different gods and goddesses to appease them. The fortune teller's prediction of Sada's death in a week's time made his entire family miserable. Shantabai has thrown brilliant light on his psyche and the superstitious community in this oeuvre. She has depicted the development of her own rationalism in the autobiography and exemplified it by taking Gangu's son to a doctor. The marriage customs of the community too are described at length.

Dalit autobiographies document the chill penury and hunger of those who lived at the lowest rung of the social ladder. Shantabai describes how left over, begged for food, was dried up and eaten later in times of deprivation. The jowar collected from the cow dung too was washed and dried to use later. How the villagers killed a buffalo to quench their hunger has been described. After delivery, how Naja and another Mahar woman had to eat raw cobs to satisfy their hunger throws light on the utter poverty of the families. The life of the women described in the autobiography is thrice cursed- firstly due to female sex, secondly due to being poor and thirdly, due to being a low caste

Mahar women. The exploitation of these women is physical as well as psychological. Kumud Pavade aptly puts it into words. Says she, "A Dalit woman suffers in the family first as she is a woman and then she has to face the society as she is a Dalit."[8] In the patriarchal, androcentric society, Dalit women are subjugated and occupy a secondary place. Shantabai's husband acquired a second wife and so Shantabai left him. She preferred to live alone in her pregnant condition with self respect. She withstood and at times, opposed and fought against the ill treatment meted out to her.

In addition to these motifs, there are umpteen number of references to the rites and rituals of the Mahar community in the text. How the caste tribunal or *Panchayat* adjudicated upon various disputes has been described at length. The occupations of the people in the community or their means of livelihood, religion, objects of worship and celebrations, the life of the people in the community and those of upper castes along with their hegemonic culture and some references to Ambedkarite movement find a mention in this female Dalit autobiography. A study of all these kaleidoscopic motifs is necessary to understand the life style and culture of the community. Language is an index of culture and so language plays an important role in an analytical study of this text.

IV

In Sociolinguistics, it is said that each individual speaker is presumably moulded much more by his experience (as a listener) than by his genetic make-up and his experience consists in fact of speech produced by other individual speakers, each of whom is unique. Yet a degree of similarity is generally found between speakers of that language in the same community. Many linguistic variables influence language of a speaker. The first and foremost is the speaker himself – the kind of person he is and his varied experiences in life. Other factors are origin or present home, socio-economic status, sex, race, age, and education. The membership of a social group or community, his home atmosphere, and social environment too influence his language.

The term 'speech community' is widely used by sociolinguistics to refer to a community based on language. A language or a dialect is used for communication in the speech community. The language of a community 'Boli bhasha' is different in its pronunciation, grammar, sentence construction, and vocabulary. Even though 'dialect' (boli) is different from the language, it is not completely different. There are similarities and differences between the two and that is why it is understood. Its vocabulary, phrases and idioms and proverbs impart a distinct touch to literature. Sampat Gaikwad has divided the speech communities described in Dalit autobiographies into four different groups. In the first group is the Savarna speech community living in the village. In the second group is the speech community living outside the village and considered Untouchable. In the third can be included those nomadic tribes who do not have a village or place outside a village to live in but who belong to a particular place and caste and in the last group are Adivasis living in hills and valleys and jungles. All these 'speech communities', whether big or small, have been moulded in the Indian social order. The Indian social order and village system has left its imprint on these speech communities vis-a-vis its language. The speech habits depend on the social content and it influences the emotions, behaviour, thought process, attitudes, customs and traditions of that community. The reality of life is expressed through language.[9] Dalit literature deals mainly with life in villages or rather outside the village bounds. Naturally the language used by the autobiographer is rural language (gramin bhasha). Three factors, society, period, and place influence a language. The language of the Dalit autobiographer depends upon the geographical locale of the writer and his community. Nagnath Kotapalle comments,

> A plane of rural society is felt here. In this society are seen the scattered islands of exploited Dalits. A different life style and dialect of that society is observed here. As the generation in this society goes on acquiring education, the pictures of that life along with its background will appear in literature.[10]

The language is used along with all its distinctive features and regional flavour. Jyoti Lanjewar opines, "The language of Dalit autobiographies is regional. The autobiographies reveal many strains of colloquial languages in Maharashtra and along with colloquialism, means of subsistence, village system, customs and economic system are also reflected."[11] The colloquial language is used naturally and simply. It is not used as a deliberate strategy; spontaneity of expression is its main feature.

V

Shantabai Kamble was born on 1st March, 1923 at Kargani, in Aatpadi taluka of Sangali District in the Mahar community. She spent her childhood at Mahud and acquired education till seventh standard, overcoming many obstacles. This self narrative is her first literary composition. Prior to this, she had never attempted any genre of literature. Shantabai Kamble herself has enumerated the characteristics of her life narrative. According to her,

1. It is the first autobiography written by a Dalit female.
2. It is an autobiography highlighting the painful lot of women.
3. The autobiography reveals the neglect, humiliation and poverty of Dalits.
4. It narrates along with individual experiences communal experiences.
5. The autobiography depicts the experiences of a female teacher who lived outside village boundary in the rural area.
6. And, the autobiography employs the 'bolibhasha' (dialect) of a Dalit female. [12]

Shantabai Kamble used a dialect of Marathi used in the rural areas of Sangali District. All her childhood and schooling experiences have been narrated in this dialect, which is quite different, form standard Marathi. Bama, a Dalit writer, well known for her autobiography entitled *Karakku* rightly points out, "the Dalits have different vocabulary and speech. They should deliberately overstep what they are permitted to write, by the rules of the 'dominant' grammar. The Dalit should write as a Dalit. The Dalit's writing should be read like the Dalit's."[13] Naturally such a language will go against the 'standard' languages, pure, classical, divine, and 'cultured'-the academic languages and the ramifications of such a language would be more vibrant and powerful.

The words or language used by Shantabai in her text can be classified as –

1. Words in the colloquial language,
2. Words used in the rural sector,
3. Words used by Dalits,

4. Standard Marathi words,
5. English words with hackneyed pronunciation,
6. Some English words.

This mixed language immediately brings to forefront the marginalized existence, humiliation and exploitation of Shantabai's community. She has also resorted to the use of many Dalit and rural words in the text. A detailed list of these words offers an insight into the want of academic and cultural refinement of her community and its marginalization. Words such as 'tadtamasha'(p.54), 'taralki'(p.59), 'rakuli'(p.93),'takkya' (p.37), 'karani' (p.44), 'kakati'(p. 06), 'lagir'(p.46), 'vakut' (p.3), 'aabdari'(p.8) , and 'kanig'(p.10) etc. are noticed. The author has also employed many idioms and phrases such as 'jibhela haad haay ka?' (p.58), 'potala adhaar zala' (p.65), 'gajarachi pungi vaajali tar vaajali nahitar modun kadhali' (p.78) , 'gaavala made zale tar tyachi lakde taku naye' (p.88), 'tya bai ekapat rahat asatil tar mee choupat rahin' (p.104), 'yacha gaavachya bori ani yacha gaavachya babhali'(p.135), 'Mahar mangana khata yeina ani kutryala paani pita yeina' (p.135), etc. There are words with distorted pronunciations such as 'sukirwari', 'abyaas' (p.41), 'piligachi'(p.41), and 'pwat'(p.44). The text is replete with peculiar verb usages like 'zopalu'(p.12), 'maraliya' (p.12), 'sangtiyach'(p.19), 'kartuya', 'aastuya'(p.29) and 'kartyati'(p.31), etc.

To highlight the subjugation of her brethren, Shantabai has employed very short sentences and simple vocabulary. Famous Marathi writer P.L. Deshpande while appreciating this autobiography remarks,

> One particular thing I felt specially. That is the language of this autobiography. Very short sentences of three – four words each. These too are devoid of ornamentation. There is no melodrama employed to create impact and yet due to the intense inherent agony of these incidences and experiences, the reader becomes restless. Such is the huge strength of this writing.[14]

A look at some sentences is enough to substantiate this comment. Describing her home, Shantabai says,

Majha jalmacha gaav Mahud Budruk
Gaav Karad Pandharpur rastyavar haay

Gaavcha aajubajula mala hayat
Kasal vada nadisarka haay (p. 11).

(My birth place is Mahud Budruk.The village is on Karad – Pandharpur Road

By the sides of the village are plantations. Kasal stream is like a river).

The use of words is bare minimum and simple yet captivating. Use of bombastic language is avoided. At another place she says,

Aamacha tanghar huta.
Chaar bhinti matichya bhendyachya hutya.
Ghar tansachya kadana shekarla huta.
Eka bajula daar. Darjaval ukaal.
Tyachya bajula jata. Jatajaval devacha devhara.
Devharyavar amachya aaja aajichya
Sonarachya rupyaachya kelelya murti hutya (p.11).

(Our house was of grass and sticks.
Four walls were made of mud and dried grass.
The house was made strong with dried stumps.
There was a door on one side. Near the door was an *'ukal'*.
By its side was a *'jata'*. Near it was the god's *'devhara'*.
On the *devhara* were the silver idols of our grandmother and grandfather made by the goldsmith.)

The picturesque style adds a touch of liveliness and raciness to the narrative. The use of words is culture specific. Addition of glossary of words such as '*Ukhal*', '*Jata*' and '*Devhara*' is also essential. Many such examples can be cited from the text. The description of how Shanta had to wear a dhotar to the school (p.17-18), that of Gangu's message to her mother (p.19), the school recess for urination (p.7), the delivery of Lalu Maharin and her starvation (p.37), the death of her mother (p.47), that of her marriage (p.70), etc. have been narrated employing the same technique. The economy of word usage is simply amazing. It is usually said that grief is verbose but Shantabai's self restrain and spontaneity of expression is heart touching. Her autobiography also acquaints the readers with the customs, traditions, rites and rituals, and culture of her community. There are umpteen number of references to 'Potraj' (p.33), 'Siddhanathachi Sasne' (p.116), 'Vasudeo' (p.24), 'Urus' and 'Piracha

Malida' (p.59), 'Devrushi' (p.47), ' Mariaai' (p.46), etc. In addition, it contains mention of 'sakharpuda' (p.68), 'haldicha Divas' (p.69), 'Mundaval' (p.71), 'mangalashtak' (p.72), 'Janvasa' (p.70), and 'karvalya' (p.37). The list is too exhaustive to be produced here. The names of eatables also hint at the culture of the community. For a middle class, urban, non-Dalit person (like me), these words pose a Herculean challenge. Some challenging names are 'gulvani' (p.71), 'kordyas' (p.75), 'telraand' (p.75), 'barbat' (p.40), 'gudsa' (p.05), and 'chanya' (p.06), etc. Dalit autobiographies have, in fact, contributed many new words to Marathi and these have enriched and enhanced Marathi vocabulary. Bhalchandra Phadke feels, "In reality Dalit autobiographies have enriched the vocabulary of Marathi language and it has also enhanced the grandeur of different colloquial languages."[15] Arjun Dangle has felt the need of a new dictionary of Dalit words.[16] Most of these words possess multidimensional religious and cultural connotations. Equivalence in English or mere translation of such terms into English by retaining the original word in Marathi fails to unfold the cultural ethnicity of the word. There are many such paragraphs in the self narrative. To give some examples, the description of Masadevi Yatra and Potraj (p. 34-35), the Sasans of Siddhanath (p.116), Yellama's Devi's Yatra and Keech (p.160), etc. can be cited.

Vijaya Joshi confesses that a middle class reader is in a fix due to this language. There are many incomprehensible words. She feels that a glossary of these words would have proved useful. She substantiates her point of view with words such as 'gudsa', 'kekati' and 'rakuli'. [17] Jadhav opines that white collared society is not able to understand this language due to differences of culture. He too concurs with Joshi in pointing out the utility of glossary.[18]

VI

The process of translation involves the transfer of meaning contained in one set of language signs into another set of language signs through competent use of the dictionary and grammar. The process involves a whole set of extra-linguistic criteria also. Edward Sapir claims that 'language is a guide to social reality' and human beings are at the mercy of the language that has become the medium of expression for their society. Experience, he asserts, is largely determined by the language habits of the community, and each separate structure represents a different reality: "No two languages are ever sufficiently similar to be considered as representing the same social reality. The worlds in which different societies live are distinct worlds, not merely the same world with different labels attached." [19] Soviet Semiotician Juri Lotman has echoed the same sentiments when he declares firmly that "No language can exist unless it is steeped in the context of culture; and no culture can exist which does not have at its center, the structure of natural language."[20] Language then, is the heart within the body of culture, and it is the interaction between the two that results in the continuation of life energy. It is this language that poses many challenges to the translator. Shantabai has incorporated many lexical items from the vernacular corroborating Prestan's view of "language shift to meet social demands."[21] *Mazhya Jalmachi* is steeped in Indian ethos and culture. All proper nouns, gods and goddesses, months of Hindu calendar, festivals, utensils, items of clothing, castes and sub-castes, appellations used, and places of pilgrimage signify this culture.

In his article 'On linguistic aspects of translation,' Roman Jacobson distinguishes three types of translation.[22] They are Intralingual translation, or rewording, Interlingual translation or translation proper and Intersemiotic translation or transmutation. Having established these three types, of which translation proper describes the process of transfer from SL to TL, Jacobson points out the central problem in all types: that while messages may serve as adequate interpretations of code units or messages, there is ordinarily no full equivalence through translation. Georges Mounin, the French theorist, perceives translation as a series of operations of which the starting point and the end product are significations and function within a given culture.[23] Dr. Leacock says, "As is the relation of hands to the body, or the leaf to the tree, so is the relation of man to society. He exists in it and it in him. As it is impossible to divorce an individual from society. ..." [24] Man is a social being. He lives in the society especially in the community, in his own caste people. Each writer has his own style and linguistic characteristics. These depend upon and are inherited from his family and social background (samskaras). These peculiar expressions reflect upon the personality of the writer. Naturally, there are many rural words used in this autobiography. They help in evoking rural atmosphere. Words in the colloquial language lend it a distinct flavor and impart a touch of reality to it. The few English words employed in the narrative occur with hackneyed pronunciation. In moments of provocation, annoyance and emotional turbulence, the use of rustic language and Dalit words is much more pronounced. The change in Shantabai, the refinement and development of her personality after joining service is well reflected in the Marathi text. P.L. Deshpande in his pertinent comment says,

> Shantabai has employed the prevalent rustic language, the language of the community in which Shantabai has spent her childhood, to narrate the initial part and used standard language after having begun her life in the profession of teaching. Thus the language of the narrative has also changed. The change in the language on the new turning of her life is so spontaneous that all incidents, environment and language in the newly begun life are blended harmoniously.[25]

VII

A deep study of the Marathi text reveals many additional features of the language. The nouns used in the autobiography are usually concrete and recognizable. The adjectives that are employed in the text are inexact and verbs too are stripped to a minimum. The simplicity of word choice is obvious and most of the sentences are short, simple sentences. Sometimes short sentences are joined with a conjunction. Subordinate clauses are rather infrequent. Thus, "this hard boiled narrative, mainly defined by its prose, involves a 'tough', 'no-nonsense' depiction of objects and people, eschewing complex verbs, excessive use of adjectives, subordinate clause and flowery effects (only one simile has been used in the text). Frequently, hard-boiled sentences which purport to be bold statements of fact can, through their juxtaposition, produce complex meanings."[26] 'Boli' language has been employed in this autobiography for the uneducated, illiterate, and rustic characters. The use of social deixis and honorifics is also noteworthy. The change in the language proficiency of the protagonist depending on her education, background, interaction with other people in villages and cities is noticed in the Marathi edition. Code mixing, code switching, and borrowing form an integral part of the narrative strategy of the writer.

All these features make the task of the translator a difficult one. Santosh Bhoomkar, translator of *The Outcaste* felt that *Akkarmashi* was a 'formidable text' and accepts having experienced a sense of inadequacy. Limbale helped him in the task and "provided me with meanings of words and phrases which were otherwise not available in any dictionary nor known to anybody around me, except him".[27] Sandhya Pandey, translator of Kale's *Against All Odds* has accepted the necessity of transcreation due to 'cultural inferences and presuppositions'. Dr. Narendra Jadhav too accepts the tediousness of the translator's task. In the English translations of other Marathi Dalit autobiographies, same titles have been retained. This holds true of *Upara (An Outsider)* and *Uchalya (The Branded)*. The English translation of these Marathi titles is also provided. The titles of *Kolhatyache Por (Against All Odds)*, *Akkarmashi (The Outcaste)*, *Amacha Baap Aan Amhi (Outcaste: A Memoir)*, and *Vasti (Growing up Untouchable in India)* have been changed. Their English equivalences fail to provide the exact nuances of meaning associated with titles in the source language. These translated titles have shifted the emphasis. Both *Vasti* and *Amacha Baap aan Amhi* symbolise togetherness, a sense of belonging, cohesion, unity as well as synergy. This aspect is completely missing in their English equivalences. The very titles *Vasti* and *Amacha Baap aan Amhi* indicate plurality - of personality and culture. *Against All Odds* has shifted the emphasis from an individual, a *Kolhatyache Por*, to his adverse, hostile circumstances and atmosphere. The word *Akkarmashi* does not possess any equivalence in English being metaphorical in nature. Its English title *The Outcaste* is applicable to all Dalit writers and Untouchables. A similar problem cropped up at the time of translation of the title of Shantabai's autobiography. It has been translated into English as *The Kaleidoscopic Story of My Life* by Sharmila Rege.[28] '*Chittarkatha*' means a picture story. 'Kaleidoscopic' hints at the range of pictures created by a child's toy. I have retained the source title and qualified it with a sub-title in English.

A Dalit autobiographer writes his text from an insider's point of view being an integral member of his community. He believes in the demand that "words and language should change their traditional roles", and in the "notion that words and language themselves are eager to cast themselves into new revolutionary roles..." [29] He knows the culture and dialect of his community along with its lexicon very well. When an outsider translates such autobiographies (but for Narendra Jadhav), he/she approaches this work of art from outside, being unacquainted with that community's culture, ethos, and lexicon. Jadhav has himself translated his text into English and a marked difference sets it apart from other Dalit autobiographies. The problems that Narendra Jadhav faced when he handed over the translation of his *Aamacha Baap* to an outsider are/ were the problems faced by others, including myself. Mere proficiency in Marathi and English and possessing social awareness does not help. The main problem crops up with the 'boli bhasha' and if it is lost, the soul of the document is lost. To Marathi readers and to a certain extent to non-Marathi Indian readers, Dalit movement, Dr. Ambedkar and his life mission are known. But for non-Indian readers, all social references, including caste system in India, its hierarchy and social relationships need much explanation and elaboration.

Marathi and its dialects follow a unique construction pattern and word order. In one language itself, many times, it is difficult to come across two complete synonyms. Naturally in another language such synonymy is difficult to obtain. The real task of the translator and his choices begin from here. In a particular language, words and groups of words possess broader and deeper meaning than their ordinary usage. This deeper meaning is imparted due to emotional, representative, symbolic, social, cultural, and aesthetic connotations. Words also acquire a different meaning due to rhythm, alliteration, etc. Then the meaning of the words is context relevant. All these complexities lead to the basic surmise that no translation can ever be perfect. The reader of a translation with an ability to read the original should not expect to be wholly satisfied with it. Sometimes a photograph appears more beautiful than the real and hence, translations need not always be of inferior quality. Sujit Mukherjee has pointed out,

> The translator is tested twice over. First he is tested in terms of reception — What he makes of the original text ... The second testing is of the

translator's command of the two languages involved – that of the original and that of the translation ... 30

The translator has made available a text for the reader which he otherwise, would not have been able to know about and read. That is why, L.W. Tancock is in accord with Sujit Mukherjee when he says, "The aim of any translator is to communicate a work of literature intact to a reader of a different language. The ideal translation, like the ideal stage play should have the power to suspend the reader's disbelief, to make him think he is reading an original piece of work written in his own tongue." [31]

English language is alien to Indian culture and ethos and hence fails to provide exact equivalents for vernacular and idioms. To capture any culture in its true essence, target language, if a foreign language, falls insufficient and inadequate. The disrespectful and informal addresses in Marathi can not be conveyed in English. The use of English words in conversation, their hackneyed pronunciation, its effect on the listener, etc. can not be translated into English. Code mixing or borrowing from other languages into Marathi is very difficult to depict in English equivalence. Mahesh Elkunchwar is of the opinion that 'while translating a work from one Indian regional language to another, alternate, equivalent words are found as the regional languages and culture possess many similarities in India'.[32] He further opined that the difficulties faced in English translations are not faced while translating into regional languages. In another interview, Mahesh Elkunchwar says, "References and allusions ingrained in the Indian psyche cannot be brought out via a foreign language".[33]

Different dialects of Marathi are very difficult to be captured in English. In almost all Marathi Dalit autobiographies, dialectical peculiarity plays a significant role. In this autobiography, language acts as an index of the narrator's development. Standard Marathi and dialects of Marathi are used effectively to shed light on such development. Such a development of character reflected through the medium of a language can not be shown into English. *Mazhya Jalmachi* does not possess long drawn symbols and images, and figurative and idiomatic language. Conflict whether psychological or social or political is also very difficult to translate as its true spirit could prove to be too elusive to capture. Each language has got its own grammar – word order, rules of gender and number. This makes the task of the translator more tedious. Some observations can be made about the difficulties faced in the translation of this Marathi Dalit autobiography into English:

1. Standard English has been used in the translation.
2. The dialect of the source language, code mixing and switching, borrowing, etc. had to be ignored in the translation to a certain extent.
3. The equivalence provided for words in the source language does not cover its features in the target language in a comprehensive manner.
4. The distinctions- both overt and covert too, subtle in dimensions of time and space have been retained so as to evoke same emotions and tensions.
5. No changes have been made in chapter-scheme, divisions and order of paragraphs. Chapter division has been indicated in a manner similar to the source text.
6. Some times transliteration and calque (literal translation) is used. It is used for expressions such as 'tya bai ekapat rahat asatil tar mee choupat rahin' (p.104), 'yacha gaavachya bori ani yacha gaavachya babhali'(p.135), 'Mahar mangana khata yeina ani kutryala paani pita yeina' (p.135), etc.
7. Some additions (very rare), omissions and emendations have been made in the translated text. Only some phrases, occasionally words and very rarely sentences have been omitted.
8. The level of vocabulary in the source language and the target language is not same in terms of grammatical features.
9. The borrowed vocabulary in the source language is, wherever possible, retained (for example words like 'ghodi'(p.17), 'dhotar'(p.18), 'lugada'(p.27), 'pairani'(p.54),) but most of the times translated into English.
10. The spelling of the borrowed vocabulary is given in the target language.

11. The vocabulary items expressed in cultural values such as eatables, etc. are retained (for example:'bhakari'(p.19),'uradi' (p34.), 'aamati', 'gulvani' (p.71), and 'puranpoli'(p.71),) as they are in the source language but sometimes they are translated into English.
12. The women characters in this Marathi Dalit autobiography use verbs in the male gender to describe their actions. This change in the gender of the speaker of the vocabulary is not noticed in the translation.
13. The spelling of the distorted pronunciation in English in the source text is given as standard spel'ing in the target language.
14. There is, most of the times, no indication as to whether the term translated into English is currently in actual use. Words such as 'kos'(p.21),and 'sher' (p.96) ha e been retained.
15. Homophonous words and puns are usually treated in a manner that is used for all other words in the translation. No special treatment has been provided.
16. The translation of pronouns from Marathi into English is very difficult. Marathi 'mee',and ' mya' is translated as 'I' and 'You' is used for 'tu', and 'tumhi'. 'Amhi' could be 'I' or 'we' depending on the context.
17. Proper nouns usually are retained as they are in the original text. Clipped proper nouns are also retained but subtle differences could not be brought to the fore. The informal ways of addressing a person such as 'Eh'(p.7), Aar'(p.12), 'Aaga'(p.6), usually attached with proper nouns,have been retained. The subtle differences in pronunciation such as 'Pandarpur' and 'Pandharpur' have been depicted and an English reader, unacquainted with the pure Marathi pronunciation, will not perhaps understand it.
18. Distorted or impure pronunciations of some Marathi words such as 'hutee' (p.3), 'huta'(p.3), 'whay'(p.4), 'haay' (p.4), 'hutu' (p.5), 'hayeet'(p.5), and 'zopalu' (p.12), 'maraliya' (p.13), 'martuya' (p.17), 'kartati' (p.31), etc. reflect upon the up

bringing, caste, class, culture and level of education of a character. Such nuances are not at all represented in the target language.

19. Sometimes, the slang words are literally translated and at other places, English substitutes are provided. Interjection and interrogations are most of the times literally translated. Idiomatic phrases are also literally translated.

20. The translator found it difficult to look into the phonology, ease of pronunciation of the word and familiarity of the form of the word, frequency of the word, familiarity of the content of the word, social prestige of that word, less number of syllables of the word for the onomatopoeic conditions, the role played by the chosen word in distinguishing the style of the author, the register of the text, etc.

21. The word order of the source language and that of the text in the target language is different.

22. Correspondence between sentence patterns and styles in the source text and target text has been retained. Usually sentences in the source language are not clubbed or split in the target language.

23. The punctuation marks used in the source text are retained most of the times in the translated version.

24. Exhaustive glossary has been provided with additional notes for non-Indian readers. Such additional notes might help in explaining the content of the autobiography and at least, acquaint the reader with the culture of the community to a certain extent.

25. Colloquial language has been used to translate conversational passages. The translation conveys the cultural situation to a certain extent. In the English translation, the words indicative of relationships such as 'Aay' or 'Ba'have been used. In the same, in descriptive paragraphs, many other Marathi words are used. These Marathi words possess cultural inferences and have been explained. Yet this kind of an attempt has resulted, sometimes, in infelicity of expression.

26. The Dalit autobiographer, in order to capture the culture, imparts a local colour and a regional flavour to the language. This was very difficult to convey in the target language for the translator. This Dalit autobiography has rustic setting and describes socio-cultural practices which are alien to many European cultures.
27. Scenes of humour (for example: one on page no.123) were perhaps most difficult to transfer or render into English. This is due to the density of cultural elements and the linguistic specificity of humour.
28. Dalit autobiographies have introduced many new words in Marathi language and have enriched it thus in the process. Some of these newly introduced words are beyond the comprehension of many Marathi readers and need an explanation. In English translation of this Marathi Dalit autobiography, these words posed a major difficulty. Such words were translated into English after a discussion with Dalit writers and scholars.
29. In the Indian social hierarchy, people belonging to different classes converse in different dialects or kinds of language. An attempt to reflect the same has been made in *Mazya Jalmachi* in English. Yet a major part of this aspect of different language usage is lost in English translations as everything has to be narrated in plain, simple English. The variety of dialects and styles used in Marathi can not be shown and translated or transliterated into English. The source document is 'polyphonic.

VIII

In any translation, grammar and lexis play an important role. Out of these two, it is the lexis or lexicon or the "words" are more important as they are the carriers of designative or referential and connotational meaning. Then the anismorphism between Marathi and English contributes to the difficulty of finding equivalence in the target language. Anismorphism is the difference between the languages, especially in lexical meaning. These include differences in the organisation of designata, absence of denotata, and difference in culture, etc. Plant, animal, and bird names in Marathi, cultural names like *mangalsutra* and *haldi- kumkum* used by a woman as a symbol of marriage, names of Gods and Goddesses specific to the culture of the community like *Mariaai*, and *Khanduba*, etc. do not have equivalence in English. Culture bound words are found in designata too inspite of the presence of denotata. Kindred relationship terms in Marathi like *anna*, *dada*, *bhau*, *mama* and *mami*, *Atya* and *mavashi*, etc. are cases of culture - bound words. The translation of any socio-cultural document is a 'Gestalt', a multi - dimensional structure consisting of more than the sum of its parts. It has to trace complex relationships and the importance of individual items has to be decided by their function in the text. The text has to be studied not in isolation but against 'a particular sociocultural background' and as a part of the given situation. The language of Dalit autobiography is an integral part of Dalit life and culture. To convey its essence, the translator of this Dalit autobiography has resorted to borrowing, literal translation and definition, substitution, omissions, and additions. Yet some 'lacunae', 'blank spaces', 'gaps', or 'voids' are noticed.

The translator (I) of this Marathi Dalit autobiography knows the source language (Marathi) and the target/receptor language (English) well. I am also familiar and acquainted with the two cultures and have interacted with Dalit writers. These Dalit autobiographies form the mainstay of that literature which has been isolated from the mainstream Marathi and world literature. The success of the translated text will have to be tested on the touchstone of the 'readability criterion' and 'the acceptability criterion'. In spite of problems of equivalences in lexicon and culture, this translated text has preserved to a certain extent the essentialities of the source text both in matter and manner. The professed aim of all Dalit litterateurs to create awareness about their plight among the local and global readers and especially among humanists and human rights activists will be accomplished undoubtedly through this translation.

WORKS CITED

1. Jain, Nirmala, "Lekhan' Kisi Ki Bapauti Nahi Hai", Hans, August, 2004, p. 213.

2. Phadke, Bhalchandra, Dalit Sahitya : Vedana ani Vidroha, (Pune: Shreevidya Prakashan, 1977), p.27.

3. Pantavane, Gangadhar, Dalit-Sahitya Charcha Va Chintan, (Aurangabad: Saket Prakashan, 1993), p.186.
4. Kamble, Shantabai. *Mazya Jalmachi Chittarkatha,* (Pune: Sugawa Prakashan, 1990), Arun Kamble's Foreword, p. n. not given. All subsequent references in the parentheses are taken from this edition of the book.
5. Kamble, Shantabai. *Sahityasuchi,* Diwali issue, 1987, p. 68-69.
6. Kamble, Shantabai. *Mazya Jalmachi Chittarkatha,* Arun Kamble's Foreword,
7. Jadhav, Manohar. Dalit Striyanchi Atmakathane: Swaroop ani Chikitsa, (Pune: Shreevidya Prakashan, 2001), p.264.
8. Pavde Kumud as quoted from Bhagwandas , ed., Dalit Solidarity, Times Messey, ISPCK, Delhi, p.151.
9. Gaikwad, Sampat, "Dalit Atmakathane : .....," Dalit Sahitya, Lekhajokha, ed. Mahendra Gaikwad, (Nagpur: Sangharsha Prakashan, 2004), p. 99-100.
10. Kotapalle, Nagnath, Gramin Sahitya : Swarup ani Shodh, (Pune: Mehta Publishing House, 1985), p.59.
11. Lanjewar, Jyoti, Samkalin Sahitya : Pravrutti ani Pravah, (Nagpur: Vijay Prakashan, 1985), p. 287.
12. Jadhav, Manohar, Annexure 2, p.265.
13. Bama, "Dalit Literature", Indian Literature, Sahitya Akademy's Bimonthly Journal, 193, Sept-Oct-99, p.98.
14. Kamble, Shantabai. P.L. Deshpande's letter to Dr. Arun Kamble,
15. Phadke, Bhalchandra, Asmitadarsh, Diwali, 1983, p.89.
16. Dangle, Arjun, Dalit Sahitya : Ek Abhyas, (Mumbai: Maharashtra Rajya Sahitya-Sanskriti Mandal, 1978), p.21.
17. As quoted in Jadhav, Manohar, p.137.
18, Ibid
19. Sapir, Edward, as quoted by Susan Bassnett, Translation Studies, (Routledge, 2003), Page 21.
20. Ibid, P.22.

21. Preston, D.R., Sociolinguistics and Social Language Acquisition, (Oxford House Publishers Inc.1989).
22. as quoted by Susan Bassnett, Translation Studies, Page 22.
23. Ibid, P. 23.
24. Manohar, Yashwant, Nave Sahitya Shastra, (Nagpur: Vijaya Prakashan, 2001), Page 182-183.
25. Kamble, Shantabai. Mazya Jalmachi—, p. no. not given.
26. Cobley, Paul, Narrative, (London: Routledge, 2001), p.232.
27. Limbale, Sharankumar. The Outcaste. (Oxford University Press, 2003). p.xi.
28. Rege. Sharmila. Writing Caste/ Writing Gender....(New Delhi: Zubaan, 2006), p.156.
29. Bhongle, Rangrao, p.172.
30. Mukherjee,Sujit, Translations as Discovery and Other Essays on Indian Literature in English Translations, (New Delhi: Allied Publishers Pvt. Ltd.), p.141.
31. Tancock, L.W., "Some Problems in Style from Translations in French", Aspects of Translations, (London: Secker and Warburg Ltd; 1958), p.45.
32. Elkunchwar, Mahesh, "... Tar Marathichya Bhavitavyala Dhoka", Tarun Bharat, Nagpur, p.9, Sunday 14 May 2006.
33. Bhattacharya, Supantha, "The English Translations of Elkunchwar's Plays: A Study in Errors", New Horizons, Vol.I, No. 11, August 1991, p.37.

15

The Vision of Darkness in *Andha Yug*

Basavaraj Naikar

Dharmavir Bharati (1926-97), the Hindi author was born in Allahabad, Uttar Pradesh. He studied there and participated in the anti-British Quit India movement. He earned a doctorate in Siddha saint literature in 1947, and then became a full-time journalist, editing the weekly *DharmaYug* from 1960 to 1989. He was a war correspondent in Bangladesh in 1971, and made a tremendous impact. He was also a poet, novelist and essayist. His two novels, *Gunahonka Devata* (*The God of Sins*) and *Suraj Ka Satvan Ghoda* (*The Seventh Horse of the Sun*) are classics of Hindi literature. He has published five one-act plays under the title *Nadi Pyasi Thi* (*The River was Thirsty*, 1954), often produced by schools, colleges and amateur groups.

He wrote only one full-length play *Andha Yug* (*Blind Age*, 1954), originally as radio drama, now recognized as a classic of modern Hindi theatre. "Set late in the *Mahabharata*, it concerns the eternal values of life that are damaged or broken and re-established again and again. Bharati was deeply perturbed about the perpetual problem of war becoming global and destroying humanity. Obviously reflecting nuclear conflict, his play also interrogated the received wisdom of Krishna's assurances. An epic drama in blank verse, it applied various forms such as folk theatre, Parsi theatre, *Katha-gayan* (singing of tales), and Western tragedy as required. The use of symbols and imagery provided a new dimension to the theme. It was a challenge to directors because the text's poetry and dramatic beauty is not easy to convey. Thus the premiere had to wait till 1962, produced by Satyadev Dubey on Theatre Unit's rooftop stage in Bombay. Subsequently the National School of Drama performed it in

1963, directed by Alkazi, and revived it several times. Many directors in other languages, like Ajitesh Bandyopadhyay (Bengali, 1970) and Ratan Thiyam (Manipuri, 1993), also staged important versions."[1]

His play, *Andha Yug*, translated into English by Alok Bhalla, deals with the epical theme of the conflict between the Kauravas and the Pandavas culminating into climax on the eighteenth day of Kurukshetra war. Although the theme is borrowed from the last part of Vyasa's *Mahabharata*, Dharmavir Bharati has accentuated it in such a way that it remains relevant even today. It was written immediately after the Partition of India, but it appeals to the reader even in the twenty-first century, which is vitiated by international terrorism and fundamentalism. Though the story of Kauravas and Pandavas is incidental to it, it achieves the universality of appeal by highlighting the metaphysical conflict between Good and Evil. It is on account of its universality that it becomes relevant in every age and nation.

The play begins with a prologue, which foreshadows the theme in advance. It says that the play is concerned with the age of darkness as described in *Vishnu Purana* in which there would be a decline in prosperity and dharma and the whole earth would slowly perish; the one, who has wealth, would rule; the one, who wears a false mask, would be honoured; the one, who is greedy, would be a king; the people, weary of misrule, would hide in dark caves and wait for their days of misery to end. It says further that it was only Lord Krishna, who was dispassionate and detached, whereas all the others were blind and self-absorbed and that the play is the story of enlightenment through the life of the benighted and the blind.

The first act begins with the narrator commenting on the central event and its negative nature, "Both sides in the war/ violated/ the code of honour/ smashed it/ ripped it into shreds/and scattered it - / the Kauravas perhaps more than the Pandavas" (P.27). [2] He comments further that it is a strange war in which both sides are doomed to fail; that blindness rules this age and not reason and that blind fear, blind love, blind power and blind justice shall prevail in the end. The Kurukshetra war is obviously an archetypal one as it suggests the metaphysical war between Good and Evil. Whereas the Kauravas represent Evil, the Pandavas represent Good. The war is necessitated by the blindness of the Kauravas and consequently the Pandavas have suffered countless sorrows. But in the war there has been a reversal of situation. So far Good was helpless against the force of Evil. But Good is slowly gaining victory over Evil. As a consequence of this unwanted war the common people feel that their whole life has become meaningless. For example, the two guards express their opinion, which voices that of the common people. They say that they are very tired but yet they have to march up and down guarding these desolate corridors. They are unhappy to learn that the Kaurava queens, who once wandered gracefully like the fragrant breeze, have become widows now. They are sad to notice that the Kaurava Kingdom is ruled by an old and blind ruler and therefore all their actions are meaningless. Now the guards are surprised to see the Kaurava Kingdom, is overcast with thousands and thousands of ravenous vultures, which are eager to feed on the dead. The guards consider them as a bad and dreadful omen. The shadow of the vultures indicates physical darkness symbolizing other kinds of darkness like ocular, psychological and one moral ones. King Dhritarashtra's blindness is indicative of ocular darkness. Queen Gandhari's voluntary blindfolding of her eyes shows her extraordinary loyalty to her husband. But both of them, in addition to being physically blind (or blindfolded) are morally blind also because of their blind affection for and attachment to their children i.e. Kauravas. The different kinds of blindness unfold themselves as the play proceeds forward.

When Vidura comes to see King Dhritarashtra, the guard tells him that the king could not see the terrifying scene of war, as he is physically blind. He is waiting for the latest news bulletin to be brought by Sanjaya. But when Vidura meets the king, the latter confesses that he is afraid for the first time in his life. Vidura tells him,

> Afraid?
> The fear you experience today
> Had gripped others years ago. (P.33)

Vidura reminds the king that the latter had been warned by Bhishma and Dronacharya and that Krishna had also advised him,

> Do not violate the code of honour.
> If you violate the code of honour
> It will coil around the Kaurava clan

Like a wounded python
And crush it like a dry twig. (P.33)

But King Dhritarashtra had not bothered to listen to this advice. On the contrary his physical blindness was accentuated by the moral blindness caused by his filial attachment to his sons,

My sons were the flesh of my flesh
They were the final arbiters of truth for me.
My love for them was my law
My code of honour. (P.34).

In other words, his attachment to his sons is an extension of his selfishness, which prevents him from understanding the world from a wider perspective. He has realized his mistake rather belatedly,

Today
I realized
That there is a truth
That lies beyond the boundaries
Of my selfhood.
I realized that only today. (P.35)

He feels terrified by what he has learnt today. Queen Gandhari also feels that the ideals like *dharma*, duty and honour are mere illusions; that there is a ferocious beast in each man; that everyone is hypocritical and self-interested. She does not have any faith in Krishna. That is why she has blindfolded herself. In the seventeen days of war, all her sons except Duryodhana have been killed one by one. Now she desperately hopes that Duryodhana will be victorious in the war. Thus when both King Dhritarashtra and Queen Gandhari are waiting for the latest news from Sanjaya, there comes a mendicant, who confesses that his prediction (that the Kauravas shall be victorious) has proved to be false due to the intervention of a stranger man like Krishna. The same view is corroborated by the Guard 2, who says, "And the one they worship as their Lord takes the responsibility for all of them!" (P.43) But those, who have no faith in the moral order symbolized by Krishna, happen to be the blind King Dhritarashtra and his blindfolded Queen Gandhaari.

The second act begins with the chorus, which describes Sanjaya, the rational sculptor of words and his bewilderment in the forest of doubt and confusion. Then Sanjaya himself comes on the stage and expresses his sense of confusion, "I have lost my way on this path of thorns and stones" (P.47). Although several soldiers have died, Sanjaya has not died. He is very sad to be alive and witness the defeat of the Kauravas by the Pandavas,

> Yes, I am still alive.
> The earth for miles around is strewn
> With the corpses of Kaurava soldiers
> Slaughtered by Arjuna.
> The Kaurava army is scattered;
> All its heroes are dead. (P.48)

Sanjaya was about to be killed by Satyaki, but Vyasa had told the latter, "Sanjaya cannot die. He is immortal" (P.49). Sanjaya was cursed by Vyasa, "You will survive disasters, floods,revolutions, and wars of annihilation so that you can tell the truth" (P.49). Sanjaya is thus destined to tell or report the whole truth of the events like the modern news reporters of the various media. Speaking the bitter truth is indeed a very unpleasant job. He finds it humiliating to tell the whole truth about Duryodhana's death to King Dhritarshtra and his Queen. But Kritavarma exhorts him to be brave enough to tell the truth.

Kritavarma is sad to learn that Duryodhana is defeated by the Pandavas and that only three of them are alive (i.e. Kritavarma, Kripacharya and Ahvatthama). Now the scene focuses on Asvatthama and his psychology of revenge. He thinks that his father Dronacharya was cut to pieces by Dhristadyumna when Dronacharya threw down his weapons on the battlefield on hearing Yudhisthira announcing triumphantly the death of Asvatthama, the elephant but giving an impression of the death of Asvatthama, the man (and son of Dronacharya). Thus according to Asvatthama, his father was killed by the Pandavas immorally and unjustly. Hence he decides to avenge the death of his father by becoming a metaphorical beast, "I decided to turn myself into a blind, ruthless beast" (P.52). He wants to be blind and ruthless like a beast and turn his hands into claws, and strangle Yudhisthira for lying and for being responsible for his father's death. In his frenzy he mistakes Sanjaya for a Pandava and wishes to kill him, but Kripacharya prevents him from doing so by clarifying to him, "Sanjaya cannot be killed as he was neutral and took no sides in the war" (P.55).

Kritavarma says that Duryodhana is still alive and intends to look for him. Sanjaya tells them about the whereabouts of Duryodhana, "With his extraordinary powers he has stilled the waters of a lake. And there unknown to the Pandavas, he sits strangely still in the floor of the enchanted lake" (P.57).

Meanwhile the Mendicant is rather unhappy to learn that his prediction about the victory of Kauravas over the Pandavas has proved wrong. Asvatthama is also terribly angry with him and finally kills him blindly and indiscriminately. Kripacharya tries to pacify him. Asvatthama confesses how he became a blind medium of revenge and does not know how he killed the Mendicant, "I did not kill him! I was blind with rage. I wanted to annihilate the future, which has been prophesied. Believe me I do not know the old man was killed" (P.63). Kripacharya suggests to them to sleep and rest for the night.

In the third act, the narrator says that King Dhritarashtra and Queen Gandhari listen to the story of the defeat of Kauravas by the Pandavas narrated by Sanjaya. "His painful story turned Gandhari into stone. Her face pale with sorrow seemed lifeless" (P.65). The Kaurava soldiers have been limping back to the city in defeat and disgrace. King Dhritarashtra is waiting to hear the news of the last battle between Bhima and Duryodhana. Meanwhile the Guard 1 tells Vidura that an enemy soldier has entered the city with their defeated army and that he is a sorcerer, a shape-changer, who can take any form at will" (P.69). That soldier is none other than Yuyutsu, the son of Dhritarashtra, who has fought on the side of truth and not on the side of Kauravas, though he belongs to their party. He expresses his views as follows:

> What is my crime?
> That I was on the side of truth?
> No other warrior—
> Neither Drona nor Bhishma—
> dared to oppose Duryodhana.
> Only I had the courage
> To declare:
>
> > I will not fight
> > On the side of untruth.
> > I may be a Kaurava

But truth is higher
Than my clan! (P.71)

Obviously, Yuyutsu is one of the Kauravas, who retains his moral integrity, loyalty to truth and rational approach to life. He has transcended the selfishness, greed and vengeance indulged in by the Kauravas. He knows that even his mother Gandhari may not like to see him. But Vidura appreciates his position and moral approach to life, "Do not say that. In this evil episode you are the only one of the Kaurava clan, who has held his head high with pride" (P.72). He asks Yuyutsu further not to bother about the people of the city, who look at him with contempt. When Yuyutsu meets his mother and bows down to her feet, she taunts him about his siding with the enemies and refuses to bless him. Yuyutsu is rather sad about his mother's undignified behaviour. He feels that "It would have been better if I had accepted the untruth" (P.75). He is so desperate that he thinks his siding with truth has earned his mother's curse and the people's hate and turned out to be a futile act in the final analysis. But Vidura consoles him by advising him, "Great suffering must be endured with grace" (P.75). Yuyutsu is sad to know that everybody hates him now. He thinks that he is damned but Krishna is victorious wherever he is.

Meanwhile the Guard 1 reports that Sanjaya has brought the news that Duryodhana has been defeated by Bhima in the final battle. The Pandavas are blowing the conch-shells and declaring their victory. But Balarama is enraged with the Pandavas because he thinks that Bhima violated dharma in defeating Duryodhana and Bhima's immoral action was abetted by the 'unprincipled rogue' Krishna known for his holiness and cunning.

Kripacharya and Kritavarma also want to take revenge upon the Pandavas, but not through treachery. But Asvatthama is terribly vindictive and wants to be declared as the Commander of the army in Duryodhana's presence. Accordingly Kripacharya is directed by Duryodhana to anoint Asvatthama as the Senapati of the army. Now Asvatthama decides to wreak vengeance the next morning and orders his soldiers to sleep that night. But he keeps watch by pacing up and down. It is at this time that he happens to see a dance of war between a crow and owl. Then the crow sleeps and the owl watches it nervously. The owl prods him to make sure that he is really asleep and then attacks him. After a ferocious fight between them, the owl kills the crow finally. Asvatthama, who is watching the scene, breaks out of his trance, laughs confidently for having found the truth. He wants to rush to the Pandava camp, where the victorious Pandavas must be unarmed and sleeping and slaughter them mercilessly in the manner in which the owl has killed the crow. He fastens his cummerbund and wants to attack the Pandavas especially when Krishna has gone to Hastinapur to console Gandhari. He says, "Like a beast I will crush Dhristadyumna with my feet – like a mad beast trampling on a lotus-flower. I will not even spare Uttara, who is carrying Abhimanyu's son and the future of the entire Pandava clan in her womb! (P.88) Kritavarma and Kripacharya try their best to dissuade him from the immoral and treacherous vengeance, but Asvatthama turns a deaf ear to them.

Meanwhile the Mendicant's ghost appears on the stage and deplores the blindness of the people and their inner contradictions. Yuyutsu's spectre deplores his stagnant life symbolized by a firm wheel fixed to a chariot. Sanjaya's spectre laments his uselessness as a decorative wheel. Vidura's spectre laments his faith in the Lord, who is like a useless axle, which has lost its wheels and cannot turn by itself. The spectral vision acts as a commentary on the overall blindness, darkness and meaninglessness of life. The Mendicant's ghost now happens to descry a peacock feather wafting in the air and understands that Lord Krishna is returning from Hastinapur after trying to console Gandhari.

In the fourth act, Asvatthama rushes to the Pandava camp to slaughter them vindictively and mercilessly, but happens to see Lord Shankara, the god of annihilation, standing guard at the gate and challenging him, "Defeat me before you enter" (P. 95). Asvatthama attacks him vehemently but ultimately accepts his defeat and begs the Lord for mercy. Then Lord Shiva blesses him, "Asvatthama, you will be victorious. The Pandavas have lost their sense of righteousness. Because I loved Krishna, I protected them, gave them victory, renewed their confidence. But they have violated the dharma of war and opened the doors for their destruction" (P.97). Thus blessed by Lord Shiva Asvatthama reaches Dhristadyumna's tent with the speed of lightning and wrings his neck mercilessly. Then he proceeds to kill the Pandava soldiers and Shikhandi also. Likewise Kritavarma and Kripacharya also slaughter the children, old men and servants heartlessly. Queen

Gandhari feels happy to learn about Asvatthama's heroic feat. Duryodhana is still alive and wants to tell something to his party men, but cannot. Kripacharya narrates to Duryodhana how Asvatthama has slaughtered the important leaders of Pandava camp. Duryodhana dies after listening to it. Queen Gandhari is so happy about Asvatthama's vindictive heroism that she wants to remove her blindfold, gaze upon Asvatthama and transform his body into a bright diamond. But ironically Sanjaya has lost his vision and therefore cannot show Asvatthama to the Queen. That is because Vyasa has granted him vision only for a limited time of eighteen days.

Now the Kaurava city is desolate and the diamond throne is empty and the people have left to perform the last rites for Gandhari's dead sons. When Yuyutsu meets his father Dhritarashtra, the latter cautions him against Asvatthama's rage and advises him to hide somewhere. But by that time Sanjaya brings the news of the unexpected transformation of Asvatthama from a hero into a fearful coward. He is hit by Arjuna's arrows. Because of his helplessness, Asvatthama releases his Brahmastra at Arjuna, not knowing the dire consequences of it for the earth and mankind. Vyasa explains sadly, "For centuries to come nothing will grow on earth. Newborn children shall be deformed. Men shall become grotesque. All the wisdom men gathered in the *satya*, *treta* and *dwapara Yugs* shall be lost forever. Serpents shall hiss from every ear of corn and rivers shall flow with molten fire" (P.114). Then Vyasa requests Asvatthama to recall his Brahmastra. But Asvatthama pleads his inability and helplessness, "Vyasa, I am powerless! I only knew how to release the Brahmastra. My father did not teach me how to recall it" (P.115). Consequently Asvatthama's Brahmastra is about to destroy the child in Uttara's womb. But again a miracle happens. Krishna saves the child in Uttara's womb by exchanging his life for Uttara's stillborn child. Then Krishna forces Asvatthama to surrender his talismanic gem in exchange for his life, under the shadow of a curse forever. Now Asvatthama bows his head in defeat and leaves the place.

Queen Gandhari removes her blindfold and wants to see Asvatthama, but the latter goes away from there. As his body is covered with boils and open sores, he smells worse than a diseased dog! Vidura tells Gandhari that Krishna has cursed Asvatthama for the sin of infanticide, with immortality and condemned him to live forever and ever. Gandhari mourns the death of her son, Duryodhana and is enraged with Krishna for his incitement of Bhima's *adharma* and his vile curse on Asvatthama. She, therefore, curses him,

You may be a god
You may be omnipotent
Whatever you are
Whoever you are
I curse you
And I curse
All your friends and kinsmen.
They shall attack and kill each other.
They shall eat each other
Like rabid dogs.

And many years later
After you have witnessed
Their destruction
You will return to this forest
Only to be killed
Like a wild animal
By an ordinary hunter! (P.122)

Krishna accepts Gandhari's curse without any grudge and even explains his divine as well as human aspects,

I may be a god.
I may be omnipotent.
But I am also your son
And you are my mother.
...
If I am life
Then, Mother
I am also death.
I accept your curse, Mother! (P.123)

The fifth act shows the victory of Pandavas and a series of suicides. Though Yudhisthira has won his throne and his kingdom, he is not really happy. He feels lonely and dejected. He is sad to know that his brothers are either ignorant or foolish; either insolent or weary. He trembles to watch the encroaching darkness and hears the sinister steps of the coming age. Yuyutsu, who upheld dharma, is taunted by Bhima and ill-treated by the beggars. He, therefore, commits suicide by plunging a spear into his own heart. Now Yudhisthira's kingdom has grown decadent.

On the contrary, the forest catches fire. Both Gandhari and Dhritarashtra are consumed by the fire. Whereas the Kaurava dynasty is destroyed completely, the Pandava kingdom also comes to an end. Yudhisthira grows increasingly dejected day by day. Slowly he loses his faith in everything and realizes the hollowness of his victory in the war. He understands that his victory is also a long and slow act of suicide.

The chorus in The Epilogue describes Krishna's death.

He leaned against the tree
Placed his left foot
Shaped like a deer's face
On his right thigh
And with a sigh whispered:
'A strange age has passed' (P.148).
...
Mistaking
Krishna's foot for a deer
He draws his bowstring
And takes aim (P.150).
...
The stars went out
Darkness covered the earth
And that forest of fear
Became even more terrifying.

The moment Krishna was killed
Dvapara Yug came to an end
And on this god-forsaken earth
Kali Yug took its first step

And that forest of fear
Became even more terrifying (P.151).

The death of Krishna represents the beginning of the age of darkness. The chorus strikes an affirmative note that in spite of the overwhelming darkness of Kali Yug, there is a seed of light buried in the human mind and might grow into a big tree of high moral ideals,

> And yet it is also true
> That like a small seed
> Buried somewhere
> In the mind of man
> There is courage
> And longing for freedom
> And the imagination to create something new (P.161).

The chorus iterates further that the seed, which is buried without exception in each one of us, will grow from day to day in our lives as duty, honour, freedom and virtuous conduct; makes us fear half-truths and great wars and always saves the future of mankind from blind doubt, slavery and defeat.

Presenting even a small chunk of the great epic, the *Mahabharata* in the form of a play is not a joke. It requires a lot of intelligence on the part of the dramatist. He has to present his vision of life through the dramatic medium by showing a few bits of action on the stage, by highlighting the moral ideas through verse, by linking the events on the stage with the off-stage one through choric narration and comments. Thus the direct (on-stage) and indirect (off-stage) action is linked intelligently and the authorial comment and interpretation is articulated through the chorus. In his note to the directors, Dharmavir Bharati confesses, "The choric songs are arranged between the acts in a style borrowed from the traditions of Indian folk theatre. The chorus is either used to give information about events, which are not shown on stage or to underline the poignancy of the action. Sometimes, it also clarifies the symbolic importance of the events" (P.19). Although the chorus is borrowed from the Indian folk theatre, it easily resembles the chorus of Greek plays and captures the attention of the spectators.

Dharmavir Bharati has shown his dramatic talent in distributing the theme conveniently into on-stage and off-stage action. For example, Duryodhana and his battle with Bhima or the murder of the Old Mendicant by Asvatthama, or the release of the Brahmastra by Asvatthama, the killing of Krishna by the hunter and such other terrible events are not shown on the stage (or in the form of direct action), but are narrated as happening off-stage (in the form of indirect action). Similarly the eagle killing the crow and the cloud-like gathering of eagles waiting to devour the dead bodies of Kauravas are shown symbolically on the stage, which holds mirror to Dharmavir Bharati's experimentation with the dramatic technique. *Andha Yug* easily attains the grandeur of a Greek tragedy and succeeds in conveying its universal message. It teaches modern man the futility of indulging in selfishness, terrorism, fundamentalism and such other evils and suggests an affirmative philosophy of life to be followed for the attainment of true happiness. It offers the moral lesson that Truth will be ultimately victorious, although un-Truth may enjoy some power temporarily. In other words the play is a dramatization of the formula, *satyameva jayate*.

WORKS CITED

1. Lal, Anand, *The Oxford Companion to Indian Theatre*. New Delhi: Oxford University Press. P. 53.
2. Bharati, Dharmavir, *Andha Yug*. Tr. Alok Bhalla. New Delhi: Oxford University Press. P. 27. (All the subsequent page references are to this edition.)

16

"The static perishes, the dynamic perishes not": Basava's Ideology in *Fall of Kalyana*

Madhavi Nikam

Mahatma Basaveswara's progressive ideology can be vividly sensed from the aphorism, "The static perishes, the dynamic perishes not." To be dynamic, one has to purify his inner self, his thoughts and his actions. Man's life and his deeds have to be untainted, virtuous inwardly and outwardly in order to achieve the spiritual contentment. Basaveswara, the great social reformer of Karnataka, (India) set an ideal before the blind followers of religion that no favoritism can be really made on the ground of caste, class or gender. Need for social reform and religious wakefulness with right perspective is an essential factor for the upliftment of the society. Basava's preaching, modern and practical is still applicable to the globalized world.

Basavaraj Naikar has made a genuine effort of making the social message of Mahatma Basaveswara reach every part of the country by translating Dr. M.M.Kalburgi's play *Kettittu Kalyana* into English as *Fall of Kalyana* (2003). Naikar has beautifully portrayed the revolution against all types of injustice and the fight that Basava gave against the corrupt system. The play conveys the social message and a vivid interpretation of life that existed during Basava's period. The expectation and the dissatisfaction with the society made Basava revolt against the religious and social hypocrisy. With the play *Fall of Kalyana* many momentous incidents that have been engulfed in history, come forth alive before our eyes. The play is based on the philosophical preaching, social reform movements and revolutionary practices of Basava, who believed that change is the law of life and need of time. Anything that is stagnant will come to an end and whatever is dynamic will survive.

Basava was the son of a Brahmin named Madiraja and his wife Madalambika of Bagewadi, in Bijapur District. His life was full of political activities as he was personally related to the King Bijjala. He was married to Gangambika, the daughter of Baladeva, the chief minister of Bijjala, the Kalachuri King of Kalyana (1145-67 A.D.) and gave his own sister in marriage to the king. He was appointed in Baladeva's place after the latter's death. After Basava's appointment, he and his nephew Channabasava began to popularize the Virasaiva doctrines and won a great number of adherents. In the process they rapidly depleted Bijjala's treasury with liberal gifts to the *jangamas*, the Virasaiva priests. This alienated the king who tried to punish Basava, was himself assassinated. Basava went to the shrine of Sangameswara at the confluence of the Malaprabha and Krishna rivers and was absorbed into the godhead.

The basic outline of the Hindu society had emerged long before the transformation of the Vedic religion into Pauranika dharma. It was based on the four-fold *Varna* system, which later on degenerated into caste or *Jati* system. There was no untouchability in the Vedic age but it had become an important feature of the Hindu society of the Pauranika period. *Fall of Kalyana* projects the various issues, which were predominant in about 1370 A.D.

The ridiculous religious and social practices needed to be uprooted and new reformative ideas to be implemented in the rigid social system. The socio-politico-cultural aspects needed terrible changes in the age-old traditional Hindu society. There was an intense necessity to orient the people blindly following the false religious traditions. Reformation was not possible without revolution and it needed a firm and skilled leader. Basava paved the way for the welfare of the mankind with his modern, liberal and munificent attitude towards the downtrodden and the marginalized sector of the society. He was aware that the class, caste, gender; economic discrimination was the root cause of the social evil predominant during that period. Justice was essential to reset the lives of many who had become the victims of the religious bigotry. In the name of preserving culture, tradition and religion, the downtrodden were kept aloof from the privileges of life and liberty.

Basava accredited the evils predominant in the Hindu society at an early age and protest against them. His was an individual revolt in the beginning, which turned out to be the protest of the masses later on. The noble man fought for the noble cause of uplifting the poor, the exploited and the marginalized. Revolution begins at home and so it happened in Basava's life. He rebelled against the age-old custom of the 'Upanayana' (investing of the holy thread in the Brahmin religion) at an early age. The sacred thread was a clear indication of caste discrimination. He was firm and adamant of not wearing the thread to an extent that he did not budge his decision even when his family was ostracized. Not unaware of the fact that the Indians bear everything in the name of fate and *karma*, he decided to revolt against it. He knew, "We earn the prestige- not by hard work but by caste discrimination. Whereas the caste-system divides society, the theories of past *karma* and rebirth fortify the division" (2). Hinduism confesses submission as a supreme responsibility; it does not furnish and support people to make choice and value judgment in times of mayhem. Basava was least bothered about his own salvation and so the warnings and threats of the elders fell on deaf ears.

No wonder the learned Brahmins felt insecure and wanted to stop Basava with emotional, social and personal persuasion. But they fail drastically and fall flat on the face with Basava's question, "In that case, is the betterment of *sudras* and women achieved if they wear the sacred thread?" (2) Unable to answer Basava's question makes them furious. Their inability to convince him results in restlessness, insecurity, rage and ostracizing the family. They experience great difficulty in handling the situation when all the ways and means looked futile. Basava had fixed goals, ideals and motives for his future and hence he proceeds to Kudala-Sangama after defying *Manu Smruti*, a book considered holy by Brahmins which upholds the *Varna*-system and caste system propagating caste, class and gender discrimination. Madarasa and Madalambika are heartbroken at their son's departure after being beaten up by the priest. The harsh cruelties of the social establishments and their set customs are a hurdle in the progress of mankind. The ostracism is not an outcome of anger but more of fear to lose control over the existing community.

Situated on the banks of Malaprabha and Krishna rivers, Kudala-Sangama was a centre for education. In spite of entreaties by the family members and relatives Basava settles in Kudala-Sangama in the humble custody of Isanyaguru. The guru was a source of motivation and helped Basava attain his goal. In the moment of distress the guru's words consoled him and helped him come back to normalcy. Isanyaguru words, "Don't you worry. You seemed to be tired. First you have your bath and food. Then I'll listen to your story. Or it will unravel itself", are really soothing. His words are like medication to the ailing heart. Spiritual growth and emancipation are possible after long hours of meditation, devotion and holy deeds. Basava was aware that the unprivileged were deceived and duped into believing that they were benefited by following the rules prescribed in *Manu Smruti.* In Kudala-Sangama he spends years in educating himself but without real satisfaction. Isanyaguru was aware that he was a different student and so never forced him to attend classes or follow the normal trends in education that the other chose. He is aware of the meaninglessness of the education he is taking there. He realizes that, "the selfsame priestly culture is very strong here also. The mechanical reading of the *rudra*, the recital of mantras, the offering of thousand leaves of *bel* and such other things have not been awakening our intelligence. The intelligence of Shaivas has been tarnished like that of Brahmins by the smoke of sacrificial fire" (12). He protested against the educational system, the temple culture and the commercialization of religion. He was aware that the soul must be purified and his ideology came to him as a magical revelation while conversing with a friend. He says:

> Yes. The soul has to be purified. The soul has to be purified like this water. The dirty water has the capacity in itself to be purified. If water has to be pure, it should flow on and never be stagnant. 'The stagnant is impure and the flow is pure. The static perishes, the dynamic perishes not' Yes. It flashed across my mind. Yes, it flashed. I understand it now. This is not mere water, but my mentor (13).

Human beings commit mistakes but not repeating them, repentance, penance, meditation, and virtuous deeds help them to purify themselves. Giving up unethical behaviour, speaking truth even in the hour of crisis, controlling one's anger, being on the part of justice, helping the poor and the needy, is a path which leads an individual towards salvation, away from the world of temptation, and immoral, irreligious activities which are solely responsible for mankind's destruction. Basava cemented a path for the well-being of the human beings. He not only preached but also practised. A few years later when Madarasa is on death bed Basava is heartbroken but shows his father the path of enlightenment by suggesting that materialistic temptations truss man in the shackles of sorrow and misery. The entanglement with the property caused grief and intense agony. So after his father's death, he hands over the entire property to the servants who served his family for many years. Generously he distributes the property amongst the servants giving up the static and moving ahead in search of dynamic goals. After setting goals and ideology of life he always followed them himself before implementing it in the society. He takes away his sister Nagalambika with him for he knows:

> I can neither live nor grow in the stifling atmosphere here. There is no other go but to go away. But it is dangerous to leave my sister alone here. That is the reason why both of us are leaving for Kudala Sangama (17).

Protest becomes an indivisible part of Basava's life. The Brahmins of Bagewadi has a soft corner for Madarasa and so after his death they decide to withdraw the ostracism and render the funeral rights. Basava refuses their favour and cremates his father with the help of the maidservants. He revolts against traditional limits of the Brahmin society. He is least bothered about the inevitable consequences and does not fall prey to the customary beliefs and burden. The Brahmins felt insulted and retorted:

> Basava, please don't be reckless. This is a very serious situation. Stand away. Don't aggravate the societal enmity further. Don't think that everything would be over now. Please remember that you have a sister and that you may have to see her suffer (15).

The rage of the community makes no difference to Basava as his goals are set and mind free of such tribulations. After gaining spiritual and ethical power, his emotions and thoughts were in his control. He teaches the same to his followers in his later life with the *vacanas* he wrote to propagate moral, religious and spiritual ideas. Changing the social trends, breaking the established norms and swimming against the normal stream were a challenge. To embark upon a new life irrespective of the caste, class, creed, culture was a Herculean task. He was an impediment to the Brahmins of Bagewadi and his quitting the place was a blessing in disguise for them.

Changing the social milieu, Basava set working against the evils of superstition, caste discrimination, violence against women, religious hypocrisy, political corruption and moral discrepancy. Standing against the superstitious rituals of sacrifice, he himself is injured and spurts blood to save a lamb from the *Vipras.* Meaningless rituals which he revolted against. took life of the innocent. While saving a lamb from the clutches of the *Vipras*, Basava is badly injured. Slaughtering an innocent lamb in the name of religious ceremony was unacceptable to him. Life is precious, and in every soul god resides, hence it is necessary to safeguard every living soul whether human or animal. Spiritually pious he cares for every one and acts in the well being of them. One should worship God by fulfilling the deeds He has given him and should not engage in false, meaningless rituals. Religious activities should be for the upliftment of the downtrodden, well being of mankind, and for the protection of nature. Man's relationship to society and his nature should be humanistic for the survival of the universe. The real quintessence of religion had tripped to the backdrop in such rituals. Real dedication and righteous life had vanished in the fake world of materialistic craze and prosperity.

Basava was a firm believer in deeds and not only in worship. He believed that work is worship and it should be done with utmost devotion. To gain the blessings and grace of god one must purify himself inwardly. Exterior worship is fruitless and does not give spiritual satisfaction. Spiritual purity is a must and so he practised it himself. One should consider one's soul as God and worship its symbol i.e. *istalinga*, was Basava's preaching and practice. The true spiritual progress is coincident with the devotion and meditation.

Fertilization of right religious culture, spiritual and moral understanding, social awareness were essential. He believed that the concrete symbol of *istalinga* is a means of self-purification. When his guru interrogates, "Isn't it another form of the sacred thread?", he answers:

> No, no. Though both are hung around the neck, they are not the same. A man becomes a Brahmin as soon as he wears the sacred thread. From that day, he starts classifying society into Brahmin, Ksatriya, Vaisya and Sudra. On the contrary, the *istalinga* removes this social division created by the Vaidic people. Whereas the sacred thread divides society, the Siva-string unifies it and considers its members as believers and the rest as non-believers (21).

Spiritual concern of Basava made Isanyaguru happy and confident that he will definitely bring social reform. His ideas were clear and he decided to dedicate his life to propagate and implement high ideals and true way of nearing god. Initiated mass action was the result of Basava's preachings. People far and near were influenced by his ideas. Basava protested against the monastery and the temple culture. Commercialization of worship hurt him. Being aware of the fact that the poor borrow money for offering their devotion to deities was humiliating. He raised his voice against the *Devadasi* system, the practice of libation, the cross-palanquin procession and other gaudy activities. He alleged that by repudiating the temple culture the negative tricks would fade away. Eradicating the superstitious beliefs was the need of the hour. Basava exposed the defects of the system and became a victim of the pontiff's rage. He is thrashed and blamed for opposing the system. He discusses the matter of commercialization of the monastery, the corruption and fake religious facades with Isanyaguru. Reformation, relocation and resetting the old ideas, traditions and order were essential. Eradicating social evils was necessary for drastic change, which was impossible without social awareness. It is not an individual's task to reform but a mass activity. He rightly points, "These days, the kings have been exploiting the subjects, the priests have been exploiting the devotees and the men have been exploiting the women. Thus, the society has been divided into two streams i.e. the exploiters and the exploited" (33). Suffering and misery of the exploited section of society and the consequent outcome of destruction and anger was actually waiting. It is the social conscience of the exploited, which prevents them from condemning outright the religious dictators.

Basava exposes the double standards of the religious authorities interested in minting money and are least troubled by the adversity caused to others by their dealings. The greedy pontiffs enthrone their own near and dear ones as their heirs who have very narrow loyalty towards the throne and are constrained either to their own interests or that of their family. Basava is more concerned about the women and the exploited class.

Basava decides to go to Kalyana for further reformative movements on the advice of Isanyaguru. Baladeva, Basava's father-in-law takes him to the court of the king Bijjala in order to procure a job for him. The king is pleased to see him and praises him, "Your son-in-law is like the sun that has appeared in the form of the moon and embodiment of compassion. You are indeed very lucky to have such a son-in-law. Your daughter, Gangambika is also equally lucky to have him as her husband" (35). Basava's life takes a major turn. He impresses the king with his efficient work and is gradually made the finance minister after Siddharasa's (finance minister) death. Basava accepts the post as a challenge for self- examination. It is an experiment in spiritual purification –'remaining clean in the midst of money'.

Social reformation and social awareness become easy for him with power and money at his disposal. He gathers the low-born and the poor and advises them to eradicate the class and caste discrimination. He offers solutions and ways out of the miserable situation. Rejecting the monasteries and the temples is the first step for relocating self and nation. He guides the poor morally, spiritually and virtually. He protests against the existing system and tells them to reject the monastery and the temple culture and treat own persons as temples:

> Your own soul. You wear the *istalinga* as a symbol of the deity. Daily service to this symbol will help you attain spiritual elevation. Since it is worn on

> the chest by everybody without any discrimination between high-caste and low-caste, it becomes a symbol of social equality also (40).

Poverty is the root cause of all evils in society. Poverty, ignorance, illiteracy are curse upon mankind. These people are easily duped by the pontiffs and priests in the name of religion. Vocal protest of the downtrodden and the exploited makes a drastic change. The society does not provide for the candid means of income. The outbreak of antagonism against the mistreatment by the upper caste, such as the Brahmins can be seen through the cry of the crowd. People see the outburst of emotions and feelings against the wrong being committed all around in the society. He gives option to the people to change the existing situation by offering them 'collective work and collective feeding.' Basava arranges to supply a house, clothing and few other things from the treasury. He trusts that the association he has urbanized among himself and the poor and low-born people is ingenious and dynamic, for in the course of action not only the individual's character and destiny will change, but more dynamic individual- helps to reform the society. He feels enthusiastic and happy to see his dreams come true. He has an intense desire to change, shape and relocate the world of the poor, to uproot the old, traditional way of looking at life. The cankerous disease of caste, class and gender discrimination infecting the masses is to be eradicated.

The economic and social change motivates the people to follow their leader. Basava introduces the concepts of *kayaka* and *dasoha*. *Kayaka* means not only physical labour but mental labour as well. It means one has to work not only for oneself but also for the society, whereas *dasoha* means ownership of an object by God and use of it for another man. There is no chance of hoarding in *dasoha*. By not hoarding material things we can live happily. Basava is convinced that a comprehensive change in our society will be possible, once the people of Kalyana become emancipated to s upervise their own dealings. People believe in themselves and have hopes that man can overcome his difficulties in spite of being born in backward class and caste.

Basava developed the socio- spiritual academy on a democratic ground. A modern outlook of life was the special feature of this academy. The basic religion he believed in was 'Kayaka- *Dasoha*' which flourished under his guidance. The *sarana,* a *Virasaiva* male, who has surrendered himself to God is, therefore, very humble and free from egoism. *Sarana*hood does not depend upon birth and caste. Basava's preaching and practicing helps the poor to be independent. He expects the women to move with equal space of that of men. The outcome of his efforts is seen in the confidence developed in women. Collective culture is encouraged making men and women feel more independent and at ease. Basava's theories in the Socio- Spiritual Academy take the forms of *vacanas,* which spread effectively. With Basava's growing influence and the change in the society, the priests, pontiffs and other Brahmins are annoyed and feel jealous. They approach the king to place their grievances against Basava, who has levied tax on the *agraharas* and also cut the royal grant nearly by half. The king leaves his throne when people agitate and speak ill about Kalyana.

Eradicating caste discrimination is a must and so Basava eats food in Nagimayya's (an untouchable) house. The Brahmins are annoyed and pass on the information to the king. He is tried for entering the untouchable lane, having food there and violating the caste-system. Rivalry is seen amongst the Brahmins and the followers of Basava. To remove the caste and class discrimination a concrete step was necessary. Basava wanted to set an example and his wife Gangambika encourages him for second marriage with a Ksatriya girl, Nilambika, sister of the King Bijjala. Even Nilambika believes:

> Yes, it is better to be the wife of a poor man with dynamic values than to be the wife of a king with static values. It is exactly for this spiritual freedom that I married that small officer. What is the meaning of material wealth for man and wife if they have no ideological companionship? I have married Basava with an intention of becoming his ideological wife (68).

Violence against women was a common phenomenon. Basava stood against the *Devidasi* system, *sati* system and also helped a prostitute to settle in happy marital life. Basava sees a woman tied in rope taken to the magistrate for judgement as she was caught throwing her newborn child in the dark. In the Socio- Spiritual

Academy the young *saranas* are put a proposal to marry the prostitute and a young *sarana* accepts her as his wife. To eradicate the *Varna* discrimination Madhuvyya, a Brahmin and Haralayya, a *sudra* decide to marry their children and set a different example for the society. Basava is ready to face anything for economic, social and religious equality.

Reformation has to pay its price and so Madhuvayya and Haralayya, have to lose their lives as per the king's order for violating the *varna* system. The noble sacrifice only proclaimed to the world the great worth of Basava's philosophy. Basava is terminated from his minister-ship and banished from the capital. Jagadeva and Mallibomma slaughter the king and a terrible massacre takes place killing many *saranas.* Basava settled in Kudala-Sangama and breathed his last there.

Fall of Kalyana translated by Basavaraj Naikar from Kannada to English is a substantial effort to reach the non-Kannada readers. The social message of Basava is effectively communicated through the work with sensitive precision and vivacity. Naikar has used simple language and every bit of idea is conveyed effectively and efficiently. He has brought to limelight the various issues, which influence the society and the systems. Writing and portraying through the characters the past details a difficult task, which is marvellously handled by him. Capturing every detail of somebody's personal life is a task in itself. The recurring subject matter touched upon has to do with the political, social, economic, religious, and cultural life of the time. The philosophy of amalgamation of various aspects is challenging, and which he has handled skillfully and done justice to the original work. The details provided against the background of historical event gives the play a touch of reality. Naikar has provided every detail required to capture the real sense of the work. Basava's mission of a new society became successful as many *saranas* took the bacanas with them when they left Kalyana and practised in various corners of the country. True devotion and righteous behaviours are the pillars of happy life and excellent society. The play reminds us of Gandhi, Mahatma Phule, Dayanand Saraswati and other social reformers, who spent their lives for the welfare of mankind.

WORKS CITED

Kalburgi, M.M. (2003) *Fall of Kalyana,* Trans.Basavaraj Naikar, Bangalore: Basava Samithi

Publication. All the subsequent references are from this edition.

17

Sufi Symbolism in Manjhan' s *Madhumalati*

Mudita Agnihotri
Alok Pandey

Translation is not only the version of other language but a strong means to connect humanity living in different cultures. It must be an urgent requirement of getting a message with deep surface of other language but the translation of a literary discourse obviously aims high as translation desires to convey the message of source text to the people who are not familiar with that language. A literary discourse appeals a sensible heart to the extent and the translator contemplates the initiative of a laudable enterprise. No doubt, a literary book is not desired to reproduce in other language unless it has a universal appeal in its contents, and the translator finds it quite useful in any time or place. Manjhan's *Madhumalati* is one of the literary sublime discourses which can be relevant in any culture or place. This book is translated by Aditya Behl, Simon Weightman with Shyam Manohar Pandey and published as Oxford World Classics. *Madhumalati* is a mystical romance composed in 1545A.D. in Awadhi (a dialect of Hindi Khari Boli) language, because Manjhan was born and brought up in the very centre of Shattari Sufism in Bihar during probably most active and influential period. His father Sayyid Muhammed Ali Manjhan belonged to Jaunpur. The poet himself writes:

Samvat nau sau baaban bhayau/sati purush kali parihar gayeu
Tao hum chit upja abhilasha/ katha ek badhahu ur bhakha
Suras bachan jahan lagi sunei/ kavi who samane hain sab gunein
Jaun sab kahein suras ras bhakhee/ sunahu kaan daie pem abhilashi[1]

(In the year nine hundred and fifty two
The man of truth abandoned this Kali age
Then a desire arose within me
To weave a tale in language full of feelings
Using the sweetest and most powerful words
That ever I had heard or stored in my heart
All who aspire to love should hear me.)

Manjhan is one of the major Sufi poets who have produced considerable Indian literature as the poets of love tales. The poets other than Manjhan attempted love poetry with a great feeling of separation but Manjhan's *Madhumalati* offers reunion of the lovers after a long separation.The happy ending of the poem shows the subjective elements in this poetry as Manjhan has incorporated his own experiences as a person. Manjhan was considered to be a person with large soul and strong faculty love. In fact, Shattari Sufi trend started in India with Shaikh Abdullah Shattar, who reached India in the later half of the fifteenth century. He adopted a unique way to link directly with the Indian folk. He went from village to village with a demand to know the persons who were interested in knowing the way to God. These practices soon progressed from ordinary prayers to the noble attempt of realization of the divine truth.

Manjhan projected his personal disposition, values and feelings in this epic. He was supposed to be the most generous among Sufi poets. This was the reason he focused the notion of love among human beings. The aim of Sufi poets was to awaken a sense of love among the people through establishing the significance of love. The cultivated reader feels the emotions of the parted lovers—— Manohar and Madhumalati in the poem. The reader response is deliberately shaped by the sources of Rasa or flavour of a poem. Manjhan's cosmology is supposed to be the base of his imagery and symbolism along with narration. These intermediaries and interpreters as the received Shattari cosmology, discussed the level of manifestations of the absolute.

The first level out of those is the idea of oneness which is beyond all attribution. This undetermined place of absolute oneness is prior to the beginning of everything. The poet tries to find all Indian approximation for the Sufi theory of wahdat al-wujud or the unity of existence. Manjhan is astonished at the contrast between the oneness of the creator and the multiplicity of created forms which could be called disguised form of God self. God pervaded everywhere though not visible, is unqualified, yet singular, closed yet manifested, without a shape yet multiple shaped.

In every state the Supreme
Lord is one
A single in many guises
In Heaven earth and hell,
Where ever space extends
The Lord ....form
He is Om, the singular sound
One light there is which shines alone,
Radiant in all the world.
How can I destroy the one
Who pervades the universe in so many forms
In the three worlds, all know his being
Whatever exists, exists in him.

....

Beginning of the, beginning
End of the end,
Many forms but only the essence,
He is one there is no other
He has neither beginning nor end.[2]

Symbolism could be called in context of this romance, an expression or representation of the invisible by conventional signs or figures, as the poet expresses the divine love. The human love of Manohar and Madhumalati is taken as a reflection of spiritual love. He uses both the poetics of Rasa and suggestion from Sanskrit poetics and mystical symbolism of Sufi literature. The approach adopted by Sufi poets is different from Islamic.They believed in Indian philosophy of Vedanta and took soul as the part of great soul. They were overwhelmed by the concept of true love and desired to meet their beloved. Sufis came to India with a single mission to extend Islam but their considerate heart and adjusting nature allowed them to be with the Indian public and win the public praise. Whole

Sufi literature is based on love, and love is founded on beauty. They tended to corporate in their poems that God himself is allured on his own created beauty and loves it with all his heart. He loves beauty and so he extends beauty in the world through generations. The central idea of love is beauty and due to this reason Sufis loved most the supreme power. The aesthetics of Indian Sufi literature aimed at suggesting a never failing relationship of love between a transcendent god and human world through the circulation of love between human beings as lovers.

O soul, you are an ocean of treasures
Why do you destroy yourself with pride?
All of creation is the mirror of your face
From it the triple world shines with light
In heave, earth and the neither world,
Your radiance gives light to all.
You alone are manifest in all creation...[3]

Madhumalati is written in Awadhi language or Eastern Hindavi. Along with Maithili, Awadhi was a major literary dialect. There are many evidences that in Manjhan's time learned scholars and poets assembled and recited their poems in Arabic, Persian and Hindavi. This rich interactive mixture of vernacular and classical literature helped to create an aesthetic culture. The Sufi is one who has two points of view, his own and that of their quality of Sufism brought them to by the people of other culture. Sheikhs used to command the spiritual jurisdiction as Guru and their disciple used to seek spiritual guidance for them. Sheikhs provided proper training to attain the entire closeness to God or Allah through music and poetry. The Sufi poets composed their poems based on love and romance by taking their heroes as ascetics who have the utmost desire for the revelatory beauty of a heroine or God. Their heroes could be called in sense Yogi but heroines were only beautiful Indain women. Their stories were narrated in different contexts. These heroes or Yogis represented a love not to worldly beloved but ultimately to God, the omnipotent.

The poem begins with the praise of God and shows the inability of the poet to accomplish the great enterprise of singing God's grace-

God giver of love, the treasure house of joy
Creator of the two worlds in the one sound Om
My mind has no light worthy of you
With which to sing your praise O Lord. [4]

The king Surajbhanu's queen gives birth to a son after a long time. The astrologers are called to predict his destiny. They name the infant Manohar and predict that he, in his fourteenth year, will meet his beloved and fall in love. For some time, they will be separated and during this time he will become a yogi. The prince was brought up well and educated as he was to be crowned at the age of twelve. The prediction of the astrologer proved true and prince in his fourteenth year fell in love with the princes of Maharas where he was transported by the nymphs with his bed to the bedroom of princess Madhumalati. The prince was amazed by astonishing beauty of the princess. After while the true love which was cultivated in their former birth, revives between them. Soon they pledge themselves for perpetual union and love. Again both the lovers fall asleep and in the meantime the nymphs take back to his palace. When he wakes up he feels acute pain in love. He narrates his maid servant the case. The king calls many doctors but all of them fail to cure him because they never had the pains of love or separation. The prince disguising as a yogi goes to the state of Maharas with his large retinue but unfortunately all of them had to lose their lives except Manohar. He was saved for two reasons namely the love of Madhumalati and mercy of God. In the forest of Kadli Vana he meets a girl Pema, who was imprisoned by a demon. She discloses before Manohar that she, the childhood friend of Madhumalati visited her home with her mother every month. Manohar is extremely happy to listen about his beloved. He soon resolves to free the girl Pema and encounters the demon. Through some tricks, he succeeds in killing the demon and takes Pema back to her parents. Her parents express their desire to get him as their son-in law but emphatically he refused as the true love for Madhumalati was beating in his heart. Next day he meets Madhumalti with the help of Pema. Old love reawakens and they take their vow not to have physical love before marriage. They sleep there and her mother queen Roopmanjari was worried not to find her in her room. She reaches the place and gets terribly angry with their union. After coming to her state Maharas she turns her daughter into a bird by uttering a spell:

> " you have disgraced your
> Mother and father
> O ruin of the family
> Why did you not
> Die at birth?
> Wicked girl, you have blackened
> Our family name.
> ....
>
> Taking a handful of water,
> The queen uttered a spell
> And sprinkled it over the face.
> The moment that is touched
> Madhumalti, the girl
> Became a bird and flew away.
> ....
> With it is, she was maddened by love
> With wings she became more deceptive
> She flew faster even than the wind
> ....
> Both father and mother wept themselves
> Senseless over their daughter.[5]

Madhumalati as a bird goes all round the world in search of her love Manohar. She suffers horribly from the pain of separation. She finds a prince who looks like Manohar and allows herself to be caught. That prince is Taracand who has a dignified soul as he, hearing her story, resolves to help her at every cost. He takes Madhumalati back to her parents. Her parents got extremely happy to get her. Soon her mother Roopmanjari restores her to the princess. The queen offers her daughter's hand to Taracand but he gently refused as he knew Madhumalti could only be happy with Manohar. The parents of Madhumalati inform Pema the happenings. Manohar appears at the scene as yogi. Somehow marriage is arranged between Manohar and Madhumalati. Pema, the friend of Madhumalati is married to Taracand.

Both the couples return to their respective kingdoms. The journey ends with entire happiness to all concerned.

The poem ends with a note of love that is a strong sign of Sufi poetry. The Sufis were well versed in various symbols and conventions of Persian poetry but at the time they were strongly fascinated by the Indian poetics and imagery of Indian classical literature. They attentively tried to mingle the notion of a person of literary taste, refinements and enough sensibility with the concept of ASHIQ or lover and the SALIK , the seeker on the mystical path, and. This poem has varied meaning as it could be simple love story of beyond that a journey to the closeness of God. In fact, Manjhan uses the quest for human love as a technique to evoke spiritual level of meaning about this world. The metaphysics of Sufism is to focus on a transcendental principal that cannot be embodied simply but could be called a process of self-transformation to make a balance in this world. The symbolism in this poem is subtle as it abounds in multiple suggestive meaning and symbols. For example his heroine sometimes is an embodiment of erotic love and on the other she becomes a sign of spiritual love. There are three stages—— the awakening time of love, the period in separation and the condition after the union of love. The first and the last are normal processes of human life but the second one of separation is quite significant as it is the only way of purification of the self. This purification, according to Manjhan, is possible through love. In Sufi terminology, wodd is the love which stimulates the lover(Mohebb)to become annihilated from his nafs'(Nurbaksh). The greatness of love is well established in the poem as the poet accepts it as the foundation of life.

The witness is that which appears after absence where God is the witness in one's inner consciousness (serr) the inner consciousness is that Gnostic is the witness that which he perceives (God) is that which is witnessed. The lover possessing pure inner consciousness describes, in terms of the transitory his vision of different aspects of the eternal as the witness.The masters say that the witness is present and whatever is present and what ever is present in your heart is your witness.[6]

Love is oriented to beloved and beauty is the cause of love. The beloved in Sufi symbolism is said to represent God that is he who is absolutely free of the need for friendship. Simultaneously, beauty is said to represent the existence of all possible perfections gathered in one being and this can apply only to God. Beauty has double functions as essential beauty that is, of course, of the divine and the other is relative beauty, which lurks from the physical body. This is why, Manjhan narrates the relative beauty of Madhumalati from her head to leg in twenty one verses from 77 to 79. The separation also is a symbol of a journey to know the self beyond everything in the world. Manjhan finds people blessed those who happen to be separated and purify their souls for ever.

> Fate gives some the pain of separation
> gives them the crown of the triple world
> Do not think separation is pain from it , joy comes into the world
> blessed is the man whose sorrow is the sorrow of love in separation? [7]

The translation of this romance serves the purpose as well but it is true that the entire notion of the poet cannot be translated because " We do not translate a word but the longest sequence or cluster of words that makes sense when checked against two realities, in L1 and L2."[8]

In fact, the translators have tried their best to bring the poem into the version of other language and it was a privilege for them that one of them was fully acquainted with culture of SL, and the other was well acquainted with the target language. But even then the complexity of inter cultural translation could not be solved;

Culture and intercultural competence and awareness that rise out of experience of culture are far more complex phenomena than it may seem to the translator. The more a translator is aware of complexity of differences between cultures, the better the translator he will be. It is probably right to say that there has never been a time the community of translator was unaware of cultural differences and their significances for translation.[9]

The typical Indian words could not be translated in English as they do not occur in the English culture. Consequently the translators have adopted the technique of literal translation but in this way the word loses its gravity for example:

> Let me first tell of the parting in her hair
> difficult of ascent as the path to heaven

As he looked at her parting and her flowing locks.
he kept straying from the path and returning to it.[10]

In Indian culture the way to divide hair for a style is not mere a parting of the hair. It is more than that as it has a ritual significance in the life of an Indian woman. At the same time it can arouse many emotions related to the well- being of Indian woman. There are some more complex words which could not be translated into English like Barahmasa, Dvapar, Om, Brahma, Kali, Gandharva, Papihas, Swati, Vedas, caki, cakor, and Yogi. These words are used as it is. Since no equivalent words are found for these words in English, it is beneficial to use the same with a note for meaning otherwise they must have lost their beauty and gravity. The other point to be noted is that he concludes his narrations with happy ending, in which no one dies, no one is sad.

The poem could be called an inter play of profane love and divine love. The ordinate love is treated as a step towards progression in Sufi treatise. The romances of this trend have more subtle symbolism as they have often more than one interpretation. This romance also has a use of suggestion and allusion to point out some symbolic levels. The total appeal of the poem is the contentment and satisfaction that can only be achieved through love.

Love is costliest Jewel in existence
The man whose soul knows love is blessed.[11]

WORKS CITED

1. Manjhan, Mir Sayyid. *Madhumalati.* (ed.)Shivgopal Mishra, Varanasi, 1957, p.14 (All subsequent quotations have been taken from Manjhan's *Madhumalati*, (tran.) Aditya Behl and Simon Weightman, Oxford World classics series, Oxford)
2. Manjhan *Madhumalati*.pp.3-4-5
3. Ibid, p14
4. Ibid, p.1
5. Ibid, pp.146-147
6. Nurbaksh Encyclopaedia, Vol.v Sufi Symbolism.pp.35-6
7. Manjhan, *Madhumalati*.p.13

8. Translation Directory. Com\Ferenc Kovacs's "Meaning: the translator's role in clarifying Some misconceptions"
9. Translation Directory. Com/ Samira Mizani' " Cultural translation"
10. Manjhan, *Madhumalati*. P.33
11. Ibid, P.13

18

Technical Features and Thematic Concerns in *Sangya-Balya*

Pratima Chaitanya

The great cultural renaissance generated during the postcolonial period brought about various innovations in the Indian theatre. The postcolonial Indian theatre saw many meaningful encounters with tradition. The drive to return and re-discover our tradition was inspired by a search for roots and identity. This was part of the whole process of decolonization of our life-style, values, social institutions, creative forms and cultural modes. (Goel 204)

The colonialist values can only be eroded by reclaiming one's own identity, one's own past. In the postcolonial scenario, an increasing number of literary artists are turning towards the rich Indian heritage to re-define their Indian identity. It appears that with this perspective in mind, Basavaraj Naikar translated a popular folk play of North-Karnataka, *Sangya-Balya* into English.

The play was originally composed by Rayappa Pattar of North Karnataka. The structure of the play is based on that of the *Sannata*, one of the folk-forms of Karnataka's *Bayalata* (open air theatre). *Sangya-Balya: A Tale of Love and Betrayal* is based on a real-life incident (which took place during the British rule) and depicts the extra-marital relationship between Sangya and Ganga,leading to Sangya's tragic murder by Ganga's husband and the betrayal of Sangya's trust and friendship by his bosom friend, Balya. The social play suggests the turmoil of its times that introduced new values of money and love, and new institutions like the judicial court and non-traditional commerce. The play is remarkably modern in its attitude and concludes with an open-ending.

The folk performances begin with the invocation of the presiding deity, which generally is the Elephant-headed Lord, *Ganapati* or *Ganesha*. *Sangya-Balya*, too begins with the observance of *nandi* (opening prayer) to Lord Ganapati and blessings are sought by the Chorus for the performance:

> Salutations to you O elephant-headed lord,
> By your grace we are staging this play
> Of Sangya and Balya, the two bosom-friends.
> We offer you a coconut and a bunch of bananas;
> Grass, bhel-leaves and flowers by way of worship.
> Kindly grant intelligence to us, the dull-witted ones,
> We bow down to your feet, Lord,
> Kindly ward off all possible hindrances. (Naikar, *Sangya-Balya* 1)

The Chorus gives a greater flexibility to the dramatic speech and an incredible variety and complexity of expression. Apart from the observance of *nandi*, the Chorus in *Sangya-Balya* also acts as a narrator and tells the audience about Sangya and Balya's visit to Bailawada and their meeting with Ganga:

> CHORUS: (*Sings*) Sangya and Balya together
> Walked towards Bailawada
> Ganga also came to the bank,
> Sangya offered her dried coconut
> And a blouse piece hurriedly. (84)

The Chorus prevents emotional identification of the audience with the scene in order that one may think dispassionately about the play.

The classical Sanskrit plays and consequently the regional folk dramas or *natyas*, unlike the Greek tragedy regard drama as drama or make-believe, and not reality. It is for this reason that their treatment of time and space is imaginative and not realistic and not conditioned by the so called unities of time and space. The same is the case with *Sangya-Balya*, where the treatment of time as well as space is imaginary. From the days of Sangya and Balya's friendship, the departure of Virabhadra to Bellary, the meeting of Ganga and Sangya at the fair at Lord Basavanna, their love-affair, the return of Ganga's husband, her subsequent abandonment, the meeting of Sangya and Ganga in Hongala, Sangya's killing and Virabhadra's confession of his crime to a government official, there is absolutely no unity of time.

Similarly, the play observes no unity of space. By simple actions like miming and gesticulating, the stage is utilized to convey a sense of movement from one place to the other. The action moves from village Bailahongla to Bailawada. Within the village different locales are suggested by making use of *kakshvibhaga* or "the imaginary division of stage into different areas by which various locales can be suggested without any scenic change." (Jain 21) The opening scene of the play is indicative of the use of *kakshvibhaga*. In the opening scene, the Chorus is present on one part of the stage while on the other the story of Sangya and Balya is being enacted. When Sangya in search of Balya asks a boy to search him out, the latter goes onto the other part of the stage, which supposedly is Balya's house, and asks him to meet his friend. Sometime later, a part of stage becomes the moneylender's shop. Sangya and Balya take a few rounds and walk from one part of the stage to the other and their walk indicates different locales. As the stage-directions suggest, "Sangya and Balya make a round of the stage and leave." (Naikar, *Sangya-Balya* 1) Stage-directions like these which suggest movement like walking around or a journey from one place to another is a direct reference to *parikrama*, a convention from the *Natyashashtra*. The play is replete with the use of *parikrama*. The journey to Lord Basavanna's fair by Ganga and Paramma is mimed and indicative of *parikrama*, as suggested by the stage directions "Both of them walk on." (26) They walk round the stage and mime that the temple is far off. Ganga sings—"How far away is the temple/ O God, how far. . . ." (27)

Thus, the play like the Sanskrit and the folk performances does not make use of many dramatic properties. Folk plays are in general actor-oriented and therefore there is no need for any realistic or any other kind of stage setting. The absence of a creative playwright in the folk theatre makes the latter so completely the theatre of an actor, who by miming and gesticulating indicates various locales. For example in *Sangya-Balya*, Lord Basavanna's temple in the fair is verbally indicated by Ganga in these words, "Here is the temple, here is the temple. . . ." (28) and described by Paramma in the following words: "The temple is beautiful and the idol too" (28). The temple is not virtually present on the stage but is to be imagined by the audience. In a typical folk theatre style, there are no dramatic settings to indicate the temple.

A folk performance is replete with songs, dance and instrumental music. Unlike a *Yakshagana* performance, where the Bhagavata or the Sutradhar does the singing, *Sangya-Balya* is like an opera, where the characters themselves sing their dialogues. In *Sangya-Balya* all characters and the Chorus sing their dialogues. The dialogues are then immediately translated into prose by the characters of the play, as in a typical *Sannata* performance. Songs in *Sannata* are accompanied by the music produced by a "small flat drum" (Naikar, Introduction v) called *Dappu*. Previously *Sannata* was known as *Dappu* and then it became *Dappanita*.

These varied techniques—the chorus, the predominance of songs, dance, gesticulation, *kakshvibhaga* and *parikrama*— borrowed from the traditional and classical Indian theatre are not only means to intrigue the audience (which they obviously did) but also correspond to the more contemporary and modern idea of defamiliarisation. By deploying the technique of defamiliarisation, the audience is made to think hard about the problems and the issues, which surround them rather than identify with them. The major thematic concerns of the play are discussed as follows.

The theme of oppression of women by the patriarchal order finds mention in the play. One commonality between the cultures of East and West is the marginalization and suppression of women. The situation is further worsened in India, the former colony of Britain, because the women of this country were doubly colonized—by virtue of being part of the colonized country and at the same time dominated and crushed by the unjust patriarchal order. Ganga appears to have a happy married life with her husband Virabhadra, but when he goes away on a business tour, she is left alone. Though she does not want her husband to go away, her opinion is not taken into consideration. As a dedicated Indian wife, she is only forced to abide by the decisions of her husband. She pleads with her husband not to leave her alone, but to no avail. She cries:

> GANGA: (*Sings*) Please don't go away from me
> O my dear husband. How shall I
> Live alone in this mansion large?
>
> . . .

> There is nobody in this three-storeyed mansion.
> I am a young lady, who cannot stay alone here.
> My body and youth will go to waste, what shall I do? (Naikar, *Sangya-Balya* 14)

She has to forgo her desires and is only supposed to follow the dictates of her husband. Like a typical Indian wife, she is reduced to the position of a house-maid, who has to execute all her duties uncomplainingly and become an epitome of *tyaga* (sacrifice), *tapasya* (penance) and *tanmayta* (dedication). Without caring for her feelings and ignoring her constant pleas, her husband takes no time in giving orders to Ganga for the maintenance of the household. That the Indian woman has to live under several restrictions and is expected to observe *purdah* is revealed by a reference to Ganga's covering her face with a veil. Paramma, the old lady, asks her to "lift up [her] face and remove [the] veil from it." (18).

Paramma's husband called "Husband" in the play is a wry comment on all husbands, who ill-treat their wives and feel that they can freely exercise power over women. Paramma's husband appears to be unthankful, mean, demanding and chauvinistic. Though the old lady is dedicated to the services of her husband, the latter is extremely demanding and constantly scares her with dire consequences if his idiosyncrasies are not fulfilled:

> HUSBAND: (*Sings*) Don't go, my dear wife, don't go,
> I cannot stand the severe cold.
> I can spend the day and night easily
> If you are within my arms
> . . .
> I cannot sit alone cross-legged at home.
> You have not given up your coquetry, though you are old.
> Nor have you give up your double talk.
> Though an old wife, you haven't learnt
> The art of staying at home with me.
> If I get angry, I shall break your teeth,
> . . . .
> Yes, please come back soon . . .
> Otherwise I will thrash you with this cane. (20-22)

A woman in Indian society is bound to be chaste till her last breath. Chastity is a myth propagated by the patriarchal order to suppress women and interestingly enough this myth has been heartily accepted by women of the whole world, so much so that some women go to the extent of ending their lives to protect their chastity. If any woman violates these rules, she is not only looked down upon but also culturally excommunicated.

Ganga claims to be chaste and committed to the cause of her husband. When at Sangya's behest, Balya acts as a go-between and requests Ganga to accept his friend's love, she gives him "ear studs" (45) and beats him up. She again turns down the offer when Sangya approaches her. It is when Paramma cajoles her to acquiesce to the proposal that she accepts it. All the time Ganga claims that she is not a woman of easy virtue and that she is dedicated to her husband and so cannot indulge in an extra-marital relationship. But more than the pricking of her conscience and her pledges to be chaste, what seems to worry her is the social implications of this affair. In fact, she shirks away from it not because of her dedication to her husband, but because she is afraid of her husband, her brother-in-laws and the society at large which idealizes chastity. In her confrontation with Sangya, she very candidly makes this confession:

> Why do you pester me, Sangya?
> How shall I bear the public charge?
> This affair cannot last long.
> You may receive a dangerous jolt. (50)

Ganga wishes to gratify her sexual desires but seems to be afraid of the society. Also she does not want to reveal to the world that she is a woman of easy virtue and therefore despite herself, keeps on denying Sangya's advances. Sangya is clever enough to observe this. After her constant denial, he says, "Do you wrinkle your nose in contempt/ Simply because I ask you openly?" (50) It is only when Paramma convinces her that she agrees to the proposal. Ganga knows that before setting off on his business tour, her husband had made the old lady her guardian. She was afraid the old woman might spill the beans of her illicit affair to her husband. When she finds that Paramma is in her support, she acquiesces to the proposal. Paramma too knows that Ganga's pleas and cries of chastity are nothing but hypocrisy. As the old lady says, "I know all your play-acting, / You are a clever young lady. I know how you beckon/ Sangya to come to your place." (64) It appears that Ganga tries to dissemble her sexual desires and sensual nature under the garb of morality. When the opportune moment comes, she completely plunges herself in lust. Inklings of her sensuality, her burning lust are given by the playwright in comparing her twice with a snake—the priest at Lord Basavanna's fair says that her "complexion is like that of a cobra?" (29) and later Sangya says that "[h]er waist is slender like a snake " (33). The snake is an archetypal symbol of eroticism and fecundity. The comparison of Ganga's body parts with those of a snake is pointer to her sensuous and erotic nature.

A woman in a patriarchal set-up is hardly conceived of as a normal human being with normal desires. She is either interpreted as a goddess or a whore. Ganga for her husband is a superhuman person, who has to control her desires, her yearnings and unflinchingly dedicate herself to the services of her husband and his family. Virabhadra leaves his young, beautiful wife without her consent and goes away to Bellary. Being unable to control her desires, Ganga liberally runs an affair with Sangya. When the husband finds out, he is furious. Virabhadra labels his wife as a whore and takes all her belongings and throws her out of the house. A woman's desires, her will, her decisions are never taken into account. It is always the husband who decides and the wife has to suffer mutely. Ganga tells Balya about her plight:

GANGA: (*Sings*) Come on, brother Balanna
See what happened to my life!
My husband and his brothers
Confiscated all my ornaments,
And drove me out of my home. (77)

Belief in miraculous powers and magical boons has been the epicentre of Hindu religion, which bears a strong influence on the Indian mind. The sudden appearances of the supernatural forces, sooth-sayers, *akashwanis* (oracles) and granting of wishes have been, since ages, an integral part of the classical and later the folk literature. This device has been successfully deployed in the play. When, after his unsuccessful attempts to convince Ganga for an affair, Sangya is utterly despondent, a *korvanji* or fortune-teller appears on the scene. The *korvanji* has supposedly the power to make prophecies and change the course of one's life. As she says:

KORVANJI:I am not a korvanji
Of this country or that.
Know that I hail from heaven.
I can know what you dream
And what you eat.

. . .

I know how to mesmerize women
And make them follow you, men. (56)

This sooth-sayer works out for Sangya the plan to get Ganga. She tells him to "make use of Paramma of the Top-House." (58) Her prophecy finally comes true, as Paramma is successful in bringing Sangya and Ganga together.

The Indian society is overtly superstitious. Belief in good and bad omens form a vital part of an Indian's day to day life. Several popular illustrations of the Indian society find mention in the play. Sangya says that he does not wish to go to Bailawada because of certain ominous signals:

My turban brushed against the door
And slipped down. It was an ominous sign.
I will not go to Bailawada.
I saw a spade on my way,
It was an ominous sign,
I will not go to Bailawada.
A cat crossed my path from right to left,
It was an ominous sign,

I will not go to Bailawada. (83)

Crushing poverty, which has become an inevitable part of Indian society, is well portrayed in the play through the characters of Balya and Paramma. It is, indeed, heart-rending to see Balya's pitiable condition, who cannot even afford food for his family. He narrates his predicament to his friend, Sangya in the following words:

BALYA: (*Sings*) I am a poor fellow, my dear,Sangya.

I went in search of work and wages,
You know how many children I have.
I have neither *jowar* to grind
Nor any food to eat at home. (4)

In the play we also get glimpses of the ill-treatment, oppression and exploitation of the underprivileged by the privileged. In Act One, Scene Two of the play, when Sangya goes to fetch money for the items purchased for his friend at the moneylender's shop, the latter ill-treats Balya. As soon as Sangya leaves the shop, the moneylender asks Balya to "sweep the floor and dust the counter." (8) He then blames Balya for not getting money for the items purchased and beats him up and "kicks Balya, who falls on the floor unconscious"(9)

The episode also reveals how such constant maltreatment by the privileged hardens and fails to affect the deprived so much so that they do not hesitate to commit crimes, trickery and treachery as soon as they get an opportunity. On being beaten by the Moneylender, Balya feigns that he has died. The scared moneylender then in desperation asks Sangya to take Balya back and agrees not only to give him the clothes purchased for free, but also some additional money. Balya seems to be a seasoned trickster. On hearing this, he immediately gets up and laughs heartily at his trickery and walks away with his friend Sangya. Later Balya does not shirk away from deceiving his bosom friend, Sangya and leads him to death for the sake of money. He is bribed by Ganga's husband Virabhadra to bring Sangya to an isolated place, where the latter plans to kill him for seducing his wife. As Balya says:

BALYA: (*Sings*) Kill me not brother Virabhadra,
I shall be meek like a lady
Of your family.
I shall bring Sangya to you,
Give me hundreds of rupees,
Mansion, land, oxen and cart
Right now in black and white.
I shall bring Sangya on Wednesday
In the evening on the way to Bailawada.
You sit in ambush behind the *kevada* thicket
With axes and sickles ready in hand. (81)

Similarly Paramma is a poor, old lady who acquiesces to ruin Ganga's marital life by convincing her to have an affair with Sangya for "a set of saris, a set of blouses, a pair of golden bangles and a pair of buffaloes." (85) The episodes clearly reveal how the underprivileged, the deprived, the needy (their needs unattended by the privileged), easily give in to temptations and treachery.

From time immemorial, the fire of lust and revenge has remained unquenched. The Ravana-myth— the downfall of an erudite scholar because of his growing lust for Sita— is oft-quoted in the text to indicate the continuity between the past and the present. The follies and crimes committed in the past are constantly repeated in the present. It appears as if human civilization has learnt nothing from past transgressions. Be it the mythological Ravana, the Sangya of the folkloric world or any lustful man in the present day, the uncontrolled fire of lust gobbles him up. Though questions in recent times are raised on the ethics of Chastity, it still appears to be accepted by the Indian society at large and its violation leads to death, ruin and misery—Sangya is killed, Ganga's marriage is irretrievably destroyed and Virabhadra is supposedly imprisoned. Revenge leads to no good: The killing of Sangya leads to no happiness for Virabhadra, his life appears to be in jeopardy and he is supposedly jailed and hanged.

Thus, *Sangya-Balya* is brimming over with concerns, which are as relevant for the present day world as they were centuries before. The play transcends the barriers of time and seems to ooze contemporaneity for all ages.

WORKS CITED

Goel, Savita. "Folk Theatre Strategies in *Hayavadana*". *The Plays of Girish Karnad:Critical Perspectives*, ed. Jaydipsinh Dodiya New Delhi: Prestige Books, 1999. 204-212.

Jain, Nemichandra. *Indian Theatre: Tradition, Continuity and Change.* National School of Drama, 2005.

Naikar, Basavaraj., trans. *Sangya-Balya.* By Rayappa Pattar. New Delhi: Macmillan Publishers India Limited, 2009.

_________. Introduction. *Sangya-Balya.* By Rayappa Pattar. New Delhi: Macmillan Publishers India Limited, 2009. v-vii.

19

The Subaltern Vision in *The Edge of Time*

Basavaraj Naikar

Generally politicians in India have no time or patience or willingness or competence to be creative writers, although they have a very rich and variegated experience of life. But Veerappa Moily is an exception to this rule. M.Veerappa Moily (1940) hails from coastal Karnataka. He was born at Mudabidri in Daksina Kannada District of Karnataka State. An advocate by profession and deeply involved in politics for the last forty years, he was the Chief Minister of Karnataka during 1992-97. At present he is working as the Chairman of the Administrative Reforms Commission in Delhi. As Chief Minister, he initiated many reforms and progressive programmes in Karnataka. Presently he is the central Minister for Law and Justice.

A gifted writer in Kannada, Moily has published three plays (*Muru Natakagalu*), three novels (*Sagara Dipa* 1986; *Kotta*, 1993; and *Tembare*, 1999) three poetry collections (*Halu-Jenu*, 1994 etc) and a compilation of his lectures. Whereas *Sagara Dipa* (*Light of the Ocean*) deals with the fishermen's life, *Kotta* depicts the life of the Koraga community. His most ambitious work is the epic *Ramayana Mahanveshanam*, a retelling of the *Ramayana* in five volumes, translated into Hindi recently. Of his novels, *Kotta* has been translated into several languages including Hindi and English. *The Edge of Time* is the translation of his fourth Kannada novel, *Tembare*.

Veerappa Moily has a rare combination of many qualities in him. Firstly, he hails from the subaltern strata of the coastal Karnataka. Hence he has a first hand experience of the ethnic community in which he is born and brought up. Secondly, his legal profession as an advocate has given him a deep knowledge of the causes and consequences of human conflicts and litigations. Thirdly, his life-long participation in the political life of Karnataka has enabled him to see the cross section of the Kannada society at its grass root level. Fourthly and most importantly he has the creative talent to transform his rich and varied experience of life into works of art. His deep commitment to human cause and strong conviction add a ring of authenticity to his writings. As Vivek Rai rightly points out, "Fieldwork in folklore, political experience and legal knowledge – all these are wedded to *dalit* and feminine sensibility to create in the novel a new worldview" (Blurb).

The original novel in Kannada entitled *Tembare* is excellently translated into English by Dr. C. N. Ramachandran, who is himself a bi-lingual scholar and critic known for his *magnum opus* translation of *Male Madeshwara* into English. As he served for about ten years as Professor and Chairman of the Department of English at Mangalore University, Mangalore, he has been able to observe the details and absorb the essence of Tulu culture prevalent in that area, which, in turn, has enabled him to translate Veerappa Moily's novel dealing with the culture of Tulu Land.

In his "Author's Note" Veerappa Moily highlights the dominant features of Tulu people and their culture:

> The land of Tuluvas, in coastal Karnataka, is renowned for its legends and folklore, and there are still many features of their traditions yet to be brought to light. The kinship-systems, the natural ways to eradicate exploitation, and the voice of revolt that constitute Tuluva society are universal values.The oral epics and narratives of *bhuta*-worship prevalent in Tulunadu, record the dynamic relationship between the past and the present. These epics and narratives lay before us moments of aesthetic delight in a day-to-day world of dry routine; like flashes of lighting, they illumine a world covered with fog. Our body is also like a *tembare*; there are many spots on this body, neither very hard nor very delicate, which can produce varied sounds and tones. I beat those spots again and again, wondering which spot would satisfy me.

> At those times, I was not myself, I was like a salt-doll that has become one with the sea. [1] (p. v).

India is a multi-religious and multi-lingual country known for its unity and diversity. That is why its ideal is tolerance as preached by the great saints like Buddha, Mahavira, Shankaracharya, Basaveshwara, Kabir and Chaitanya and so on. All these great men taught universal brotherhood and humanitarianism. But in spite of these high ideals, there has been repeated violation of them resulting in injustice, suppression and murder of the helpless people. The writers should be aware of the harsh social reality and try to write about it honestly and boldly. Art should serve the purpose of social amelioration. Veerappa Moily believes in this philosophy of art, "Unless writers have such consciousness and the determination to fight against injustice, they end up as hypocrites. Writers, who cannot respond to the social changes, are like dead wood, and their works too will be lifeless. A work that cannot absorb the spirit of truth and righteousness from a community is as dry as a desert. And, works of literature should be like oases, sources of love and life. The great French writer-philosopher, Romain Rolland has declared that 'India is the country in which for the first time, Man's dreams come into existence.' *Tembare* attempts to catch and record such dreams" (P. ix). He continues to clarify his intention behind his writing and to suggest the manner of responding to the novel by the reader, "My novel intends to capture that vision and unveil the dreams of the future. I have spread my dream carpet on the ground. My appeal to readers is: tread softly on the carpet because you will be treading on my fond dreams. The silk with which this carpet is woven, has not come down from the heaven; it is the essence of thousands of ordinary workers, who have sacrificed all towards this vision. This silk, which was rough and knotty, has been refined to make it artistic." (p. ix).

Another important feature of the novel is that it is not a work of romantic imagination, but one based on the brass tacks of social reality supported by fieldwork and research. Veerappa Moily states honestly,

> The subject of this novel is the product of research, and it is always a challenge to give such a subject the form of a poetic and artistic novel. In fact, it is not a work of fiction; truth has transcended and transformed

> the fictitious nature of the work. There is the hard work of five years behind this novel. After I gathered relevant ideas and information from books, fieldwork and personal interviews, I took a year to write this novel. (p. x).

As the translator, C. N. Ramachandran clarifies further, "*Tembare* is not only a fine work of imagination, it is also a work of deep research in folklore and anthropology. As the readers can see, the novel extensively makes use of myths, *pad-danas* about various *bhutas*, and history. All are integrated into one organic whole in the novel... Arguably, the 'new novel' in the new millennium has to be, besides being a work of imagination, a historical document, a political tract and a sociological study. *Tembare* is one such multifaceted work" (p. xx).

The novel deals with the life of the people belonging to Pambada caste and culture, which is one of the subaltern groups in coastal Karnataka, especially Tulu Nadu. The coastal Karnataka is known for two cultural channels: one, *Yaksagana*, the folk-theatre and the other, *Bhutaradhane* or Spirit-Worship. Whereas *Yaksagana* is a means of (relatively secular) entertainment, *Bhutaradhane* is an expression of ecstatic religion testifying to the folk beliefs and superstitions. Thus *Bhutaradhane* has many dimensions like the mystical, the social, the moral and the judicial. The spirit-impersonation is itself a dramatization of myth. As Peter J. Claus says,

> Dramatization of myth in a ritual context is familiar enough. Often, I would think, the ritual tradition (the context) and the mythic tradition (text) have somewhat independent existences. This is the case with Tulunad's *siri* rituals and the story of the *siri* spirits. The myth is part of a woman's narrative song tradition, while the rituals are managed by men."[2]

Peter J. Claus adds later:

> Paddanas are closed connected with this ritual. As Peter J. Claus clarifies, "Tuluva paddanas are sung narratives, which are a part of several closely related singing traditions and which could be called ballads or epics or ritual songs, depending on the context or purpose in which they are sung.[3]

Both *Yaksagana* and *Bhutaradhane* are so specific to the coastal culture and interesting in their own ways that they have attracted the international attention of anthropologists and folklorists. *Tembare* may be described as an ethnic novel depicting the life of the subaltern strata of society belonging to the 'little tradition' as contradistinguished from the so-called 'great tradition' of Brahmanical Hinduism. In almost all the Indian regional literatures the great tradition has had a lion's share so far. Now it is high time to bring the marginal little traditions to the center, in order to know and recognize all the possible varieties of human experiences instead of hanging on to the already familiar and overdone great tradition. In the postcolonial era, thanks to Derrida and his tribe, there is no question of superiority or inferiority of cultures. Neither the great tradition is superior nor is the little tradition inferior. All these traditions or cultures are simply different from one another. In the multi-cultural context of India and in that postcolonial situation, recognition of the otherness of cultures assumes enormous significance. *Tembare* also testifies to the fact that a man (novelist) from the subaltern strata of Indian society can not only speak but also write artistically about his experiences. *Tembare* easily brings to our mind similar ethnic novels from Africa like those of Chinua Achebe and Ngugi wa Thiang'O.

As the translator explains the central thematic concern of the novel, "*Tembare* depicts the experiences of one such exploited caste called Pambada, the members of which community are the traditional impersonators of a *bhuta* called Panjurli, an animistic spirit... Since the writer has an intimate knowledge of this community, he authentically depicts the nature and degree of exploitation of this community. These Pambadas have no land of their own, have no means of education and have to depend on casual labour for their daily bread. When they impersonate the *bhuta*, people show respect and devotion towards them; but once the ritual is over and the impersonator comes out of his role, he continues to be an 'Untouchable' " (pp.xvii-xviii).

The novel delineates the tension between tradition and modernity in the Pambada caste and culture. In other words it shows a contrastive picture of conformity and non-conformity to the tradition of *Bhutaradhane* or Spirit-Impersonation. Whereas Aitha stands for the tradition of spirit-impersonation and has a firm faith in its sanctity and validity, Pambada rebels against the hereditary profession of Spirit-Impersonation and goes in for modern education and civil service. Like him, his sister Thomu also rejects her family tradition of possession dance and goes in for modern education and legal profession. Thus in the same family there are three different paths followed by three persons i.e. two brothers and a sister. These three different paths followed by the members of the same family may be discussed in some detail in the following paragraphs. The novelist offers some ethnological details of the Tulu society (just as Chinua Achebe and Ngugi wa Thiang'O do in their novels about Yoruba and Gikuyu cultures). For example there are many communities in Tulu Nadu like Pambada, Parava, Nalike, Paanaara and Ajila that conduct and participate in the worship of spirits. There seems to be a class division among the spirits also. While the Paravas conduct the worship of the 'royal' spirits like Jumudi, Kalkuda and Panjurli, the Nalike community has a limited field and can participate in the worship of the 'lowly' spirits like Chamudi.

Monta Pambada, like his forefathers, had considered the worship of spirits a sacred ritual and had unalloyed faith in the spirits as another form of truth. That was why even the British courts in India permitted as credible evidence what was sworn in front of the spirits. That was an attempt to transform a spiritual forum of justice into a social system of justice. The vows taken by the leaders of communities, villagers and towns in the presence of spirits would get spiritual legitimization.This is the positive aspect of the spirit-worship.

But there is also a negative aspect to it. Whenever people have no real faith in the spirit-worship, they use the so-called sacred occasion to indulge in violence, wreak vengeance upon their enemies and immorally tilt the judgement of the spirit-impersonator in their favour. In such desecration of the holy ritual, moral principles are suppressed by immoral and selfish considerations.

Although spirit-impersonation is of great importance on the scheduled day and time, the impersonators are revered on that day and during the programme; they are totally forgotten and conveniently neglected by the society, because the spirit-impersonators belong to untouchable castes.This kind of contradiction between the professional importance and holiness enjoyed by the impersonators and the social negligence suffered by them is exemplified by Pijina. "When Pijina, Lakana's father, impersonated the *bhutas* during the ritual at night, all those assembled looked on him with fear and reverence. But during the day, the same people treated him as an 'untouchable.' Pijina, of course, had accepted such treatment as a way of life..." (P. 26).

In spite of the awareness of their low status in the society, the spirit-impersonators engage in the holy ritual because it gives some social elevation at least temporarily. As Pijina says to his son, "But for our participation in the *bhuta*-worship, we would have remained *parayas*, untouchables. What has elevated us socially is the *bhuta*" (P.42). There seems to be a close connection between the spirit-worship and the subaltern status of the participants in many societies of the world. As I.M. Lewis rightly opines, "Such peripheral cults... also commonly embrace downtrodden categories of men, who are subject to strong discrimination in rigidly stratified societies."[4] Referring to the similar examples from India Lewis continues to say, "All the elements we have so far discussed are particularly well displayed in the context of the Hindu caste-system. Several recent writers on Indian communities comment upon the predilection, which peripheral spirits show for men of low caste. Through possession such lowly orders are allowed a limited franchise to protest against their menial circumstances. One of the best analyses of this pattern of ritualized mutiny is that provided for the Nayars of Malabar by Kathleen Gough." [5]

The impersonators are proud of the sacred profession and fight for their rights when the conventional law of inheritance is violated due to the exigencies of life. For example when Monta Pambada, Lakana's grandfather, helped Suranna Alva to reclaim his position of impersonator from Deju Alva, the latter took revenge on Monta Pambada when the possession-dance was in progress, "Mangu's recitation reached its crescendo, and the frenzied sounds of the *tembare* reverberated everywhere. Suddenly in a flash, Deju snatched the sharp sword that was in the hands of the *bhuta* and with one stroke, slashed both Monta Pambada's arms. The people, who had assembled there stood transfixed as Monta's hands fell in front of Kodamanittaaya. Blood began to flow like an incoming wave of the Nandini River. The *tembare* fell silent and Mangu, Monta's wife, fell on the ground, unconscious" (P.30).

The spirit-impersonator's life is restricted by many a rigorous rule. He must lead a stoic life in order to achieve efficacy in his religious profession. "The *bhuta*-impersonator's life was hedged in by too many restrictions and conventions: he had to maintain a stony silence even when there were births and deaths at home. Even if somebody died in his own family, he was not supposed to go near the survivors and comfort them; he had to move out of his house, build a separate hut for himself, cook his own food, and thus spend the forty days of ritual impurity like an outcast. Whether it was his own mother or father or his wife and children, who had died, he could not touch the dead body, let alone carry it on his shoulders. He had to live his life cut off from all human relationships" (P.32)

A conspicuously ironic feature of the spirit-impersonation is that on the one hand it has a mystic connection with the supernatural world, on the other it has an ugly connection with the caste-hierarchy and the resultant exploitation of the low by the high and a means of punishing or wreaking vengeance on the poor people by the rich ones. "In order to reach that mystic stage, which is in between this world and the next, he has to pass through many other stages; he has to make the transition from the mundane to the spiritual gradually, step by step. The stylized recitation of *pad-dana* and the *tembare* beats aid the impersonator in achieving such a transition" (P.43). The mystic and supernatural aspect of spirit-impersonation involves some kind of fear psychology also. "As a matter of fact, the people of Tulu Nadu have more faith in *bhutas* than in gods, and out of fear, they follow whatever is dictated by the *bhutas*. For *bhutas*, unlike gods and goddesses, are intimately connected with the day-to-day happenings of this world; and the rituals of *bhuta*-worship have achieved both popular respect and credibility" (P.36).

There are different varieties of spirit-impersonation having different degrees of effectiveness and purposes. For example, the ritual of Pilibhuta is especially connected with death. "Contact with the Pilibhuta was like playing with death, he said. It was believed that the Pilibhuta impersonator had to touch somebody before the completion of the ritual, otherwise he would die soon. Hence, the impersonator would move heaven and earth to touch somebody. And because of the belief that whoever happened to be touched by the impersonator would die within a year, everyone was on guard not to be touched by the *bhuta*. Consequently, the ritual of Pilibhuta could end only with the death of the one or the other: the impersonator, or the person, who was touched by him" (P.32).

Another negative aspect of the spirit-impersonator is that he "has always to be under the shadow of fear from the village chief or the administrator. The fear and anxiety are doubled if one is initiated into that cult of *bhuta*-worship. For once he is excommunicated from the cult; he gets no further invitations from anybody. Hence most of the time, he is not free to act as per the dictates of his conscience, he has to blindly obey whatever the elders or the leaders order" (P.40). Although the spirit-impersonation involves strict discipline, ritual purity and a sort of mystic communion with God or supernatural world, at a higher level, it is also, ironically enough, subjected to a sort of colonialism or exploitation by the village chief or the administrator on the social level. Thus there is an unhappy contradiction in the whole process of possession/impersonation due to the desecration of the holy practice into a tricky game of exploitation, over the years. Lakana remembers this gradual desecration as follows, "To my grandfather, he thought, impersonating the *bhuta* was not a profession, it was a means of worship, it was a way of penance and contemplation. Although his honesty and truthfulness ended in a tragedy, he persisted in the path of truth throughout his life. Pijina, my father, was helpless and desperate owing to the tragic end of his father; hence he became a pawn in the power games of the administrator" (P.42). If the spirit-impersonation involves social exploitation along with some sort of ecstatic experience, then why should the people of these subaltern communities go in for this profession? One is easily tempted to ask such a question. But the answer is also provided by the same people. As Lakana's father tells him, "But for our participation in the *bhuta*-worship, we would have remained *parayas*, untouchables. What has elevated us socially is the *bhuta*" (P.42). Now the whole thing becomes clear. The spirit-impersonation elevates the social position of an untouchable, gives him a chance of mystic experience and security of religious faith and yet occasionally forces him to be exploited by the socially powerful people. For example when Mohanaraja's sister Vimala and his uncle's son Shekhara was in love with each other, his uncle was against their marriage. He, therefore, arranged a *bhuta*-ceremony to decide the feasibility of the marriage.

Though Pijina, the spirit-impersonator was in favour of the marriage, he was pressurized by the uncle (of Mohanaraja) to give a negative verdict. Consequently Pijina announced at the end of the elaborate possession-dance, "It is impossible. If the marriage takes place, it will destroy both the families" (P.45). As a result of this negative verdict the lovers committed suicide by hanging themselves from the ceiling of the house. Here Pijina's holy dance (of spirit-impersonation) is used as a means of social exploitation, selfishness and vested interest by the rich or high caste people. Pijina becomes a helpless victim of such a negative system.

The gradual transition from the mundane world into the mystic state is to be specially noticed by the reader as it can be compared and contrasted with the practices of ecstatic religions of other parts of the world. As the novelist explains, "A person from such communities like Parava, Pambada and Nalike has to act as a 'representative' of the *bhuta* in the rituals of *bhuta*-worship. In order to reach that mystic stage, which is in between this world and the next, he has to pass through many other stages; he has to make the transition from the mundane to the spiritual gradually, step by step. The stylized recitation of *pad-dana* and the *tembare* beats aid the impersonator in achieving such a transition" (P.43).

Maire and Pijina, the parents of Lakana, Aitha and Thomu are the chief exponents of spirit-impersonation in this novel. Maire, as a young girl was attracted to Pijina as a spirit-impersonator and married him in course of time with parental approval. She played a supportive role in Pijina's professional life as a singer, but was not conscious of the gender-discrimination at all. She brought up her three children – Lakana, Aitha and Thomu – by sacrificing a lot for them. She tolerated her husband's alcoholism. But her husband died in a mysterious way. Different people attributed his death to different causes like his alcoholism, strain of dancing barefoot, singeing his chest with a burning torch, lack of observance of ritual purity and Jumadi *bhuta's* anger etc. "Maire sees in his death a modern variation of the '*Parati Mangane* narrative'. Her heart tells her that, when the master cast covetous eyes on her, Pijina attempted to kill him with the *bhuta*-sword, and the master's slaves caught him at that time and killed him" (P.49).

Having lost her husband, Pijina, Maire is deeply disturbed. "She had realized the awful truth: that the god, to whose service Pijina had devoted his entire life, had not come to his aid at the critical moment. While her father-in-law, Monta Pambada had lost both of his arms for the sake of truth, her husband had lost his life itself for the same truth" (P.55). She had realized the bitter truth that the spirit-impersonator has to be a puppet in the hands of his masters. "She knew the naked truth: be it Pambada or the spirit itself, as long as he danced to the tune of his masters, uttered the oracular words that satisfied them, and thus played the role of a lawgiver, he was respected during the performance and would get enough to eat. But once he differed from his masters, he had no place on the earth" (P.56). The same fate has happened to Koraga Taniya, Kalkuda and Kallurti.

Now Maire has the responsibility of bringing up her children i.e. two sons, Aitha and Lakana and a daughter, Thomu. She sends them to far-off schools to educate them. As all the three children grow into young men and women they wish to give up the hereditary profession of spirit-impersonation and follow modern ways of earning their livelihood. For example, the eldest son Aitha begins to work as a casual labourer under a contractor. The younger son, Lakana wants to be educated and become a District Collector. The youngest daughter, Thomu wants to be educated and become a lawyer. Thus all the three of them choose three different paths.

The three ways of life followed by the three persons are beset with their own distinctive hindrances and challenges and demand some kind of sacrifice or the other. Whether their ways of life are traditional or modern, it makes no difference. We may examine their three different ways one by one.

Aitha, the eldest son in the family, cannot be educated as he is mentally not smart. He, therefore, chooses a simple life of a labourer and overseer under a contractor called Raghurama Shetty. But his deep faith in Kodamanittaaya prevents him from practicing the corrupt method of keeping false records/accounts of daily expenses. Aitha is a man of high morals and sterling conviction. When the engineer threatens him of the loss of his job, Aitha replies boldly, "No, sir, I cannot do it. Once I have sworn on Kodamanittaaya, I can't go against it even if my tongue is slit"(P.61). The engineer taunts him as the grandson of King Harishchandra and persuades him to sign the false record of expenditure in the register, Aitha replies firmly, "The Master of all masters is Kodamanittaaya. He is the one, who grants food for all. I cannot sign this register" (P.62). Obviously the engineer is disarmed by Aitha's answer expressing his strong moral conviction. Aitha also feels a righteous satisfaction. His strong faith in Kodamanittaaya is highly appreciated by his mother.

The importance of Kodamanittaaya is narrated in the pad-*dana*, which is oft sung in Tulu Nadu. According to the *pad-dana* Kodamanittaaya is a royal spirit and has the tiger as his mount. Gangadhara, the manager of the shrine of Kodamaittaaya, knows the pain and suffering of the Pambada family. He also knows that nowadays Pijina's sons do not actively participate in the spirit-worship. But he does not like this fact. He, therefore, goes to Aitha's house with ritual materials of formal invitation and requests him, "Kodamainttaaya visited me in my dream. His wish is that Aitha himself should impersonate him during the ritual" (P.67). He consoles Maire, "Please forgive me. In the name of Kodamainttaaya, I swear that no unjust or untoward incidents will occur as has happened in the past" (P.67). In spite of Gangadhara'a persuasion, Aitha does not agree to impersonate the spirit. He and his mother remember all the tragedy that had befallen her husband and fathe.-in-law.

Aitha undergoes a moral dilemma. Being a formally educated man he thinks deeply about the course of life that he has to follow. He knows that his brother, Lakana has warned him against the traditional spirit-impersonation. When Aitha's mind is oscillating between two opposite directions i.e. tradition and modernity, he is pleasantly surprised to learn that his younger brother Lakana has been appointed as the Assistant Commissioner. Thus Lakana's choice of a modern way of life is confirmed. But Aitha is still uncertain about his profession. Thus when he is undergoing a sort of dark night of the soul, he suddenly has a mystic experience of illumination and call of the divine spirit,

> In the moments just before dawn, Aitha saw a vision: a huge round mass of bright light shone before him and he slowly became a part of it. Immediately, huge waves that one witnesses at the end of the world enveloped him and he felt suffocated. Within no time he fell unconscious. Then,

> gradually, there came to his ears from a distance the mellow notes of Kodamanittaaya pad-dana and the slow rhythmic beats of the tembare. He saw Kodamanittaaya coming to him through those notes, riding on a tiger, and beckoning him with love and affection (P.73).

This mystic experience of Aitha naturally reinforces his faith in the spirit-god, resolves his dilemma and inspires him to resume the family tradition of spirit-impersonation. With the consent of his mother, Aitha goes to Gangadhara's house and tells him, "Master, as per the wishes of Kodamanittaaya, I agree to participate in the *bhuta*-worship" (P.74). Then Gangadhara encourages him and strengthens his faith in God by narrating the instance of Vibhishana and Kanakadasa. Aitha returns home with a sense of joy and contentment.

But when Aitha writes to his brother, Lakana to attend the initiation ceremony, Lakana writes a caustic reply accusing him of being entrapped again in the spider's web and of falling a victim to their selfish goals. Finally the day of initiation arrives, and as expected, Lakana remains absent. But Aitha is formally initiated and he wears the ritual bangles. On the day of the *bhuta*-worship Aitha puts the saffron–paste on his face and feels a wave of excitement surging through his body. He dances ecstatically and captivates the audience. It is indeed a noteworthy personal triumph for Aitha. "By any account, it was a indeed a noteworthy personal triumph for Aitha. He, who had been an anonymous casual labourer till then, joined the legends built around old traditions. Some very old people remembered the grace and dignity of Monta Pambada; they said Aitha was just like his grandfather, and spared no words of praise for his total commitment, artistry, faith and linguistic propensities" (P.78). Thus Aitha and his mother are ecstatic about the successful ritual. Gangadhara is also very happy about it. "After the ritual, Gangadhara, who had gone through the thrilling experience of a nuclear explosion, heaved a deep sigh of relief like a philosophical scientist. He had the satisfaction of having led what he had undertaken to its successful conclusion" (P.79).

As days go by, Aitha strengthens his faith in the spirit-worship, extends his impersonation to the royal spirits like Kodamanittaaya, Kukkinandaaya, Jumadi and Rakteshwari. He cultivates strict discipline prescribed by tradition. He puts on the anklets by reciting the '*paari*', tries the *ani* on his back, wears a mask and holds the weapons of the deity. This is the stage of transition from the concrete to the abstract, in which Aitha attains a mystical state. His strong conviction is expressed in his words, "I feed the virtuous with the divine nectar from my full pot; but I will feed the evil-doers with poison that is in my breasts. I always uphold justice; and I will destroy all kinds of injustice" (P.83). Thus Aitha becomes the sword of justice and the wall of protection. "He has grown from ritual to vision and from a mortal to the stature of a deity. He is the 'Kodimara', the flagpole of the whole village" (P.83).

There is, thus, a striking difference between the two paths chosen by Aitha and Lakana. There is a partial break of tradition and partial continuation, but with a strong conviction and righteous determination. The novelist himself comments on this phenomenon critically,

> As if the two chopped off arms of Monta Pambada had taken a new form, Lakana and Aitha took two different paths. In a sense, the tradition of Monta was completely broken. Aitha did not continue bhuta worship in the naïve and innocent manner of his grandfather. His fidelity and devotion were to his own soul and not to his masters. Hence, though Aitha seemingly continued his grandfather's occupation, he followed a different path and held before him a different goal. However, if one, considered Aitha's honesty, integrity, and faith, one could see that one arm of Monta had indeed blossomed as Aitha (P.84).

Whereas Aitha stands for tradition, Lakana stands for modernity. "For all appearances, Lakana had broken away from Monta's tradition; he had nothing but contempt and anger toward the whole system called *bhuta*-worship. But from a different point of view, Lakana also continued Monta's tradition in a new form. The kind of honesty and principles that Lakana displayed in his field as a revenue officer demonstrates that he was indeed Monta's grandson" (Pp. 84-85).

Lakana being educated in a modern way begins his service as the Revenue Officer at Basavakalyana taluk of Bidar District in North

Karnataka. His modern education enables him to analyze the problems of Indian society like religion, caste, gods and race. In order to understand these issues he sets aside some time regularly to study the Bhagavad Gita, Manu Dharma Shastra and the works of Dr. Ambedkar. Consequently his study of these classics and serious cogitation make him sadly aware of the internal contradictions to be seen in the lives of great men like Lord Krishna. He is rather confused and confounded by such contradictions. Similarly, the system of caste-hierarchy propounded by Manu makes his blood boil with rage. He experiences intense anguish. Likewise his reading of Ambedkar's works makes him very unhappy about the panchamas. "Lakana remembered the term panchama – he and his caste belonged to the fifth, the 'untouchable' caste. As Lakana continued to read Ambedkar's opinion about varna and caste, he came to understand, gradually, the cunning stratagems that the priestly and the ruling classes have always employed in order to control society" (P.87).

Although Lakana is disturbed and depressed by such irrational ideas of the past, he remembers his profession of a Revenue Officer and defines a new role for himself. It is a happy coincidence that he is posted to Basavakalyana, a city named after Basaveswara, the great social reformer of the twelfth century. There is a great similarity between Basaveswara's ideas against social injustice and caste-discrimination masquerading as religion and those of Lakana. Basaveswara had declared thus,

> I will put the Vedas to the sword,
> I will pierce all the sastras,
> I will whip logic and break its back,
> I will chop off the nose of Agamas,
> Behold, O generous God of Kudala Sangama,
> I am the beloved son of Chennayya, the tanner.

In course of time Maire arranges the marriage of her two sons, Aitha and Lakana with two rural brides, Chennu and Taniyaru respectively. But the contrast between Aitha's traditionalism and Lakana's modernity is to be seen in their behaviour, "When all the ceremonies were over, as per the custom of the village, the newly married couples had to go and get the blessings of their masters. Lakana refused to do so, stating that he had no master, but Aitha and his wife went and were blessed by Gangadhara" (P.90).

Lakana does not like religious hatred that has been erupting in India repeatedly. He is keenly aware of the demolition of the Babri Masjid in New Delhi on December 6, 1992 and the consequent religious riots between Hindus and Muslims all over India. Lakana, the Revenue Officer of Basavakalyana does not wish to allow any religious conflict to crop up in his jurisdiction. "He had taken a vow that he would not allow anyone to create an atmosphere of religious hatred in the place, where Basavanna had worked and the famous Kalyana Revolution had taken place" (P.123)

In order to forestall any communal clash on December 6, he holds a peace march through all the major lanes of Basavakalyana. The people take a vow to forget the differences of caste and religion and work together for peace. But after the meeting is over, Lakana hears the rumour that people are coming from Bidar to Basavakalyana carrying long swords with them and that they had plans to burn mosques and stone temples and ransack petty shops. Listening to such information Lakana feels deeply disturbed. Rumours about Hindus and Muslims accusing each other reach him. He, therefore, feels helpless like Abhimanyu caught inside the *chakravyuha*.

But in spite of all these problems, Lakana decides firmly to prevent the communal clashes, even at the cost of his life, "Yes, I have to go, and I have to fight it out even if it means losing both of my arms, or losing my life,' resolved Lakana; and on the night of 5 December, he personally visited many people as he could and talked to them. He talked to men, women, and children; he took up one piece of rumour after another and demonstrated how they were only rumours. He went to mosques and prayed there with Muslims; he went to the temples and prayed there with Hindus; and thus Lakana, who was an atheist in principle, became a theist for his people. His first priority was to protect the minds of the people, besides their bodies. He knew that the police or military force, however big in number, could not control fanatical mobs. Their minds had to be cleansed and protected" (P.126). On December 6, while Lakana is touring the whole city with police and military escort, he receives the news that all the domes of the Babri Masjid have been demolished. Similarly he hears the reports of looting and killing, of setting fire to houses and shops etc. But Basavakalyana remains calm and peaceful. Lakana is happy to realize that, even after eight centuries,

Bassavanna was alive. "On that terrible night of 6 December, though violence spread like wildfire throughout the country, Basavakalyana remained calm, like an iceberg calmly floating on the sea" (P.127). Though he has controlled the situation at Basavakalyana, he is deeply depressed by the reports of religious clashes taking place throughout the country. He becomes rather helpless and begins to recite a *vacana* of Basavanna: The rich build temples to Siva, / What can I do, a poor man?

But Lakana's profession involves several hazards. His adherence to truth and justice causes serious problems for him. Now his wife is none months' pregnant after the tragedy of three miscarriages. His wife stays alone in the government quarters and there is no relative to take care of her when he is away at his office. But Lakana cannot neglect his official duty as a Revenue Officer. One night he boldly raids Girijapati's rice mills. Girijapati happens to be the President of the District Council and belongs to the ruling party. He confiscates the huge stocks of rice that are being illegally stored there, prepares the relevant documents, seals the mill and transports the whole stock to the granary of the Food Corporation of India. After completing the whole task, he reaches home at 2 P.M., he finds his nine-month pregnant wife, Taniyaru lying down exhausted, her face having lost its colour and turned white. When he tries to awaken her, he receives an urgent call from the Minister-in-Charge of Bidar District. Lakana explains to the personal assistant of the Minister that his wife is in a stage of advanced pregnancy and asks if he could meet the Minister after a few days. But the assistant tells Lakana in a stern voice, "No, you have to come here immediately. Otherwise, it will be registered that you have disobeyed orders and you will be suspended" (P.157). Hence Lakana helplessly leaves his wife alone at home and goes to Bidar to meet the Minister. It is common knowledge that in India bureaucratic power is controlled by political power. Hence the government officers have to dance according to the tunes of politicians. When Lakana meets the Minister after three hours of waiting, the latter roars at him, "How dare you raid this man's mill?" (P.164) Lakana replies, "When there are unaccounted stocks illegally stored there, how can one close one's eyes to it?" (P.165) Lakana speaks in a professional and legal manner, but the Minister talks his own political language. The administrative discourse and the political discourse are at loggerheads with each other. The Minister orders Lakana to open the locks of the mill, but Lakana boldly refuses to do so. The Minister threatens him, "If you don't listen to me, I will have to transfer you to a place devoid of even water. I will have to suspend you and send you back to your *bhuta*-worship. Be careful" (P.166). But Lakana is an officer with such a strong conviction and sterling morality that he refuses to obey the order of the Minister, "I shall never do such a shameful thing, Sir, please excuse me... I cannot allow the lamp of my conscience to be put out. My body may burn, but not my soul" (P.166).

As the Minister's anger explodes, he calls the Chief Minister in Bangalore on the phone and tells him, "The Tahsildar of Basavakalyana is a very arrogant man. Either I continue as Minister or he does as the officer; both of us cannot stay in the same district. Before he reaches Basavakalyana, his suspension order should reach him" (P.166). Then the Minister tells him the harsh political truth of our country, "You are the enemy of my community and wherever you go, my people will hunt you down. What do you think you are doing? Do you think that our party is going to lose power and another party is going to support you? Yu are under the illusion. Governments may come and go, but caste equations don't change. People of every single caste stick together and protect each other. This is the unwritten constitution of this State or of this country"(P.166).

It is said that sorrows always come in a chain fashion. This is especially true in the life of Lakana. He has to face different kinds of evils or challenges in his professional, familial and social life. Some of them are attributable to political evils, some to social evils and some to his fate. What is most conspicuous about his life is that all these evils occur in a chain fashion. For example, Lakana returns home at Basavakalyana after refusing to yield to the local Minister's pressure. Then he is upset to learn that his wife had labour pains at night, but no doctor attended to her until the next morning. Though he is happy to have a child, he is very sad to know that the child is disabled due to the nurse's indifference and negligence. But Lakana takes it as a challenge in his life. The birth of a disabled child is ultimately ascribable to his fate. As already mentioned, sorrows rush in his life in a chain fashion. Before he is reconciled to his disabled child, he receives a telegram, from his brother, "Start immediately, mother serious." He, therefore, rushes in his car from Basavakalyana to his village Padiyuru and is shocked to learn that his mother is burnt to death by the local hooligans,

> Just then, Aitha and Thomu ran up to Lakana and embraced him. Tears had dried up in their eyes and their faces were swollen. Lakana took a few steps toward a body covered in cloth: it was his mother's body, charred and unrecognizable (P.172).

Shocked beyond measure by the mother's death, Lakana asks his brother how it had happened. Then Aitha tells him in brief,

> He was told, as briefly as possible, that Chaluvayya Shetty's bodyguards had first murdered Buda Mulya and cut off his wife's hand, and then, in the evening, they had locked Aitha's house from outside, poured kerosene oil and set fire to it. Maire, trapped in the burning house, and the cattle in the shed had died amidst helpless screams. Aitha and his wife had survived a similar fate because, at that time, they had gone to the Kodamanittaaya shrine to offer their prayers. On their way back, they had seen from a distance, red tongues of fire rising high above their house. By the time they hurried home, everything was over; there was only a deadly silence. Their neighbours had helped them put out the fire with great difficulty. When Aitha was finally able to enter the house, he could only see his mother's charred body (P.173).

Lakana, Aitha, Thomu and Chennu are heartbroken and listless. Unwilling to take shelter in anybody's house, they spend the whole night under the mango tree near the burnt home. When Lakana gets up in the morning, he receives a telegram. "It read that he had been suspended with immediate effect and that he should vacate his quarters within two days. There at Basavakalyana, his wife and child lay like orphans in a hospital; and here his mother had been a victim of an inhuman crime. All the villagers knew the truth about the ghastly crime, but were silent owning to their fear of power" (P.174). Growing desperate, Lakana meets the Superintendent of Police and tries to persuade him to conduct a proper inquiry, but the Superintendent turns a deaf ear to his request. Thus Lakana receives shock after shock and feels righteous anger at all the man-made brutalities. "When he realized that even a rage that yearned to explode the whole police station with bombs, how could he judge the Naxalite violence as wrong? That was the question that raged in his mind" (P.176).

Thus although Lakana has chosen the modern way of life by rejecting the heritage of spirit-impersonation, he is not altogether happy. He undergoes many sorrowful experiences due to political evils and social evils, which are ultimately ascribable to his fate. As the novelist comments upon his life, "Lakana's life should have been smooth and peaceful at Basavakalyana, the center of Sri Basavanna's socio-religious movement, but it was not. On the contrary, it was marked by one misfortune after another. Due to the negligence of a doctor, his wife became almost insane, his child was crippled, and he was suspended from his job for no fault of his" (P.191). But in spite of all this suffering, Lakana does not lose his courage, but files a writ petition in the High Court challenging his suspension order. After a minimal enquiry the court passes severe strictures against the callous action of the minister and the government, and passes an order that Lakana should be reinstated in his position in the same town. Accordingly Lakana reports himself to duty and continues his sincere work. After a few days he is promoted to the post of Assistant Commissioner and transferred to Mandya.

Though Lakana is happy about his promotion and transfer, his wife Taniyaru is not happy at all. As her bouts of depression increase, she starts taking the sleeping pills without her husband's knowledge and suffers from frequent fits of rage. Occasionally, she would weep for hours and sometimes even abuse and beat her child. There starts a quarrel between Lakana and his wife, which may be described as a conflict between skepticism and faith. Taniyaru attributes all her suffering – like her depression and having a crippled child – to her husband's skepticism, "This is the result of your hatred of the spirits. You lost your mother, you turned me into a mental patient, my child became a cripple, and now we have to move to a strange place – all because of your lack of faith in god and spirits" (P.192). Although Lakana reasons with her from his agnostic point of view, Taniyaru does not accept it, because she has her own bitter and painful experience of life."Everyday in the morning, Taniyaru would experience intense pain as though she was being bitten by scores of scorpions all over her body, as though she was being struck by numerous arrows coming from different directions. She had to free herself from such pain at any cost" (P.194)

Lakana has spent all his time in discharging his professional duty and neglected his wife and home. It is only now that he understands his wife's terrible loneliness and the 'household syndrome.' That is why he obliges his wife for the first time in his life and takes her to Padiyuru in his car before joining his new post as Assistant Commissioner at Mandya. He looks at life now from his wife's perspective. "Now, it was Taniyaru, who was Lakana's teacher; she was the rainbow ushering in a new awareness, and his life, freed from his own self-centred black clouds, began to sight a new horizon" (P.196).

When Lakana and Taniyaru reach their village and stay with Aitha in the parental home, Lakana realizes the pleasures of a joint family, which has been slowly disappearing in the modern days. Lakana's son Shyama sleeps happily between Aitha and Chennu, while Aitha's son Somu sleeps soundly in the arms of Lakana and Taniyaru. "The question of who were whose parents appeared inconsequential in the moonlight that had serenely spread everywhere" (P.201). Although the life styles of the two brothers have changed from each other conspicuously, they realize the pleasures of family reunion and hope for frequent opportunities of coming together. Taniyaru feels very cozy and satisfied in the traditional atmosphere. One morning Aitha carries Shyama to the shrine near the river by the side of the banyan tree. He applies the juice of some plant on the child's body and dips the child in the water thrice. Taniyaru, who has followed Aitha silently, screams in fear. But as she sees Aitha take the child to the shrine, rolls on the ground three times as part of the ritual and worships the spirit, Taniyaru is disarmed by Aitha's attachment to her child and consequently she develops great respect and admiration for her husband's elder brother,

> Having reached the shrine, Aitha, holding on to the child, rolled on the ground three times as part of his service to the spirit. Still the child was not scared. Aitha stood in front of the spirit, the child in his arms and his eyes closed, and prayed to the spirit silently. Then he worshipped the spirit, took from the priest what was given to him as a token of the spirit's

> grace, ate it and made the child eat it as well. When he turned to return home, Taniyaru ran up to him and prostrated herself before him (P.203).

Aitha feels rather embarrassed by Taniyaru's prostration and requests her, "Please don't do this. You, the wife of my elder brother, are like a mother to me. Please get up" (P.203). But Taniyaru is overwhelmed with a sense of gratitude and considers Aitha to be the spirit himself. Her faith in the traditional religion is reinforced. Then Aitha consoles her, "Be patient. This cripple-state of your child is only temporary. By the grace of Kodimanittaaya, he will be free from it, just as a lotus opens itself as soon as the rays of the sun touch it" (P.203). Taniyaru tells Aitha, "I will not leave this place until the child is cured. I have come here with this firm resolve" (P.204). But Aitha's advice to her opens her eyes and gives her a new realization of her husband's role in the society, "Don't behave in such a manner. Lakana's work is also a form of worship; he hopes to glimpse truth through his service to society. Our goals are the same. While I seek god in the symbol of the spirit, he seeks god in his duty and service. The only difference between us is that his work is greater because his world is bigger than mine. You have to be with him always and you shouldn't disturb his peace of mind. If you do, I may not succeed in my endeavour" (P.204). His advice enables Taniyaru to understand her husband's greatness and nobility and her respect for her husband increases suddenly, as a consequence of her repentance over her folly, "As she neared her husband, Taniyaru tightly clasped his hands and leaning against his chest, sobbed, 'I have erred. I didn't understand you, and hence, not only did I suffer, but I made you suffer as well'" (P.204).

Now Lakana and Taniyaru begin to look at life from a fresh perspective. Aitha's advice to Lakana comes from the bottom of his heart and is deeply philosophical, "Brother, you and your wife can leave for Mandya today itself. Your place of work is Mandya; there is not much you can do here. Now, consider this: our life-span is woefully short; in this short period, whatever we can do for people in general and the degree to which we enrich their lives – that is the only thing, which survives us" (P.205). Thus there is a sort of mutual recognition of and transformation between tradition and modernity. Just as Lakana realizes the importance of traditional life, Aitha recognizes the importance of modern life. Then both the brothers exchange their sons for looking after them. Lakana's son Shyama is left with Aitha, and Aitha's son Somu is taken by Lakana. "Lakana and Taniyaru were overcome with emotion in the presence of those two great souls. They fell dwarfed by their love and attachment" (P.205). Lakana and Taniyaru feel a great sense of satisfaction from the reinforcement of human bondage. They leave happily for Mandya.

After reporting to duty as Assistant Commissioner of Mandya, Lakana participates in the festival of folk performances organized by the Kannada and Culture Department. Prof. Neelakanthappa, an expert folklorist, stresses the need for revival of the folk arts. But Lakana expresses his frank views in his concluding speech. He says, "These folk arts have been exploiting the lower classes and Dalits for centuries together. However, they have masked their social behaviour and various forms of exploitation with paints and clothes, and they have maintained them by calling them dance, ritual and art. It is wrong to glorify these arts" (P.209). Prof. Neelakanthappa admires Lakana's realistic views about the folk arts.

Lakana has a depressing experience when he sees the houses of Dalits being burnt to ashes. He pacifies the crowds and makes arrangements to send all the wounded Dalits to the nearby hospitals. After a short while he witnesses the clash between upper caste people and Dalits finally resulting in police firing. When the upper caste youth begin to pelt stones at Dalit youths and the police force, a few policemen and youths are hurt. "The enraged policemen, without giving any preliminary warning, opened fire. Within a few seconds, about fifteen Dalits and a few policemen, including a Sub-Inspector, had died. Within no time all the Dalit houses were set on fire and there was awful commotion everywhere" (P.213).

Lakana is deeply disturbed by the unhappy communal clash. He begins to brood seriously about the yawning gap between the upper caste/class and the lower caste/class people and the consequent clashes, hatred and misunderstanding. He could not arrest any of the perpetrators of violence as the whole thing was attributed by the authorities to mob hysteria: "There were many occasions on which Lakana had to accept defeat, but he never went against his conscience and weakly surrendered to them" (P.216). Once Mailarayya, a leader of Dalit Sangharsha Samiti meets him and asks him to join the association of officers belonging to scheduled castes as a member by contributing two percent of his salary as membership fee. But Lakana suspects it to be an open invitation for corruption. He tells him frankly, "If we begin such a movement, we will be corrupting honest officers also. No problem can be solved through publicity, processions and press statements" (P.217). He tells Mailarayya further that struggling for eighteen percent reservation in legislature and administration will not help them have permanent power. He accuses his own people of distancing themselves completely from the community that trusts them. But Mailarayya comments on his ideas, "But your objectives are too remote and too Utopian" (P.218). But Lakana conveys his clear vision to him, "Self-help, self-respect and acquisition of knowledge – these have to be our immediate concerns" (P.218). He insists that Dalits should develop legal consciousness, and extend it to the other members of their community, but they do not do it at all. "This is the tragedy of our community and other marginalized communities" (P.221). Lakana speaks like a visionary when he says that the Dalits should have their goals clearly defined and that their society needs a major surgery.

As some years go by, Lakana and Taniyaru grow ripe with the experience of life and look at life from a broader perspective. "Lakana's voice also has undergone recognizable changes, it does not have now its earlier harshness and shrillness... Lakana has now learnt to possess many different voices – those of his duty to the government, love of a husband, affection of a father, and concern of an elder brother – and still harmonize them" (P.224). Similarly Taniyaru has regained her gusto for life. She loves and respects her husband for his conscientious behavior, worships Panjurli, and teaches the traditional arts of the Pambada community to the children in the neighbourhood. Thus, there is a kind of reconciliation between husband and wife and between their agnosticism and faith respectively.

Thomu, the youngest daughter of Maire completes her elementary school education in the village and wants to continue it further in the city, but Maire pressurizes her to get married. Finally she is married off to a young man called Angara, much against her wish and will. In the patriarchal society a bride has no choice to select her husband, but she has to accept a man selected and approved by the parents. Thomu is no exception to this patriarchal rule at least initially. But as days go by, Thomu's real nature reveals itself clearly. Temperamentally there is a similarity between Thomu and her brother Lakana in that both of them protest against the tradition sooner or later. Thomu's marriage with Angara turns out to be a mismatch, as there is no temperamental compatibility between the two. She has voluntarily learnt a bit of dance by observing her father and other bhuta-impersonators. She has developed an artistic sensibility and is deeply interested in singing and paiting. But on the contrary her husband Angara, being just a casual labourer, cannot appreciate her art as it is beyond his comprehension. When people appreciate her songs and paintings, he grows suspicious about her character. Being a beast, he considers her art as redundant and inconvenient to him. He destroys her painting tools and objects to her singing. He becomes an alcoholic and starts beating her. On top of that, he degenerates into a womanizer. Thomu confirms her suspicion about him when once she sees him in the arms of another woman. Finally she realizes that far from being a loving husband, he is only a wild beast.

Now that Thomu has discovered her identity through the bitter experiences with her drunkard husband, she decides to discontinue her life with him. She, thus, becomes a modern woman, who can live independently without a husband. For her bold decision, she draws inspiration from the pad-dana or narrative about Siri, the first woman to rebel against patriarchy. Thomu's awakening of self-respect is admirable. She enjoys the moral support of her brother, Lakana. Consequently she takes a bold decision and walks away from her husband for good.

Lakana takes Thomu not to the native village, Padiyur, but to Susheela, a dynamic activist in the women's movement in Bangalore. Guided by Susheela, Thomu joins a high school and pursues her interest in music, dance and painting. Later with the help of Lakana, she joins a college for a B.A Degree. Gradually she develops her musical talent to a great extent, presents folk dances like kanyaapu, trains the members of her own troupe in folk songs and folk dances. She realizes her potentiality to a great extent, consolidates her identity and shapes her career meaningfully. "In the college atmosphere, Thomu was a singing cuckoo, a dancing peacock and occasionally a roaring tigress. As a student of science, she absorbed the precision of logic and the force of arguments based on evidence, which gave her words the sharpness of a knife and the sudden flash of lightning" (P.107). After the completion of her B.A. Degree, she joins a law college, makes a steady progress and takes special interest in the problems of women, dalits and rural people. Soon after graduating from Law College, she begins to practise as a lawyer and takes special interest in the cases of the poor and women. "Even here she was different from others: she would not accept the briefs of rich clients. Her clientele consisted of only the poor and women. Owning to the Land Reforms Act, a large amount of litigations on behalf of former tenants began to enter the court, and most of such cases, on behalf of the tenants, would have Thomu as their advocate" (P.110). Thus she dedicates her legal career for the betterment of poor and helpless people thereby rendering her service to the society.

When Cheluvayya Shetty wants to buy his land back from the tenant, Buda Mulya for Rs. 15000/- and manages to get him arrested, many shameless lawyers help him to do so. Buda Mulya is so helpless that he can have neither the court nor the lawyers to help him. But Thomu, who has set up her office at Karkala, recently, takes up Buda Mulya's case. She gets him released on bail and succeeds in getting the injunction quashed. As a result she incurs the wrath of other lawyers. A few strangers raid her office and break all the furniture. One day a bog lorry is made to collide with the riksaw in which she is moving. On some other occasion a hired murderer sneaks into her house and alerts her to be careful and refuses to murder her because of his respect for her and her social concern. But Thomu survives all attempts on her life and continues to fight for justice.

After some time Cheluvayya Shetty and his gang of goondas murder Buda Mulya and sever an arm of Korapolu (wife of Buda Mulya) and burn Maire to death. Now the criminal tries to escape. But Thomu lodges two complaints in the Magistrate's court under CRPC 200. One complaint is on behalf of Korapolu and another, on behalf of Aitha. The Magistrate happens to be an honest and upright officer, who never succumbs to any kind of pressure. The very next day he posts the case as per CRPC 202, for preliminary hearing. The news spreads immediately like an electric flash. That night a stranger meets the Magistrate privately and tries to offer a bride of five lakhs rupees for not admitting the case. But the Magistrate does not yield to the temptation. Then the Inspector of Police, Hemant meets the Magistrate and alerts him to handle the case of Chelvayya Shetty with extreme care. But the magistrate reminds him of his own duty and silences him.

On the day of preliminary hearing, Thomu pleads with the judge to admit the case, record all of their statements, to issue an arrest warrant against Cheluvayya Shetty and to hand over the case to the COD, or to get the investigation conducted by the court itself. Within half an hour or so the Superintendent of Police, the Deputy Commissioner, the Public Prosecutor and some legal experts enter the court to defend the criminals by their intervention. But Thomu opposes their intervention strongly. She insists that the statements of the complaint should be recorded. She pleads further,

> I have come here with the hope that I can get justice here and I know the price of justice and truth. This tahsildar here has been suspended because he stood for truth; Aitha Pambada lost his mother only because he upheld what was just and right. Buda Mulya lost his life because he fought for the land that was rightfully his under the Tenancy Act and his wife, Korapolu, has lost her hand. How many more lives and limbs of innocent people does the government desire? Let the public prosecutor clarify this. I am aware that the gigantic arms of corruption have embraced most people; I implore that the sword of law should cut off those hands. There is neither tomorrow nor yesterday for this urgent task – it has to be done now, and at this moment. This is my plea (P.182).

The public prosecutor, two other lawyers, Chinnappa and Dejappa Shetty try to intervene unnecessarily and influence the magistrate not to admit the case. But the magistrate, being a man of sterling morality and uprightness, can see through the corruption of hired defenders of the criminal. He, therefore, admits the case and gives his justification as follows:

> The police officers, who have intentionally ground the wheel of law to a halt, are also deemed to be active accomplices of such an act. In fact, this is a clear instance of police inaction. Hence I have admitted this case as per the provisions of section 204 of CRPC. Having admitted this case, I order that Cheluvayya Shetty and the concerned police officers of this district be served non-bailable arrest warrants and that they be produced in the court at the time of the next hearing (P.190).

The gang of criminals is shocked and surprised by the magistrate's admission of the case. But Thomu is thrilled to the core to have achieved a tremendous victory, which reinforces her faith in the judiciary because of such rare magistrates of strong morals.

Thomu continues her lawyer's profession by devoting her time to help the poor women and *dalits* seeking justice. "Alone. She is moving forward like the River Nandini, jumping over boulders and rocks and cutting through jungles and forests. Thomu's voice is the voice of protest against injustice, and empathy for those seeking justice" (P.225). She can argue forcefully on behalf of the women, who are subjected to male atrocities. She becomes an active member of an organization called Naari (Women) and volunteers to help the helpless women. Being a dedicated soul she is neither interested in nor worried about marriage, although she can caress and play affectionately with her nephews. In addition to these, she is also an artist, who sings only the songs of protest and resistance. Thus, Thomu has given up the traditional way of life and chosen the modern way of life. Being educated in law, she has led a life of dedication. She has shown the courage of remaining single as a divorcee without depending upon any man or lover and fulfilled her dream of becoming an artiste. She has actualized her potentiality, achieved and asserted her identity and attained a sense of fulfillment in spite of her frustration at the initial stage of her married life. She has been a real practitioner of feminist self-reliance without unnecessarily tom-toming about it — a fact that is more than admirable.

The Edge of Time, thus, offers three different ways of life followed by the three members of the same family traditionally connected with *bhuta*-worship. *Tembare* or the drum symbolizes the ritual of possession-dance. Though all the three of them follow their own paths – of conformity (like Aitha) or of protest (like Lakana and Thomu) they have to face the inevitable challenges and hazards indigenous to their chosen professions, apparently caused by upper caste and class people and their selfishness but at a deeper level by their fate.

Veerappa Moily deserves our congratulations for giving such a beautiful provincial and ethnic novel richly textured with Tulu culture, which includes their rituals, songs, dances, oral epics, beliefs and superstitions etc. The novel captures the ethos of Tulu Nadu in its transitional period in which tradition and modernity collide and complement each other paradoxically. One is easily reminded of Chinua Achebe's *Arrow of God* as far as the conflict between religiosity and secularism is concerned. The novelist has offered an insider's picture of the life of the subaltern category of *bhuta*-worshippers, which comes like a fresh wind in the Indian fiction, as it brings the marginal group to the center-stage and decentres the Brahmanic hegemony in the realm of letters. It highlights the experience of *dalits*, which is conspicuously opposed to that of the upper caste Hindus of India.

In this sense it is indubitably a novel of social realism with a strong dose of ameliorative intention. Veerappa Moily, who hails from the subaltern section of Indian (Karnataka) society, happens to be a lawyer by training and a politician by profession and a social reformer by vocation, has written this novel with a consciousness of his social agenda. He has employed the technique of omniscient point of view and chronological narration in the novel. The narration is generally fast and has a mixture of (the present) experience and (the past) memories of characters. The stress is more on the socio-political than on the psychological aspect of life. That explains the reason why Veerappa Moily, the socio-political leader sometimes tries to override the novelist in him by his unwanted authorial interventions, pontification and generalizations about the evils of Indian, Hindu caste system. Instead of leaving the narrated experience to the judgement of the reader, Veerappa Moily begins to offer his satirical, general and didactic remarks in-between the narration thereby hindering the flow of particularized experience. That is why a perceptive critic like A. A. Mutalik Desai asks a question, "Is Moily's

The Edge of Time a novel? Do his efforts contribute more anthropologically and socio-economically? Is the author engaged sufficiently as a man of creative literature?"[6] One wishes at least the so-called copy-editor of Rupa & Co had scissored off such interfering remarks from the otherwise facile narration.

Although the novelist has offered a very detailed realistic and ethnic picture of Tulu culture, including its sub-castes, he fights shy of mentioning the exact caste of the owner of the rice mill, Girijapati and the local minister at Basavakalyana. He only mentions that the man belongs to the upper caste. One wonders why the novelist should have the fear of mentioning the name of the community in an ethnic novel? One may easily guess that he is referring to the Lingayat community, but that he has no courage to hurt the feelings of the people of the said community. The novel cannot be half ethnic and half neutral, hence colourless.

The Edge of Time translated by Dr. C.N.Ramachandran from the Kannada novel, *Tembare* is a very significant contribution to the realm of Indian Literature in English Translation. But one wonders why the translator has used the cheap Hindi film-type of spellings for elongated vowel sounds like 'Kodimanittaaya', or 'Aarati' instead of using the internationally recognized diacritical marks. One wonders what the publishers and their editors must be doing with their ignorance and indifference to the conventions of publishing. But such minor irritants do not diminish the bewitching beauty of the translation. Dr. C. N. Ramachandran deserves our congratulations for liberating the local text from the regional bondage releasing it into the global realm of letters thereby giving it an opportunity of international recognition.

WORKS CONSULTED

1. Moily, M. Veerappa, *The Edge of Time*, Tr. C. N. Ramachandran. New Delhi: Rupa & Co. 2006. (All the page references are to this edition.)
2. Claus. Peter J. "Ritual Transforms a Myth" in Kumar and the *Siri* Myth/Ritual. hmt. P.1.
3. Claus. Peter J. "Variability in the Tulu Paddanas," in Gundert-m.htm P.1.

4. Lewis. I.M. *Ecstatic Religion.* Harmondsworth: Penguin Books Ltd. 1971. P.32.
5. *Ibid.* P. 114.
6. Mutalik-Desai. A.A. Review of *Tmbare* in *Deccan Herald.* Bangalore. 22 April 2008

20

Journey of Soul towards the Supreme in the Poetry of Sant Kabir

Swatantra Asija

Sant Kabir, popularly known as Kabir Saheb, was a fifteenth century sage, social reformer, spiritual guide and poet. He was also the founder of a sect known as the "Kabir Panth". In the religious history of India, Kabir is a unique figure as Ch. Vaudeville also comments:

> ...to the Hindus, he is a Vaisnava *bhakta*, to the Muslims a *pir*, to the Sikhs a *bhagat,* to the sectarian Kabir-panthis, an *avatar* of the Supreme Being; to modern patriots, Kabir is the champion of Hindu-Muslim unity, to neo-vedantins a promoter of the Universal Religion or the Religion of Man...[1]

The appeal of Kabir's poetry makes him close to the people of every sect. Hence, the journey of soul towards the Supreme unfolded in the poetry of Kabir reflects the different facets seen by every individual beyond the discrimination of caste, creed and sex. The study of this path in the poetry of Kabir can be outlined in six stages as given below:

1. Awakening of the Self
2. Purgation : the state of search and effort
3. Illumination : a glimpse of unification
4. Dark Night of soul : the state of purification
5. Pre-phase of union
6. Unification

Awakening of the Self

Leaving aside the exceptional cases, it can be commented that the journey of every mystic begins with an ardent inquisitiveness to know the Real. While leading an ordinary life in this world and enjoying worldly pleasure, there comes a juncture when the soul becomes conscious of some higher reality and perennial pleasure and the search for the Ultimate Reality begins. This consciousness must also be taken as the benevolence of the Almighty. With His grace Kabir becomes aware of the darkness and dimmers of the world and strives for the shelter of the Almighty. The poet avows:

> All my life, I saw for myself,
> Whole of world is dark and dim,
> Says Kabir, do take shelter of God
> You shall not return earthward again.[2]

This consciousness leads the soul to search for a real guru (guide). There is a dire need of real guru (guide) and a deserving disciple for attaining substantial spiritual gains or the apple cart of aspirations may be upset. Kabir says:

> When his Guru is blind, what can the disciple do?
> The blind urges on the blind, both fall into the well.[3]

The essential factor to kindle the spiritual spark in the heart is love and it is the guru who bestows this element to the soul. Kabir got devotional love and Rama-Rasayan (spiritual wine) through his guide to whom he ever remained indebted. In fact, the soul is awakened with the help of Guru only. When he gives a mantra (incantation) to his disciple, he inclines towards the search of reality. He gets the ability to discriminate between various contradictory objects, i.e. *sat* and *asat* (truth and falsehood), the Real and the unreal, pleasure and pain, eternity and transitoriness, etc. This state is characterized in the poetry of Kabir through his pronouncement that the light of knowledge bestowed by the guru made him follow the right path by renunciating the path of evil.

The grace of Guru (guide) awakens the soul and starts considering Govind (Lord) as the only reality. In this way guru, who works as a mediator between the soul and God, finally brings about their union. That is why, Kabir considers guru greater than even Govind

(Lord). It is only by virtue of his kindness that the soul identifies the illusive nature of *Maya* (worldly illusion). Man, under the effect of illusion and ignorance, is like a moth making continuous bids to mount the lamp of *Maya* and meets his fatal end, i.e., death. The thought of death makes Kabir's soul restless as he takes cognizance of wasting precious life in worthless deeds. His highly worried heart makes him raise a query:

> When will you start
> Meditating the Almighty Lord,
> ....
> In play with friends you spent your childhood
> In youth a prey to lust
> In old age weakness overtook you
> Lost your heydays all.
> Lost sight that body is all false
> And death was the certain end;
> Says Kabir, do listen all wise men
> Forget not your transience here.[4]

Being awakened, Kabir intends to enlighten others too. He utters:

> O visitor, do wake up !
> Why are you so much in slumber?
> You have yet to go far my friend
> Do not lose your senses sleeping![5]

Purgation: the state of search and effort

Mystics have been recognized as the highest saviours of the world. The contention is based on perhaps the preaching nature of mystics who, after attaining perfect knowledge, develop this attitude in them. On the one hand, they construe the transcience of this world, and, on the other side, they put emphasis upon rectitude. Kabir firmly believes that by abnegating *kama* (sensual pleasure), *krodh* (anger), *trishna* (craving), one can certainly meet the Almighty.

Since there is no certain device which can be used for the purification of self, every individual adopts a different path for it. Instead of emphasizing any theory in particular, Kabir talks about morality in this regard. He tells us about the advantages of *satsangti*, i.e., good company, which is always essential as it definitely casts its inescapable effect upon an individual. It transforms a man into an individual with *sanmati* (good sense). In one of his couplets, he tells us that it is the power of *satsangati* (good company) that changes even a neem (the margosa tree) plant into a sandal tree.

> Says Kabir, the company of the saint
> Never goes in vain
> Bitter "neem" near sandal plant
> Becomes sandal, not "neem" again.[6]

The outer objects of the world exert a tantalizing impact upon an individual while the attainment of the goal of mystic journey is possible only by controlling the senses. Kabir tells us that only through the slow and steady pursuit of devotion; man can be one with the Supreme. The process of taming the senses is very difficult and Kabir prescribes *prapatti* i.e., elusive devotion, the easiest way to attain this end. He says that we should abnegate all the doubts of the heart and start *bhajan*—chanting devotional songs which make us seek the grace of the Supreme. It is the utter humility of Kabir that he views himself as the 'dog' of Rama as a mark of his deep devotion.

Knowledge is also an important factor in this regard. Without a dust storm of knowledge, the shade of doubts can never be dispelled. Knowledge facilitates an individual with the capability of listening to *anahadnad* (a particular sound that is heard during the journey of consciousness) which drives off *trishna* (craving). Besides the importance of knowledge, Kabir also lays stress on the importance of devotional love, which he terms as a heaven for all the *bhaktas* (devotees). All these ways are like the small tributaries flowing towards the main river of yoga and love which are the most effective and significant elements of Kabir's emotiveness.

Love is such an essential factor of Kabir's life and poetry that he compares a heart without love with a graveyard. Again he says that it is like a piece of flesh in the house of a blacksmith. Love purifies the soul enabling an individual to attain perpetual pleasure and peace. Like *Sufis* (a sect of Muslim saints), Kabir emphasizes the significance of virtuous love and maintains that life without love is futile.

The summit of love-based devotion can be viewed in the form of marital love which is expressed through various symbols by Kabir in his poetry. There is an abundant use of such symbolic expressions of love in Kabir's poetry. "Young bride!/ do sing the welcome song",[7] "O my love! Do come to my hut"[8] and "The Lord is my Love, O friend/ Lord Hari is my Love"[9] are some of the beautiful symbols expressing mystic love. As a lover, Kabir also values and deeply understands the prick of separation. Various inner states like love's insatiety, aspiration, agitation, guilt, helplessness, doubts, oblivion, pleasure and pain, etc. have been penetrated minutely in Kabir's poetry.

The ideal of his love is *sati* (a loyal woman) and *sura* (a brave man) whose qualities are elaborated in his poetry. It is expressed through symbols and metaphors. His love is filled with intoxication, enchantment and fascination at the same time; it also requires the spirit of extreme sacrifice and penance, deep devotion and complete surrender. He does not consider love a child's game and says that only a fellow, who has prepared himself for rigorous devotion, can enter the house of love. Kabir utters:

> Kabir this is love's house dear
> Not house of aunt
> Only who doth his head surrender
> Can enter the house, others not.[10]

In the path of this love man has to fight the evil forces enforcing the vitiating effect of senses. A fellow possessing the attributes of a chaste and loyal woman, will emerge victorious in this battle of love which requires knowledge coupled with devotional love. A true devotee wishes to sacrifice all that he possesses. The fear of deatn cannot frighten him owing to his intense urge to attain the supreme pleasure after death. Like a *sati* when a devotee's heart becomes fully engrossed in the Almighty, the difference between the two vanishes. Kabir depicts his devotion, purity and penance-based quality of love towards the Ultimate. Indeed, his love is ineffable and pure.

Another important way of self-purification propounded by Kabir can be viewed through yoga. The literal meaning of the term yoga is 'to add up' or 'to unite'. Thus the spiritual or physical devotion,through which the soul is united with the Supreme, is yoga. It is considered successful when the soul, eradicating the impressions of Maya on it, comes to understand the ultimate truth and absorbs in the Almighty through *samadhi* (meditation).

There are various kinds of yoga, viz, *Jnanayoga, Rajyoga, Hathyoga, Mantrayoga, Karmayoga,* etc. (different practices of yoga leading to unification with the Ultimate through knowledge, concentration, corporeal discipline, remembering the Lord and detached actions respectively) which are different ways of attaining the same secret goal. Through the gradual increase of knowledge, the soul becomes oblivious of its existence and the prick of separation is increased. It views the Almighty in every particle of the universe. Thus both attain unexplainable unity which is *Jnanayoga*.

In *Karmayoga*, the soul mingles with the Supreme through the deeds done with *nishkam bhav,* i.e., detached feelings. *Mantrayoga* denotes that through regular remembrance of God or regularly chanting a particular line in His praise, the soul absorbs in Him through *dhyan*, i.e., speculation. The way of unification through controlling body organs and breath and transacting them in an appropriate way is known as *Hathyoga*. According to *Rajyoga,* unification with the Supreme can be attained through constant concentration on the Divine Light. In fact, *Hathyoga* and *Rajyoga* are inter related as it is essential to control body organs (theory of *Hathyoga*) to tame the heart (theory of *Rajyoga*).

All the ways of unification of the soul and the Supreme mentioned above are directly or indirectly embodied in Kabir's poetry. Therefore, it reveals the impact of the various exercises of *yoga* to some extent on him, though there is no clear indication of the poet's adherence to any such theory in particular. Like an essence-taker, Kabir extracted useful things from different theories and evolved a new system which may be known as project whose purpose is to provide an innate or natural tendency to the heart, mind and soul making them free from all illusions. Kabir's early poetry tells us that in the beginning he was definitely impressed by *Hathyoga* (stoic theory) which was a popular methodology adopted by most of the sages at this time.

He stresses on the spiritual bath at a three-dimensional place where *ida, pingla* and *sushmna* (three important nerves) conjoin. He says "Mind bathes at the meeting point of three nerves (nadis), viz. the *ida, pingla* and *sushmna* and sees the one unperceivable Absolute".[11]

Describing the way of the soul's elevation, Kabir says, "Sun (breath of right nostril) got absorbed in Moon (breath of left nostril) and lastly both made one house i.e., entered in Sushumna".[12] Kabir further holds:

> O Avadhu! make thy residence in the firmament Where there is always rain of nectar and enjoy bliss by drinking it through back passage and by pressing the middle point of body between the anus and scrotum (performing *moolbandha*). *Tadagi-Mudra* is created and the vital airs have all gone to the brain (sky) and the *sushmna* has become active by the fire kindled by burning sex-passion (*kama*) and anger (krodh) and the serpent power (*Jogin or Kundalini*) has been aroused. Mind stuff has been restrained and is in the main market now calmly enjoying the taste of nectar. The unbeaten sound has begun and all the doubts are removed.[13]

In this way, Kabir's relationship with the theories of asceticism cannot be ignored. But a deep study of his poetry tells us that he judged the inappropriateness of *hathyoga* (stoic theory) and left it very soon. At this juncture, he added the concept of love to yoga. Assigning a better place to love-devotion than stoic theories, Kabir propounded a new theory of love-devotion with the help of complete single-minded devotion and brought out its simple form for the betterment of the masses.

As soon as, Kabir moved ahead on the path of obscure unity with the Almighty through devotional love, he became disinterested in the piercing technique of *chakras* (cardinal plexus) of *hathyoga* (asetic theory) and its various ostentations. Here, Kabir propounded the theory of *Shabd Surat Yoga* (a kind of yoga in which the spirit has to be united with the *anhadnad* (a particular sound heard during the journey of consciousness) of its inner self which arises continuously in it). This was the stage when Kabir detached himself completely from *Hathyoga.* In this way, "starting from *ingla-pingla* and passing through *aasan* and *pranayam*, Kabir concentrated on *trikuti* and attained the stage of Mantra Yoga".[14] At this point he emphasized the importance of *ajapjap* (a natural way of remembering Lord wherein neither the tongue nor the lips move nor any sound is produced in it) and *sumiran* (reciting the name of Lord) which are very close to *Sahaj Yoga* (a kind of yoga that puts emphasis on steady conversion of sensual pleasures instead of the subjugation of senses). Considering *Sahaj Yoga* as the best mode of concentration and contemplation, Kabir suggests, "O Sadhu, / In a simple manner cleanse yourself".[15]

Sahaj Yoga is a kind of yoga in which a devotee does not need to make undesirable efforts to meet Him. In Kabir's *sahaj yoga*, there is no need of suppression or oppression of senses. It is known as *sahaj* because every moment man can devote himself to Rama, the deity. While performing worldly duties, man does not forget or become oblivious of the Supreme. This is the easiest form of yoga in which emphasis is laid on the taming of the heart and the senses.

If we try to establish a relationship between Kabir's poetry and various theories of *yoga* of his age, it can be stated that neither the *Yogasutra* of Patanjali nor *Shivsahita* nor Hathyoga Pradeepika will suffice to provide a clue to a proper understanding of Kabir's yoga philosophy as none of them has touched the height of Kabir's love. Indeed, Kabir's concept of yoga is much related to devotional yoga of Guru Gorakhnath (Head of Nathpanth) which too lacks in that tender, melodious touch of love which is easily detectible in Kabir. Thus Kabir's yoga is a beautiful blend of various yogic theories culminating into his own theory which can aptly be termed as *bhakti-yoga* (devotional yoga).

Kabir's yoga seems to have undergone a continuous change as it journeyed a long distance from "*Hathyoga* to *Layayoga*, from *Layayoga* to *Sahaj yoga* and from *Sahaj yoga* to *Mantra yoga*. Again this *Mantra yoga* is developed as *Sahaj yoga* and at last it was termed as *Bhakti Yoga*."[16] In this way, Kabir's poetry brings forward numberless ways of purification of the self, yet the most significant among them all is his devotional love. He avows:

> Shed all your doubts and strife of mind
> Take the Lord's Name with love-devotion
> Salvation will be yours for ever.[17]

Illumination: a glimpse of unification

The stage of purgation mentioned in the preceding pages is not only a gateway to the illumination of the soul and the self but also an ascending to the divine aura. Kabir is dazzled to have a sight of the eternal light. He perceives the place of his Lord illumined without the sun or the moon. There is "no beginning nor middle nor end" to that region. Neither death nor disease nor any other calamity exists there. Kabir delineates:

> There is no land or sky there
> Nor Sun or Moon in that country,
> ....
> With eternal brilliance is that land lighted;
> ....
> There is no beginning nor middle nor end
> Nor death or disease exist at all; [18]

Kabir is thrilled to envision the light hovering all around. In his attempt to explicate the lusture of the Lord, he compares it with "a million suns". :

> A million suns are ablaze with light,
> The sea of blue spreads in the sky,
> ....
> Rains pour down without water, and
> the rivers are streams of light.[19]

Having a glance of that splendid region through meditation, Kabir believes that each and everything of the universe can be viewed in the body itself, but it is essential to be blessed with the grace of *Guru* and shun the five distortions. Kabir sketches a beautiful picture of the presence of *brahmand in pind,* i.e., the reflection of the universe viewed in the body.

> In this body is the celestial park
> And therein the Lord Almighty !
> In this body are the seven seas
> And all the nine lakh stars;
> In this body are all gems and diamonds
> And the tester thereof too.
> Here the celestial music swells
> Springs gush here everywhere.[20]

The spiritualistic magnetism blended here is termed as Kabir's illumination in which nothing else but only silvery encircling remains between the yogi in Kabir and the targeted penetration of point. This mystic allurement brings the poet close to the unification along with the brightest floating of the highest stream of consciousness. Here lies the glory of all the stages ascended by a devotee in order to attain *sahaj samadhi* and bathe in the rays of the illumined inward glory. While being at this stage, the devotee automatically recognizes its spiritual identity: though, on the other hand, the worldly existence prevails as such. To Kabir, this is the stage, wherein a new span of mystic experiences starts expanding and a unique and highly subjective leading towards the "Dark Night of soul" begins.

Dark Night of Soul

The state of pleasure and joy attained through constant contemplation under the stage of illumination, does not last long as, at times, it is disturbed by the interception of *Maya* (worldly illusion). Kabir describes *Maya* in various peculiar terms. He depicts it as a wicked lady with the five distortions, *i.e., kama (desire), krodh (anger), moh (attachment), lobh (greed), ahankar (ego)* as her sons who make everybody dance to their tunes. *Maya* ensnares a man in various ways. She entraps all the human beings, but is afraid of saints who cause a crushing defeat to her in most of the cases. Even if she somehow succeeds in entangling them, she has to leave the scene because of the *Guru's* scare.

When *Maya* impels a devotee away from partial experiences, he becomes restless due to the anguish of separation. In fact, the element of separation is a significant factor in the devotion of a mystic. While expounding its significance, Kabir asserts that *virah* (prick of separation) of God should not be equated with the *virah* of this world as this *virah* (separation from God) in itself is a form of Lord. The poet personifies the *virah* and depicts it giving command in the following manner:

"Biraha" calls out to Kabir and says
Don't you leave me alone
I will take you within the Lord's rays
And leave you on your own.[21]

Therefore, the anguish of *virah* should not be condemned. *Virah,* the purifier of a man's soul, is the easiest way to attain the Almighty while leaning towards worldly pleasures lead him astray from the path. That is why a real devotee considers it better to renunciate the worldly involvements and absorb himself in the service of the Supreme even during the phase of separation. Without weeping or crying, a devotee can never attain his Rama, i.e., the Lord.

Kabir depicts this stage of soul in a very effective language. Each state of a separated soul, i.e., agitation, filthiness, quivering, insanity, anxiety, annoyance, helplessness, perplexity, confusion and restlessness, etc., is penetrated minutely. Kabir's separated soul seeks information about Lover from every passenger. She addresses her Rama who has been the object of her concern for a long time. Her heart is restless and it craves for Him. Kabir can be seen making all possible efforts to meet his Rama or even for a glimpse of Him. He wishes to set himself ablaze so that the sky is covered with the smoke of his body and his Lover (Rama) may have pity on him and the agony of separation may be mitigated or removed completely through His Kindness.

In a very famous stanza, Kabir's soul complains to the Supreme that everybody considers her to be His wife but He does not care for her. He contends that there is no use of this kind of relationship between the lover and the beloved unless both are united:

> My body and mind are grieved
> for the want of Thee;
> O my Beloved ! come to my house.
> When people say I am Thy bride, I am
> ashamed; for I have not touched
> Thy heart with my heart.
> Then what is the love of mine ? I have
> no taste for food, I have no sleep;
> my heart is ever restless within
> door and without.
> As water is to the thirsty, so is the
> lover to the bride. Who is there
> that will carry my news to my
> Beloved ?
> Kabir is restless : he is dying for sight
> of Him.[22]

The use of language in the above lines though in translations clearly exhibits the intense agony and prick of separation. He has deployed this picture to denote the state of hope and wait.

The mere recognition of its enemies, i.e., the five distortions (*kama, krodh, etc.*) and *Maya* impels the soul to launch its spiritual battle against them. The devotee fixes the goal of his life to remove all the obstacles. At this juncture, all the doubts are dispelled and the devotee asserts firm faith in the Supreme. The soul wishes to attain victory over these enemies as it is the only source of attaining the everlasting oneness. Being inconsiderate of death, the soul views it as a source to attain the eternal pleasure.

Thus, on one hand the devotee wishes to absolve himself of the prick of separation, on the other side, he emerges victorious over his senses. Thereafter, he circumscribes the path of exclusive devotion with single-mindedness. Kabir seems to be familiar with the significance of this oneness which has been highly emphasized in the scriptures of ancient India. That is why, he also urges others to leave all the doubts and seek the shelter of the Almighty by remembering only Him. At the extreme of his devotion, Kabir finds himself as the slave to Lord Rama and wishes to be disposed of according to His desire. His heart, mind and soul are for Rama only.

Pre-phase of Union

In this way, owing to its victory over both *Maya (worldly* illusion) and the petty desires of this world and complete surrender to the Supreme, the soul succeeds in acquiring a proper position in the realms of the spiritual world. It is filled with the light of knowledge and becomes face-to-face with the enlightened Supernatural Power. "Millions of suns are shamed by the / radiance of a single hair of His / body".[23] He further contends that he catches a glimpse of light without the sun and the moon. The light which he perceives is infinite giving the impression of a constellation of suns, though it is not the point where the soul merges into the Supreme.

While respecting the Indian traditions and values, Kabir has not shown union without marriage. Hence, the preparation of marriage with the Supreme begins. During this stage, instead of seeking the house of her father, the soul craves for the husband's abode for her own betterment. The domain of her husband is splendid, while the only way leading to the husband's home is through *bhajan* (reciting the name of Lord). It is majestically kindled with the lunar and the solar lamps.

It is the state wherein *virhani* (the separated soul) dreams of her union with the Lord. In fact, assumption of love is more melodious and sweet than the union itself. Kabir has portrayed the inner state of the beloved in categorical terms when the soul thinks, "I am not able to understand how He will behave with me"[24], a fear, because of which she undergoes the trauma of tremendous shivering day and night.

There are numerous detailed references to the encounter between the soul and the Supreme in the works belonging to ancient Indian literature. With the *darshna* (holy glance) of the Almighty, the tissues of attachment are lacerated. All doubts become baseless and futile and the web of *karmas* (deeds) is dismantled. Kabir, too, depicts that with union of soul and the Almighty, the soul becomes blessed and it gets absorbed in the ocean of pleasure day and night.

Unification

The last stage in the journey of a mystic's life is that of unification. Kabir has put to use vigorous and virile language to reveal this state. With the help of symbols related to conjugal love, Kabir's expression becomes highly touching, striking, impressive and effective. The poet projects himself as a bride while he lends the status of a bridegroom to his Rama. Kabir does not forget referring to various rituals performed in marriage while describing it in his poetry. He deems himself to be a *dulhan,* i.e., bride, and says that they should chant benedictory recitations as Lord Rama has arrived at her place as husband. Imparting an extraordinary character to the union of the soul and the Supreme and considering it much different from an ordinary marriage, Kabir recounts it in a superb figurative language:

> Young bride
> do sing the welcome song !
> My Love has come to my hut today
> in procession of the elements five.
> He is my honoured guest tonight
> my youth and love are willing up
> I shall cling to Him to body and mind.
> My body I shall cause to be the altar
> where Brahman will chant the Vedas

and with my Love and I shall go round
the round
the sacred fire
to celebrate my wedding with Him !
Gods and goddesses and countless sages
Have come from far to see the wedding
Says Kabir – O my luck!
I am going to wed my dear Love
The Lord Supreme![25]

Thus, it is the initial stage of a soul's union with the Almighty where her friends (other souls) inspire her to be happy as Lord Rama Himself has come to wed her. The soul is overwhelmed with happiness because of the advent of her Rama and other distinguished and gracious guests. Even *Brahma* (the Creator) himself is chanting *mantras* (Vedic hymns). The soul enjoys the state of blessedness on her marriage with an immortal entity, i.e., God. Kabir's description denotes this union as strange and the soul gets an ineffable pleasure through it.

Adding another dimension to the spiritual marriage, Kabir maintains that, as the newly married soul is ignorant, she finds the path leading to union with the Ultimate absolutely different from the normal one. She also experiences that the path is difficult to tread. With many efforts she reaches there, but now her *ghunghat,* i.e., veil is an obstacle in the way of direct meeting. As the marriage is a spiritual one, the face veil is not cloth but of *karmas* (deeds) and illusions. Her friends prompt her, "Remove the veil / you will meet your gracious Lord."[26] In the end, the soul attains her love and it manifests its joy in terms of the following musical outburst :

I shall sing the welcome song
steeped in the Nectar of His Name
My Lord, my Love, He has come !
My heart is shinning in His glow
I shall place Him on the throne there.
My precious Love I have got today !
without my effort it is all His grace
my Love. my Ram put the consort's mark
on my face.[27]

In this way, Rama bestows his company to the soul irrespective of her undeserving efforts. Avowing her devotion to Him obsequiously, she implores Him to lend immortality to her love. She prays to the Supreme to dwell in the temple of her heart forever. In this way, after enjoying the taste of Nectar, the soul tries to make it everlasting. Thus this union comes up as a glorified one with the help of marital symbols.

After marriage, the soul gets absorbed in the Supreme and loses its individual identity. Monism or absence of duality is a very popular belief of almost all the religions. Kabir describes this monastic state through the symbol of drop and the ocean. As the drop loses its separate identity after merging into the ocean, in the same way, the soul loses its separate existence after meeting Him. In the poetry of Kabir, the absorption of individuality has been unfolded in numberless ways, yet its emotional description is marvellous and matchless. When the lover and the beloved are unified, there remains no difference between the two. If the Lover (Supreme) dies, the beloved (soul) will also die, otherwise she, like her Lover, will remain immortal. Since 'Hari' is immortal and universal, there is no question of the soul being subject to death. The poet elucidates that he will not die even if the whole world dies as he has got his Lord to bestow him immortality. Thus death can never take him away.

In this way, the poetry of Sant Kabir brings forth varied stages of soul's journey towards the Supreme, among which significant ones are awakening of the soul, purgation, illumination, dark night of the soul, pre-phase of union and finally, unification.

The terminology used in the description of all these stages is a mixed version of various languages spoken in the age of Kabir. It is called *saddhukari, i.e.,* the language of saints which is open to all other dialects and slangs. Basically, the language of his poetry is Hindi influenced by various regional languages like Rajasthani, Bhojpuri, Avadhi, Punjabi and the Hindi spoken in eastern states. The terms of Urdu and Persian are also used in the poetic outpourings of Kabir. Addressing to the common masses of his age, Kabir never paid heed to ameliorate or polish his language. Nowhere has he seemed to be following rules and regulations of grammar. One can easily comprehend the colloquial touch throughout his poetry. The beauty of his language is enhanced with the frequent use of idioms and phrases. Being open to all the languages, Kabir's phraseology, at times, embraces the vocabulary of *yogis* (ascetics). It also reveals the influence of the *Siddhas* and the *Nathas*. Their influence can be viewed upon his mode of expression too as in *Ulabansiyan* he makes an abundant use of paradoxes and it proves for from the easy access of a scholar. Truly, his language is in complete harmony with his thought. At times, it does not appear to be literary because the poet never considered it essential and did not strive for it. His language is successful in attaining its basic concern, i.e., striking the very idea conveyed through the group of words.

In order to establish Sant Kabir as a mystic poet, it can be stated that he never followed or presented any steadfast theory or philosophy for union with the Almighty. His poetry unfolds various paths to be united with the Supreme and the reader is free to choose one according to his capability and convenience. He considers that the path of love-devotion and complete surrender is the best and the easiest to attain unification with the Lord.

To depict his unification with his Lord, Kabir uses a versatile language which is called *saddhukari* open to many other dialects and vernaculars. The dominance of colloquial terms and day-to-day usages make his poetry close to the masses. He is a believer of monism, but from the point of view of commoner, we find the traces of the relationship of *bhakta* (devotee) and *bhagwan* (Supreme) in his poetry. Indeed, all is subtle and mystic as he himself says "Nobody understands the state when Kabir and Rama, bhakta and bhagwan are united."[28] Moreover, Kabir's mystic poetry apart from his didactic tone and candid communication as a social reformer, need not be measured in any perspective other than the unification, oneness and embodiment with his Lord, the Supreme.

REFERENCES

1. Vaudeville, Ch. *Kabir* .Vol.1.Oxford: Clarendon Press. 1974, p.3
2. Das, G. N. *Mystic Songs of Kabir*. New Delhi : Abhinav Publications. 1996 p. 29
3. Shah, Ahmad. trans., *The Bijak of Kabir.* Delhi: Low Price Publications. 1997. P.199.

4. Das, G. N. Mystic *Songs of Kabir*. New Delhi : Abhinav Publications. 1996 p. 48
5. Ibid., p.25
6. Das, G.N. *Maxims of Kabir.* New Delhi: Abhinav Publications. 1999. p.33
7. Das, G.N. *Love Songs of Kabir*. New Delhi: Abhinav Publications. 1994. p.39
8. Ibid, p.42
9. Ibid, p.94
10. Das, G.N. *Maxims of Kabir*. New Delhi: Abhinav Publications. 1999. p.63
11. Quoted by Kanhaiya Lal Kalla, The Influence of Yoga Philosophy on Hindi Poetry. Dehradun : Sahitya Sadan. 1967. p.120
12. Ibid, p. 117
13. Ibid, p.118
14. Sharma, Yagya Dutt. *Kabir: Sahitya Aur Siddhant*. Sonipat : Aksharam. 1990. p.97-98
15. Das, G. N. *Mystic Songs of Kabir*. New Delhi : Abhinav Publications. 1996. p. 87
16. Sharma, Yagya Dutt Kabir. *Kabir Sahitya Aur Siddhant*. Sonipat: Aksharam, 1990. p.98
17. Das, G. N. *Mystic Songs of Kabir*. New Delhi: Abhinav Publications .1996. p. 41
18. Ibid, p.52
19. Tagore , Rabindra Nath. trans., *Songs of Kabir*. New Delhi: Cosmo Publications. 1985. p.142
20. Das, G. N. *Mystic Songs of Kabir*. New Delhi: Abhinav Publications. 1996. p. 116
21. Das, G.N. *Maxims of Kabir*. New Delhi: Abhinav Publications. 1999. p.78
22. Tagore, Rabindra Nath. trans., *Songs of Kabir* .New Delhi : Cosmo Publications. 1985. p.82-83

23. Ibid, p.120
24. Das, Babu Shyam Sundar. ed.. Kabir Granthavali .Varanasi: Nagari Pracharini Sabha, Sanvat 2025. p.226
25. Das, G.N. *Love Songs of Kabir* .New Delhi: Abhinav Publications. 1994. p.39
26. Ibid, p.67
27. Ibid, p. 46
28. Das, Babu Shyam Sundar. ed.. Kabir Granthavali .Varanasi : Nagari Pracharini Sabha, Sanvat 2025. p.226

21

Is the Subtle Cultural Matrix of Godaan Untranslatable?

Neeta Modi

Translation is not an easy art because the translator is consciously or unconsciously always within the confines of the original.Translation means 'to carry across', 'to transfer'. John Dryden represented translation as a judicious blending of 'paraphrase' and 'metaphrase'. But he cautioned against 'imitation' i.e. adapted translation. "When a painter copies from the life...he has no privilege to alter features and lineaments."[1] However there is a common misconception that translation is a straight forward verbatim replacement between any two languages. In fact, translation involves lot of "spilling over" not only of languages but also of cultures.

Culture is the sum total of signs, beliefs, artefacts, social arrangements and customs created by human beings. Today people of different nations, races, genders, religions, languages and cultures have merged together into a global village. So now when languages and cultures are constantly coming in close contact, the role of the translator has become not only very crucial but also very arduous. Translation involves transposition of not only words, expressions, ideas and thoughts from one language (source language) into another (target language) but also of cultures. The cultural aspect of the text also has to be borne in the mind. The process of translation i.e. recoding across cultures should correspond to the target culture to make it credible and comprehensible to the target readers. A good translator is one who is not only bi-lingual or multi-lingual but also bi-cultural or multi-cultural. He is the bridge between cultures and civilizations. He shapes the target language and also enriches his own (source) language with ideas, thoughts, loan words, calques, grammatical structures, idioms and vocabulary from the former.

It is almost impossible to translate words and phrases that are heavily and exclusively grounded in a culture. When to paraphrase, when to use the nearest local equivalent, when to coin a new word, when to transcribe, when to add an explanatory note or glossary, has created a lot of controversy and confusion. The culture-bound words or phrases which defy translation have always fascinated the translators.

When the writer and the reader share a common cultural background they comprehend the text easily. But when their cultural background is different or unfamiliar there is difficulty in proper interpretation. During translation if some culture specific elements in the source language are not dealt with properly the target language reader finds them insensible, incomprehensible and may face "cultural shock". "Cultural shock" is a common experience for a person from another culture. To avoid it, translators should have a thorough knowledge of the culturally derived values, attitudes and outlooks in the two languages concerned. A translation should be faithful, expressive and close to the original work. Thus, it is the job of the translator to bring together two different persons, his author and reader and to help his target reader understand and enjoy the author of the source text as correctly and completely as possible.

But translation should never be the replica of the original. As a French critic, Gilles Menage rightly remarked that translation is like women, who can be either beautiful or faithful but never both at the same time.

India has an ancient tradition of translation but it was never thought of as something different from creative writing. In ancient times much translation was done between allied languages like Sanskrit and Praakrit. Such translations were 'shadows' of the original texts.

Creative translations of ancient Sanskrit spiritual texts like the Ramayana, the Mahabharata, and the Geeta are generally termed as "Transcreation". Transcreation if understood as 'rebirth' of the original text is the best solution for the problems faced in translating culturally oriented texts. According to G.Gopinathan, it can be defined as "an authentic re-interpretation of the original work suited to the readers or audience of the target language in the particular time and space"[2]. This re-interpretation has a social purpose and includes explanations, summarization and aesthetic innovation in style and techniques. Poets like Tagore, Aurbindo, Ramanujan, Agyeya and Dharamvir Bharati also used this technique. Through it the problems of 'untranslatability' can be solved to an extent.

Every society has its own unique mythology, history, and way of life, culture and language which differentiates it from others. While translating, a translator must have essential knowledge of all these elements of the source language text so as to do justice to them in the target language.

In Literature, especially translation brings societies and people nearer. Tagore, Sharat Chandra, Premchand, Tolstoy, Gorky, Shakespeare, Milton, Wordsworth are all familiar and dear to us in spite of cultural and linguistic barriers. However, it is very difficult to find proper parallels for words, phrases and expressions to re-code them in the target language. It is difficult to capture and communicate the cultural gestures and elements of a work in the receptor culture.

A translator has to face many problems and challenges while rendering Hindi or any Indian language text into English. Translation is beset with not only linguistic snags but also cultural ones. It means transmission of culture as well. It involves two different languages and two different cultures, so it is translation of language as well as of cultures. The cultural factors are difficult to handle, and the problem of untranslatability increases all the more if the differences between the source and the target languages and their respective cultures is too much.

Godaan, the swan song of Premchand poses many challenges during translation into English as it is deeply embedded in Indian culture. The culture incorporates language, dialect, native food, garments, folk music, musical instruments, native kitchenware, customs, traditions, social structure, relations and their terminology. It also includes natural world, flora-fauna, seasons, festivals, mythology, beliefs, omens, superstitions, native medicines and even the games and sports played in that region. Therefore, culture is 'all inclusive' and encompasses anything and everything that is specific to the region and related to the life and living of its natives. It is, thus, imperative that the translator has, preferably first hand knowledge of the source culture to do justice with the job at hand. But the problem still remains at the other end, i.e. with the target language and the target readers. Generally, there are no exact parallels of many culturally related terms in the target language and this causes the untranslatability.

The novel *Godaan* is in Hindi but has been liberally sprinkled with many dialectical words and phrases. Premchand has even used Sanskrit-influenced words and phrases in *Godaan* but very dexterously and tactfully so that they nowhere hinder the free flow of the narrative.

Chirasthayi jeernavastha (p.5), kolaahal pratikshan prachand, krishak-prakrati (p.43), samashtivaad, apmaan aur aaghaat ko dhairya aur udaarta se sahne ka abhyaas (p.53), manodgaaron par kathor nigrah (p.56), Eershyamishrit vinod, shraddhapoorn swar (p.65), laalsaapradipta netra, shishta prem ki durbalata aur nirjeevata (p.73), saadhvee, papishtha, trast hriday (p. 123), Bhishagaacharya (p.192), dharmabhiru man trast, aartswar (p. 221), aardrkanth (p. 229), duraasha (p. 244), kushkanya (p. 256), vilasini ramani (p. 289), ahamanyataa ka dhwansa (p.342) etc. are some of the examples.

Godaan is full of Sanskrit principles and maxims. Hori – Gobar dialogue on page 10 "Vrikshon mein fal lagate hain, unhain janata khaati hai, kheton mein anaaj hota hai, wah sansaar ke kaam aata hai, gaay ke than mein doodh hota hai, wah khud peene nahin jaati, doosre hee peete hein; meghon se varsha hoti hai, usase prithvi tript hoti hai" reminds us of

"Pibanti nadyaha swaymeva nodakam swayamna khaadanti falaanivrikshah.

Dharadharo varshati natmhetve paropkaraay sataam vibhutayah"

And *"kheti mein jo marjjad hai wah naukari mein to nahin hai"* echoes in the famous sentence from Upnishads

"Krishimitkrishasva, vitte ramasvah bahu mattyamaanah".

The sentence *"aurat ko bhagwaan sabkuchh de, roop na de, nahin to wah kaaboo mein nahin rahati"* (p. 260) is a reflection of Sanskrit maxim

"*Bhaaryaa roopwati shatruh*" and seems culturally untranslatable. It has no significance or meaning for a Western reader.

Premchand has written *Godaan* in the backdrop of villages like Belari and Semari near Lucknow but his graphic description represents the culture not only of this region but of the whole nation. Most of the characters are illiterate and hence use incorrect words in the name of dialect like "*parsan* for *prasann, niyav* for *nyaya, ser* instead of *sher, bamhanai* for *brahmanitva, partach* for *pratyaxa, vises* for *vishesh, paraschit* for *praayashchit, saraarat* for *sharaarat, kaasi* for *kaashi, kulachchani* for *kulaxani, istaam* for stamp, *kagad* for *kaagaz*." Regional words are used thus in plenty and are difficult to translate. Major characters of the novel Hori, Dhaniya, Sona, Jhuniya, also make use of regional dialect. Some examples are noteworthy:

Hori - *natan kheti bahurian ghar (p.23)*
londe kaheen fad par jame honge (p. 23)
jal mein rahakar magar se bair budbakpan hai (p. 26)
shaaid bhinsaar ho raha hai (p. 27)
Dhaniya - *andhe kookar ki tarah hava ko bhoonka kare (p. 42)*
Dekho apne sapoot kee leela, usey apni sel se chhutee nahin (p. 111)
Vah muaa bahattar ghaat ka paani piye hue (p. 111)
Jhunia - *baithane ko maachi doongi (p. 26)*
Sona - *jaa tu gobar path (p. 36)*
Dr. Mehta's dialogues in the guise of Afghan
Amse poochhata hai kaisa loot, kaisa daaka?....
Am yaan se kissi ko nahin jaane dega (p. 73)

Such lines lose their beauty as well as cultural connotations when translated.

The childish prattle of Shilia's son Ramu is quite humorous, relaxing and it defies translation. He calls *roti – oti, doodh – tut, saag – chhag, koudi – toli*. When asked his name, pat comes the reply '*Lamu.*'

Rural life and culture is highlighted by Premchand through the effective tool of language. Influence of city on the language is also evident. The rural characters speak Hindi sprinkled liberally with regional words and thus make their language more natural, realistic and effective. Cultural meanings are woven intricately into the texture of the language.

Aber, bhurkas, gapadchoth, darsan, asnaan, parsaad,muskiraana, durdasaa, tirasanaa, rapot, kamisnar and many more are all used naturally and spontaneously by the characters. Translation may hinder the spontaneous natural flow of the narrative.

The abundant but specific kinship terminology of India shows the value and importance attached to it in our society, whereas in the West it is quite general and vague. The feelings, the association, the affection, the reverence and the awe attached to these terms resist translation. *Naana – naani, dada – daadi*, become merely grandfather-grandmother. Same is the case with *maama-maami, kaaka-kaaki, foofa-bua, taau-taai, mausa-mausi*, they are uncle-aunt. They simply lose their rich associative connotations and evocative value when translated. We in India still have joint families and extended relationships. We cannot do without our specific terms. Western culture does not give much importance to family or blood relations and hence have no specific and a very limited kinship terminology which is insufficient to convey the wide range of Indian relationships.

Several terms of kinship in the novel like *Dada, Amma, Kaka, Kaki, Beta, Bahu, Bhai, Bhabhi, Jeeja, deedi, Saala, Saali, Saas, Sasur, Devar, Devarani,* and *Sasuraal* are extremely culture specific and are loaded with emotional effervescence. They convey feelings of respect, dignity and intimacy. Affection, motherliness, concern, innocent cajolery, security, awe and a lot more are the associations connected with these terms. Translation can hardly do justice to the rich and varied sentiments evoked by them.

In *Godaan,* the protagonist Hori on meeting Bhola greets him thus *" raam raam Bhola bhai"* (p. 8) In India certain conventional societal or community addresses are also prevalent. They may sound weird to the Western reader who is unfamiliar with the social hierarchy of India.

The Zamindaar is addressed as "Rai Saaheb" by the villagers out of respect. Hori is "Bhaiya" for his younger brothers. Bhola, Damdi Bansor and others call Hori "Mehto". Datadin is a brahmin, highest in the social ladder so villagers address him as "maharaj" as a mark of honour.

Educated characters like Mehta and Khanna are addressed as *Mehtaji, Khannaji, Bhai Saheb.* The women are "*Deviji*" and Malti is "*Baaiji*" for the illiterate young black woman. The police inspector is addressed as "sir" by Hori and others.

As a part of our culture, we in India address our elders as "*Aap*" to show respect. The difference between honorific "*Aap*" and familiar and intimate "*tu*"/ "*tum*" cannot be rendered in English. If we try to translate such things, the idea and the sense behind this plural honorific address would be lost.

Proper names also reflect the culture of an area or country. *Godaan* has many proper names with rural touch like *Hori, Dhaniya, Gobar, Jhuniya, Bhola, Sona, Roopa, Dulaari* and many more.

Food is a very important part of culture and varies from region to region. Some food items are related with a season or festival and remind us of some story behind them. This again is culture specific and cannot be experienced by one who is not familiar with that culture.

Godaan also has some specific food items especially rural like *'jowar – roti', 'arhar – dal' with raw mangoes, 'laddus', 'halwa', 'puri', 'gulaab jamun', 'sherbet', 'chapatti', 'gur', 'sattu', 'chaat', 'ras', etc.*

Not only food items but native kitchenware, things of daily use, dress, medicines, musical instruments, religious rituals are all culture bound and defy translation. Dress materials and clothings like *khaddar, achakan, pyjama, saari, chunari, dhoti, pagadi, dupatta, mirjai, kachhani, kurta* and *salwar* are all referred in the novel. *'Dhol-Majeera'*, the native musical instruments, *'bailgaadi', 'ikka', 'tonga'*, etc. are the rustic means of transport while '*gulli-dandaa*' and '*kabaddi*' are native sports. '*Beedi*', '*chillum*', *'paan'*, *'gilori'*, all these are untranslatable and can only be transliterated.

Caste, customs, traditions, and social-structure also challenge a translator. Caste system and social hierarchy are quite strong in India even today. The Brahmin father and son Pandit Datadin and Matadin would not accept food or even water from Shilia as she was a cobbler by birth and hence impure, untouchable. Hori is ostracized for giving shelter to pregnant Jhuniya. Datadin, the Brahmin Pandit asks him to distribute rice to the community and feast the Brahmins to save his Dharma.

Datadin's son Matadin has an illicit affair with a cobbler girl Shilia. To atone his sin he reads the Geeta, observes all religious rituals, has a dip in Holy Ganga, performs a big Yajna and feasts many Brahmins and is taken back in the fold of his caste. Dhaniya and Gobar are outraged by this hypocrisy. Dhaniya realizes that the society judges the rich and poor by two different moral codes. Gobar remarks "the world sides with those who have money". So community and ostracism becomes silly. Hori is forced to pay a fine of Rs. 100 and 30 mounds of grain by the Panchayat, whereas Matadin goes scot-free. Still Hori believes that "It is the voice of God that speaks through the Panchs". This shows his implicit faith in the age old customs and traditions.

It is very problematic to portray culturally bound aspects. Though Hori's life is full of sufferings and miseries, he has a unique self-complacency and fatalism. Complacency is an integral part of Indian philosophy. His fatalism also becomes his plus point as it helps him in facing his sorrows and despair. He attributes his miseries to his fate or destiny and faces them calmly. The socio-economic system of India makes the role of fate all the more important as it has the capacity to make the life of thousands and lakhs of people tolerable. Hori has faith in life. He does not know what will happen tomorrow and is perhaps not even worried about it as he has no such foresight. He is an optimist and has great faith in God and this keeps him alive and going. Hori symbolizes the farmers of the older generation and Gobar represents the labourer of the new generation. We are all aware how Gobar is replacing Hori in Indian culture. Hori is an individual as well as representative of a class. He has many qualities of a typical Hindu. Indian culture is reflected in his complacency and fatalism. Like other Hindus he has his own beliefs, faiths and superstitions. He has Hindu culture too in his blood. He cannot keep a penny of a Brahmin even if the Brahmin is dishonest. Pandit Matadin charges exorbitant interest on the loan but Hori pays without any doubt or question. He tells Gobar that he cannot forget '*Neeti*'. "*Neeti haath se na chhodana chhahiye beta! Humne jis byaaj par rupaye liye hain, voh toh dene hee padenge. Phir Brahman thahare! Inkaa paisa hume pachegaa? Aisaa maal toh inhin logon ko pachata hai*". In this way he is a staunch Hindu and believes in "*Varnaashram* system" and therefore considers a Brahmin important in the social hierarchy.

But when the issue of sheltering Jhuniya comes up, Hori is not afraid of the '*varnaashram* system' or of being ostracized by the society. He listens to his heart, gives shelter to Jhuniya and also repents and pays for it a lot. He does thus everything to save Hindu culture and even becomes a mere labourer from a farmer. All these are very tricky and sensitive issues for a translator. He has to be very cautious while trying to translate culture.

Every society or nation has its own customs and traditions which give it an identity. In India people greet one another with *'Namaste'*, *'Jai Shri Krishna'*, *"Har Har Mahadev'* or '*Ram Ram'*. *"Ram Ram Bhola Bhaiya*"; says Hori on meeting Bhola in the opening of the novel. Gobar touches the feet of his parents before leaving for the city and so does Jhuniya. The elders in turn bless them. This is a mark of respect unheard of in the West. It may look ridiculous to them but it is part of our culture. Similarly women cover their heads and even their faces with 'sari' as a decorous tradition. Nohari, Jhuniya, Sona, Dhaniya, cover their heads in keeping with the custom. The lady of the house is referred to as '*Lakshmi*'. Bhola tells Hori that "A good wife is a *Lakshmi,* bhai," and when Hori thrashes Dhaniya, Datadin asks him not to beat 'the *Lakshmi* of the house'.

Indian woman has a weakness for ornaments. Sona mentions '*Nathunia'* and *'Kanthaa'*. After marriage she wore '*Hansali*' and '*Hemul*' in the neck, *'Karnaphuli'* in the earlobes, silver bangles, '*kaajal'* in her eyes and vermilion in the parting of her hair; a true picture of a 'happily married woman'. Some ornaments can be worn only by a woman whose husband is alive. There are several restrictions for a widow; not only in ornaments but also in dress, colours, and even her appearance in social functions and religious ceremonies. The pain, the agony and the sufferings of a widow cannot be understood by the readers unfamiliar with this culture.

All these things are deeply embedded in culture. One who is well versed with Indian culture can only understand their significance. So a translator has to be careful while translating them in the target language and culture. 'To bring fire from the *chulhaa'*; 'to draw water from the well'; 'to carry the water-filled pitchers on one's head' and treating the guests like a God *(Atithi Devo Bhav);* are all illustrations of typical Indian culture. Dhaniya tells Hori, "either do no invite a guest, or if you do, feed him well", when Bhola comes to their house.

The villagers were orthodox, superstitious and believed in *'Nazar'*, *'Tona-Totaka'*(black-magic), *vaidyas, hakims* and faith-healing. When

Gobar-Jhuniya's son falls ill they show more faith in black magic and faith-healing than in medicines. Translation of popular beliefs, superstitions, omens, etc. is difficult. It is a good omen to see a cow, and a married woman early in the morning. Sight of a widow, a cat walking across the way, wailing of dogs, all these are supposed to bring disaster or ill-luck.

It is auspicious to have a Tulsi plant in the front courtyard of a Hindu house. Shilia spots one in Sona's courtyard in the novel. It is highly revered, associated with purity and is worshipped. The Goddess ruling Tulsi is known as the personification of bhakti to the Supreme Being. Such cultural patterns which do not belong to the target language culture are difficult to translate.

There is description of the spring season, the romance, the joy and fragrances lavishly falling on the world. The Koel perched on the mango branches cooed softly, sweetly touching the heart with its harmonious melodies, awakening several desires and hopes; Mahuwa branches were cluttered with a flock of Myenas; Neem, Sirus,Karounda and mango trees were laden with sweet intoxicating flowers; Hori's troubled heart, drowned in so much colour, broke into a song. Even when translated, such culturally loaded portrayal fails to evoke and convey the associative emotions, the wealth of connotations and cultural details in a person unfamiliar with our culture.

Indian mythology is one of the richest elements of Indian culture that enriches it further and makes it a unique one in the world. Bhola tells Hori that there was no one to look after his house and family after his wife's death: "*Ghar mein Mahabharat machaa rehataa hai*". Later Datadin cites instances from Mahabharat and Puranas enumerating the Brahmins who had married girls of lower castes and their children were accepted as Brahmins.

A scene from the Ramayana is enacted at the function organized by Rai Saheb. References to mythology too create difficulty for a translator. Transmitting culture through translation is quite complicated as well as significant.

Customs and traditions are part of culture and we the Indians are steeped into them right from birth to death. There is hardly any occasion that does not have elaborate ceremony, be it birth, *naamkaran*, thread ceremony, engagement, marriage or any other festival. Even after death certain rituals are performed. The significance or the value or the latent symbolism behind them becomes a stumbling block for a translator. They can be transliterated and then explained in the glossary if they have no equivalents in the target language and culture.

Proverbs and idioms are storehouses of wisdom accumulated over centuries. These often have "proper nouns with history or cultural significance which can't be mapped on another linguistic and cultural space."[3] Premchand has effectively used several proverbs and idioms in Godaan. Viz –

Talve sahalaanaa (p.1)
Pet – tan Kaatnaa (p.1)
Ek- ek koudi daant se pakadanaa (p. 1)
Bin gharani ghar bhoot kaa deraa (p. 10)
Baal ki khaal nikaalanaa (p.12)
Paanv mein shanichar honaa (p. 16)
Choti ka paseenaa aedi tuk aanaa (p. 18)
Man bhay mundia hilay (p.19)
Laad de, ladaa de, laadne wala saath kar de. (p. 21)
Naak kaatanaa (p. 28)
Pagadi neechi hona (p. 28)
Gardan par savaar hona (p. 29)
Gale par chhuri chalaanaa (p. 30)
Dwesh ka mayajaal badi-badi machhalion ko hee f ansaataa hai. (p. 36)
Kafan ko koudi nahin. (p. 37)
Khoon khoulanaa (p. 39)
Munh sikodanaa (p. 53)
Dwaar par naak ragadanaa (p. 215)
Munh dhonaa (p. 217)
Kaha-sunee honaa (p. 218)
Munh dekh kar beeda denaa (p. 219)
Rupayaa haath ka mail hai (p. 219)
Naak sikodanaa (p. 219)
Bhoot sawaar honaa (p. 219)
Haath paon foolanaa (p. 221)
Jaisaa baap waisaa betaa (p. 222)
Anguli par nachaanaa (p. 224)

Cultural implications are subtly woven thus in the very texture of the language and it depends on the translator to project them or reflect them in the translated work. It is his duty to initiate the target language readers into the sensibilities and deeper nuances of the source language and culture.

A brief but captivating and graphic description of festivals of *Holi, Phag*, singing of *Aalha* in the month of *Aashaadh, Kajli* in the months of *Saavan – Bhadon* and then recitation of the Ramayan during Navratri are cultural identities and hence untranslatable. In villages native musical instruments like *Dhol* and *Majira* can be heard for six months out of twelve in a year. There is one occasion or the other to celebrate, to sing and to enjoy forgetting all sorrows and tensions.

Religious culture relates to the religious beliefs and faiths of a society which are quite specific. *Ganga* is the holiest river for Indians. It is believed to take the soul to the doors of Heaven. Similarly *'Gangajal'* is an essential ingredient of every religious offering. The villagers follow dharma strictly. Pandit Datadin wants Heera to swear by the holy water of the *Ganga* if he has not poisoned the cow. When Heera is found missing, his brother Sobha suggests that he might have gone to take a dip in *Ganga* to atone his sin.

Hori has great faith in God and religion (dharma). He is ready to pay the fine imposed on him by the panchayat as he believes that 'it's the voice of God that speaks through the *Panchs'*. Again when Bhola comes to take away his bullocks Hori says that he will be ruined if the bullocks go but if Bhola's dharma sanctions it then he may take them. So implicit is Hori's faith in dharma and God.

Reading the Geeta, swearing by the holy water of *Ganga*, and the holy thread is also religion (and therefore culture) bound. Thakur Dhyansingh performs a *pooja* and sends sweets to each house. Hori feels it would be insulting to attend the *pooja* without offering any thing for '*Aarti*'. He was worried more about his social prestige than the religious sanctity involved.

Pandit Datadin refers to the present age as 'dark age- *Kaliyug'*. He goes to Benaras with his son for expiation of his sin. But Dulaari feels sin cannot be atoned by money. Once the dharma is gone it is gone. One can't buy it with money. After spending a huge amount on the pandits of Benaras, Matadin is again declared a Brahmin and taken back into the fold. A big 'Yajna' is performed, many Brahmins feasted and mantras are chanted. As a part of purification ceremony Matadin has to taste cow dung and urine. This is supposed to purify him by killing the bacteria of defilement in his soul. But Matadin revolted against this penance, dharma and discarded his sacred thread as he knew his patrons would neither accept water from him nor allow him to touch their utensils or food. And therefore he returns to cobbler Selia and eats food cooked by her.

Nokheraam, a Brahmin fasted on every '*ekadashi*' and feasted five Brahmins. Pateshwari, a Kayasth held the recitation of '*Satyanarain*' every full moon and invited ten Brahmins. Both vied thus for superiority. These cultural elements do not have equivalents in the target language culture and hence are almost untranslatable.

Religious beliefs, customs, rituals, ceremonies present hurdles in translating a text. Such sensitive and cultural issues demand full attention of a translator. Weddings are a grand affair in India as they follow different customs and traditions. "*Kanyaadaan*" has great importance attached to it. It is not merely a marriage of two persons as in the West. It is again a very culture specific term full of associations and rich symbolism. It can be fully comprehended and appreciated only by one acquainted with our culture.

Hori also has great faith in the Indian tradition of *'Kanyaadaan'* and wants to marry off his daughters as lavishly as he can with good dowry. The idea of Sona's *'kushkanya'* wedding saddens him and Dhaniya. But Nohari helps them with money. Defeat comes in the form of Hori's helplessness when he is forced to sell his second daughter Roopa. This is Indian culture, this is their religious belief. All these ceremonies, beliefs, faiths and rituals are so deeply rooted in the culture that the efforts to translate them render them culturally incomprehensible and the readers may get "cultural shock".

'Gobar', 'Gobar paathanaa', 'Kande', 'Uple' lose their resonance when translated as 'cow- dung cakes'. So holy is the cow and its dung and urine that they are used as purifiers during religious ceremonies and rituals. When Heera poisons the cow out of jealousy it is regarded s a heinous crime, because great religious importance is attached to a cow in India. It is considered as a mother, very holy, very sacred. Premchand's novel 'Godaan' amply exemplifies this. The protagonist cherishes only one desire in life – to own a cow and serve it. He considers it a great honour and prestigious to have a cow and

also very auspicious to see the cow very first thing in the morning. For him and others cow is a Goddess from Heaven. But even that remains unfulfilled and he dies an untimely tragic death. Out of four basic components of Indian culture- *Geeta, Ganga, Gau and Gayatri*, Hori chooses only one and is defeated even in that.

Like "Kanyadaan", *"Godaan"* also has cultural implications. '*Daan*' is neither charity nor donation; it is not even gift or endowment. Mere lexical equivalents of cultural patterns or contexts or references are not adequate enough for the target language readers to interpret culturally loaded words, lines or text.

The very title of the novel "Godaan" defies translation. It is so culture-bound that it has no English equivalent. In Indian (Hindu) culture "Godaan" is very significant after '*Yajna*' or any other auspicious function. "Godaan" by a dying person helps him to cross the dangerous *'Vaitarini'* river while going to Heaven. He only has to hold the tail of the cow and she takes him safely across the perilous river, as per *"Garud Puraan"*.

The title "Godaan" reflects satire, pity, hollowness, hypocrisy, social evils, rural life and agrarian culture. A person who fails to fulfil his only dream wish to buy a cow has to give a cow in charity before breathing his last just to improve his next life. It is a sharp satire on religious rituals which touches our heart and moves us to tears. The irony is that when Hori is about to die Dhania has to part with the only *20 annaas* she possesses; the '*purohit*' takes it in the name of *Godaan!*

A translator has to perform a dual function of translating the local colour as well as the meaning. He should himself be thorough with both the languages and cultures involved in order to be credible and comprehensible to his target language readers. It is his job to bring home the culture by interpreting the text linguistically and culturally. A translated work, as stated earlier cannot be an exact copy of the original. But a good translation can serve as a bridge between two languages and cultures and help the target language reader comprehend and enjoy the text as much as the source language reader might have. Translation of cultural elements is complicated but vital task to attain this goal.

Untranslatability can be dealt with by using innovative devices and procedures like: Transliteration, Adaptation, Borrowing, Substitution, Omission, Addition, Compensation, Reduction, and

Deletion. It can also be by the Calques, Paraphrase, Cultural equivalents, Descriptive equivalents, Translator's note, Glossary etc.'

The enigmatic question —— should one translate culturally loaded or culture specific words, phrases, elements and aspects or leave them as such, does not have universal answers. It depends upon the translator and the text. The best solution is to leave it at the discretion of the translator.

WORKS CITED

1. Kasparek, Christopher, "The Tıanslator's Endless Toil", p. 84
2. Gopinathan, G. Translation, Transcreation and Culture: The Evolving Theories of Transltion in Hindi and Other Modern Indian Languages.
3. Desai, H. Muse India. 2007
4. Premchand, Munshi. *Godaan* (Hindi), Saraswati Press, Allahabad.

22

Translation: Significance and Problems

N.Sharda Iyer

Indian literature has a great tradition in each of its languages, reaching back to several centuries. There are a number of masterpieces in each one of them having locked treasures to readers who are unaware of the language in which they have been enriched. The world outside which imagines that in a multilingual country like India the slender sense of unity is lost in a bewildering diversity, will realize the essential principle of unity that runs through all regional literatures if these works are available through translation and feel the heartbeat of our nation. For, as Srinivas Iyengar wrote, "One touch of nature makes all world kin, but it is in the literature that the heartbeats of a nation are heard; and it is through the medium of a commonly inspired and shared literature that we can exchange pulses as it were and realize, while the differences are on the surface, the sense of unity flows as in an underground river".

Indian literature is a vast storehouse of epic compositions based on ancient myths and legends presenting a sustained allegory of the political history of the time in a panorama of socio-cultural life like the Mahabharata of Nannaya in Telugu, Pampa in Kannada, Kambar and Valmiki in Tamil. There are the didactic and philosophical poetry like Tirukural in Tamil, Viveka Sindu in Marathi, Hitopadesh in Sanskrit, the secular Champu epics like Sandesha poem in Malayalam, the devotional lyrics of great poets Narasi Mehta in Gujarati, Tukaram in Marathi, Kabir and Tulsi in Hindi, Shankaradeva in Assamese, the Vachanakaras and Dasa schools in Kannada and Chaitanya in Bengali. There are poetic biographies of saints in all languages. There are prabandhas in prose and poetry dealing with contemporary political theme; considerable literatures reflecting the attempts at synthesizing

Hinduism and Islam; satirical and neo-classical poetry in medieval period; and writers of the 19th and 20th century, who reflect the changing socio-economic, cultural and political scenario to be read by everyone and which could be made possible only through a faithful translation that would be a significant contribution to knowledge and to the library of world literature.

Translation actually brings into play the creative ability of a person, wide scholarship, a critical insight and a capacity for organization of material which would bring into focus not only the work to be taken for translation, but also the milieu/background, placing in its proper context in world literature, evaluating the tradition to which it belongs in its own literary setting and assessing its intrinsic qualities of form and substance. It brings into play the creative ability of a translator.

Translation in India began after Independence, as a step towards erasing boundaries by taking literary works across regional, national and international borders; for, translations go beyond a mere literary and aesthetic value. It plays a far more significant role. In a country like India rife with myriad forms of linguistic, cultural, religious, caste class divisions, translations can contribute to the formation of a literary democracy.

In 1947, when faced with the bewildering mass of languages, the prospect of forming commonalities – the question of how to make the culture/language, literature of one state familiar to another, how to make one aware of the underlying unity and the concept of one India – figured, translation was felt as being a positive major step in this direction. Unity in diversity motif governed formation of institutions like The National Book Trust, Sahitya Academy in 1950, which strove to knit India into one through literature, by translating from all official and unofficial languages. Most of the translation is carried out by using English as a conduit language.

The choice of English cannot be explained satisfactorily only in terms of the colonial predicament. The issue of linguistic choice is also part of a language problem involving a power relation between the major and minor languages. A major language does not necessarily mean a language spoken by the majority, over a large territory or a language rich in literature and philosophy. To be a major language it must be anointed with power: political, economic and ideological. None of the Indian languages, despite their long and distinguished literary history and enormously large number of speakers is a 'major' language. An Indian writer, i.e. a writer who writes in an Indian language, either by choice or accident, is fated to be unknown to the rest of the world irrespective of his literary accomplishment when he is translated into a 'major' language. English came to India not as the language of Shakespeare, Milton and Bible alone; but primarily as the language of East India Company promising new financial prospects and political patronage. Even the teaching of English was part of a larger political project. India had its bilingualism or multilingualism even before the introduction of the English language. But, there was a hierarchy, each having its importance as means of communication; each having more or less clearly defined social function. English being the language of the ruling Power, altered and that hierarchy were turned into a relation of opposition between 'major' and 'minor' language The opposition was later redefined as that of 'international', 'national' and 'regional' by the ruling elite of India after independence.

It is not true that major-minor opposition is true only of colonial India or post colonial third world. It is also true to some extent of smaller nations of Europe. Being powerful, politically and economically, these nations could not be monolingual and were obliged to learn a 'major' language. However, very few writers from Romania, Poland, Czechoslovakia or Bulgaria, Holland, Scandinavia, Greece or Iceland, would have thought of abandoning their mother tongue in preference to a 'major' language like English, French or German. Fortunately for them, there always existed a group of intermediaries including translators, critics and publishers, who tried to overcome the constraint of 'minor' language. The function of such intermediaries has been patronized by the 'major' languages, mainly because they are components of the Western World. But, India's situation was entirely different. India was not only part of the exotic Orient, but also a colony. The Orientalists, of course translated ancient works; but, their interest with a few exceptions, as usual, was not exactly literary. The Sanskrit or Tamil texts that were translated for the Western audience did not go beyond a microscopic community. There was hardly any attempt by the Western scholars to translate the vast literary treasure that India has, or even to acquaint the Western public about its nature and quality. That was left to the Indian themselves. While it is the normal practice all over the world to translate foreign texts into one's own language, seldom is the practice revered in India. Literatures composed in 'minor' languages were and still are translated by Indians themselves into a 'major' language. It seems that one has to come to terms with the 'major'/ 'minor' linguistic opposition.

It is sad to see how forms of knowledge and experience lie unnoticed and unacknowledged because they have not been translated into the global language. Literature written in the 'Bhashas' want to enter the public domain through English, in order to ensure visibility and what Walter Benjamin refers to as 'after life'. Since 1996 there has been a tremendous upsurge of Indian literature translations into English, an activity that was not only marginal, but also perceived as unnecessary in the decades after independence, has acquired in the last decade and half both a cultural and economic validity. It makes sense for publishers to invest in English translations for this would attract reading public as well as it is hoped that some of the titles would be absorbed in canons of subaltern literature or find a place in the syllabus of South Asian literature in universities in India or abroad.

As for translation into and from Indian languages, which get woefully left out from most overviews of translations, they happen in a smaller and less noticeable way. The story of intra-India language for translation is far from uniform. A lot depends on the language of the source text – its readership and the dynamic use of that language. Though the scheme of *Aadan-Pradan*, initiated by Sahitya Akademi and National Book Trust, concerns with inter language translation, yet they are affected by three things – general apathy among writers in accepting translation as a literary activity; secondly, there are not many writers who know languages other than their own; and lastly, the problem of marketing regional language books.

Brahmabandhab Upadhyay (1861-1907) a radical political activist of Bengal described Tagore as 'the world poet of Bengal' in the editorial of his journal *Sophia* dated 1st September 1900. "If ever the Bengali language is studied by foreigners it will be for the sake of Rabindra. He is a world poet. He is like the Devdhara which has roots deep down, down the lowlands but which threatens to pierce the sky – such is its loftiness ..." Upadhyay was not alone in making such a claim. Ten years later, a younger contemporary of Tagore, rapturously declared during a public reception given to Tagore on his fiftieth year, "Jagat Kabi Sabhay mara tomar kore (we boast of you in the assembly of the poets of the world).

Unlike some of his predecessors and contemporaries, Tagore did not have any ambition for fame as a writer in English. He had visited England twice, responded to English literature and music, he knew the anglicized elite of Calcutta quite intimately. But, in his choice of language for his literary expression he had no dilemma. He wrote in Bengali. His international reputation, however, rests entirely on 'Gitanjali' in English and other works in English that followed it. Even in many parts of India and the world he is known mainly through these English translations and translations of these translations.

The tremendous response from the West prompted him to translate more of his writings. He is the only major writer in literary history of any country, who translated his own works to reach a larger audience. His decision to become his own translator and subsequently to write in English, though not entirely beneficial to him, was nevertheless a momentous one. The citation of the Nobel Prize (1913), awarded to him for his English Gitanjali (1912), praised his "profoundly sensitive, fresh and beautiful verse by which, with consummate skill, he has made his poetic thought expressed in his own English words, a part of the literature of the West". Whether he made his poetic thought a part of the literature of the West is a different proposition. But with the English translation his transition from a Bengali writer to a world figure was made certain.

In a letter dated 6th May, 1913, to his niece Indra Devi, he wrote the story of the genesis of translation of Gitanjali, "on the day I was to board the ship I fainted due to my frantic efforts at leave taking and the journey itself had to be postponed. Then I went to Sealdah to take rest. It was the month of Chaitra (March-April). The air was thick with the fragrance of mango blossoms and all hours of the day were delirious with the song of birds. It is an odd habit of mine, as you know that when the air strikes my bones, they tend to respond in music. Yet I had not the energy to sit down and write anything new, so I took up the poems of Gitanjali and set myself to translate them one by one. You may wonder why such a crazy ambition possessed one in such a state of health. But believe me I did not undertake this task in a spirit of reckless bravado. I simply felt an urge to recapture through the medium of another language the feeling and sentiments which had created such a feast of joy within me in the days gone by ..."

This account of the genesis of the English translation of Gitanjali is certainly of great documentary value. Although tne translation began rather suddenly, that exercise was really the culmination of efforts started at least a decade earlier. It began around 1890 when he himself translated a poem titled 'Nishpal Kamana'. This was, however, a stray and solitary example without any follow up. From the early years of the twentieth century, however, Tagore gave some thoughts to translation of his works mainly because of his admirers like Jagdish Chandra Bose, the natural scientist, who said "I will not allow you to remain in obscurity in the countryside" and who himself translated a few of Tagore's stories which remained unpublished. Others like Bipin Chandra Pal, Pramathalal Sen, also translated his poems and stories and were keen in presenting him before a larger world outside Bengal.

Around 1909-1912, concerted efforts were made by Roby Dutt, Ajit Kumar Chakravarti, Ananda K Coomaraswamy, Sister Nivedita, and who were joined in these efforts by young Bengali scholars living abroad. All these made Tagore realize the necessity of translation of his works. Though he left the work of translation to his admirers and well wishers, yet when a request for publication of translation came from Rothenstein, Tagore gave serious thought to translation, he for the first time expressed his dissatisfaction with the translations done by others; he disapproved of all metrical translation and wanted the poems to be translated in prose. In a letter to Pramathalal Sen, dated 14 May, 1912, he expressed not only his dissatisfaction, but what was most crucial was his desire to translate his own poems. He wrote, "if possible I will try myself when I reach England." It was a kind of creative impulse that had been simmering within him for a long time and finally burst out in the open.The excitement and the joy with which Tagore began translating his poems in the quiet surroundings of rural Bengal continued throughout his long voyage to England.Within a week of his arrival he was the centre of attraction of the most powerful literary elite in

England. Gitajnali with Tagore's unique blend of longing devotion, faith in God and simple love of created beings made it an instant success. He became a spokesman of an India which was basically humanist and universal, simple yet profound.

Rothenstein, the painter said "here was poetry of a new order which seemed to me on a level with the mystic". A.C. Bradley remarked "It looks as though we have at last a great poet among us again". W.B.Yeats felt that "these lyrics display in their thoughts a world I have dreamt all my life long". Ezra Pound pinpointed the chief literary interest of Gitanjali – the use of prose poetry. "Gitanjali in English is prose rendering of songs that by their very nature are untranslatable". Fr. Fallen in his book, *Tagore in the West* wrote; "for once a miracle has been achieved. Although lacking much of the musical beauty and evocative power of the original in Bengali, is yet a jewel, even an English religious poetry ...".Today, still Tagore for the West, is the author of Gitanjali.

Tagore in his translation chose the prose poem because he felt he would not be able to give effective metrical rendering to them in English. They were prose poems of the images of powerful evocation in the model of Vaishanava lyrics combined with a stream of the influence of folk tale and folk poetry. The non-Bengali reader misses the musical movement of the original as Yeats ruefully referred to the subtlety of the rhythm which he could not enjoy as he did not know Bengali. The English translation reads like a prose poem, but the Bengali version makes the phrase glide into one another. The accent is as much on the music as on the poetry as Subramaniam Bharati's. The stillness is disturbed by a dance or rhythm, the ear is charmed and enraptured, there is a quick passage through the door of the sensibility, and the chords reach the souls sanctuary at last. This is the main reason why a Tagore or Bharati defies translation into English, even when the attempt is by the author himself as A.E.Houseman reiterates, "poetry is not the thing said but a way of saying it. The Gitanjali in Bengali, is, as told by Yeats 'full of subtlety of rhythm and untranslatable delicacy of colour'. What is true of Gitanjali is true of all the poems of Tagore; they are richly decked in the intricate beauties of time and rhythm and the 'language is more than usually coy and unwilling to yield to her secret to alien vestment". Aurobindo writes "... one has only to compare this

English prose with the original to see how much has gone out with the change, something is successfully substituted which may satisfy the English reader, but can never satisfy the ear or mind that once listened to the singer's own native and magical melodies". As Toru Dutt wrote in *Mon Pere*:

> The flowers look loveliest in their native soil
> And their kindred branches, plucked, they fade
> And lose the colours Nature on them laid
> Though bound in garlands, with assiduous toil
> Pleasant it was, afar from the turmoil.
> To wander through the valley, now in shade
> And now in sunshine, where these blossoms made
> A Paradise, and gather in spoil
> But better than myself no man can know
> How tarnished have become their tender hues
> Even in the gathering, and how dimmed their glow
> Would'st thou again new life in them infuse
> Thou who last seen them where they brightly blow
> Ask Memory. She shall help my stammering Muse.

Translations are always like wearing gloves that blunt our sense of touch and prevent out taking hold of the words with sensitive bare hands, all important words because only the poet can build with them a fragile bridge, between the intangible reality of poetry and the tangible unreality of our matter of fact daily life. (Victoria).

Tirupavai is a vernacular Veda composed by Kodai, popularly known as Andal – the ruler of hearts – the only female saint among the twelve Alwar saints. A fondling fostered by Periyalwar, a Vaishnava saint poet, Tirupavai works out the desire of Andal for Sri Krishna in his manifestation as Lord Ranganatha – Vishnu. According to legends she is supposed to have merged into the idol. It is a complex poem which the sensual and the sexual merge with the spiritual and the religious. It is a dream love embodying desire and its complications at various levels, modulating into a great poem of spiritual ecstasy.

Mohan Ramanan in his translation of this great devotional epic of the 8th century observes that a reader of it becomes a sahrdaya (a person after Andal's own heart) which is central to Indian aesthetics. Indian poetics has a lot to offer in respect of reader response criticism because it gives an exalted position to the reader. He is a Sahrdaya "one with a kindred heart" in whom the poet's outpouring will find its completion and fulfilment. The poet and the reader are the two aspects of a single entity. The poet and the reader participate in Sarasvata-tattava. They participate in this virtue by the creative imagination and the responsive imagination, the two possess respectively. An attitude before the text will provide the necessary attitude. Bhakti in Andal is fused with Bhakti in the reader who must humble himself before Andal's devotional intensity and her superior spiritual claims.

Andal adopts the Nayika-Nayaka Bhava, a mode where the devotee transforms himself into a bride to the Lord. It is a central mode in Vaishnavism adopted by Mira and Jaidev. The dominant rasa Sringara is a means to an end which in Indian tradition is Atmananda (Spiritual bliss) and Rasanubhava (aesthetic experience). Poetry becomes a means for Divine realization and the Tirupavai becomes a means for the attainment of beatitude. Andal's literary offer is much in the nature of pure surrender. Tirupavai is a complex interplay of Sringara-love with surrender to the highest form of spiritual evolution, which makes a psychological reading, however insidious in its charm, ultimately impoverishing Andal's poetic offering, which imaginatively and with poetic strength weaves a saga of spiritual consciousness, creates in the Sahrdaya a corresponding exploratory mood. To translate or read Andal is to translate oneself from 'Sdoth' (asat) to the full alertness of consciousness (sat). Translator becomes a sacrament, an act of piety. Such a relation between the original author and contemporary reader/translator produces a vibrant exchange making for the proper internalization of the 8th century text and amalgamation of it with a modern notion of family, the radical questioning of the manner of patriarchal society, the democratic aspiration for a new social order based on the reorientation of human relations devoid of manipulation, exploitation and tyranny. Andal's Tirupavai is a love poem giving full play to the erotic motif. She was clearly rebelling against the repressions imposed on women by the society. Her feminism has a familiar modern ring to it. Andal represents a radical revolutionary from the modern point of view.

The difficulty that one experiences while translating from a superior literature with a rich language into a language and literature of the same stature is reconciled by Edward Noronha, Institute of Konkani, Mangalore. Naronha, who translated the Kannada poem Golgother athava Yesuvina Kadeya Dina in Govinda Pai's Golgotha mattu Vaisakhi (Mysore Kavyalaya 1965 p.17-31) into Mangluri Konkani in which quality literary work has not been very rich and the literature tended to be jejune, satisfied with mere, and often cleverly set up rhymes, limited to religious and devotional themes, with a spare sprinkling of comments on nature and its beauties.

The Kannada text, translated, is a narrative poem in regular meter. The content of the poem is the last day of Jesus - Jesus being questioned by the Pilate; Pilate's effort to save him; the wrath of the Jews; the scourging and the crucification. The description of these events is interspersed with comments on the state of Pilate's mind, verbalizing of his thoughts and the figure of Christ. Since Konkani was not of the stature of Kanada, therefore, it was not in a position to modify in any significant manner what it received by way of translation from Kannada. Therefore, it had to be very faithful to the original while translating.

The difficulties faced were, in several instances, the intensity and the flow of the original could not be retained in the translation. The reason being Konkani does not use Sanskrit words in the same measure in which Kannada uses; even when the Sanskrit words were retained they looked ill at ease. In contrast the flow could be retained when the words used were already familiar in the language. Where the original has powerful visual auditory effect, translation has failed. Neither could the compactness be retained. An intensively poetic passage is much easier to translate than passages which are relatively dry, where the translator works and even literally hacks his way, causing a perceptible measure of unease to the poem.

In conclusion it could be said that a receptor language still in building a serious literature offers several advantages as well as disadvantages. The main advantage is because of its still immature state of the language and its literature, the translator needs to stay very close to the original which belongs to a more developed language and literature. The disadvantage is that this burden of setting up literary devices is left to the translator and adds to his difficulties.

******

INDEX